Egbert C. Smyth, William J. Tucker

In the Matter of the Complaint Against Egbert C. Smyth and Others

, professors of the Theological Institution in Phillips Academy, Andover. The

Andover defence. Defence of Professor Smyth, arguments of Professor Theodore

W. Dwight

Egbert C. Smyth, William J. Tucker

In the Matter of the Complaint Against Egbert C. Smyth and Others
, professors of the Theological Institution in Phillips Academy, Andover. The Andover defence.
Defence of Professor Smyth, arguments of Professor Theodore W. Dwight

ISBN/EAN: 9783337179410

Printed in Europe, USA, Canada, Australia, Japan

Cover: Foto ©Andreas Hilbeck / pixelio.de

More available books at **www.hansebooks.com**

In the Matter of the Complaint against Egbert C. Smyth and others, Professors of the Theological Institution in Phillips Academy, Andover.

THE ANDOVER DEFENCE.

DEFENCE OF PROFESSOR SMYTH; ARGUMENTS OF PROFESSOR THEODORE W. DWIGHT, PROFESSOR SIMEON E. BALDWIN, HON. CHARLES THEODORE RUSSELL, AND EX-GOVERNOR GASTON;

EVIDENCE INTRODUCED BY THE RESPONDENTS;

Dec. 28, 29, 30, 1886;

TOGETHER WITH

THE STATEMENTS OF PROFESSORS TUCKER, HARRIS, HINCKS, AND CHURCHILL;

Jan. 3, 1887.

BOSTON:
CUPPLES, UPHAM, AND COMPANY,
The Old Corner Bookstore,
283 Washington Street.
1887.

CONTENTS.

		PAGE
I.	PROFESSOR DWIGHT'S ARGUMENT	5
II.	EVIDENCE INTRODUCED BY PROFESSOR BALDWIN	92
III.	PROFESSOR SMYTH'S DEFENCE	97
IV.	TESTIMONY OF NEWMAN SMYTH, D.D.	181
V.	TESTIMONY OF PROFESSOR HARRIS	184
VI.	TESTIMONY OF PROFESSOR HINCKS	187
VII.	TESTIMONY OF PROFESSOR TUCKER	189
VIII.	PROFESSOR BALDWIN'S ARGUMENT	191
IX.	HON. CHARLES THEODORE RUSSELL'S ARGUMENT	209
X.	EX-GOV. GASTON'S ARGUMENT	256
XI.	STATEMENT OF PROFESSOR TUCKER	272
XII.	STATEMENT OF PROFESSOR HARRIS	284
XIII.	STATEMENT OF PROFESSOR HINCKS	300
XIV.	STATEMENT OF PROFESSOR CHURCHILL	307

PROFESSOR DWIGHT'S ARGUMENT.

To the Reverend and Honorable Board of Visitors of Andover Theological Seminary:

THIS is an extraordinary case in many of its aspects. I call your attention in the first place to the mode in which it has been presented to your Board by the self-constituted accusers of the Professors.

In doing this I refer to nothing outside of the papers before your Honorable Board.

MODE OF PRESENTING THE CASE.

In a paper dated July 23, 1886, four gentlemen, viz., J. W. Wellman, H. M. Dexter, O. T. Lanphear, and J. J. Blaisdell, presented a paper to your Board making so-called " charges " against five Professors in the Andover Theological Seminary, whom they named. They stated in this paper that they were *constrained* "from a sense of duty " to bring complaints against Professors Smyth, Tucker. Churchill, Harris, and Hincks. After setting these complaints out at some length, one of them, J. W. Wellman, signed his name as trustee of the seminary, and the others, viz., Messrs. Dexter, Lanphear, and Blaisdell, signed their names as a " *committee* of certain of the Alumni."

I do not propose now to speak of the intrinsic nature of the charges themselves, on which comment and criticism

were made before your Honorable Board at a recent meeting
on October 25th. These gentlemen, however, under an order
or intimation made on November 8th by you, amended or
attempted to amend their complaint in a way hitherto unexampled in legal practice, apparently dividing a joint complaint into separate proceedings against each Professor.
What was, however, worse than all, they ceased to describe
themselves as a *committee*, and henceforward appear in their
own individual names by an attorney.

To this course of proceeding the Professors by their counsel make and have constantly made strenuous objection. I
call particular attention now to the evidence of duplicity and
underhanded methods on the part of these complainants in
having with apparent untruth described themselves as a
" Committee of the Alumni." The object of this description
apparently was to gain a credit for their charges by appearing to act in a representative character. There was in the
statement an implied suggestion of a meeting of certain
Alumni, by whom they were appointed a committee. This
number was shadowy and uncertain, it is true, but the statement that there were Alumni behind them was calculated
and, it is believed, designed to make an impression upon the
community. As it now appears, these four men comprise all
the Trustees and all the Alumni who engineer this movement. If three of these men are a committee at all, they
are self-appointed — "a committee of the whole." The men
asserted by implication to be behind them are "men in buck-
ram "— like the eleven of the immortal *Falstaff*, at one time
formidable in their indefiniteness, but now subsiding into
three. I say that for such conduct these signers have forfeited the confidence of all candid, truth-speaking men, and
I add, with *Prince Hal*, " What slaves are ye to hack your
swords as ye have done and then say it was in fight? What
trick, what device, what starting-hole can you now find out
to hide yourselves from this open and apparent shame?"
Conduct like this at the Bar would gain the scorn of the
legal profession. We believe that before your Board it will
receive the treatment it richly deserves.

It is unfortunate for the interests of the respondents that in a tribunal like this there are no settled rules of practice. We are driven to supposed analogies with other branches of law more or less similar. The closest analogy seems to be that of the practice in the English Ecclesiastical Courts, or in Admiralty. In fact, Chief Justice Shaw, in *Murdock* v. *Phillips Academy*, 12 Pickering, 262, 263, refers to the rules to be found in Burns' Ecclesiastical Law.

According to that case, these things must concur before your Board: "1. A monition or citation of the party to appear. 2. A charge given to him which he is to answer, called a libel or complaint. 3. A competent time assigned for the proofs and answer. 4. A liberty for counsel to defend his cause, and to except against the proofs and witnesses. 5. A solemn sentence, after hearing all the proofs and answers."

There is absolutely wanting in the present instance the first two of these. There has been no citation, and there is in the *proper sense no libel.* What we have to do with at the present moment is *the libel,* or, in more ordinary language, the complaint. This is vital, for in the same connection the court in the case cited from Pickering's Reports says, on p. 263: "These rules indicate the course which must in substance be pursued by *every tribunal* acting judicially upon the rights of others." And this remark, by the precise terms of the decision, includes proceedings by the Boards of Andover Theological Seminary.

A "libel" implies three things: A plaintiff, or "promoter;" a statement of a cause of action, or ground of proceeding; and a defendant, or respondent. One of the fatal defects in this proceeding is that there is no legal representative of the interests adverse to the respondents.

To define a "libel" we turn to the source of information indicated in the case in 12 Pickering, viz., Burns' Ecclesiastical Law: "A libel is a declaration or charge drawn up in writing on the part of the PLAINTIFF, unto which the defendant is OBLIGED to answer." This statement of course implies that there must be both plaintiff and defendant, and that the latter is required by *some rule of law* to answer.

This is not a case in which your Board can proceed of its own motion to a trial of the respondent.

There may be cases in which an ecclesiastical judge may proceed *ex officio*. Burns, however, says that proceedings which touch *freehold*, debt, trespass, and the like, concern matters between *party* and *party* (Lond., 1797, 6th ed.).

There is substantially a freehold in the present case, as the Professors hold office *during life*, and accordingly have a freehold or life interest in their office. This interest is pronounced by the court in 7 Pickering, 380, 1st paragraph, to be a " valuable property." Even if an *ex-officio* proceeding were proper, it has not been resorted to in the present case. The ordinary method of proceeding by parties has been selected. But this theory is impossible, for these signers have no interest in the matter and cannot possibly be parties "aggrieved." If the case be wrongly conceived, the names of the signers cannot be ignored.

But what is still more decisive is that an *ex officio* proceeding is solely applicable to a *criminal* case. The ecclesiastical law follows the canon law in this respect ; and the bishop or his official proceeds " from the mere office," induced by public fame or the relation of credible persons to inquire into the innocence or criminality of persons within his jurisdiction (Browne on the Practice of the Ecclesiastical Courts, bound up with Browne on the Civil and Admiralty Law, 1st Am. ed., vol. i., pp. 502, 503).

The present case, however, is not to be regarded as a charge of crime. It has no resemblance to the ecclesiastical case of deprivation. The object of "deprivation" was not to unseat a person from a particular benefice, but to deprive a clerical person of his office as minister. Loss of a particular benefice would follow, as well as incapacity to be admitted to any other like position. When Chief Justice Shaw, in 12 Pickering, 262, refers to "deprivation" in ecclesiastical cases, it is only to show the necessary elements of any prosecution in a special tribunal like this, whether the proceeding be criminal or civil. Moreover, "deprivation" before an ecclesiastical tribunal is a breach of the law of England on

account of the relation of Church and State. It is termed
the "king's ecclesiastical law." There is no ecclesiastical
law in this sense in the United States.

The subject of "deprivation" in English ecclesiastical law
is treated with fulness in Godolphin's Abridgment of the Ec- .
clesiastical Laws, London, 1680, title Deprivation (p. 306).
He reduces all causes of deprivation to three : (1) want of
capacity ; (2) contempt ; (3) crime. The crimes are true
crimes in the ordinary sense of the criminal law, such as mur-
der, forgery, and the like, or the violation of some statute
prohibiting criminal acts. The proceeding in the present instance is not for a crime in the domain of criminal law. It
is impossible for this Board to try a criminal case. At most,
this proceeding is for the violation of a trust, which by the
common law is not criminal, but only the subject of a civil
action. It has been declared by one of the signers to be a
scandalous violation of a public trust. It will be shown hereafter, if it be a valid trust, to be a charitable use or trust.
These trusts have for centuries been supervised, controlled,
and superintended in England by the High Court of Chancery, as well as other courts having equitable powers. No
other court has assumed jurisdiction to superintend them or
to correct abuses in their management. All trust law originated with the Court of Chancery, and trusts still remain the
principal objects of chancery or equitable jurisdiction.

It is a mistake to suppose that your Honorable Board, if it
has original jurisdiction, represents simply the visitatorial
power of the common law. This is a statutory tribunal having powers beyond those conceded to visitors at common
law. One very marked distinction between it and the common-law visitor is this : your decisions are reviewable on
appeal, while no appeal lies in the case of a visitor. His is
a domestic forum. He acts summarily. This is not the
case with you. You must follow rules ; you must conduct
yourselves as a court, for so the law of Massachusetts, as
expressed in the statute-book, as construed by the Supreme
Court in 12 Pickering, 262, has provided. Considered as a
court or legal tribunal, so far as you review the management

of trusts, your jurisdiction is in the nature of equitable authority.

Now, it is perfectly well settled that the jurisdiction of equity over trusts is in no respect criminal, but purely civil. A court of equity is not a criminal court. ' Its jurisdiction as a whole is purely civil. It is a property court. Your power to inquire into "heterodoxy" is not a general power extending to all trusts of a charitable nature. It is for the purpose of determining whether the rules of a particular foundation in Andover Seminary have been violated, and nothing more. The creed which you examine need not be in itself a truly Christian creed. It is not because it is Christian that you are reviewing the conduct of the respondent. You are sitting here because certain men having money at their command long ago concluded to make use of it in a special way, and you are inquiring whether the trust that these men now dead imposed upon the property, so far as it is lawful, is being carried out faithfully by the beneficiaries. That is a pure civil inquiry, in the same way as if the trust had been for instruction in medicine or law. That would be so if a court of equity in Massachusetts were to-day engaged in doing the same thing that you are. Why should you be regarded as holding a criminal court, when the Supreme Court holding precisely the same inquiry for the same purpose would be deemed to be holding a civil court?

I cite the following authorities to show that a court of equity has no criminal jurisdiction:

Attorney-General v. *Utica Insurance Co.*, 2 Johns. Ch., 379.
Phillips v. *Stone Mountain Railroad*, 61 Ga., 386.
Life Association v. *Beogher*, 3 Mo. App., 173.
Davis v. *American Society*, 75 N. Y., 362.
Cohen v. *Commissioners of Goldsboro*, 77 N. C., 2.
Cope v. *District Fair*, 99 Ill., 489.
Moses v. *Mobile*, 52 Ala., 198.
Attorney-General v. *Tudor Ice Co.*, 104 Mass., 239, 240.

Special reference is made to the case in 2 Johnson's Chancery, and that of the *Attorney-General* v. *Tudor Ice Co.*, *supra*.

The first of these cases was decided at an early day by Chancellor Kent while presiding in the New York Court of Chancery. He says, on p. 378 of the report, "if a charge be of a criminal nature or an offence against the public, and does not touch the enjoyment of property, it ought not to be brought within the direct jurisdiction of this court, *which was intended* to deal only with matters of civil right resting in equity or where the remedy at law was not sufficiently adequate." The Massachusetts case is still more emphatic. The court said:

" This court, sitting in equity, does not administer punishment or enforce forfeitures for transgression of law; but its jurisdiction is limited to the protection of civil rights, and to cases in which adequate relief cannot be had on the common-law side of the court or of the other courts of the commonwealth " (p. 240).

The administration of trusts in equity is not, accordingly, a criminal proceeding, though it may perhaps be held to assume, as a matter of form, a criminal aspect in certain cases prosecuted in the name of the Attorney-General. These cases are very rare in Massachusetts, and do not include such cases as the present (104 Mass., 239, 240, 244). The last page cited is particularly in point.

No support can be derived for a criminal theory based on the doctrines of an information in the nature of a *quo warranto*. That is a proceeding in a court of common law (not equity) to inquire by what warrant a person occupying an office retains possession of it, and may in case of misconduct result in forfeiture. It was originally *in form* a criminal proceeding, because if the office was forfeited a fine might be inflicted. It is now unanimously recognized by jurists as in substance a civil proceeding, and has by statute been stripped of all criminal aspect in a large number of the American States as well as in England. (See, in England, 47 and 48 Vict., c. 61, § 15, where it is declared that proceedings in *quo warranto* shall be deemed to be *civil* proceedings for all purposes; N. Y. Code of *Civil* Procedure, § 1983, § 1990; followed in many other States.) Moreover, there is nothing to show in the amended complaint that the present proceeding is to obtain the forfeiture of an office. The *quo warranto*, too, is in the name of the *commonwealth* before a court of criminal jurisdiction.

The result is that the present is a civil case, and that there should be, as in all other civil cases, a *true party* to the record, prosecuting it because he has some *interest* in the subject-matter.

The course of proceeding, adopted in a New York case, has been approved in an emphatic manner by the Supreme Judicial Court of Massachusetts, in *Murdock* v. *Phillips Academy*, 12 Pickering, 265. Reference is there made, with marked approval, to the case of the *Dutch Reformed Church in Albany* v. *Bradford*, 8 *Cowen* (N.Y.), 457. There the *consistory*, consisting of the deacons and elders of a church, made a *specific charge* against their minister to the classis, the court having original jurisdiction in such matters. The consistory, as representing the church where the minister was serving, had *an interest* in the question. It was in substance the same as if the church itself had appeared as complainants, or much the same as if in the present case the Trustees of Andover Theological Seminary had in their official capacity presented the case before your Honorable Board.

It ought never to be overlooked that the relation between the Professors and Trustees of Andover Theological Seminary originated *in contract*. It is not like the origin of title to a public office, in which there is simply an appointment, and in general no contract. How can a dissolution of a *contract* justify a criminal proceeding? Suppose that a similar contract had been made by a college where there was no Board of Visitors, and dissolution of the contract was claimed in the ordinary courts, would there be any criminal element in the proceeding? Even if the dissolution were for some crime, the *proceeding for dissolution* would not be criminal, but only for breach of contract.

There is nothing in the remarks of the Supreme Court in the case of *Murdock, Appellant,* etc., 7 Pickering, 330, opposed to these views. The court at this point was discussing the necessity of making the articles of charge definite and particular, and in enforcing that requirement remarked that, *by analogy* to trials on criminal accusations in the courts of justice and the principles of the constitution, no man can be deprived of his office, which is a valuable property, without having the offence with which he is charged "fully and plainly, substantially and formally, described to him." This remark is by no means equivalent to the assertion that a proceeding before the Board of Visitors is a criminal proceeding. Criminal proceedings are referred to simply as sources of our ideas of justice, precisely as the reference in the same breath is made to the principles of the State constitution.

Moreover, the constitution of the State prevents you from holding a criminal court. (See Art. 12.) This provides that no person shall be deprived of his property or estate except by the "judgment of his peers or the law of land." This phrase is uniformly held to guarantee trial by jury in criminal cases.

There should also be mentioned in this connection a most serious practical objection to this proceeding, if it be right, as we insist, to regard it as of a civil nature. Suppose that this proceeding should not be successful, what is there to prevent four other Alumni from instituting a similar proceeding and treading the whole ground over again ? In regularly instituted suits between proper parties a former judgment is a bar to another original proceeding. This is one of the strongest reasons for having formal parties upon the records of the court. But it is an inflexible condition of the application of this rule that the parties should be the same. If four new Alumni should proceed, the parties will not be the same, and the respondent may thus be subjected to repeated litigations. This tribunal should pause before it faces such consequences.

The Charges Considered.

I next proceed to consider the charges themselves.

As the matter now stands in the so-called amended complaint, there is great uncertainty prejudicial to the defence of the respondent. Does the old " complaint " remain? It is not expressly disposed of. Is the new one valid? If so, two cases are pending before the same tribunal for the same cause. This we have objected to, and the two cannot be properly carried on together. Perhaps the amended complaint is a substitute for the old one, and that the validity of further proceedings must now be tested by that. We have a right to demand that the court shall require an election by the signers on which they will stand; and we now demand it.

If the amended complaint be a substitute, we insist that it was not competent for the signers to proceed as they have done. They have apparently assumed to divide the former joint proceeding into five separate proceedings. This cannot be lawfully done. This rule has been applied in equity in a case like the present, except that the names of the *plaintiffs* were divided instead of the respondents. The court would not hear the subdivided cases without the general consent of all parties interested. *Appleton* v. *Chapeltown Paper Co.*, 45 Law Journal, Ch., 276, decided by a great judge, Sir George Jessel, Master of the Rolls. Instead of assenting to the division in this case, the respondent has constantly objected.

But assuming for the moment that the original case can be split into five separate proceedings against the will of the respondents, and that it has been successfully divided, I now reach the amended complaint considered as to its subject-matter, and insist that several cardinal rules of pleading are violated.

Violation of Rules of Pleading as to Subject-Matter.

I. The first three charges are without specifications. They are mere conclusions of law instead of statements of fact; or it may be said that they are mere inferences of the signers, without giving any facts from which the inferences are de-rived. It is true that the expression "hereinafter enume-rated" is used in each case, but that is not enough. Accord-ingly, the words "hereinafter enumerated" in each of the first three charges must be confined to what is set forth in each charge by itself. The result as to these is that there are no specifications as to those charges. There is no enumera-tion *in connection* with the charge. It is required by the sim-plest rules of pleading that each charge should be *complete in itself* (Gould on Pleading, c. iv., sec. 3). The rule is there stated in this form : " In all cases in which there are two or more counts, whether there is actually but one cause of action or several, each count purports *upon the face of it* to disclose a distinct right of action, UNCONNECTED WITH THAT STATED IN ANY OF THE OTHER COUNTS ; so that upon the face of the declaration there appear to be as many different causes of action as there are counts inserted " (4th ed., by George Gould, 1861).

Moreover, if each of the charges is distinct, it is impossi-ble and absurd to assume that the same specifications and quotations from the writings of the Professors will prove each. If the charges are not distinct, but are mere idle rep-etitions, then the first three ought to be stricken out, and we ought to be relieved from the trouble and expense of contesting them.

II. If, however, the fourth charge, with its specifications, be not obnoxious to any criticism of indefiniteness of a vital nature (as we contend that it is), still it is clear that no offence is charged of which this Board has original jurisdiction, even though it be assumed that in certain cases the Board pos-sesses such jurisdiction. It is not one of the cases specified in the article from which original jurisdiction is assumed to be derived.

The distinction between the plain original jurisdiction of the Trustees and the assumed jurisdiction of this Board I now place in view by extracts from the statutes. Article 14 of the Constitution of the Theological Seminary provides that a professor may be removed by the *Trustees* "for gross neglect of duty, scandalous immorality, mental incapacity, or any other just and sufficient cause." Article 20 of the statutes concerning the Associate Foundation confers whatever power of removal is vested in the Board of Visitors, in the following words, " to remove him (a professor), either for misbehavior, heterodoxy, incapacity, or neglect of the duties of his office." A glance will show that the power of the Trustees is broad and wide, while that of the Visitors is specific and restricted. Of the four instances named, only one can possibly be aimed at in these proceedings. This is " heterodoxy."

The powers of the Board of Visitors cannot be extended beyond those named, as they form *part of the original contract between the Trustees and each Professor*. The Visitors have no connection with that contract. They are only to see to its observance. As we have stated, none of these specified grounds of removal can exist in the present case but " heterodoxy." " Heterodoxy," however, is not charged. It is only alluded to in the fourth " charge " (marked IV.), in the following indirect manner : " We charge that the several particulars of the ' heterodoxy' of the said Egbert C. Smyth, and of his opposition to the creed of the Seminary, and to the true intention of the Founders, as expressed in their statutes, are as follows, to wit." This is not a *charge* of " heterodoxy." It plainly assumes that " heterodoxy " has been charged in some prior paragraph. On examining the prior paragraphs no charge whatever of " heterodoxy " appears.

III. But assuming that there is a charge of "heterodoxy " sufficient in form, there is a preliminary inquiry. What is " heterodoxy " within the meaning of the Founders? Does it mean a denial of the principles of the Christian religion, or simply a denial of the doctrines contained in the particular Andover creed which the Professors are required to sign? Reference is now made to the Associate statutes, and to a Professor on the " Associate Foundation." This is a highly penal charge. A Professor's contract, made for life, is to be dissolved by a *quasi*-judicial proceeding. These

" Founders " drew their statutes themselves. The Professors had nothing to do with them. The benefactors, of
course, selected their own words.

In such a case as that, the settled rule of law is that the
instrument and its interpretation is to be taken most
strongly against the party who selected the words in question (Broom's Legal Maxims, 529, and cases cited). The
rule finds strong illustration in such cases as policies of
insurance, where one party to the contract, viz., the insurers,
almost invariably selects the general words used in the
instrument. (See *Harmon* v. *Mut. Ins. Co.*, 81 N.Y., 184,
where this rule is rigidly adhered to.)

It is also a rule that an obscure contract is to be interpreted most strongly against the party to whom the obscur-
ity is attributable (*Wetmore* v. *Pattison*, 45 Mich., 439–441).

In the present case the rule of the so-called Founders has
remained for about eighty years unaltered. The word " heterodoxy " has during all this period remained undefined and
unexplained. Several generations of professors have passed
away without their beliefs being judicially called in question. The word " heterodoxy " *seems to be too vague to
become the subject of judicial inquiry.* Observe that *no power
of* removal is granted to the VISITORS because the party
believes or teaches *in opposition to the creed.* The ground
for removal before this Board is HETERODOXY, and there is
no mode of ascertaining what " heterodoxy " is unless resort
be had to the ordinary meaning of the word.

" Heterodoxy," as commonly understood, is a deviation
from the *established* opinions on the matter of religion.
(See Worcester's Dictionary, title Heterodox.) This would
not fairly include the present case, for there is at most only
a deviation from a special creed, established by three or four
persons, having no correspondence with any creed in general
use among the members of the particular denomination to
which the Founders belonged. It is an eclectic creed, made
up, as will be hereafter shown, from divers and even contradictory sources. If deviation from the creed had been
intended, the Founders should have said so. Power to

remove for that cause may, perhaps, be conferred upon the *Trustees* under the words "other good and sufficient cause." All that we urge now is, that it is not conferred upon the *Board of Visitors.*

Still we cannot refrain from expressing our belief that the "Founders" did not intend to guard assent to their creed by a threat ever suspended over the Professors of removal for "heterodoxy." Their reliance was upon the general character of the Professor and upon his being an "orthodox and consistent Calvinist," and upon his solemn declaration made when he entered upon his duties and repeated every five years. If these could not secure his adhesion to the creed, nothing of a minatory nature could.

The fair conclusion, then, is that the word "heterodoxy," as used in Article 20, refers to a departure from the established tenets of the denomination of Christians to which the Professor belongs. In that view, reference to the creed of the "Founders" is immaterial.

THE GENERAL MERITS OF THE CASE.

While having perfect confidence in the foregoing views, I proceed to argue this case on the theory that "heterodoxy" includes the case of departure from the special creed of the Founders. In that view I shall maintain that no ground exists for the charges set forth in the fourth (IV.) article of the Amended Complaint.

Before taking up this article in detail, it will be necessary to show the precise scope and bearing of the matters in controversy.

This case presents purely a legal question. Has there been such a departure by Professor Smyth from the aims and purposes of the foundation on which he is placed as to violate the contract between him and the Trustees of the Seminary, and to prevent him from enjoying the benefits of the foundation upon which he is placed. This question involves to some extent the law of charitable trusts, and the power of a Board of Visitors acting partly under the com-mou law and partly under provisions of a Massachusetts statute.

The first branch of this subject to be considered is the meaning of the expression " charitable trusts."

The Law of Charitable Trusts Stated.

The first branch of this subject to be considered is the meaning and effect of the expression "charitable trusts," under which it will be claimed by the signers that the present foundation is to be ranked. The word " charitable " is here a purely technical word, and not to be confounded with its popular meaning of bestowal of alms upon the poor. The great element in a " charitable trust " is that it is public in its nature, and in some form beneficial or useful to mankind. Such trusts existed as far back, in England, as there is clear historical light, being undoubtedly borrowed from a highly developed system on this subject in the later Roman law, attributable to the general spread of the principles of Christianity, and to the necessity of endowments for the support of hospitals, care of the poor, houses of rest for wayfarers, support of churches and priests, redemption of Christian captives, etc.

These trusts, introduced into England no doubt by the clergy, have been mainly for the promotion of practical good deeds among men. But few, comparatively, have existed for the mere spread of opinions. An attempt, rude it must be admitted, to classify them is found, in England, in a statute of the 43d Elizabeth (A.D. 1601), Chapter IV. It is by reference to the classifications of this statute that English courts have been largely guided in determining whether a gift is charitable or not. It is a significant fact that none of the enumerations in that statute has any connection with the spread of religious opinions. The poor are referred to, education, public works, relief of prisoners, marriage portions of poor maids, support of young tradesmen, and the like. It is only by inference that religious opinions are included. Before the year 1600 such foundations can scarcely have ex-

isted, or they would, if common, no doubt have been referred
to in the statute of Elizabeth.

There is a peculiarity about trusts for these purposes,
which sets them apart from all of a private nature. They
ask *the protection of the law* for the continuance of the foundation *forever*. The fund is to be forever intact, and only
the income, as it accrues from time to time, is to be appropriated to the "charitable" use. The long line of beneficiaries
beginning to-day, it may be, stretches on to infinity. Nothing of this kind is tolerated in the case of private trusts.
They must end at the termination of a specified number of
lives in being when the trust is created, and a moderate term
of years in addition (twenty-one years). Every such trust
may thus be challenged as to its validity. What is its object?
Is it to found a family, to promote the ends of private persons, even to found a library or a picture-gallery for their exclusive use? If so, it cannot be perpetual. On the other
hand, is it to found a public library, public schools, give employment to the poor, to establish a public hospital? Then
it may last forever, for public uses and public necessities
never end.

In fact, the distinction between private trusts and charitable trusts depends on large views of public policy. It is
contrary to the best interests of a State to permit an owner
of property, by any deed, will, or other instrument whatever,
to keep the estate forever devoted to private uses. In the
nervous language of the old judges, they who attempt to do
this "fight against God," who decrees in human affairs muta-
tion and instability instead of fixedness and stability. To
this general rule of invalidity of permanent trusts, the special rule as to charitable uses is the only exception.

Now, what is the underlying thought that lends to these
charitable trusts a practical immortality, and to this end sum-
mons the law to their protection and support? To this inquiry there is but one answer. It is the element in them of
public utility. Let them be beneficial to the public; they
may be allowed to exist. Let them be pernicious to the
public; they should be unsparingly condemned and rooted

out. Public utility is thus the condition and the law of their existence.

Perhaps no case shows this more clearly than the very peculiar foundation of Thomas Brown, established by the Court of Chancery in England, in the case of the *University of London* v. *Yarrow*, 23 Beavan, 159, and on appeal in 1 De Gex & Jones, 73. The testator made a bequest to a corporation for founding, establishing, and upholding an institution for studying and endeavoring to cure maladies of any quadrupeds or birds *useful to man.* The Lord Chancellor said, in this case : "I cannot entertain for a moment a doubt that the establishment of a hospital in which animals which are *useful to mankind* should be properly treated and cured, and the nature of their diseases investigated, with *a view to public advantage*, is a charity" (1 D. G. & J., 80).

This being the crucial test of a charitable institution, it would follow that no establishment of this kind pernicious to mankind, or even of doubtful utility, could be upheld for a moment by the courts. The institution must be able to vindicate its right to a perpetual existence, by showing that it is presumably for the public advantage.

Such a principle as this is peculiarly applicable to a perpetual foundation for teaching and inculcating opinions. It surely cannot be for the public advantage to have erroneous opinions propagated among the young. The theory of one of the counsel for the complainants cannot be upheld, to the effect that it is immaterial whether the opinions are plainly erroneous or not. No charity could reasonably be upheld which was established for the perpetual instruction of youth in the Ptolemaic theory of astronomy, or its modern Ethiopian revival under the proposition "that the sun do move." What has been won from the darkness of ignorance ought to be retained, not merely as the knowledge of scientists, but as the common property of the people.

I quote some valuable remarks upon this subject from a work by the present Lord Hobhouse, formerly Sir Arthur Hobhouse, long an active member of the Board of English Commissioners of Charities, and a high judicial officer. No person in England, where charitable institutions number forty thousand at least has more knowledge or experience of their practical workings than he. I refer now to his work called the Dead Hand (published in London, by Chatto & Windus, 1880). He says, on p. 123: "There is a subject on which very few can speak plainly without giving offence. It is asked as though the question were unanswerable whether a public tribunal shall interfere with foundations for the support of opinions? The opinions for which foundations are established are usually of a theological character, and it is thought that foundations for this purpose are more valuable and sacred than others. Now, as to their being more valuable I will not hesitate to say that foundations attaching endowments to the holding and teaching of prescribed opinions *are, if they are to be unalterable*, the very worst kind of foundations that can be conceived; for experience shows that the opinions to which men have attached property change and become extinct (sooner or later, according to their depth and force), and then you have a direct premium on profession without belief. But that which tends to corrupt the noblest part of man, the very eye of the soul, his perception of truth, is as evil a thing as can be imagined. Suppose, for instance, that a large estate had been settled in the sixteenth century for maintaining the geocentric theory of the universe. It was believed implicitly; it was supposed to rest on the clearest testimony of revelation; to doubt it was impious. Suppose, then, that this had been done, and that now, when every child at a national school knows the contrary, solemn lectures were delivered to show that in some sense or other — astronomical, metaphorical, or mystical — the sun travelled around the earth. Is any public authority to interfere with so degrading a mockery? It is said 'You cannot interfere with the authority of the founder.' I venture to say, you can and ought. As long as any man believes any opinion whatever, let him proclaim it, without molestation, from the house-tops. But to allow that property shall be devoted forever to bribing people into teaching what they do not believe is monstrous."

These are wise words, searching the matter to the core.

No doubt the English Court of Chancery has frequently followed the intentions of the founders of a charity with great closeness, even when lamenting their unwisdom. There are thus all over England charitable institutions founded in form on the theory of public utility, which are now on long experience producing most pernicious results — encouraging pauperism, opposed to sound theories of political economy, promoting ignorance, or fomenting domestic discord, or gratifying personal rancor and bitterness. An instance of the last is that of Thomas Nash, of Bath, who gave a perpetual annuity to the ringers of bells at the Abbey Church, Bath, " who were to ring from time to time forever a whole peal of bells, with muffled clappers and various solemn and doleful changes, on the anniversary of his wedding-day for twelve hours ; and on the anniversary of the day of his death to ring a grand bob major, with merry, mirthful peals, for the same space of time, in joyful commemoration of his happy release from domestic tyranny and wretchedness." These are his own words (Lord Hobhouse's Dead Hand, 102, 103). This bitter-minded testator was thus allowed to inscribe on the records of the court a perpetual and apparently malicious libel on the character of his wife, in the technical form of a charity, because the gift was to sustain in perpetuity the bell-ringers of a church.

The Parliament has been compelled to interfere with the galling chains of this severe construction as far as opinions are concerned, and in the Dissenters' Chapels Act, 7 and 8 Vict., c. 45, to provide, by way of partial relief, that unless there is in the deed of trust an express requirement that particular religious doctrines be taught or observed, or be forbidden to be taught, the usage for twenty-five years immediately preceding any suit shall be taken as conclusive evidence that doctrines in accordance with the usage may henceforward be taught and observed.

It is certainly well worth while considering by the courts of this country, so far as the question is still open for consideration, whether it is judicious to adopt a literal and ironclad construction of these creeds, which may foster litigation, and even in the absence of litigation check the educational movement of the time and prevent thorough educational training.

It is to be carefully observed that the present case is *not* distinctively that of a *religious creed*. It is not imposed, as is usual in such cases, upon a congregation of believers. It is meant as a clog upon *instruction*, and may turn out to be a prohibition against instruction in the truth. It says to a body of teachers " You must not teach doctrines because they are true, but because we, the ' founders,' impose them upon you." It says to pupils, " You must not hear from your instructors the truth simply and solely because it is the truth, but only so far as we, the ' founders,' allow your instructors to impart it." The teacher is thus emasculated, and the growth of the scholar is one-sided and dwarfed. In the name, not only of the professors under trial, but of all the teachers of the land, including, I hope, the chairman of this Board, I respectfully protest against such shackles of iron upon education.

Let us consider precisely what this creed means to teachers. Here is a class of blameless and highly intelligent men, who think that their true vocation is education of the young, and that in some of the noblest branches of knowledge — theology, ecclesiastical history, homiletics, and in the art of skilful and persuasive public speech. They are invited to pursue their calling at Andover Theological Seminary. They are met at the entrance with a ponderous creed, smelling of antiquity and the outcome of the fiery struggles of ancient days — contests of which we have little or no knowledge, and with which we have as little sympathy. Its words are technical and uncouth. Its clauses are confused and con· tradictory. Yet all must alike adopt this creed, *the real meaning of which has never been interpreted.* If such a creed is good for instructors in theology, why will it not answer in medicine or law? Why will it not be useful to instructors in art? One of these Professors really teaches a fine art — rhetoric and elocution. Now, it is said to him in substance:

" You must not comment upon the graceful style of Addison, nor the gorgeous diction of Jeremy Taylor, unless you combine in your mind the utterances of Augustine, Athanasius, and Calvin, with the metaphysical observations of the elder Jonathan Edwards, and the correct exposition of the phrase 'corporeal strength' as coined by Dr. Samuel Spring. You must not refer to the eloquent speech of Chatham or Erskine, of Webster or Choate, until you renounce the heresy of the Sabellians and all the wicked works of the Arminians and Pelagians. This you and your successors must do from time to time forever." If such a check on instruction is good at Andover, why wouldn't it be useful at Harvard, Amherst, or Williams? To tie an institution to such a creed seems like anchoring a vessel in the swift current of a flowing stream amid the mud and rubbish of bygone ages. So the Phillipses, Browns, and Abbots, noble in their intentions and sincere Christians, but erring in sound judgment, bedded their little institution on the hills of Andover, among the mud and rubbish of extinct controversies. There is no comparison between the effects of a stationary creed upon education and upon a church. The former is open to the charge of misleading youth — one of the gravest offences known to the commonwealth of ancient Athens. Should the present or a similar case reach the Supreme Judicial Court, it may be worth while for the judges to consider the legal effect of imposing a non-elastic creed, religious or otherwise, upon teachers in our great theological or other professional or literary institutions.

It serves my present purpose to point out some of the far-reaching questions of this painful case, and to suggest that if this creed is to prevail it should have a liberal interpretation, that technicalities should not bear sway, that contradictions or modifications should be reconciled and adjusted, that the substance of the creed should be only regarded, and above all, where the creed is silent, that the principles of justice and the general spirit of Christianity be followed.

Let your Honorable Board remember that this creed having never been judicially interpreted as to the *specific meaning* of phrases used, the professors in considering its meaning had the right to give it all the breadth allowed by rules of liberal interpretation as applied by good-sense, honesty of purpose, and the rules of courts having jurisdiction over such subjects.

The general correctness of this line of argument is affirmed by an important decision of the Supreme Judicial Court in a case concerning this very creed. I refer to the case of *The Trustees of Phillips Academy* v. *James King, Executor*, 12 Mass., 546 (A.D. 1815).

This case is of so much consequence, from the point of view now before your Board, that I ask your indulgence if I state it at some length.

The controversy arose out of the will of Mary Norris, dated March 21, 1811, who bequeathed to the Trustees of Phillips Academy, in Andover, thirty thousand dollars, for the benefit of the Theological Institution, so that the income might be received from time to time and the principal kept invested. She expressly directed that her bequest should "enure particularly and exclusively (so far as may be consistent with the constitution of the said associates) to that part of said institution commonly called the *Associate Foundation*."

The facts were submitted to the court upon an agreed case. It is referred to at this point in the argument to show the rule of construction adopted in determining the validity of the bequest. It was claimed on behalf of the executors that the will of Mrs. Norris was void, on the ground that the Trustees of Phillips Academy, by the Act of the Legislature of June 19, 1807, were made capable only to hold property for the support of a theological institution agreeably to the will of the donors IF CONSISTENT with the ORIGINAL DESIGN of the founders of the Academy (see Deeds and Donations, 68, 69; Act of 1814, p. 132; Act of 1824, p. 164), that this design was to propagate *Calvinism* as containing the important principles and distinguishing tenets of the Christian religion as summarily expressed in the Westminster Assembly's Shorter Catechism, and that the design of the donors of the associate foundation was to add to Calvinism the leading principles of Hopkinsianism — a mixture inconsistent with the original design of the founders of the Academy.

It is to be observed that Mrs. Norris made her will with all the associate statutes before her. These were adopted March 21, 1808. Her will was dated March 21, 1811, precisely three years later.

Now mark what the court, speaking through Judge Thatcher, says as to the objection of the executor's counsel (p. 562 of the report).

" The counsel for the defendant brought forward in the argument, and urged upon the consideration of the court with great force, several specific propositions or articles of two opposing creeds, or which the counsel contended were directly contrary to each other, insisting that the intent of the founders (Mrs. Phillips, John Phillips, Jr., and Samuel Abbot) was to maintain Calvinism, or the theology of Calvin ; and if there were but one single article or proposition in the creed of the associate founders contrary to Calvinism, the Trustees of the Academy would have no right to take and appropriate the legacy in question ; and should the creed imposed by the associate founders omit a single article contained in the creed of Calvin, or as Calvinism was understood at the time of the foundation of the Academy, it would be such a departure from the intent, design, and plan of the *original founders* that it must intercept the extended legacy and prevent any right from vesting in the plaintiffs. It was then stated to be an essential article in the creed of Calvin, and what all Calvinists must necessarily believe to make them Christians according to the Calvinistic theology, that 'the original sin of Adam is imputed to all posterity in some way or manner ; that they are all and every one actual sinners — whereas the associate foundation did not admit this article in the creed taught in their branch of the theological school, but substituted the following article in lieu thereof, and made it a necessary part of the religious creed to the professors, and to be by them taught to the students in the institutions, viz., Adam, the federal head and representative of the human race, was placed in a state of probation, and in consequence of his disobedience all of his descendants were constituted sinners' — which latter article, it was urged, is not only an article of a system of religion called Hopkinsianism, but is inconsistent with and contrary to the system of Calvinism in general, and particularly to the foregoing article of the creed of Calvin, or of a Calvinistic Christian, as taught in the Assembly's Shorter Catechism, as could not be taught in consistency and harmony with the design, views, and intentions of the *original founders* of the Academy, and thus the legacy being given to promote Hopkinsianism, in opposition to Calvinism, as explained in the said catechism, is void."

Before going further in this case, it must be stated, by way of explanation, that three distinct classes of donors have been referred to by the court in this decision: (*a*) the early or true founders, of April 21, 1778; (*b*) the donors of August 31, 1807, Madame Phœbe Phillips, John Phillips, and Samuel Abbot, who may be called the Calvinistic donors; (*c*) the donors of March 21, 1808, called the Hopkinsian or associate donors.

Now, the objection that was urged upon the court was, that there was an inconsistency between the requirements of the Calvinistic founders marked above (*b*) and that of the associates marked (*c*), and that as the legislative act of June 19, 1807, required *consistency*, there was no "consistency," and the plan of the associates could not be carried out. If the legacy of Mrs. Norris necessitated Hopkinsianism, so much the worse for it. It was void.

Now, observe the way in which the court answers this apparently formidable objection. It holds that the counsel missed *the true point* of the case, for the act of the Legislature (June 19, 1807), in referring to the *original design* of the founders, means the founders above marked (*a*) — the founders of 1778 — and each of the creeds (of 1807 and 1808) now before your Board must be consistent with that design. This was beyond doubt the meaning, for the creed of 1807 was not adopted until August 31st, while the act of the Legislature was enacted June 19th, forty days before.

The Constitution of 1778 prescribed no creed. It declared

in two places, and with much emphasis, that "the *first* and *principal* object of the institution (italics by the founders) is the promotion of true piety and virtue."

Now, the question is, Does the associate creed of March, 1808, square with that "*original* design"? In deciding that point the court applies a rule of construction which we invoke in our behalf, using the following language:

"There is a clear and intelligible meaning consistent with the whole course of the providential government of God over the natural and moral world by general laws, so far as the subject has been investigated, which may be applied to the two articles attempted to be contrasted *with no greater latitude in the use of language* than is frequently applied by *orthodox divines* to words and phrases in the Bible not always to be taken literally, in which sense these propositions or articles will mean the same thing. And in such sense they are consistent with the revelations contained in the Bible, which revelations make up the fundamental principles of the religion of Jesus. Hence there is no necessity of conjecturing a variety of meanings which the words may *possibly* be susceptible of in minds more habituated to dwell on the theories of certain divines than on the religion of Jesus as delivered by himself and those who were authorized by God the Father to preach it. AND I HESITATE NOT TO SAY THAT IN ALL CASES LIKE THIS we ought to be satisfied whenever we can reconcile the language of honest Christians by that CHARITY of CONSTRUCTION which it is allowed by all that we should apply to the Holy Scriptures."

"For myself," Judge Thatcher continues, "I confess that I do not clearly perceive any other sense than that in which the two articles mean *substantially* the same thing, notwithstanding some diversity of expression in which they can be said to be true and consistent with the Christian religion; and knowing as we do the founders, as well as the after benefactors who have set up the associate foundation, to be persons of great piety and most sincere believers in the religion of Jesus, and that the *first and principal object with all of them* has been to establish, teach, and enforce the belief and practice of that religion on the students of the institution, and through them on the whole world of mankind — why should we now be called upon to apply an *astute, narrow, and uncharitable* construction upon a few technical propositions, merely to divert the legacy of a pious woman from an object nearer to her than life itself? And let me add, in this case the object is great and noble beyond almost anything in our country."

These are, indeed, noble and statesmanlike words. They establish several propositions closely related to this case. They allow a latitude in the interpretation of this very creed, looking more to the fundamental principles of the Christian religion than to the mere words of the creed itself. Christ is greater than the divines who resort to certain theories in the interpretation of his words. There must be charity of construction, and substantial agreement with the creed is sufficient. We must reflect that the men who framed the creed were men of great piety and sincere believers, and their leading end and aim was not to exalt their creed, but to promote the religion of their Master. Why, then, is this court called upon to adopt an " astute, narrow, and uncharitable construction," to subvert a legacy? It is on this reasoning that the legacy is valid, for there must be a *substantial* agreement with the original design. Without this mode of construction there would be at this moment no associate foundation in existence. We ask in a like spirit, why should an " astute, narrow, and uncharitable construction " be now adopted to impair the reputation and to take away the property of men who are equally pious and sincere believers, and who have a similar intent to promote the religion of their Master?

We have only to add that this opinion of Judge Thatcher is the *law of Massachusetts* as applied by him to this particular creed. As law, and as announced by the highest appellate court, the views there set forth are binding on this Board. It would be a breach of judicial subordination not to follow them. You are required by this decision to adopt a liberal and charitable construction as opposed to one astute and narrow; you are to regard substance rather than the mere technical meaning of words; and you are to do this because the principal object of the founders was to teach the students the belief and practice of religion rather than to teach a creed, and because without this liberal construction there would to-day be no associate foundation in Andover Theological Seminary.

We accordingly stand upon this rule of construction, insisting that we have a right to its benefits throughout this present controversy.

THE CREED CONSIDERED AS A LEGAL DOCUMENT.

Taking up now for discussion the specific points involved in this case, we can but be struck with the strictly *legal* aspect of this creed. It abounds, yea, superabounds, with legal terms and conceptions. Adam is declared to be the *federal* head and representative of the human race. God, it asserts, entered into a *covenant* of grace with those whom of his own good pleasure he elected to everlasting life. His covenant with them was to deliver them of this state of misery by a *Redeemer*. This Redeemer made an *atonement* for the sins of all men, etc.

Mr. Maine, in his masterly work on Ancient Law, was the first to point out how all such creeds as these are saturated with the rules and principles of Roman law. None of these questions were discussed or even broached in the Eastern Church. That was governed by the Greek spirit, delighting in pure metaphysical speculations and in theology, engaging in profound controversies as to the divine persons, the divine substance, and the divine natures. The men of the Western Empire were of a more practical nature, looking at the problems which beset man in his daily life and the rules which are to be applied to govern them. Their vocation was jurisprudence. During the middle ages, while nearly every other source of knowledge was eclipsed, they had at hand a vast store-house of refined and masterly legal speculations in the books of Justinian and the commentaries upon them. It is a mistake to suppose that the Pandects were lost during this dark period and then found, as some writers maintain. They were always at hand to guide opinion, and moulded the ideas of theologians.

The Latin language furnished a copious and accurate vocabulary to express theological ideas. To quote a passage from Maine: "The nature of sin and its transmission by inheritance; the debt owed by man and its vicarious satisfaction; the necessity and sufficiency of the atonement; above all, the apparent antagonism between free-will and the Divine Providence — these were points which the West began to debate as ardently as ever the East had discussed the articles of its more special creed. Why is it, then, that on the two sides of the line which divides the Greek-speaking from the Latin-speaking provinces there lie two classes of theological problems so strikingly different from one another? . . . I affirm without hesitation that the difference between the two theological systems is accounted for by the fact that in passing from the East to the West theological speculation had passed from a climate of Greek metaphysics to a climate of Roman law. . . . Almost everybody who has knowledge enough of Roman law to appreciate the Roman penal system, the Roman theory of the obligations established by contract or delict, the Roman view of debts, and of the modes of incurring, extinguishing, and transmitting them, the Roman notion of the continuance of individual existence by universal succession, may be trusted to say whence arose the frame of mind to which the problems of Western theology proved so congenial; whence came the phraseology in which these problems were stated, and whence the description of reasoning employed in their solution?" (Maine's Ancient Law, Scribner's ed., ch. 9, pp. 329–347). It is in singular conformity with these views that we find that John Calvin was a great jurist and thoroughly versed in the subtleties and refinements of the Roman law, which are plentifully exhibited throughout his writings (4 Ency. Britannica, 9th ed., 714, title John Calvin). It may be added that the conception of Adam as the " federal head" of his race is a plain Roman-law notion; for that system assumes that a family is a corporation represented by its head, and that this corporation is immortal, and that rights and liabilities are transmitted by succession to the ever-changing members of the family. It grows more and more clear on careful study that the principles of the Roman law colored theology after the Reformation as well as before. An important inference from these views is, that these Roman-law conceptions may be true for us, but may not be suited to all men; that they may, and probably will be, to a certain extent, shifting and transitory. Some wisdom in the framers of this creed is, as we think, accordingly shown in requiring the Professors to maintain and inculcate, not only the Christian faith as expressed in the creed, but also all the other doctrines and duties of our holy religion so far as may appertain to their office, ACCORDING TO THE BEST LIGHT GOD SHALL GIVE THEM. Here is a sufficiently wide door opened for a professor to compare the creed with the Scriptures, and to determine whether its formal and legal words are the final and the absolutely authoritative expression of Christian thought. In adding this last-named clause, the founders would seem to have "builded better than they knew," awarding to honest-minded and candid teachers the range of study and expression which their vocation necessarily requires.

RELATION OF THE CREED OF THE ASSOCIATE FOUNDERS TO THE WESTMINSTER SHORTER CATECHISM.

I now approach the topic of the relation of the Associate Creed to the formulas of the Westminster Shorter Catechism. It is highly noticeable that there is not one word concerning the Westminster Catechism in the constitution of the original founders. That all came in with the donations of the later donors, and especially with those of August 31, 1807. It will be found that in some respects not touched upon by Judge Thatcher in the case in 12 Mass., 546, there is a serious modification of one by the other, and this modification, it is believed, lies at the very root of some of the matters now in controversy.

I shall contend, among other things, that no professor on the Associate Foundation is required to subscribe to the

Westminster Assembly's Shorter Catechism, and this largely on the ground that the Associate Founders in making up their creed selected from the Shorter Catechism certain passages *verbatim*, omitting others, and that it is impossible to reconcile the creed with the catechism. What they expressly used, they of course adopted; what they omitted, they rejected.

It will be incumbent upon me to give some account of the history of the production of the Westminster Catechism and its associated document, viz., the Westminster confession of faith. This account will shed light on the reasons why it was so mangled by the Associate Founders.

The Westminster Assembly, a grave and dignified body of men, was by no means simply an assembly of divines or a church convocation. So far was it from anything of that kind, that it was a political body, much resembling a constitutional commission in one of the American States to form or to revise a State Constitution. It was called in a dark and lowering time in English history, when the bands of the old royal government were being shaken, and the pressing question in men's minds was as to what would succeed it. The established religion had been abolished ; and the inquiry was as to its successor, also to be established by Act of Parliament. The Ordinance for calling the Assembly was passed June 12, 1643, by both Houses of Parliament. It was an Ordinance and not a law, for the king would not assent to it. It is entitled, " An Ordinance of the Lords and Commons in Parliament for the calling of an assembly of learned and Godly divines, and others to be consulted with by the Parliament, for the settling of the government and liturgy of *the Church of England*, and for vindicating and clearing of the doctrine of the said Church from false aspersions and interpretations " (see Rushworth's Historical Collections, where the Ordinance is published at length). Among the delegates are noblemen, noted lawyers, heads of colleges, statesmen as well as divines.

Their function was to discuss and advise as to such matters as were *proposed* to them by *both Houses of Parliament, and no other*, and in particular to come to a nearer agreement with the Church of Scotland. The persons named in the Ordinance were required to attend. They were also required to divulge none of their doings without the consent of the Parliament. Their presiding officer was named in the Ordinance. The expenses of the divines were borne by "the commonwealth" at the rate of four shillings per day, and they were relieved from all loss and forfeiture by reason of non-residence and absence from their churches or cures. What was this but to create a great governmental machine with the view of establishing a National Church? It was that and nothing else.

Every one versed in the history of the time knows that this was a sagacious scheme to establish a Parliamentary Church of the Presbyterian type. This was the reason of the existence of the Assembly and the law of its being. The first attempt was to revise the Thirty-nine Articles of the Church of England. After proceeding some way with these, this plan was abandoned.

There were two parties in the Assembly — the Presbyterians and the Independents, or "Congregationalists," the former far outnumbering the latter. There were in all one hundred and forty-nine persons named in the Parliamentary Ordinance. All decisions agreed to by the majority were to be reported to Parliament as being agreed to by the Assembly. The Parliament had determined, as far back as 1641 (December 2d), that there should be throughout the whole realm religious conformity, stating that they would not let loose the golden reins of discipline and government to leave private persons to take up what form of divine service they please (Petition and Remonstrance, 4 Rushworth, 438–451; Proposition 185, on p. 450).

Professor Masson (Life of Milton, vol. ii., p. 514) rightly says that "this Assembly, sitting for more than five years and a half, holding one thousand one hundred and sixty-three sessions, side by side with the Long Parliament, and in constant conference and co-operation with it, has left remarkable and permanent effects in the British Islands. Its history ought to be more interesting in some respects to Britons now than the history of the Council of Basel, the Council of Trent, or any other of the great ecclesiastical councils, more ancient and ecumenical, about which we hear so much." It may properly be added, more interesting to ourselves; for we are to-day feeling its influence in the charge against five Professors in Andover Theological Seminary for "heterodoxy" in not adopting its shibboleth and swearing by its precise forms.

The enormous preponderance of the Presbyterian element in the Assembly is shown by the fact that of the one hundred and five divines who were members, one hundred were of that sect and only five were Independents. They were collected to revise the national creed, and to establish new forms of worship in place of the disowned liturgy. English politicians still thought that there must be a national church, and that no person in the country should be permitted to be out of it. It was the prevailing notion that it was possible to frame propositions respecting all great religious problems — concerning God, the creation of man, free-will, sin, and man's destiny — that should be so true and fixed that the nation should be bound to them, and that no person subject to English law should be permitted to swerve from them (2 Masson, Life, etc., 525). This was certainly the view of the Presbyterian party in the Assembly. Now mark the precise difference between this idea and the contemporary notion of the New England Independent divines as represented by their leader, John Robinson. When, in 1620, he prayed with the emigrants departing from Delfthaven in Holland, and gave them his parting blessing, he exhorted them to openness of mind and candor of thought. His memorable words were: "I cannot sufficiently bewail the condition of the reformed churches, who are come to a period in religion, and will go at present no further than the instruments of their reformation. The Lutherans cannot be drawn to go beyond what Luther saw; and the Calvinists, you see, stick fast where they were left by that great man of God, who yet saw not all things. This is a misery much to be lamented; for though they were burning and shining lights in their times, yet they penetrated not into the whole counsel of God; but were they now living, would be as willing to embrace further lights as that which they first received. I beseech you, remember it as an *article of your church covenant* that *you be ready to receive whatever truth shall be made known to you from the written word of God.*" He adds, by way of caution, that they should take heed as to what they receive as truth, examining it, considering it, and comparing it with other Scriptures of truth before they receive it (Neal, Hist. Puritans, vol. ii., pp. 120, 121).[1]

---

[1] Since the preparation of this argument, I have met with additional evidence that there was a strong party of the ablest religious Protestant and orthodox thinkers opposed to non-elastic religious creeds, about the time of the formation of the Westminster Catechism. I refer for a single instance to a passage in the famous work of Mr. William Chillingworth entitled "The Religion of Protestants a Safe Way to Salvation." Speaking of creeds he says, "This presumptuous imposing of the senses of men upon the words of God, the special senses of men upon the general words of God, and laying them upon men's consciences together under the equal penalty of death and damnation ; this vain conceit that we can speak of the things of God better than in the words of God ; thus deifying our own interpretations and tyrannous enforcing them upon others ; this restraining of the Word of God from that latitude and generality and the understanding of men from that liberty wherein Christ and the apostles left them, is and hath been the only fountain of all the schisms of the Church, and that which makes them immortal; the common incendiary of Christendom, and that which tears into pieces not the coat, but the bowels and members of Christ, *vidente Turco nec dolente Judæo.* Take away these walls of separation, and all will quickly be one. Take away this persecuting, burning, cursing, damning of men for not subscribing to the words of men as the words of God; require of Christians only to believe Christ, and to call no man master but him only; let those leave claiming infallibility that have no title to it, *and let them that in their words disclaim it,* disclaim it likewise in their actions. In a word take away tyranny, which is the devil's instrument to support errors and superstitions and impieties, in the several parts of the world which could not otherwise long withstand the power of truth ; I say take away tyranny, and restore Christians to their just and full liberty of captivating their understandings to Scripture only, and as rivers when they have a free passage run all to the ocean, so it may well be hoped by God's blessing, that universal liberty, thus moderated, may quickly reduce Christendom to truth and unity. These thoughts of peace (I am persuaded) may come from the God of peace and to his blessing I commend them." Answer to Fourth Chapter of "Charity Maintained by Catholics," Section 16. These are noble words for the year 1637, and one can well understand from them why John Locke treated Chillingworth as his master. Chillingworth as he states in this connection was referring to some existing Protestant creeds. It is interesting to trace the close resemblance between these thoughts and the views of Judge Thatcher in the case of Trustees of Phillips Academy against King, 12 Massachusetts Reports, 559, 563.

Here we have two opposing and warring elements in the Westminster Assembly — the one party insisting that truth could be positively stated in a fixed form of words, to be binding on every person, and that they could and would fix the form; the other party urged that no man or set of men could see all things, and that no fixed and immutable creed could properly be made. What was the claim of the Calvinists but a claim to infallibility? Well says the historian Gardiner of that period, "the men of culture and education in England stood between two infallibilities — the infallibility of Calvinism and the infallibility of Rome" (Gardiner's England under the Duke of Buckingham, etc., vol. i., p. 213, Longmans, London, 1875). We must now count it as a misfortune, I think, that the great and growing element of New England Independency was not represented in this Assembly. It would have been perfectly proper for the colonies to have been represented there, for they were still in law and fact a part of England, and liable at any time to be governed by imperial authority.

A pressing invitation was sent from England by noblemen and other leading men to Mr. Cotton, of Boston, Hooker, of Hartford, and Mr. Davenport, of New Haven, to come over to England to assist " in settling and composing the affairs of the Church." They probably regarded the Assembly as a political expedient. Hooker said that he " liked not the business, and did not think it any sufficient call for them to go three thousand miles." At all events they did not go. One must now think that if these able men had attended, and pressed the views of Robinson, there would have been a true religious progress. But it was not so to be.

Five men of tolerant opinions must bear the brunt of the struggle alone. They were Congregational ministers recently returned from Holland. Their names should be mentioned: Thomas Goodwin, Philip Nye, William Bridge, Jeremiah Burroughs, and Sidrach Simpson — men able, learned, and distinguished. But what were they among so many?

I would not be understood as stating that the five representatives of Independency above named stood for absolute liberty of religious opinion. The divines of that time were not so far advanced.

They, however, had some latitude of view as to requirements of uniformity. They had avowed it as one of their principles, that they would not commit themselves that the views they then held would remain always unchanged (3 Masson, Life, 89). They allowed liberty of religious difference to a certain extent, while the leading spirits of the army, going further, supported that liberty without qualification.

The great majority of the Assembly favored an absolute and complete conformity of the English people to the church about to be established by them. The Shorter Catechism was but a minor branch of a great and comprehensive scheme, including doctrine, discipline, and worship. They reckoned, however, without Oliver Cromwell, and in the end had to take his views into account. The House of Commons, at his instigation, on September 13, 1644, passed an order to the effect that the Assembly should endeavor to reconcile their differences of opinion; and if that cannot be done, should endeavor to find out some way how far tender consciences, who cannot in all things submit to the common rule which shall be established, may be borne with according to the Word.

The Assembly reported progress from time to time to the Parliament. Their scheme was taken up and discussed proposition by proposition. On the 28th of January, 1644–45, the Scotch system of Presbyterianism was established by law, with Presbyteries (or classes), Synods, and a National Assembly.

John Milton could not endure the political windings and turnings of the Westminster Assembly. In a famous sonnet he describes their plots and packings as worse than those of the Council of Trent.

From time to time the Assembly continued to report, and the Parliament continued, even during all the excitement and confusion of the civil war, to discuss and adopt. On the 1st day of May, 1648, they passed the terrible Ordinance for the Suppression of Blasphemies and Heresies, so that it became the law of England. It provided "that whoever should teach, print or write, maintain, and publish that there is no God, or that God is not present in all places, doth not know and foreknow all things, or that he is not Almighty, that he is not perfectly holy, or that he is not eternal; or that the Father is not God, the Son is not God, or that the Holy Ghost is not God, or that the three are not one Eternal God; or shall in like manner maintain that Christ is not God equal with the Father, or shall deny the manhood of Christ, or that the Godhead and manhood of Christ are several natures, or that the humanity of Christ is pure and unspotted of all sin; or that shall maintain and publish, as aforesaid, that Christ did not die, nor rise from the dead, nor is ascended into Heaven bodily; or shall deny that his death is meritorious in behalf of believers; or shall maintain and publish, as aforesaid, that Jesus Christ is not the Son of God, or that the Holy Scripture, *videlicet* (here follows the list of the canonical books), is not the Word of God, or that the bodies of men shall not rise again after they are dead, or that there is no day of judgment after death: all such maintaining and publishing of such error or errors, with obstinacy therein, shall by virtue hereof be adjudged *felony*. It is further provided that if such person be convicted and does not abjure his errors, he shall suffer *the pains of death*, as in case of felony, without benefit of clergy."

For certain minor errors, one of which is that a church government by Presbytery is unchristian or unlawful, the offender is to be committed to prison.

I do not overlook the fact that there is in the Westminster Confession of Faith (chap. 20, paragraph 2) a noble statement that "God alone is lord of the conscience, and hath left it free from the doctrine and commandments of men which are in anything contrary to his word or beside it in matters of faith and worship." Placed where it is, it is an abstract proposition; and if it means the liberty of the individual conscience, it is not consistent with the Acts of Parliament adopting this creed, nor with the general purpose of the Assembly.

Such was the final outcome of the attempt by Parliament to prescribe a fixed formula for Christian faith. It was scarcely ten years later when all its works and doings passed out of legal existence. Its bloody statute of Conformity is absolutely blotted out from the statute-book with its other laws. It fondly supposed that it had settled religious belief forever. Its bigotry and intolerance produced no effect except to hasten its own destruction. The work of its commissioners, called the Shorter Catechism, remains, having no more value with modern men than its merits justly win for it.

It would thus seem that the words in which the Westminster Assembly framed its creed were not so framed as the weapons of Christ. They were forged as thunderbolts of war. They stood for a new State Church in opposition to the old, and the question really was, to which would the war incline. When King Charles II. was restored, the Thirty-nine Articles again prevailed. Had the Parliamentary party finally succeeded, the Shorter Catechism might to-day have been the creed of the National Church of England.

Personally, I have no controversy, at this time, with the Shorter Catechism. What I now say is, that it did not accord in its spirit with the Congregationalism of John Robinson and others whom he represented. Congregationalists had no hand in framing it. It does not agree with the Congregationalism of to-day. Witness the creed of the American Congregationalists of 1883 — broad and comprehensive, sliding smoothly and skilfully over controverted points, omitting the hard phrases written into the Andover Creeds, and commending itself to the consciences and judgment of reasonable men. I was glad to see the name of one of this prosecuting committee signed to this creed, and will still hope that he will yet mete out to these accused Professors the same latitude and tolerance of opinion which he has liberally accorded to himself (3 Schaff's Creeds of Christendom, p. 913).

Still, I do not mean to deny that the people of New England did for a time, at least to a considerable extent, commit themselves to the Shorter Catechism. This seems to have been due to the sagacity of the Assembly in preparing a catechism as well as a creed. This catechism was almost necessary to their design in forming a National Church embracing all the people. The children could thus more easily be kept within the pale of the church; so could their elders, not versed in theological opinions, have at hand the simpler forms of religious expression. The Shorter Catechism, for this and perhaps other reasons, became, at least for a time, acceptable here. Perhaps, one of these reasons was that the Independent party occupied to some extent a negative position, and put forth no catechism.

Still, there was in the Congregational body a far more tolerant opinion than that which governed the authors of the catechism. One has but to read the preface to the "Savoy" declaration of the Congregationalists of 1658 to be convinced of this. This paper insists that there shall be no force or constraint in confessions. With such constraint, they degenerate from the *name* and *nature* of confessions, and are turned into *exactions* and *impositions* of faith. There must be inward freeness, willingness, and readiness of the confessors to contribute to the beauty and loveliness of the confession. They herald it as a great principle that among all Christian saints or churches there should be vouchsafed a forbearance and mutual indulgence unto saints of all persuasions, holding fast the necessary foundations of faith and holiness. There is quoted and adopted the famous requirement of Cromwell, already alluded to, that some way is to be found out whereby tender consciences, who cannot in all things submit to the rule which may be established, may be borne with according to the Word. There is a fine spirit of charity and toleration running through this entire document (3 Schaff's Creeds, 708-718, A.D. 1658).

The same view appears to be upheld by the ponderous lectures of Rev. Dr. Willard, at one time pastor of the South Church, Boston, and Vice-President of Harvard College. The preface to the lectures, as published by Joseph Sewell and Thomas Prince, refers to Dr. Willard's explanation of the catechism for the use of children, and then to the more elaborate lectures for the use of the people. The first of the lectures were delivered in 1687, about forty years after the catechism had been adopted by Parliament.

It would appear that there was never any slavish adherence to the letter of the catechism in Massachusetts. Dr. Willard delivered a course of two hundred and fifty lectures on the Shorter Catechism. We may shudder to think what a course by him would have been on the whole body of Westminster divinity. Messrs. Sewell and Prince say that it was esteemed in their time (A.D. 1725) one of the noblest and choicest bodies of theoretical and practical divinity anywhere to be met with. It seems, however, that a question had been raised, even in their day, of the value of works on systematical divinity, to which they reply, "if by systematical divinity be meant a mere slavish confinement to any schemes thereof whatever, conceived or published by the mere wit of man, though founded in their own apprehensions on divine revelation, *without a liberty reserved of varying from them upon further discoveries*, our author was too generous and great a soul, and had too deep an insight into the present imperfection and fallibility of human nature, than to be capable of such a slavery. He was indeed a recommender of divinity systems, even to all sorts of persons, and especially young students, in order to methodize their inquiries and conceptions, to keep their minds from wandering and inconsistency, etc., but without obliging them to an implicit, servile subjection to any mere human compositions; and whatever system he fell into, it arose from a careful scrutiny into the genuine meaning of the Holy Scriptures, . . . and not from any mere previous veneration of the systems themselves, or their renowned compilers or abettors, though worthy of ever so much esteem." . . .

There speaks forth the spirit of John Robinson of a hundred years before. No human composition whatever, call it creed or what you please, is to be considered as conclusive evidence of the doctrines of the Christian religion. Such documents are aids to the correct understanding of Scriptures, and nothing more. They never can properly become substitutes for it. In the same spirit it was proclaimed by a

Council of Congregationalists, at Saybrook, Conn., in 1708, that "the Bible is the only sufficient and general rule of religion."

What, then, did Mrs. Phœbe Phillips, Mr. John Phillips, and Mr. Samuel Abbot mean when, in the instrument of September 2, 1807, they required (Article 12) that every professor in the Seminary on their foundation should make and subscribe a declaration of his faith in divine revelation, and in the fundamental and distinguishing doctrines of Christ as summarily expressed in the Westminster Assembly's *Shorter Catechism*, while requiring him, in the next breath, to make a solemn promise that he will *open and explain* the *Scriptures* to his pupils with integrity and faithfulness, and that he will maintain and inculcate the Christian faith as above expressed, etc., *according to the best light God shall give him?* Surely nothing less than John Robinson meant; nothing less than the framers of the Savoy declaration meant; nothing less than Samuel Willard meant; nothing less than Joseph Sewell and Thomas Prince meant, when they used the language to which I have already had the privilege to refer. These men and this woman lived but a few years later than Messrs. Prince and Sewell, in the same vicinity, and breathed the same Massachusetts air of Congregational liberty. Finally, I ask what did the Associate Founders mean when they required, at the close of their dreary creed, by like form of words, that the professors should open and explain the Scriptures with integrity and faithfulness, and should maintain and inculcate the Christian faith, ACCORDING TO THE BEST LIGHT GOD SHOULD GIVE THEM? Surely nothing less than Madam Phillips and her associates meant, when they placed themselves on line with those noble men — Robinson, Willard, Sewell, and Prince. That is indeed a far-reaching phrase — "according to the best light God shall give them." These words relax the bonds of tyrannous opinion and set the captives free from the bondage of men, bringing them into the glorious freedom of the sons of God. This phrase is taken *verbatim* from a fine and glowing paragraph of John Milton. It is worthy of perpetual remembrance. "The whole freedom of man consists either in spiritual or civil liberty. As for spiritual, who can be at rest, who can enjoy anything in this world, who hath not liberty to serve God and to save his own soul, *according to the best light which God hath planted in him* for that purpose, by reading of his revealed will, and the guidance of his Holy Spirit?"

Is it not strange that this little plank of Milton's religious platform has floated down the stream of time and at last lodged on the hills of Andover, and has been taken up by subtile theologians and bedded in their creeds? It is as near live oak as anything to be found there.

I must pause here to sketch the Abbot foundation, the Associate foundation, and the creeds which the respective founders require.

There is some difficulty in making this whole subject clear, owing to the fact that the Andover Seminary has not been developed upon any preconceived and systematic plan. It is rather a growth from the ideas and benefactions of different sets of men, all of whom were believers in Christianity, but among whom prevailed quite diverse theological opinions. Then, again, at its very origin there was an academy — Phillips Academy — since become famous for the accuracy of its classical and other instruction, upon which the Theological Seminary was grafted. One would perhaps think that here is an incongruity. This was not the view of the founders. The Hon. John Phillips, of Exeter, N.H., must be considered as the true Founder of the institution, since on May 29, 1777, he entered into an obligation to pay a sum of money to trustees whom he named. He then went on to declare the trust. This was mainly for the support of the school, in which various subjects enumerated by him were to be taught. Among others, as "many of the students may be devoted to the sacred work of the Gospel Ministry," the master was to instruct them, not only in the truth of Christianity, but in certain great Scripture doctrines which he enumerated, including that of the Trinity, that of the depravity of human nature, the necessity of an atonement, repentance, and redemption through Jesus Christ. At the same time he was careful to say emphatically that the first and principal object of the institution was the *promotion of true piety and virtue;* the second, instruction in the English, Latin, and the Greek languages, together with writing, arithmetic, music, and the art of speaking; the third, instruction in practical geometry, logic, and geography; and the fourth, in such other liberal arts, science, etc., as the Trustees shall direct.

There is no hint here of a *Theological Seminary*, but simply a plan for promoting a liberal education. It was substantially a "Grammar School," with instruction in the leading topics of religion.

The same inference is to be derived from the donation of the Hon. Samuel Phillips and the same John Phillips, April 28, 1778 (Deeds and Donations, pp. 16–28). An instrument (really a declaration of trust in its nature) called a "Constitution of Phillips Academy" was at this time executed by these founders, substantially identical with the declaration of trust of May 29, 1777; this last-named paper was executed by John Phillips alone, but without signature.

Matters being in this condition, an act of incorporation was obtained from the State, October 4, 1780. The Preamble to that expressly sets forth that the rents, etc., of the funds are to be forever laid out for the support of a *public Free School or Academy in the town of Andover.* The first section declares that the Academy is established for the purpose of promoting true piety and virtue, and for the education of youths, enumerating the subjects already named as in the Founder's Constitution. In this incorporating act the Trustees are required to conform to the true design and intention of the founders, as expressed in the Constitution (Section 3). The eighth section provides that neither the said Trustees nor their successors shall ever receive any grant or donation the condition whereof shall require them, or any others concerned, to act in any respect counter to the design of the first grantors or of any prior donation.

After the Act of Incorporation there were other donations, such as a legacy of Hon. John Phillips, April 28,

1795, for the benefit of charity scholars who were hopefully pious and designed for the Gospel ministry, who might be assisted in the study of divinity under the direction of some eminent *Calvinistic* minister of the Gospel, until such time as an Orthodox instructor shall be supported as a Professor of Divinity, etc.

The next donation of importance is Lieutenant-Governor Samuel Phillips' *first* donation, December 12, 1801. This was a foundation for the supply of certain religious books (specified) to be delivered from time to time to inhabitants of the town of Andover. His *second* donation, January 27, 1802, was for the same general purpose, with a wider list of books, his object being to counteract the dispersion of such theological treatises or speculations as tend to undermine the fundamental principles of the Gospel plan of salvation, or to reduce the Christian religion to a system of mere morality. The Westminster Shorter Catechism is named as one of nearly a score of books. There are other donations made from time to time to the Academy, which need not be specified.

There is no official recognition of a " Theological Institution" until June 19, 1807, when an application was made by the Trustees of Phillips' Academy for an act additional to the original Act of Incorporation, to enable them to receive further donations of charitably disposed persons for the support of a theological institution, and thus to complete the design of the pious founders and benefactors.

The Legislature passed an act the same day reciting the substance of the petition, and allowing the Trustees to hold real and personal estate of a prescribed amount of income, provided the income of the said real and personal estate be alway applied to the objects named, agreeably to the will of the donors, *if consistent with the original design of the founders of the said Academy.*

Down to this point, it is manifest that no foundation is authorized by law, to be thereafter made, unless it is consistent with the ORIGINAL design of the founders, as expressed in their deeds of trust. The word " original " must be held to refer to the first documents executed by them, or one of them, in 1777 and 1778.

There is no later statute of Massachusetts changing the rule of the act of June 19, 1807.

. The theory of the Supreme Judicial Court, hereafter referred to, based on the statute of 1807, is in perfect accordance with the law of the English Court of Chancery in administering charitable trusts. Thus the Master of the Rolls (Romilly) says, in a comparatively recent case : " What this court looks at in all charities is the original intention of the founder, and, apart from any question of illegality and various other questions, this court carries into effect the wishes and intentions of the founder of the charity; and where it sees that those intentions have not been carried into effect, it rectifies the existing administration of the charity for that purpose. If it cannot carry them into effect specifically, it carries them into effect as nearly as may be, and with as close a resemblance as it can." This statement is from a great master of this branch of law (*Attorney-General* v. *Dedham School*, 23 Beavan, 354).

All the later foundations, viz., among others, that of Madam Phœbe Phillips, John Phillips, Esq., and Samuel Abbot, of Aug. 31, 1807, as well as that of the regulations of March 21, 1808, called the statutes of the Associate Foundation of that date, must be submitted to this test — are they *consistent* with the *original design* of the founders, viz., John Phillips and Samuel Phillips, founders of the Phillips Academy, of May 29, 1777, and April 21, 1778? This was the real point of the important case of *Trustees of Phillips Academy* v. *King*, 12 Mass., 546, already cited for another purpose. This point is fully developed in the case on pp. 559, 560. The court draws a sharp and well-defined distinction between these original founders and all the later contributors to the institution, calling the latter "after benefactors," making even John Phillips in his legacy of 1795 an "after benefactor," as distinguished from the same John Phillips in April 21, 1778, who in his donation of that date was an "original founder" (p. 560, 2d paragraph, middle of page). It is declared that the words "Calvinistic Minister," used by him in 1795, are no part of the original foundation in 1778.

We thus come down to the bare question, Are all the specific creeds of the later days *consistent* with the *original* foundation? They are only so, considered *as modes* of "carrying out the first and principal object of the institution, viz., the promotion of true piety and virtue." They are but instrumental and accessories to that principal design.

The "principal design" of the Founders will now be stated in some detail, with the view of showing that it is derived from the writings of John Locke.

Resemblance between the Theory of Education sketched by John Locke and that of the Original Founders.

As has been stated, the "original Founders" were the Hon. John Phillips and the Hon. Samuel Phillips. Though thoroughly Christian men, they were also men of affairs, and attained political distinction. They not only founded an academy at Andover, but they, or one of them, also established one at Exeter, New Hampshire.

Their great desire was to promote a sound education, and to teach students "*the great end and real business of living.*" The italics are their own.

Their view was that the success of their institution depended, under Providence, much upon a discreet selection of the principal instructor. He was to be a professor of the Christian religion; of exemplary manners; good natural abilities and literary acquirements; of a good acquaintance with human nature, and of a natural aptitude for instruction and government.

It was ever to be considered as the first and principal duty of the Master to regulate the tempers, to enlarge the minds, and form the morals of the students. He was to give especial attention to their health, to encourage a habit of industry, and to that end to encourage them to perform some manual labor, such as gardening. Above all, he was to pay attention to their minds and morals, considering that goodness without knowledge is weak and feeble, and knowledge without goodness is dangerous; and that the two would lay the surest foundation of usefulness to mankind.

Accordingly, he must frequently delineate the deformity and odiousness of vice, and the beauty and amiableness of virtue; the indispensable obligation to avoid the one, and to love and practise the other — including the great duties they owe to God, their country, their parents, their neighbors, and themselves. He should observe the varieties of their tempers and bring each of them under such discipline as tends to develop them most fully; early enure them to contemplate the various scenes incident to human life, and furnish them useful general maxims of conduct.

It is further required, in order that the true and fundamental principles of Christianity may be cultivated and perpetuated in the Christian Church, as far as the Seminary has influence, that not only instruction be given in the truth of Christianity, but certain special doctrines (enumerated) be inculcated, including the doctrines of the Trinity, the Fall of Man, the necessity of an Atonement, etc., etc. The reason given for this branch of instruction is that many students may be devoted to the sacred work of the Gospel Ministry.

It is at the end stated that "in order to *prevent the smallest* perversion of the true intent of this foundation, the *first* and *principal* object of the institution is the promotion of *true piety and virtue* — the secondary object is declared to be instruction in the English, Latin, and Greek languages, and other branches of knowledge specified.

The Founders reserved to themselves the power during their lives to make rules for the perpetual government of the institution, but no rule subversive of the *true design* should be made.

Thus, with the most pains-taking carefulness and frequent iteration, they announced that their great aim was the "promotion of piety and virtue," and the expected result was to teach the students "the great end and real business of living."

Let us now compare with this the "Thoughts on Education " of John Locke, of some sixty or more years before. Treatises on education were not as common then as now. Locke treats of these very topics as no other writer of his day had done. Of course, he enters far more into detail than the Founders would be likely to do, but there is a striking resemblance between the general drift of each, too close to be attributed to accident.

He, too, lays great stress upon physical education, habits of industry, manual labor, and practice in the art of gardening, mental and moral culture, repetition of lessons under the eye of the instructor (strongly insisted upon by the Founders). He recommends that the instructor should study the nature and temper of each child, with a view to giving him individuality of training. Good manners should be cultivated by reiterated actions in their presence. Above all, his advice, repeated in various forms, is that the pupils should be instructed in "piety and virtue." "Virtue," he says, "is harder to be got than a knowledge of the world, and if lost in a young man is seldom recovered. Everything should be bent to the acquisition of virtue." "That which requires most time and pains and assiduity is to work into them" (the young) "the principles and practice of virtue and good breeding. This is the season that they should be prepared with; this they had need to be well provided with." In another place he says, "I wish that those who complain of the great decay of Christian piety and virtue everywhere . . . would consider how to retrieve them in the next generation. This, I am sure, that if the foundation be not laid in the foundation and principling of the youth, all other endeavors will be in vain."

Then, in § 64, comes this fine utterance: "It is virtue, then, direct virtue, which is the hard and valuable part to be aimed at in education. . . . *All other considerations and accomplishments should give way*, and be postponed, to this. This is the solid and substantial good, which tutors should not only read lectures and talk of, but the labor and art of education should furnish the mind with and *fasten* there, and never cease till the young man had a true relish of it and placed his strength, his glory, and his pleasure in it." This is the precise idea of the Founders in their requirements of inculcation and repetition, while the diction of Locke is superior.

Locke's notion of a good master for the scholars is the same as that of the Founders, though worked out with more detail. He must be a man of good manners, knowledge of human nature, well versed in the subjects to be taught, apt to teach, etc. (§ 86, § 87, § 88).

The final point to which I refer in Locke's view is the relation which virtue holds to all other matters of instruction, and that on which it rests. He arranges all subjects of instruction in four classes as to their *relative* importance: virtue, wisdom, breeding, and learning. Virtue is in the first rank. He says: "I place virtue as the first and most necessary of those endowments that belong to a man or a gentleman, as absolutely requisite to make him valued and beloved by others, acceptable or tolerable to himself. Without that, I think, he will be happy neither in this nor the other world." § 129.

Upon what does he rest virtue? The answer is a true notion of God, as of the independent Supreme Being, author and maker of all things, from whom we receive all our good, who loves us and gives us all things; and consequent to this, there should be instilled into the pupils' mind a love and reverence for the Supreme Being.

At the same time, he does not think that youth should be too curious in their notions about a Being which all must acknowledge to be incomprehensible. § 130. Locke seems to say that, as between theological metaphysics and practical piety and virtue, preference is to be given to the latter. So the Founders, after referring to great theological subjects as to be taught, lay the principal stress upon piety and virtue, and the acquirement of such manliness, sobriety, and good sense as would tend to form a class of honorable and Christian gentlemen, who had "learned the great end and real business of living."

These Founders also followed Locke in the tolerance of

religious opinion, and in making "piety and virtue" superior to doctrines.

There is thus a marked distinction between the theory of the Founders of 1778 as to education, and that of the creed builders of 1807 and 1808; the first were men of breadth of view, conversant with the writings of philosophers, and particularly with those of John Locke; the others were adepts in theological controversy, and determined to conserve the precise technical forms of statement of their day in the instruction of youth for all time. Fortunate it is, that the law of Massachusetts holds that the will of the Founders is supreme, and that the *great end*, even of instruction in the Theological Seminary, grafted upon the original foundation, still is, and must continue to be, the promotion of "piety and virtue."

The result is that there is and can be no "misbehavior, or heterodoxy," under the Twentieth Article of the Associates' Creed, on the part of a Professor, unless he wanders from the *principal design* of the institution, which is true piety and virtue. This liberal plan of the "original founders" is wholly in line with the words of John Robinson and Messrs. Sewell and Prince, already quoted, and with the generally progressive spirit of New England Theology. I admit that there is color for the view that some portions of the creeds of August 31, 1807, and March 21, 1808, are born of a different spirit, and represent to an extent what may fairly be called the intolerance of Orthodoxy, but the general outcome of them can be reconciled with a progressive view.

In a portion of this argument I have proceeded upon the view that the Westminster Catechism was imposed upon the Professors on the Associate Foundation, and have argued that even then the current of religious thought and certain qualifying words in the creeds do not bind them to a verbal acceptance of all its propositions. I have now arrived at a stage where I absolutely combat that proposition, and deny that any Professor, except he be upon the Abbot Foundation (and he only in a qualified manner), has any thing to do with the Shorter Catechism.

This branch of the discussion naturally leads to a statement of the origin and distinctive character of these foundations and creeds.

After the Legislature of Massachusetts had, on June 19, 1807, enlarged the capacity of Phillips Academy to hold property, and to use it "consistently with the original design of the founders of the Academy," the donation of Madam Phœbe Phillips, John Phillips, and Samuel Abbot were made —August 31, 1807; and a separate donation, on March 21, 1808, by Moses Brown, William Bartlett, and John Norris. The first is commonly called the Abbot Foundation; the second, the Associate Foundation.

THE ABBOT FOUNDATION.

The donors in this matter gave twenty thousand dollars to the Trustees, *in trust, for* the establishment of a Theological Institution in Phillips Academy. This gift was accompanied with a so-called "constitution" for the Seminary, which, however, from a legal point of view, is a "declaration of trust," consisting of Thirty-four Articles. So far as these articles concern the management of the institution, they may be termed "statutes" (Blackstone's Commentaries, Book I., 483, 484), the word "statutes" here being used simply in the sense of rules or ordinances. This "constitution" recites, in its preamble, the leading purpose of the foundation of 1778 as being the "promotion of true piety and virtue," and also refers to the later bequest of John Phillips of 1795; and then, in the Eleventh and Twelfth and Thirteenth Articles proceeds to set forth the duties and obligations of Professors in the "*Seminary*," not including (as is supposed) the teachers in the Academy as it had previously existed and still continued to exist. The substance of their requirement was that the Professor should be in communion with either the Presbyterian or Congregational Church, an honest, learned, and pious man, and of sound and orthodox principles in divinity, according to the system of evangelical doctrines stated in the Westminster Assembly's Shorter Catechism and more concisely delineated in the Constitution of Phillips' Academy.

It is due to truth to say that *there is not in the Constitution of Phillips Academy one word* concerning the Westminster Shorter Catechism. Certain doctrines are simply mentioned by way of enumeration, but none of them are set forth with the definitions of the catechism. With due respect to the memory of these worthy donors, long since passed away, we affirm, without fear of successful contradiction, that this reference is unwarranted by the facts, and to uphold it in this discussion is a pure case of " begging the question."

To resume the rules of the " Abbot Foundation." The Twelfth Article provides that the Professor shall make and subscribe a solemn declaration of faith in divine revelation, and in the fundamental doctrines of the Gospel as summarily expressed in the Westminster Assembly's Shorter Catechism, at the same time requiring him to maintain the Christian faith in the discharge of the duties appertaining to his office, *according to the best light God shall give him.* He is required to oppose certain specified heresies and errors. He must repeat, in the presence of the Trustees, the declaration prescribed in Article Twelfth every five years.

So much for the Abbot Foundation. Next in order is

THE ASSOCIATE FOUNDATION.

The Associate Foundation and its Statutes (March 21, 1808).

The origin of this foundation is a matter of history. It involves an account of a long and complicated negotiation between theologians of great ability and astuteness in drawing fine-spun distinctions. The two parties, so far as they had opposing views, were respectively called Calvinists and Hopkinsians. The former had followed the doctrines of John Calvin ; the latter modified the Calvinistic view owing to the speculations of the elder Jonathan Edwards and other acute metaphysicians. On the points upon which they differed they could no more coalesce than oil and water. The Calvinists, however, were in possession of the Phillips

Academy and of the embryo Theological Institution. The Hopkinsians had no Theological Seminary, though as a party they were extremely desirous to have one; still two seminaries were not needed at that time in that vicinity, and would be likely to languish or to die out for want of adequate support. One might be made strong and efficient. The interests of the two parties drove them together. Neither would consent, specifically, to abandon its views. The great problem was to find some form of words under which each party could claim that its own views were tenable. Comprehensive, or, one might perhaps be pardoned for saying, elusive phrases were sought for. Words were *inserted* which would satisfy the Hopkinsians; old phrases satisfactory to the Calvinists were not stricken out. The contradictory element in them was, perhaps, not perceived. If observed, it was overlooked. There then emerged from the struggle the Associate Creed — something new and unexampled in religious creeds of modern days. When we look at the Hopkinsian statements crowded in among the Calvinistic propositions, one is reminded of a phrase used by Edmund Burke: The clauses are "crossly indented and whimsically dovetailed."

I shall soon proceed to compare this creed, step by step, with the Shorter Catechism. But I have now reached the point where it can be affirmed that no statement in either of these creeds can change the bearing of the original foundation of 1778, not even though *the heirs of all the founders consent;* for the law of Massachusetts still declares, by the statute of July 19, 1807, that every thing shall be done consistent with the original design of the founders.

That statute is the sheet-anchor of Andover Theological Seminary. Nothing done by the trustees, founders, or others can make the smallest alteration in the principal design, viz., the promotion of piety and virtue. Before that can be done the people of Massachusetts must signify in a legal and official way what their wishes are, and repeal that beneficent statute.

The history of the negotiations are stated at length in the work of Dr. Leonard Woods upon the history of Andover

Seminary. It does not fall within my purpose to refer further to this work, leaving its consideration to others.

The Associate framers of the statutes incorporated into their creed such parts of the Westminster Shorter Catechism as they approved, rejecting others, and made their creed a substitute for the catechism.

In order to show the truth of the above proposition, I place the material part of the catechism and this creed in parallel columns, italicizing some of the leading passages incorporated. It should be observed that while the catechism is expository, and contains many definitions, the creed proceeds mostly by way of enumeration, as the definitions are no doubt assumed to be known by the Professors, who are to be regarded as experts.

In the column giving the catechism the questions are omitted, as the answers are intelligible without them. The Roman numbers correspond with the numbering of the questions.

Westminster Shorter Catechism.

I. Man's chief end is to glorify God and enjoy him forever.

II. The Word of God which is contained in the Scriptures of the Old and New Testament is the ONLY rule to direct us how we may glorify and enjoy him.

III. The Scriptures principally teach what man is to believe concerning God, and what duty God requires of man.

IV. God is a spirit, infinite, eternal, and unchangeable in his being, wisdom, power, holiness, justice, goodness, and truth.

Creed of Associate Founders.

I believe that there is one and *but one living and true God;* that *the Word of God contained in the Scriptures of the Old and New Testament is the only* perfect rule of faith and practice; that agreeably to those Scriptures *God is a spirit, infinite, eternal, and unchangeable in his being, wis-*

V. There is *but one* only, *the living and true God.*

VI. There are three persons in the Godhead, the Father, the Son, and the Holy Ghost, and these three are one God, the same in substance, equal in power and glory.

VII. The decrees of God are his eternal purpose according to the counsel of his will, whereby for his own glory he hath foreordained whatsoever cometh to pass.

VIII. God executeth his decrees in the works of his creation and Providence.

IX. The work of his creation is God's making all things out of nothing by the word of his power in the space of six days, and all very good.

X. God created man, male and female, after his own image, in knowledge, righteousness, and holiness, with dominion over the creatures.

XI. God's works of Providence are his most holy, wise, and powerful preserving and governing all his creatures and all their actions.

XII. When God had created man, he entered into a covenant of life with him, upon condition of perfect obedience, forbidding him to eat of the tree of knowledge of good or evil upon pain of death.

XIII. Our first parents, left to the freedom of their own will, fell from the estate wherein they were created by sinning against God.

dom, power, holiness, justice, goodness, and truth; that *in the Godhead there are three persons*, the Father, the Son, and the Holy Ghost, and that *these three are one God, the same in substance, equal in power and glory;*

That *God created man after his own image, in knowledge, righteousness, and holiness;* that the *glory of God is man's chief end*, and the enjoyment of God his supreme happiness; that this enjoyment is derived solely from conformity of heart and character to the will of God;

XIV. Sin is any want of conformity to or transgression of the laws of God.

XV. The sin whereby our first parents fell from the estate wherein they were created was their eating the forbidden fruit.

XVI. The covenant being made with Adam, not only for himself, but for his posterity, all mankind descending from him by ordinary generation sinned in him, and fell with him in his first transgression.

XVII. The fall brought mankind into a state of sin and misery.

XVIII. The sinfulness of that estate whereinto man fell consists in the guilt of Adam's first sin, the want of original righteousness, and the corruption of his whole nature, which is commonly called original sin, together with all actual transgressions which proceed from it.

XIX. All mankind by their fall lost communion with God, are under the wrath and curse, and so made liable to all the miseries of this life and the pains of hell forever.

that Adam, the federal head and representative of the human race, was placed in a state of probation, and that in consequence of his disobedience all his descendants were constituted sinners; that by nature every man is personally depraved, destitute of holiness, and opposed to God, and that previously to the renewing agency of the divine spirit all his moral actions are adverse to the character and glory of God; that, being morally incapable of recovering the image of his Creator which was lost in Adam, every man is justly exposed to eternal damnation, so that except a man be born again he cannot see the kingdom of God;

XX. God having, out of his mere good pleasure, from all eternity elected some to everlasting life, did enter into a covenant of grace to deliver them out of the state of sin and misery, and to bring them into a state of salvation by a redeemer.

XXI. The only redeemer of God's elect is the Lord Jesus Christ, who being the eternal son of God, became man, and so was and continues to be God and Man, in two distinct natures and one person forever.

XXII. Christ, the son of God, became man by taking to himself a true body and a reasonable soul, being conceived by the power of the Holy Ghost in the womb of the Virgin Mary, and born of her, yet without sin.

XXIII. Christ, as our redeemer, executes the offices of a prophet, of a priest, and of a king, both in his estate of humiliation and exaltation.

XXIV. Christ executes the office of a prophet by revealing to us, by his word and spirit, the will of God for our salvation.

XXV. Christ executeth the office of a priest in his once offering up of himself a sacrifice to satisfy divine justice and reconcile us to God, and in making continual intercession for us.

XXVI. Christ executeth the office of a king in subduing us to himself, in ruling and defending us, and in restraining and conquering all his and our enemies.

That God, of his mere good pleasure, from all eternity elected some to everlasting life; and that he entered into a covenant of grace to deliver them out of this state of sin and misery by a redeemer. That the only redeemer of the elect is the eternal son of God, who for this purpose became man, and continues to be God and man in two distinct natures and one person forever; that Christ as our redeemer executeth the office of a prophet, priest, and king : that agreeably to the covenant of redemption, the Son of God, and he alone, by his suffering and death, has made atonement for the sins of all men ; that repentance, faith, and holiness are the personal requisites in the Gospel scheme of salvation ; that the righteousness of Christ is the only ground of a sinner's justification ; that this

XXVII. Christ's humiliation consisted in his being born, and that in a low condition made under the law, undergoing the miseries of this life, the wrath of God, and the cursed death of the cross, in being buried and in continuing under the power of death for a time.

XXVIII. Christ's exaltation consists in his rising again from the dead on the third day, in ascending up to Heaven, and in sitting at the right hand of God the Father, and in coming to judge the world at the last day.

XXIX. We are made partakers of the redemption purchased by Christ, by the effectual application of it to us by the Holy Spirit.

XXX. The Spirit applieth to us the redemption purchased by Christ by working faith in us, and thereby uniting us to Christ in our effectual calling.

XXXI. Effectual calling is the work of God's spirit, whereby convincing us of our sin and misery, enlightening our minds in the knowledge of Christ, and renewing our wills, he doth persuade and enable us to embrace Jesus Christ, freely offered to us in the Gospel.

XXXII. They that are effectually called do in this life partake of justification, adoption, and sanctification, and the several benefits which do in this life either accompany or flow from them.

righteousness is received through faith, and that this faith is the gift of God, so that our salvation is wholly of grace ; that no means whatever can change the heart of a sinner and make it holy; that *regeneration and sanctification are effects of the creating and renewing agency of the Holy Spirit ;* and that supreme love to God constitutes the essential difference between saints and sinners; that by convincing us of our sin and misery, enlightening our minds, *working faith in us,* and renewing our wills, the *Holy Spirit makes us partakers of the benefit of redemption ;* and that the ordinary means by which these benefits are communicated to us are the word, sacraments and prayer; that repentance unto life, faith to feed upon Christ, love to God, and new obedience

XXXIII. Justification is an act of God's free grace, wherein he pardoneth all our sins and accepteth us as righteous in his sight, only for the righteousness of Christ, imputed to us and received by faith alone.

XXXIV. Adoption is an act of God's free grace whereby we are received into the number and have a right to all the privileges of the Sons of God.

XXXV. Sanctification is the work of God's free grace, whereby we are renewed in the whole man after the image of God, and are enabled more and more to die unto sin and live unto righteousness.

XXXVI. The benefits which in this life do either accompany or flow from justification, adoption and sanctification are assurance of God's love, peace of conscience, joy in the Holy Ghost, increase of grace, and perseverance therein to the end.

XXXVII. The souls of believers are at their death made perfect in holiness, and do immediately pass into glory, and their bodies being still united to Christ, do rest in their graves till the resurrection.

XXXVIII. At the resurrection, believers being called up to glory shall be openly acknowledged and acquitted at the day of judgment, and made perfectly blessed in the full enjoyment of God to all eternity.

XXXIX. The duty that God requireth of man is obedience to His revealed will.

are the appropriate qualifications for the Lord's Supper; and that a Christian Church ought to admit no person to its holy communion before he exhibits credible evidence of his godly sincerity; that perseverance in holiness is the only method of making our calling and election sure; and that the final perseverance of saints, though it is the effect of the special operation of God on their hearts, yet necessarily implies their own watchful diligence; that *they who are effectually called do in this life partake of justification, adoption, and sanctification, and the several benefits which do either accompany or flow from them that the souls of believers are at their death made perfect in holiness and do immediately pass into glory, that their bodies, being still united to Christ, will at the resurrection be*

XL. The rule which God at first revealed to man for his obedience was the moral law.

XLI. The moral law is summarily comprehended in the ten commandments.

XLII. to LXXXI., both inclusive, concern the ten commandments.

LXXXII. No mere man since the fall is able in this life perfectly to keep the commandments of God, but daily doth break them in thought, word, and deed.

LXXXIII. Some sins in themselves, and by reason of several aggravations, are more heinous in the sight of God than others.

LXXXIV. Every sin deserveth God's wrath and curse, both in this life and that which is to come.

LXXXV. To escape the wrath and curse of God due to us for sin, God requireth of us faith in Jesus Christ, repentance unto life, with the diligent use of all outward means whereby Christ communicateth to us the benefits of redemption.

LXXXVI. Faith in Jesus Christ is a saving grace whereby we receive and rest upon Him alone for salvation as He is offered to us in the Gospel.

LXXXVII. Repentance unto life is a saving grace whereby a sinner, out of the true sense of his sin and apprehension of the mercy of God in Christ, doth with grief and hatred of his sin turn from it unto God with full

raised up to *glory*, and that the saints will be *made perfectly blessed in the full enjoyment of God to all eternity*, but that the wicked will awake to shame and everlasting contempt, and with devils be plunged into the lake that burneth with fire and brimstone for ever and ever. I, moreover, believe that God, *according to the counsel of His own will and for His own glory, hath fore-ordained whatsoever cometh to pass*, and that all beings, actions, and events, both in the natural and moral world, are under His providential and moral direction; that God's decrees perfectly consist with human liberty; God's universal agency with the agency of man, and man's dependence with his accountability; that man has understanding and corporeal strength to do all that God requires of him; so that nothing but the sin-

purpose of and endeavor after new obedience.

LXXXVIII. The outward and ordinary means whereby Christ communicateth to us the benefits of redemption, are his ordinances, especially the word, sacraments, and prayer, all of which are made effectual to the elect for salvation.

LXXXIX. The Spirit of God maketh the reading, but especially the preaching of the word, an effectual means of convincing and converting sinners, and of building them up in holiness and comfort, through faith unto salvation.

XC. That the word may become effectual to salvation, we must attend thereunto with diligence, preparation, and prayer, receive it with faith and love, lay it up in our hearts, and practise it in our lives.

XCI. The sacraments become effectual means of salvation, not from any virtue in them, or in him that doth administer them, but only by the blessing of Christ and the working of His Spirit in them that by faith receive them.

XCII. A sacrament is a holy ordinance instituted by Christ, wherein by sensible signs Christ and the benefits of the New Covenant are represented sealed and applied to believers.

XCIII. The Sacraments of the New Testament are Baptism and the Lord's Supper.

ner's aversion to holiness prevents his salvation; that it is the prerogative of God to bring good out of evil, and that He will cause the wrath and rage of wicked men and devils to praise Him, and that all the evil which has existed, and which will forever exist in the moral system, will eventually be made to promote a most important purpose under the wise and perfect· administration of that Almighty Being who will cause all things to work for His own glory, and thus fulfil all His pleasure.

XCIV. Baptism is a Sacrament wherein the washing with water, in the name of the Father, and of the Son, and of the Holy Ghost, doth signify and seal our ingrafting into Christ, and partaking of the benefits of the Covenant of grace, and our engagement to be the Lord's.

XCV. Baptism is not to be administered to any that are out of the visible Church till they profess their faith in Christ and obedience to Him; but the infants of such as are members of the visible Church are to be baptized.

XCVI. The Lord's Supper is a Sacrament, wherein by the giving and receiving bread and wine according to Christ's appointment His death is shewed forth; and the worthy receivers are, not after a corporal and carnal manner, but by faith, made partakers of His body and blood with all His benefits to their spiritual nourishment and growth in grace.

XCVII. It is required of them that would worthily partake of the Lord's Supper that they examine themselves of their knowledge to discern the Lord's body, of their faith to feed upon him, of their repentance, love, and new obedience, lest coming unworthily they eat and drink judgment to themselves.

XCVIII. Prayer is an offering up of our desires to God, for things agreeable to his will, in the name of Christ, with confession of our sins and thankful acknowledgment of his mercies.

And furthermore, I do solemnly promise that I will open and explain the Scriptures to my pupils with integrity and faithfulness; that I will maintain and inculcate the Christian faith as expressed by me in the creed now repeated, together with all the other doctrines and duties of our holy re-

XCIX. The whole Word of God is of use to direct us in prayer; but the special rule of direction is that form of prayer which Christ taught his disciples, commonly called the Lord's Prayer. (C. to CVI., both inclusive, devoted to analysis of Lord's Prayer.)

ligion so far as may appertain to my office, according to the best light God shall give me, and in opposition, not only to atheists and infidels, but to Jews, Papists, Mahometans, Arians, Pelagians, Antinomians, Arminians, Socinians, Sabellians, Unitarians, and Universalists, and to all other heresies and errors, ancient or modern, which may be opposed to the Gospel of Christ or hazardous to the souls of men; that by my instruction, counsel, and example I will endeavor to promote true piety and godliness; that I will consult the good of this institution and the peace of the churches of our Lord Jesus Christ on all occasions; and that I will religiously conform to the constitution and laws of this Seminary, and to the Statutes of this foundation.

No candid person can fail to acknowledge, on contrasting these two instruments, that the latter is intended as a substitute for the former. The Westminster Shorter Catechism and the Associate Creed at Andover cannot possibly be reconciled. To assert that they can be, after due examination, is to act in bad faith.

Nothing is so notable as the statement in the Associate Creed that, "agreeably to the covenant of redemption, the Son of God and he alone, by his suffering and death, has made atonement *for the sins of all men*." This is in absolute contrast with the doctrine of limited atonement for a few of the elect. There is no trace of this doctrine of universal atonement in the Westminster Shorter Catechism, nor in other creeds adopted in England at that time. Found where it is, it is a breath of the sweet air of heaven over a barren waste where even the Rock of Israel scarcely casts a shadow to allay the fierce and constant heats that beat upon the unconverted. True, John Milton, with poetic insight, perceived it when in his early youth he sang his glorious hymn upon the Nativity, coupling his rejoicings with a far-seeing prophecy :

> " Yea, truth and justice then
> Will down return to men,
> Orbed in a rainbow, and like glories wearing;
> Mercy will sit between,
> Throned in celestial sheen,
> With radiant feet the tissued clouds down-steering;
> And heav'n, *as at some festival,*
> *Will open wide the gates of her high palace-hall.*"

Yes, open wide and forever, as the festival will be everlasting. No doubt this was regarded in his time as the glowing rhapsody of fervid youth. Only a few men saw this for a long time in New England, but these Associates saw it, rejoiced at it, hung it up as their banner, and inserted it in this creed. For many years these five Professors have been working out deductions from this immortal principle. Then there are three leading postulates which they well might pin up on the walls of Andover, as the great Luther raised his theses aloft; three great and central doctrines, everywhere presented by them — the universality of sin, an universal atonement, and the indispensableness of faith. Not one of these can be spared. They are to be inscribed on the banners of the great Christian army. What minor points they believe or hope for, such as probation after death, are inferences or deductions from these great central truths. Such inferences are not central, but inferior and subordinate.

And yet here are these prosecutors demanding that the respondent shall be an " Orthodox and CONSISTENT Calvinist." Orthodox and consistent Calvinist, indeed! Why, in this Andover Associate Creed is the very principal proposition against which John Calvin struggled with all his might. If permitted, he would lift himself from his grave to rebuke the utterance that Christ died for the sins of all men. He fell back on God's eternal, sovereign purpose whereby he has predestinated some to eternal life, while the rest of mankind are predestinated to condemnation and eternal death. Those only, he argues, whom God has chosen to life he effectually calls to salvation, and are kept by him in effectual grace and holiness to the end (Institutes, Book III.). And yet in this Andover Creed is imbedded the proposition that Christ made atonement for the sins of all men. It was on this very point that the Saxon Visitation Articles of the year 1592 contested Calvinism, affirming that Christ died for all men, and as the Lamb of God took away the sins of the whole world; condemning, in terms, it must be admitted, with some bitterness of expression, the Calvinistic doctrine as heretical that Christ did not die for all men, but only for the elect. The expression in the Andover Creed that in consequence of Adam's disobedience all his descendants were " constituted sinners " would have been abhorrent to the nature of Calvin. His was a frank and outspoken nature — despotic and intolerant, it is true, but never using words to conceal his thoughts, nor did he ever take an unfair advantage of an antagonist. The Andover Creed does not represent the original seamless robe of Calvinism, but rather Joseph's coat of varied colors; one patch of royal purple in its very centre, one wholly colorless, viz., the " corporeal strength " to repent, surrounded, it may be, by a dark, cold border of unmitigated Calvinism.

Some one may ask, Why, then, did the creed-builders require a professor to be an "orthodox and consistent Calvinist"? That is one of the mysteries of the case. Many men complain of the mysteries of theology ; they, however, are trifling when compared with the mysteries of theological creeds; and the Andover creed is the most mysterious of all.

In whatever sense the phrase " Orthodox and Consistent Calvinism " is used by the associates, it is certainly no part of the creed to be taken by the respondent. It is simply descriptive of a professor's qualities, and to be considered by the trustees at the time of his election, in the same way as another requirement in the same sentence, that he should be a " Master of Arts." I can see no other meaning to the phrase " Orthodox and Consistent Calvinism," as here used, except compliance with the creed.

I also insist upon the validity of the defence made by Professor Smyth (filed November 30, 1886), to the effect that the *words* of the associate founders expressly place him upon their creed, and their *creed alone*, and that by a fair construction of their words the intention was to exclude the Westminster Shorter Catechism. This remark applies to all the professors except Dr. Harris. The fact that Professor Smyth and other professors on the associate foundation have taken that declaration alone before the Board of Trustees and the Board of Visitors, is very cogent and decisive. It is a settled rule of construction that contemporaneous practice is "very strong in law" (Broom's Legal Maxims, 608; 1 Kent's Comm., 465). Moreover, as former Boards of Visitors have given a construction of this kind to the words of the associate foundation, it would be unjust to the respondent to adopt a different view, as he has made his declaration according to the construction accepted by all as proper at the time it was made.

CHARGES REVIEWED.

I only propose in a brief way to go over the charges under Number IV. (Amended Complaint), as they will receive ample and full refutation at the hands of Professor Smyth.

It is proper to make a preliminary remark applicable to all the charges. The creed of the associate founders is, as has been already shown, purely an *educational* creed. It has no support or analogy in any religious historic creed. It is not imposed upon the professors as religious men or members of churches, but as *teachers*. This is shown in the promise as follows: "I will open and maintain and explain the Scriptures to my *pupils* with integrity and faithfulness; I will *maintain* and *inculcate* the Christian faith as expressed in the creed by me now repeated, together with all the other doctrines and duties of our holy religion *so far as may appertain to my office* according to the best light God shall give me," etc. The words "maintain" and "inculcate," as here employed, refer solely to acts done in the course of instruction. The word "maintain," as here used, means to "assert as a tenet" (Worcester's Dictionary). The word "inculcate," equivalent "to enforce on the mind by frequent repetition" (same dictionary) is peculiarly applicable to instruction in the class-room. From this point of view, I claim that citations from the work called "Progressive Orthodoxy," or from editorial articles in the *Andover Review*, are without pertinence in establishing the charges.

But if I am wrong in this respect, I still claim that the extracts from the book and *Review* articles do not establish the propositions for which they are cited. They are wrenched from their connections. The context is not taken into account. There is no rule better settled *in all* interpretation than that the context is to be regarded. It is not a rule of law merely, but of logic, fair dealing, and common honesty (Lieber on Hermeneutics (Third or Hammond's Edition, 1880), pp. 114, 115; 1 Kent's Comm., 461, 462).

I now proceed with the specifications.

First Specification. — In the article itself cited to sustain

this specification, or in the extracts, it is submitted that there
is not the smallest ground for the assertion that the respondent holds that there is any other perfect rule of faith and
practice than the Bible, or that the Bible is not such' a rule.
It is absolutely without foundation to state, as the signers of
the charges do, that the extracts cited show that the respondent holds that the Bible "is fallible and untrustworthy,
even in some of its religious teachings." The words "fallible
and untrustworthy" certainly are not used by the respondent.
Where are their equivalents? The only imperfection in the
Sacred Writings stated by the respondent, is "lack of ideal
symmetry." Whatever imperfection there may be short of
absolute perfection is stated to have no "living interest."
The writers of the Books of the New Testament are stated
to have been chosen by Christ Himself to reveal Him. It is
also stated that their spiritual sympathy would prevent them
from attributing to Him any teaching or deed not worthy of
His character. All of this and more is utterly inconsistent
with the charges and cannot, by any proper reasoning, be
made to support them.

Second Specification. — The second specification is that the
respondent holds that Christ was not, during his earthly life,
" *God and man.*"

It is absolutely certain that nowhere in " Progressive Orthodoxy " does he say so. In many places he says directly
the opposite. Thus on page 22, " Progressive Orthodoxy,"
he says: " The uniqueness of Christ's *humanity* appears in
this, that its *entire* existence is in personal union with the
divine nature." " The *divine* and *human* relations in Christ
are *essentially* (*i.e.*, in their essence) related to each other."
P. 28. The signers seek to infer his heresy, in this direction,
from some two or three passages *cited*, none of which sustain their allegations. The most that can be made of these
is, not that they do not assert both the divinity and
humanity of Jesus, but that they uphold a *growth* in his
humanity, and its *progressive union* with the divine. That is
a totally different thing from asserting that there was *no
union at all.* This last is what the signers claim. Precisely

what the respondent affirms is, that "the facts show the limitations of Jesus' knowledge, the perfect human reality of his earthly life, the veritable growth of his consciousness and personality from the moment of the incarnation." Do the signers deny this as to his human nature? "What, then, becomes of the statement of the Evangelist, that Jesus increased in *wisdom* and in stature and *in favor with God and man*? The signers, in asserting "heterodoxy" in this respect, fly in the face of the Bible, and by their disbelief and *disregard* of it, themselves affirm that it is not a "perfect rule of faith and practice."

Third Specification. — This is that the respondent holds that no man has power or capacity to repent *without knowledge* of God in Christ.

The passages cited under this head do not sustain it. There is not one word in any of them concerning the "knowledge" of God. This is an instance of what frequently occurs in the "charges," viz., extreme carelessness or, rather, recklessness in making citations. What appears to be affirmed is, that "man of himself cannot repent." Taking this brief assertion and without the context, it is not "heterodoxy." Witness chap. 9th, Paragraph III. of the Westminster Confession of Faith. "Man by his fall into a state of sin hath wholly lost all ability (*potentiam*) of will to any spiritual good accompanying salvation, so, as a natural man, being altogether averse from that good and dead in sin, is not *able by his own strength* to convert himself, or to prepare himself thereunto" (3 Schaff, Creeds, etc., 623). It does not lie in the mouth of the prosecutors to deny the Westminster creed, as they insist that the respondent is *bound* by the "Shorter Catechism," made by the same men. The creed of the Associate Founders itself alleges that man is *morally incapable* of recovering the image of his creator, though he may have the "corporeal strength" (whatever that may be) to do all that God requires of him. The creed further says, "that previously to the renewing agency of the Divine Spirit, *all his moral actions* are adverse to the character and glory of God." The most that can be said of the creed is, that it affirms, in an obscure way, the *natural* ability of man to repent, while it asserts his *moral* inability. This view is held by the respondent as he himself affirms, and by all rules of law he is entitled to show his intent in such a case as the present, where the sole inquiry is, What did the respondent mean by certain passages of his writings? He positively says that he recognizes and affirms the theological distinction between natural and moral ability to repent. Accordingly, from every point of view, this charge is without significance.

Fourth Specification. — This is that mankind, save as they have received a knowledge of the " historic Christ," are not sinners, or if they are, not of such sinfulness as to be in danger of being lost.

The citations under this specification lend no support to it. The very first sentence quoted alleges " that man left to himself cannot have a repentance which sets him free from *sin* and death." The word " death," as here used by the respondent, cannot mean death in a physical sense, but must necessarily refer to death in the sense of being lost. The extract is to the effect that repentance without Christ is unavailing for the redemption of man. This passage, instead of showing that men *without a knowledge* of Christ are not " sinners," shows the despairing condition that they are in *through sin* without Christ.

Fifth Specification. — This is, that no man can be lost without having had knowledge of Christ.

To establish this specification, a single sentence is taken from " Progressive Orthodoxy," p. 250: " We have been *endeavoring to show* that no one can be lost without having had knowledge of Christ." The meaning here is finally lost at the last judgment. This remark is merely an inference from a course of reasoning based on the revelation in the scriptures of Christ to mankind. It is not an assertion of a fact, as the specification would lead one to believe. It is really an inference from the *universality of the atonement* as set forth in the creed itself. If incorrect, it is but a failure in a process of reasoning. I shall, however, insist that it is correct more at large hereafter.

Specifications from Sixth to Tenth. — I have carefully considered the charges from the sixth to the tenth, both inclusive. They appear to me to be either unsustained by the citations given or to be frivolous. The eighth and tenth particularly seem to be frivolous. The tenth is not supported by any citation. I leave them for the consideration of the respondent and others, if they are deemed to be worthy of attention.

Specification Eleventh. — The eleventh specification demands more consideration.

This is, that the respondent holds, maintains, and inculcates that there is, and will be, probation after death for all men who do not decisively reject Christ during the earthly life; and that this should be emphasized, made influential, and even central in systematic theology.

This is a charge which, in some form or other, has not only been brought before your honorable Board, but also before the community, at various times and places, within the last few months, and has been hitherto designated as the special heresy of the Andover Professors. The other charges appear to be in the nature of an after-thought. They are rather raised as dust to conceal a retreat upon this eleventh or main specification.

I shall consider this topic under the following subdivisions:

First. — The theory of competent theologians believing the doctrine of limited atonement, as to the necessity of knowledge of Christ to a saving faith on the part of the elect.

Second. — The necessary extension of this doctrine to *all* persons, since the theory of universal atonement has been established.

Third. — Historical reasons why the fact that probation involved a knowledge of Christ on the part of the heathen was not present to the minds of creed-builders and Christians until recently.

Fourth. — The reason why it has been an object of attention within these later years.

First. — While the doctrine of limited atonement prevailed, *knowledge of Christ* was deemed necessary on the part of the elect to a saving faith.

The witness that I shall summon upon this point is Dr. Samuel Willard (already referred to), in his ninety-sixth sermon on the Westminster Shorter Catechism (p. 437, paragraph 1, subdiv. (2)). There he says: "*Faith in Christ must be built upon the knowledge of him.* [The italics are his own.] If ever a sinner be persuaded to venture himself upon Christ for life, it must be upon a discovery that is made to and in him that Christ is such an object as is every way fit for him so to do. The act of the will cannot be called a human act any further than as it follows the dictates and direction of the understanding. Faith, indeed, is a confidence, but it is ever built upon knowledge; so that till there be a discovery made of Christ to the man, by which he apprehends him to be able to save him to the uttermost, he will not cast himself upon him for eternity." He then goes on to state "that this knowledge must be by revelation; that God hath chosen the Gospel to be the instrument in and by which this revelation was made; and that God sends the Gospel to men by men whom he employs for that end; and that their errand is to publish the glad tidings of peace, and invite men to accept it. Their commission is to all that come within their hearing, without restriction; and they are not to meddle with the secret purposes of God, as to whom he has elected to everlasting life."

He displays in this connection his belief in a "limited atonement," by stating that God brings not the Gospel ordinarily to any people but where there are some to be effectually called by it. " It cannot be instanced where the Gospel offer ever was made to men merely for condemnation. God knows who are his according to the purpose of his grace before they are so called, where they live, and accordingly orders the Gospel to come to them or them to come to it" (p. 437).

He recurs to the same point on p. 439: "That men may comply with this way as reasonable creatures, the terms of it *must be opened* to them. An human choice, though it be an act of the will, yet to render it human it must be guided by the practical understanding ; nor can it otherwise be denominated an election. That, therefore, men may be capable of making such a choice they must be acquainted with it, that so they may have the knowledge of that about which it is to be made (Psalms ix. 10). The man must apprehend the thing to be good, in order to his closing with it ; whereas that which he knows nothing of he can neither determine to be good or evil, and so cannot exert an act of his will about it."

Though this good Doctor believed in a limited atonement, it was plainly a great trial to his faith. He argued that there was virtue enough in the atonement to prove a satisfaction for all as well as for a few; that the justice of God would not have suffered any injury by the delivery of all ; and that the mercy of God would have had so many the more everlasting monuments, for all were alike involved in guilt and exposed to his wrath. If any caviller then asked him why so few, his simple and invariable answer was, " it was HIS good pleasure so to do."

That is Calvinism in its logical development. Who will say it is not dreary to the last degree ? Limited atonement ; knowledge (for the elect) of Christ ; no knowledge of Christ for the non-elect. " Die, ye accursed, die in your sins ; ye shall not know, for ye cannot believe and knowledge would be useless." Such is the word for the non-elect.

Here, in December, 1697, not long after the publication of the Shorter Catechism, we find a distinguished divine lecturing upon it, and maintaining that there could be no elect except they had knowledge of Christ, and asserting that election implied knowledge of him. His great celebrity and the wide acceptance of his views without objection indicate that he truly represented the contemporary opinion of the New England churches. His view as to the necessity of knowledge of Christ to a saving faith is eminently reasonable, and accords with logic and good-sense.

There is, in my opinion, nothing more saddening than to consider the condition of these God-fearing men of New England when they embraced, with all sincerity of faith, the doctrine of limited atonement. It cut right through the heart of society. It laid bare its most sensitive and quivering nerves. It entered into the family and divided brother from brother; yea, infant from infant. The horrible phrase "elect infants" appears in the Westminster Confession of Faith. The religion of Christ as then understood had in it all the elements of civil war, for it desolated the hearth-stone in nearly every household. It was a brave thing for the men who sustained dreadful mental sufferings from it to say, with cheerfulness, "it is His good pleasure." Still they insisted that there was no true faith, nay, no election, no *elect*, without knowledge. The only difference between the affirmation of these strict Calvinists and the alleged heterodoxy of this respondent is, that while they affirm that there can be no "elect" without knowledge of Christ, he inferentially affirms that no one can be finally lost without having had knowledge of Christ, and this because the atonement is universal. These are but different roads to the same result, viz., the necessity of the knowledge of Christ to a saving faith. The only difference is in the *number* who will have knowledge of Christ.

Second. The necessary extension of this doctrine to all persons, since the theory of universal atonement has been established.

If, now, we reject the doctrine of limited atonement and substitute for it an universal atonement, as does the creed of the associate founders, the same argument remains and is still irresistible. If Christ died for the few, then faith is brought into being in them only in connection with knowledge; if he died for all, faith is required of all to make it available to the extent that Christ designed. And this, as has been seen, implies knowledge of Christ on the part of all. If any cannot receive the knowledge, the design of Christ is to that extent fruitless. While probation after death to those who have no opportunity here cannot be strictly proved, it is rendered probable from the fact that it cannot be supposed that Christ would see His great plan frustrated by lack of suitable opportunity, even on the part of a single soul.

He intrusts it to His believing children to bring the knowledge home to every creature. But what if they do not? Because they are remiss, shall Christ's plan be frustrated? Nay, verily. To borrow the nervous language of the elder Edwards in a somewhat different connection : " This would be to frustrate all those great things which God brought to pass from the fall of man to the incarnation of Christ. It would also frustrate all that Christ did and suffered while on earth ; yea, it would frustrate the incarnation itself." He adds, " All the great things done were for that end that those might be saved who should come to Christ " (History of Redemption, Period II., Part III., Sec. II.). But we ask, in all sincerity, how shall they come to Christ unless they know ? The fact is, that the proposition inserted in this creed that Christ made atonement for the sins of all men, cuts deeper than the founders knew. They, for a special reason, established a creed mainly remarkable for its glaring inconsistencies. Into a vessel, part of iron and part of miry clay, they cast a precious seed, perhaps without thinking of its mighty possibilities. Now, it has grown to be a huge and symmetrical tree, demanding the earth for its roots and heaven for its branches. The great postulates of religion will forever remain : Universal sin, universal atonement, and universal opportunity for rational faith. When " Heaven opened wide the gate of its high palace hall " it also opened wide the gate of knowledge of Him who, standing at the very opening of the gate, announced His universal offer of pardon. As to suitable opportunity to know Him, the Head of the Church will provide, if not by probation after death, in some appropriate way. We may be certain, and be joyful in the assurance, that He will not allow "the design of His incarnation to be frustrated."

Third. I now propose to consider the historical reasons why the case of the heathen and their knowledge of Christ was not present to the minds of Christians until a comparatively recent period, and how it happened that our creeds are comparatively barren upon this subject.

In reading the various creeds that have been adopted by

the Christian Church, one is struck with the paucity of references to the case of the heathen. The great majority of the human race is entirely ignored. This is perhaps partly attributable to a contempt for barbarians derived by succession from the Roman Empire; in part to the terror and detestation inspired by the life and death struggles, long-continued, and with almost balanced fortune, between Christendom and the Turks; partly to intestine struggles in each Christian nation of a most threatening and perilous nature. Religious belief could find no place for them in the other world. This is shown in quite a remarkable manner in the Westminster Confession of Faith (not the Shorter Catechism).

In Chapter 32 (Confession) it is laid down that the " Bodies of men, after death return to dust and see corruption, but their souls, which neither die nor sleep, having an immortal subsistence, immediately return to God who gave them. The souls of the righteous, being then made perfect in holiness, are received into the highest heavens where they behold the face of God in light and glory, waiting for the full redemption of their bodies, and the souls of the wicked are cast into Hell, where they remain in torments and utter darkness, reserved to the judgment of the great day. *Besides these two places for souls separated from their bodies, the Scripture acknowledgeth none.*"

So to escape this last named difficulty, the souls of the wicked must be condemned to Hell *before* the judgment, and those of infants (other than " elect infants," described in Chapter 10) must be sent there also, because the Scripture only acknowledged two places for souls after death. Not a word of this destination as to the souls of the wicked after death is to be found in the Shorter Catechism, while that of the righteous is made substantially equivalent to the statement in the Confession of Faith. This is a significant omission, apparently showing that the view taken in the " Confession " was not firmly held, or that it was considered not to be a fit doctrine to be presented in a popular form, and especially among the young.

The general question still remains as to the principal reason why no general interest has been taken in the Church, until the present century, in the fate of the heathen after death, or, stated in a broader form, in the fate of the heathen in any respect.

One leading ground undoubtedly was that there was assumed to be perpetual enmity between Christians and heathen. I may refer to a great legal decision in the time of King James I., but a few years before the Westminster Catechism was composed, viz., Calvin's case, argued before the Lord Chancellor Ellesmere and the twelve judges of England. Lord Coke, the reporter of it, says that it was the weightiest case that ever was argued in any court. It had points in it of the highest general interest, and, among others, the relations according to the law of nature of Englishmen to aliens were discussed. The general sentiment was, according to Coke, that Christian kings and princes were, though aliens, friends of England, unless in time of war, while there was a perpetual, everlasting enmity between Englishmen and infidels, that is, heathen. Let us listen to the words of the report: " All infidels are in law perpetual enemies (for the law *presumes not that they will be converted, that being a remote possibility*), for between them, as with the Devil whose subjects they be, and the Christian there is perpetual hostility, and can be no peace, for, as the Apostle saith, ' What concord can there be between Christ and Belial ? ' " (7 Coke R. p. 17, b.) Further on, he says, " The laws of the infidel are not only against Christianity, but against the law of God and of nature," contained in the Decalogue. It must be remembered that the men who uttered this, as it now seems to us, atrocious sentiment, this bloody proclamation of everlasting war, were professed Christians, and men of the first rank for ability and statesmanship. The Westminster Assembly sat only thirty years later than this utterance of the twelve judges in Calvin's case, having among its members noblemen, statesmen, and great lawyers, among others John Selden. It is not conceivable that this view was not present to their minds, making the condition of the

heathen, whether before or after death, of no possible consequence to Englishmen. Their conversion was *too remote a
possibility* to be entertained.

Here was a sentiment, if it "did not cut the nerve of missions," prevented any such nerve from developing. Why
was the conversion of the heathen "a remote possibility," in
the language of Lord Coke, or a "possibility upon a possibility," in other forms of statement? This was undoubtedly
derived from some form of the doctrine of limited atonement.
It was scarcely conceivable that Christ would *elect* such children of Belial to be his adopted sons, and pass by men in a
Christian land who had the means of grace offered them. All
the encouragement that could be given to one living in a
Christian land, was that he might, if he used such means of
grace as were open to him, be elected, or God in his good
pleasure might, after all, "pass him by." What, then, were
the chances for election of the poor heathen, ranked among
the devil's servants? Was not Lord Coke correct in calling
it a remote possibility — not worth taking into account? —
was he not right, on that theory, of proclaiming against them,
as the mouthpiece of the justice of England, eternal war?

As late as 1744, the view taken in Lord Coke's time was
still under discussion, and the Court of Common Pleas, speaking by Lord Chief Justice Welles, took much pains to refute
the doctrines advanced in Calvin's case, so far as the right of
a Gentoo to be a witness in an English court, was concerned.
Omichund v. *Barker*, Welles R., 538. Even down to the
time of Lord Mansfield, near the close of the last century,
African slavery was justified in England by many on the
ground that the negroes were not Christians, but infidels, of
course, arguing by implication that infidels had no rights as
against Christians. It had become a current notion that if
a negro became a Christian he was emancipated, though Lord
Mansfield himself tells us that there was no ground for this
in law, and that it was so resolved "upon a petition in Lincoln Inns Hall *after dinner.*" Being rendered in that way,
little attention was paid to the decision, and the question
was not really disposed of until *Somerset's* case (cited below).

He adds that it is remarkable that before this decision the English "took infinite pains" to prevent their slaves being made Christians, so that they might not be freed. *Somerset* v. *Stewart*, Lofft's Reports (fol. ed.), London, p. 8 (A.D. 1763).

Lord Mansfield had moral courage enough to dispel this delusion, although there were fourteen or fifteen thousand slaves in England, held there on that basis. He rendered his decision with a fine, tragic air, crying out, "Let justice come, though the heavens fall." It came, and the heavens did not fall. His decision did not merely emancipate the slave It had a far wider sweep. It emancipated the Christian from his bondage to the accursed theory that the heathen had no rights, legal or moral, that could be urged against the brute force of the Christian. Lord Mansfield was in a mild way the precursor of Abraham Lincoln. Each professed to proceed according to law. The one gave the death-blow to the slavery of African heathen in England; the other destroyed the servitude of African Christians in the United States.

Now, can any one seriously contend that while this state of things continued there could have been any earnest missionary spirit in the way of converting the heathen? Most assuredly not.

Jonathan Edwards, writing his History of Redemption, not far from this period, earnestly favoring missions, could but give the most meagre accounts of them. There was some interest concerning the Indians in North America; something doing in far-off Muscovy; something among the heathen in the East Indies, particularly in Malabar. This was a most meagre exhibit. He was looking forward *to the future*, to the time when "Antichrist" was overthrown, and the heathen were emancipated "from the cruel tyranny of the devil, who has all this while blinded and befooled them, domineered over them, and made a prey of them." He burst forth into a rhapsody: "*Then* shall the many natives of Africa, who now seem to be in a state but a little above the beasts, be visited with glorious light, and delivered from all their darkness, and become a civil, Christian, understanding, and holy people; *then* shall the vast continent of America, which now in great part is covered with barbarous ignorance and cruelty, be everywhere covered with glorious Gospel light and Christian love, and instead of worshipping the devil, as they now do, they shall serve God. So we may expect it will be in that great and populous part of the East Indies which are now mostly inhabited by the worshippers of the devil. . . . Thus will be gloriously fulfilled Isaiah xxxv. 1: 'The wilderness and the solitary place shall be glad for them, and the desert rejoice and blossom as the rose.'"

But if he had disclosed his whole feeling he would have said: "This shall be *hereafter*, but alas! not now, not now. Christ is in conflict with Antichrist, and when in that conflict he is crowned victor all this will come. Till then we must wait." It was like two opposing sovereigns disputing every inch of territory, with varying successes, except that prophecy gave the assurance as to which would be ultimately successful. It was this feeling and the cognate feeling, that the heathen were not likely to be God's elect, that strangled the missionary spirit in its birth. It is easy to understand why at the close of the last century only seven missionary (Protestant) societies were in existence, and four of these in the tenth decade.

It was precisely as the strict Calvinistic doctrine began to lose its hold upon the consciences of men, and the glorious truth of an universal atonement not merely dawned upon their minds and hearts, but shone upon them and irradiated them with its full effulgence, that this other great truth possessed and animated them, that the heathen were not, in fact, the children of the devil, but rather the children of a common father and their own brethren, for whose destiny they should feel the most tender and affectionate solicitude.

Fourth. — It is time now to inquire why the missionary spirit has been so ardent and continuous since the beginning of the present century.

This is no doubt attributable to a variety of causes, including the extension of commerce, the increase of facilities for travel, increased wealth, and the prevalence among civilized

men of the tenderer and more feminine qualities, such as are
evinced in the establishment and large development of societies for the prevention of cruelty to animals or cruelty to
children. This tender sentiment has extended to their far-
away and dusky brethren, and stimulates them to reach forward and lend a helping hand for their civilization, and for
the removal of the dreadful evils which blight and consume
their lives. More than all is it to be attributed to the new
and noble feeling that Christ died for them as well as for
civilized men. To the enlightened modern Christian, Satan
has no pretence to share the honors of sovereignty with
Christ. His reign ended when Christ died. The offer of
pardon is unlimited on reasonable terms. There is nothing
left but to proclaim it with all zeal and discretion. If there
are any sinners that cannot be reached during life, let the
believer hope, or feel assured if he can, that the offer will
still be held out, and the opportunity to embrace it be
afforded, even though it be styled probation after death.
This respondent presents this probation simply as a probability, a hope. We insist, therefore, that on general grounds,
as well as on this guarded commitment to the doctrine, there
is no " heterodoxy " (Progressive Orthodoxy, 248–254, and
the article considered as a whole).

Specification Twelfth. — The next specification is, that the
respondent holds, maintains, and inculcates " that Christian
missions are not to be supported and conducted on the ground
that men who know not Christ are in danger of perishing
forever, and must perish forever, unless saved in this life."

The respondent claims that this subject is not embraced
within this creed, and is not therefore within the scope of
the present inquiry ; still, he admits that he does not hold
that the ground for supporting and conducting Christian
missions is the *absolute certainty* that all must perish forever
who are not saved in this life. The discussion of this subject has been partly anticipated, and it is only proposed to
offer a few suggestions concerning it.

Some will say that even this qualified statement "cuts
the nerve " of Christian missions. The principal objection

to it, I presume, is that the tendency of the doctrine will be to paralyze Christian effort in sending money to the heathen, or to lessen interest in the cause. Such an objection is, of course, without avail if the doctrine of " probation after death " be proved to be true. But as it cannot positively be proved to be true (though we affirm that there appears to be ground for it in Scripture as well as in reason), such an objection is to be carefully considered in weighing probabilities. There must, however, be taken into account, on the other hand, the duty of Christians to obey the divine command to preach the Gospel to all, the influence of Christian love in breeding a desire to extend to others the blessings of Christianity, the impulses of a spirit of humanity in averting cruelty, and the natural and earnest wish of all good and intelligent men to reduce the earth to a well-ordered scheme of civil and religious liberty instead of leaving it in the shadow of ignorance and disorder.

These influences are potent enough to develop Home Missions. Why not Foreign Missions?

The real difficulty is that Christians are not yet emancipated from the bondage of fear. They have not yet accepted love as the element which should control their lives. And yet, while fear was the sole prevailing impulse there were no missions of consequence. It was only after love for far-away brethren began to be the controlling element in men's lives that missions started forward to their present glorious development.

A passage from Dr. Schaff's History of the Creeds of Christendom is singularly apposite. No one will suspect this thorough student in ecclesiastical history of any thing like partiality or bias. He, from the nature of his work, must sum up conclusions as a judge. After surveying the view of the church as to the salvation of the heathen, he says : " During the period of vigorous scholastic orthodoxy which followed the Reformation in the Reformed and Lutheran Churches Zwingli's view " (favorable to the heathen) " could not be appreciated, and appeared as a dangerous heresy. In the seventeenth century the Romanists excluded the Protestants, the Lutherans the Calvinists, the Calvinists the Arminians, from the kingdom of heaven; how much more all those who never heard of Christ? This wholesale damnation of the vast majority of the human race should have stirred up a burning zeal for their conversion; and yet during that whole period of intense confessionalism and exclusive orthodoxism there was not a single Protestant missionary in the field, except among the Indians in the wilderness of North America" (Schaff's Creeds of Christendom, vol. i., p. 384, 4th ed.).

Who were the missionaries to the Indians in North America referred to by Dr. Schaff? John Eliot and David Brainerd, Congregationalist ministers, inspired with the spirit of John Robinson. We know from Mr. Brainerd's own writings what measures he pursued. In teaching the Indians doctrines that had a legal aspect, such as "justification by *imputed* righteousness," he made but very little headway. In his own words, "I found it extremely difficult to treat with them upon this great doctrine" (Brainerd's Journal, Appendix II., Sec. 4). Where he succeeded was, first, in teaching them the sinfulness and misery of the estate they were *naturally* in; and, secondly, in frequently opening to them, in his own words, with his own italics, "the *fulness, all-sufficiency* and *freeness,* of that *redemption* which the Son of God has wrought out by his obedience and sufferings for perishing sinners; how this provision he had made was suited to all their wants, and how he called and invited them to accept of everlasting life freely, notwithstanding all their sinfulness, inability, unworthiness, etc." (Journal, Appendix III. short account of Missions).

Did Brainerd preach "orthodox and consistent Calvinism" to these poor Indians? Wouldn't he have found the among of limited atonement extremely difficult? It may be unhesitatingly affirmed that while truly "consistent Calvinism" was the general doctrine of the Church not one missionary was sent to the heathen, nor was that doctrine ever preached to them.

There is another thing which the friends of Missions

must take into serious consideration. What will be the probable effect upon the loyalty to Christianity of many reasonable men on learning that the doctrine of "universal atonement," to which they now cheerfully give the adhesion of their hearts and lives, is in respect to the vast majority of the human race substantially a mockery? There are and always have been practical limitations upon the power of Christians at once to obey the command, "Go, teach all nations." We hope and believe that these are provisional. In the mean time shall they suffer eternal punishment? Can the church afford to alienate men who have a high sense of justice, without the clearest reason? It is not necessary for the members of this Board to hold the opinion concerning probation attributed to the respondent. All that any can ask is that it shall be a tolerated opinion for those whom it satisfies, and that they shall not by reason of it be adjudged to be "heterodox."

What we desire to say upon this point in more full statement is this:

It is possible to understand, on the theory of a limited atonement, how a great ruler of the universe might extend a pardon to some rebels against his authority and positively exclude others. This has been done scores of times by earthly monarchs, not in general arbitrarily, but with some shadow of reason — perhaps reasons of state. But to say that a Supreme Being offers pardon to all his subjects on certain specified and *equal* terms, and then refrains from communicating the terms to some, so that they cannot accept it if they would, is incomprehensible and abhorrent to the sense of justice implanted in the breast of man by that very Supreme Being. Communication is the very first element of human law. Why not of the divine? If these signers say otherwise, I will not believe them. Nor will I believe that the eminent and merciful Christian men who drew this Associate Creed would have said otherwise, had their attention been called to the proper inferences to be drawn from an Universal Atonement. Let us rid our minds of fallacies. The great Emperor Justinian wrote on the front of his code of Roman law the sentence: "Justice is the unflagging and everlasting purpose to render to every one his due." With a human judge, justice is rightly defined to be a *purpose*, because it may sometimes fail of accomplishment, while with God it is an assured result. No rebellious subject has a claim to a pardon ; but when offered, if it is not communicated, it is, we insist, a hollow mockery of justice, particularly in the case of an omnipotent God.

Some may object that this whole theory of probation after death is quite unnecessary, since the heathen have a law written in their hearts which they ought to obey; and if they do not, they deserve everlasting punishment. The difficulty with this view is, that it introduces into the divine plan two different modes of treating sinners — one by the doctrines of grace, and the other by the feeble fluctuating light of nature's law. Let it be said with reverence, that this is but a human device or makeshift to help God out in an imperfect system of government. The Supreme Being has but one system of government. It is reasonable to think that his plan of atonement will be made known in some way to sinners, be it by "probation after death" or in some other way that he may establish. It is not for us to make a definite assertion as to the mode of accomplishing the divine purpose. We have a right to form and entertain a hope, or even a belief, as to the probabilities of the case.

Either side to this controversy, naturally, seeks the aid of Scripture. There is in my view nothing decisive to be found there, still I think that the verses often cited from the First Epistle of Peter iii. 19 and iv. 6, are by no means adverse to the theory admitted by the respondent, but favor it rather than otherwise.

There is plainly nothing in " the Associate Creed " to exclude this doctrine ; I quote the words bearing on this subject: " The souls of believers are at their death made perfect in holiness and do immediately pass into glory; that their bodies being still united to Christ, will at the resurrection be raised up to glory, and that the saints will be made perfectly blessed in the full enjoyment of God to all eternity; but that the wicked *will awake* to shame and everlasting contempt, and with devils be plunged into the lake that burneth with fire and brimstone for ever and ever." The position of the righteous and the wicked are here strongly contrasted. The souls of the righteous pass *immediately* to glory, and only their bodies await resurrection; the wicked apparently are not to have their destiny fixed until they *awake*, presumably at the time of the general resurrection. It is very plain that there is nothing in this statement to exclude probation after death. Moreover, it is not stated who are "the wicked." The word may mean only those who, having had the offer of pardon made known to them, have decisively rejected it. This view is confirmed by the associated words "shame and everlasting contempt," which cannot with propriety be applied to those who have not known the offer of pardon and its terms.

In view of the word "heterodoxy," it seems eminently proper to state that the theory of the respondent is in accordance with the growing consciousness of the modern Church, or at least is not rejected by it.

(1.) I respectfully refer to the American Congregational Creed of 1883, and in particular to Article VII. in the statement of doctrine. It is there set forth that "we believe in the ultimate prevalence of the kingdom of God over all the earth; in the glorious appearing of the great God and our Saviour Jesus Christ; in the resurrection of the dead, and in a final judgment, *the issues* of which are everlasting punishment and everlasting life." (Vol. iii., Schaff's Creeds, p. 915.)

The question of the final destiny of mankind is thus left open until the final judgment. There is, of course, room for the doctrine of "probation after death," between the time of death and the day of final judgment.

The first name attached to this creed is that of the honored Chairman of this Board; the third name is that of one of the prosecutors of this proceeding. Is it impertinent to ask why did not Henry M. Dexter close up this doctrine of "probation after death"? If he and other representative men left it open, is it "heterodoxy" for a member of the Congregational Church to believe and inculcate it? Is it "heterodoxy" to write in a magazine that it is within the bounds of hope?

(2.) I refer to Dr. Schaff as allowing a *ray of hope* in his discussion of creeds. After referring to Zwingli's views and the revival of them among evangelical divines in Germany, partly in connection with a new theory of Hades and the Middle State, he continues:

"This is not the place to discuss a point which, in the absence of clear scripture authority, does not admit of symbolical statement. The future fate of the heathen is wisely involved in mystery, and it is unsafe and useless to speculate without the light of revelation about matters which lie beyond the reach of our observation and experience." Then he adds: "But the Bible consigns no one to final damnation except for *rejecting Christ in unbelief,* and gives us at least a *ray of hope* by significant examples of faith, from Melchizedek and Job down to the wise men from the East, and by a number of passages concerning the working of the Logos among the Gentiles" (citing the passages). He thus closes: "We certainly have no right to confine God's election and saving grace to the limits of the Visible Church. We are, indeed, bound to his ordinances, and must submit to his terms of salvation; but God himself is free, and can save whomsoever and howsoever he pleases, and he is infinitely more anxious and ready to save than we can conceive."

This author does not commit himself to precise methods. It is plain, however, that he has no controversy of "heterodoxy" with those who hope that the gospel plan of salvation will be submitted in some form or other to the knowledge of all mankind.

(3.) The creeds of the Baptist denomination, including both the so-called Calvinistic and Free Will branches of it, admit of this same view. The former state that the final judgment will fix forever the final state of man, in heaven or hell, on principles of righteousness (Schaff, iii., 748). The latter are still more specific, stating, in chapter 21, that there will be a general judgment, when time and *man's probation* will close forever (Ibid., 756).

It is much that these great denominations of Baptists and Congregationalists, with similar lines of historical develop·ment, should have come to a like general conclusion, that the matter of probation of the heathen cannot as yet be dogmatically stated. It is enough, for this respondent in the present inquiry, if the subject can still be considered open for discussion and reasonable ground of hope.

In closing this argument, I must express my deep regret that the prosecutors of this proceeding should have thought it necessary to bring this painful topic before your honorable Board suggesting it as a matter of heterodoxy. I do not desire to question their motives, but I cannot fail to deprecate the spirit in which they have made unwarranted charges against the character and deeds of five distinguished men, who represent the worth and intelligence of the denomination to which they belong, and who have long been successful instructors of youth. Such proceedings shake the confidence of men in the stability of the Christian system of truth. The charges turn out to be of slight moment, and not within the true scope of the trust imposed by the original founders. It is to be earnestly hoped that this Board, acting in a spirit of catholic forbearance and true wisdom, will reach a conclusion at once just to the accused, and calculated to subserve the interests of the cause which I assume that we all have greatly at heart.

EVIDENCE INTRODUCED BY PROFESSOR BALDWIN.

Professor BALDWIN. *Mr. Chairman, and Gentlemen of the Board : —*

We now proceed to introduce the evidence, both documentary and oral, and both brief, in support of the answer of the respondent. Our evidence will be confined to what we deem the main point to be considered by the Board of Visitors; namely, whether Dr. Smyth has in any manner violated by his publications the obligations he has assumed to the Trustees of Phillips Academy in Andover according to the Statutes under which the Seminary is constituted. We believe that the Creed is a broad and not a narrow one; that it is a practical and not a scholastic one; that it does not speak a mediæval theology, but a true and progressive orthodoxy. Other questions have been suggested to you at great length by my learned associate, with all the fulness of research that characterizes whatever comes from his hand; but the particular question to which our evidence will apply is a narrow one, — simply whether our client can take his stand with security and serenity, as we think he can, upon this ground: That he has made a full and unanswerable declaration of his acceptance of the Associate Statutes and Associate Creed, in the manner in which we think they ought to be understood by every one who reads them, who reads their history, who reads their very words, or who is cognizant of the uniform construction and usage which has interpreted them for nearly a hundred years.

Our first exhibit will be the record of the proceedings of the Board of Trustees, already introduced by my friend Professor Dwight, on Dr. Wellman's resolution. . . .

Exhibit 2 is a record of the action of the Board of Trustees on Sept. 27, 1826, and again on April 19, 1842, both together on the same paper. This is the record of the meetings of the Trustees, in which action was taken to determine whether the associate professors were or were not bound to subscribe to the Westminster Catechism. At the first meeting it was held they were; at the second meeting it was held they were not. . . .

Sept. 27, 1826. [1] "*Voted*, That in the opinion of this board the Constitution of the Theological Seminary, as expressed in the original and associate statutes, requires that the declaration made and subscribed by every Professor in this Seminary shall be in the following terms, viz.: I, —— Professor ——, do make solemn declaration of my faith in divine revelation, and in the fundamental and distinguishing doctrines of the Gospel of Christ as summarily expressed in the Westminster Assembly's Shorter Catechism.

"*Voted*, That the above declaration shall be hereafter subscribed and repeated according to the requisitions of the Constitution and the respective statutes; with the exception that the terms ' Papists ' and '' Sabellians ' be not inserted in the declaration of any Professor on the Original Foundation."

A true copy from the Records.

C. F. P. BANCROFT, Clerk.

April 19, 1842. [2] "*Resolved*, That the vote passed Sept 27, 1826, by this Board, requiring every Professor in the Seminary to make a declaration of his ' faith in Divine Revelation and in the fundamental and distinguishing doctrines of the Gospel of Christ as summarily expressed in the Assembly's Shorter Catechism, and that the above declaration shall be hereafter subscribed and repeated at every successive period of five years ' be rescinded, so far as relates to every Professor on the Associate Foundation — so that each Associate Professor shall only be required to subscribe and repeat the creed as it stands in article second of the Statutes of the Associate Foundation in the Theological Seminary."

A true copy from the Records.

Attest: C. F. P. BANCROFT, Clerk.

Exhibit 3 is a certified copy of the doings of the Board of Trustees in the matter of the inauguration of Professors Taylor, Hincks, and Harris, June 12 and 13, 1883.

[1] Records, Theological Seminary, Vol. I. p. 238.
[2] Records, Theological Seminary, Vol. II. pp. 3, 4.

June 12, 1883. [1] "The Board attended the inauguration exercises of Professors Taylor and Hincks at the chapel Tuesday evening. The exercises were as follows: . . . Reading of the Creed by Rev. John P. Taylor, Rev E. J. Hincks standing by and consenting thereto. The President then propounded to each the following constitutional question: 'Do you now make and subscribe a solemn declaration of your faith in Divine Revelation, and in the fundamental and distinguishing doctrines of the Gospel as expressed in the Creed which you have now read?' To which each responded, 'I do, believing that the Creed expresses substantially the system of truth taught in the Holy Scriptures.' Each then subscribed as constitutionally provided, and the President declared them duly inducted into office as Professors in the Seminary."

June 13, 10.30 A.M. "Inauguration of Professor George Harris. . . . Reading of the Creed by the professor elect. The President then propounded the constitutional question as follows: 'Do you now make a solemn declaration of your faith in Divine Revelation, and in the fundamental and distinguishing doctrines of the Gospel of Christ as summarily expressed in the Westminster Assembly's Shorter Catechism, and as more particularly expressed in the Creed you have now read?' To which the candidate replied, 'I do, believing that this Creed expresses substantially the system of truth taught in the Holy Scriptures.' Mr. Harris having then subscribed as required, the President then declared him duly inducted into office as Abbot Professor."

A true copy from the Records.

Attest : C. F. P. BANCROFT, *Clerk*.

We read that to show the contract under which three of the later professors have entered the service of the Seminary, and the manner in which they were inducted into office ; and we shall have further evidence to show what was the understanding on the part of these gentlemen, as to the effect of their assent to the Statutes and Creed and Catechism, in the case of Dr. Harris, and as to the action of the Trustees and Visitors upon the same, and that all this happened prior to Professor Smyth's taking the last declaration upon himself to the Associate Creed, and prior to the publications complained of by the learned gentlemen who propound this libel.[2]

As Exhibit 4 we will lay in a letter from the Rev. Samuel Spring, D.D., to the Rev. Dr. Jedidiah Morse, written Dec. 16, 1808, and printed in Wood's "History of Andover Semi-

[1] Records, Theological Seminary, Vol. II. pp. 492, 493.
[2] This testimony will be found on pp. . .

nary," p. 623. We offer this in order to show the practical construction put upon the Creed by one of the first Visitors, Dr. Spring, while he was a Visitor; he also being, as we all know, one of the main founders of the institution, and Dr. Morse another.

In explanation I may say this was written after the article in the "Anthology," which is familiar to many gentlemen here, in which the foundation of Andover Seminary is very severely criticised. It was said in the "Anthology," a Unitarian magazine then published in Boston, that Andover Seminary was a bundle of contradictions, and that the Calvinists had given themselves away to the Hopkinsians, and that you could not reconcile the Westminster Catechism and the Associate Creed. . . .

EXHIBIT 5 is a sermon by the Rev. Dr. Moses Stuart, Associate Professor of Sacred Literature at Andover Seminary, at the ordination of Pliny Fiske in 1818; and I direct especial attention to p. 17. . . .

EXHIBIT 6. Professor Stuart's Letters to Channing, second edition, particularly pp. 21 and 23. These will be commented on hereafter by Dr. Smyth, and it is perhaps unnecessary to call attention to them at this time.

EXHIBIT 7. Dr. Woods's Letters to Unitarians, 1820, particularly pp. 44 and 45.

EXHIBIT 8. Dr. Stuart's Letters to Dr. Miller, referring particularly to pp. 18, 122 and 124, comprised in the volume marked "Miscellanies No. One."

EXHIBIT 9. Dr. Miller's Letter to Professor Stuart, 1823, referring particularly to pp. 16 and 290.

EXHIBIT 10 will be the Biblical Repository, vol. 1, p. 261, and vol. 2, p. 26, containing Professor Stuart's articles on "What is Sin?"

EXHIBIT 11 will be Dr. Dana's Letters to Professor Stuart, criticising his statements in the Biblical Repository, 1839, with special reference to pp. 24 and 25.

EXHIBIT 12 will be Professor Stuart on the Old Testament Canon, with special reference to pp. 386, 391, 404, 405, 413 to 419.

Exhibit 13 will be Professor Stuart on the Apocalypse, with special reference to his comments on chap. 20, verse 4.

Exhibit 14 will be Rev. Dr. Dana's "Remonstrance to the trustees of Phillips Academy," and the "Additional Remarks," so called, which form a sequel to it, and a postscript, which forms a subsequel to it, all by Dr. Dana, published in vol. 9 of "Miscellanies," with special reference to pp. 8 to 10, 13, 18, 19, 23 and 24. These contain Dr. Dana's accusations against Professor Park, more particularly, for his heterodoxy at that time.

I believe that includes all the documentary evidence we shall trouble the Visitors with. Dr. Smyth will make an address to you, and after his address we shall have some other testimony of an oral character to make to you.

Mr. HOAR. Does Dr. Smyth appear as a witness?

Mr. BALDWIN. You have charged certain particulars of heterodoxy upon Dr. Smyth. He has denied the charge, and he is now going to make a statement in support of his denial of your charges —

Mr. HOAR. As a witness?

Mr. BALDWIN. —supposing that in this court, as in all courts where I have had the honor to appear, the party accused has a right to be heard, and the Court is glad to hear him.

Mr. HOAR. We still desire to know whether he is going to submit argument or testimony.

Mr. GASTON. I suppose he has a right to submit both.

Mr. HOAR. Not together.

The CHAIRMAN. Dr. Smyth may proceed.

PROFESSOR SMYTH'S DEFENCE.

May it please your Reverend and Honorable Body:

BY the Statutes of the Associate Foundation it is made your duty "to take care that the duties of every Professor on this Foundation be intelligibly and faithfully discharged, and to admonish or remove him, either for misbehavior, heterodoxy, incapacity, or neglect of the duties of his office." By the Statutes of the Brown Professorship, which I have the honor to hold, this Foundation is made "subject to visitation" in the same manner with the Associate Foundation. In the libel filed by the complainants and which defines the present issue I am not charged with misbehavior, incapacity, or neglect of official duty. The sole issue is one of "heterodoxy."

I desire to call your attention to the fact that I am not charged with "neglect of the duties of my [his] office." It is certainly possible that a Professor, enamored of some new opinion neither out of "harmony with" nor "antagonistic to" the Creed of the Seminary, might spend so much time in maintaining and inculcating it as to neglect his duty in respect to other truths. If this were the accusation in the present case I am confident that I should have no difficulty in meeting it. But wide as is the range of the present libel it nowhere ventures upon such an aspersion. I stand before you, even in these calumnious days, absolutely without reproach from any quarter in this particular.

I am charged before you with "heterodoxy"—nothing more, nothing less, nothing other. If I am guilty of "heterodoxy" you can remove or admonish me as the issue of this trial, according to your judgment and discretion. If I am not guilty I am entitled to a clear acquittal.

It has been said that this is not a trial for heresy, but for a breach of trust. A suit for a breach of trust would lie more properly against the Trustees or Treasurer of the Seminary. Not a cent of the Seminary Funds comes into my hands save as I receive it from said Treasurer, who acts by order of the Trustees. If there has been a breach of trust in the management of the funds the custodians and disbursers of those funds are guilty of this offence, and there are available and natural methods of prosecution. The arraignment of five professors, and the interruption of their work in the midst of a term of study, is not one of these natural methods. This is a trial for heresy, or it is nothing. The violation of solemn promises which is charged is simply an issue of interpretation of a creed. The only charge in essence and in form is the accusation of " heterodoxy."

It may indeed be suggested in qualification of what I have said, that " heterodoxy " in the present instance is to be determined by an unusual, particular and remote standard, and that this criterion is not the test which would now be imposed, so that I might be orthodox according to the rule which would be applied to-day, and yet heterodox according to the rule prescribed in the Seminary Creed. I do not admit that such a distinction is applicable in the present case. I am advised by eminent legal authority that the word " heterodoxy " in the Statutes cannot be thus limited and defined. But irrespective of this objection I must say that I think better of our Creed, better of the Founders of the Seminary, than such a contention would admit. The Creed bears traces, doubtless, of controversies which no longer interest the public, and unadjusted and even irreconcilable conceptions linger in some of its phrases. But to whatever criticisms it is fairly exposed, I " hold, maintain, and inculcate," Mr. President, that it does not bind the Seminary to an antiquated phase of belief, or to the " warts and wens " which a living theology knows how to get rid of, but on the contrary, that it logically leads to those adjustments of orthodox thought and belief which are now necessary, and in general leaves an open path for such as the future may require. Such a statement doubtless will strike with surprise some who are the friends of doctrinal progress. There is abroad an opinion which is founded, I am persuaded, upon *a priori* reasoning, and not upon scientific examination. It is like certain theories of inspiration which are derived from what men think the Bible ought to be and not from what it is. It reasons thus: The human mind has made doctrinal progress since the century opened. A creed written eighty years ago must be antiquated. That depends. An *a priori* "must be," science has taught us, is not always an "is so." It depends on who says it, still more on what has been said. I am not a eulogizer of the Andover Creed. Clothed in phraseology which it requires much special learning accurately to interpret, composed as a compromise, designed to admit under it a great variety of philosophical theories and beliefs, expressive at certain points by its silences even more than by its utterances, balancing traditional statements by novelties of doctrine, inserting some words to bar against regression and others which make progress necessary, confessing the authority of Scripture but not failing to emphasize the constant revelation in creation, providence and redemption, it cannot be rightly understood without a more careful study than its critics have usually given to it, and whatever else it may be I am persuaded that it is not the symbol of an antiquated phase of orthodoxy, nor the chain and ball of an imprisoned theology. I appear before you of necessity to make personal answer to charges most of which are utterly false, charges some of which, if true, would justly expose me to the accusation of heresy under the standards of a catholic orthodoxy, but I have a larger contention and a deeper interest. I desire to secure by your decision for those who may come after me the rights of a reverent scholarship in the study of God's word; the liberties of thought and life which are necessary to fruitful biblical study; the opportunity for that spontaneity and freedom in the discovery and acquisition of sacred truth, without which the articles of any creed however excellent can never become the reality of present, personal convictions and the living springs of knowledge, but must always remain the dry and barren deposit of a dead past. I believe the result at which I aim expresses the only correct interpretation of the duties and rights of a Professor in Andover Seminary, as these obligations and liberties are defined and guaranteed in the Creed and Statutes of the Founders.

Before, however, I venture out upon this larger field of thought, I desire to meet the complainants upon the narrowest line which they may select. I shall attempt to show that, even when every indication from the Founders is disregarded which points to that nobler conception of the function of the Creed at which I have just hinted, the present complaint is still futile and void.

In order to convict me under the present libel the complainants must prove that I hold beliefs which are inconsistent with a valid acceptance of the Creed, or that I have violated my solemn promise " that I will maintain and inculcate the Christian faith as expressed in the Creed . . . so far as may appertain to my office, according to the best light God shall give me, and in opposition to " various heresies and errors specified and unspecified, ancient and modern.

The first requirement pertains to belief, the second to official conduct in matters of faith.

To establish my guilt under the first requirement the complainants must prove at least two things: that I hold an alleged belief, and that this belief is contrary to the Creed. As I have intimated it will be contended in my behalf that there is still a further condition of the validity of the accusation, viz., that this particular belief be shown to be heterodox by a yet higher and more continuous and potent standard of orthodoxy. Without waiving this point I shall not press it in what I here present. I am content to insist at the present stage of the argument upon the two conditions first named, the necessity of proving that I hold what is charged, and that such a belief contravenes the Creed.

To prove my guilt under the second requirement, — that of official conduct, — still more must be established than under the first. My official promise must be considered in all its parts, and as a whole. No one can rob me of the conviction that whatever have been my deficiencies I have endeavored to maintain and inculcate so far as pertains to my office "the fundamental and distinguishing doctrines of the gospel" as expressed in the Creed, "according to the best light God" has given me, and in opposition to the various errors by which history shows that these truths have been confronted. I have preferred, however, to try and show what neglected element of truth heresy may be thriving upon, and how it may be healed by a larger truth, rather than merely to antagonize it. I submit to your careful consideration this test of the validity of any proof, advanced by the complainants, of my "heterodoxy" as a teacher. It is a three-fold cord. Each strand is necessary. It is weak as a broken thread if either fails. It must be shown that I have "maintained and inculcated," that is, taught purposely and urgently, what is charged; that I have done this in my work as a Professor in the Seminary; and that this deed is a violation of my promise to teach the Christian faith as expressed in the Creed "according to the best light God shall give me." I ask you in simple justice rigidly to apply this test to what on this point the complainants may offer as proof.

You will pardon me also if I request you to bear in mind that I am not on trial before you as an editor of the *Andover Review*, or as a joint author of a volume called *Progressive Orthodoxy* published by Messrs. Houghton, Mifflin & Co., 4 Park Street, Boston. I would not draw any fine or artificial distinction between my utterances in the *Review* and in the Lecture Room. No honest man, certainly no trustworthy religious teacher, can hold a double and mutually contradictory set of opinions, one for his pupils, another for his own privacy or for some other use. If I have taught in the *Review* what is contrary to the Creed, I shall not plead that I have been more reserved or utterly silent in my lectures. I have, however, a point to make which may assume impor-

tance. It is this. In the field of literature I am amenable
to your jurisdiction only so far as it can be proved that what
I publish is contrary to the Creed, or actually violates, or
necessarily and evidently tends to violate, my obligations as
Brown Professor of Ecclesiastical History in the Theological
Institution in Phillips Academy in Andover. In a volume
or review, for instance, I am perfectly at liberty to dwell *ad
libitum* on a single topic. I might co-operate in a temperance
journal, or one devoted to Civil Service Reform, and write
on one or the other of these subjects every month, provided
I neglected none of the duties of my office. Much more on
some living theological or religious question, under the same
condition. But it would be contrary to the duties of my
office to give such prominence to these questions in my lecture room. So far as the *Review* or *Progressive Orthodoxy* is
now before you, the issue is not what prominence is given to
a subject, but whether any thing is taught which shows a
belief or beliefs contrary to the Creed, or a violation of my
promise as to conduct in my office.

Indulge me in one other preliminary remark. I regret
that the number and variety of the charges in the libel make
it impossible for me to be brief. I am charged with heterodoxy upon nearly all the distinguishing doctrines of our Holy
Religion. The indictment seems to be constructed on the
plan of somebody's note-books of a course of lectures in Systematic Theology, embracing the leading topics from the
Being of God to the final resurrection and the contrasted
eternal states. One of the signers, in the original complaint,
wrote " Trustee " under his name. He is a Trustee of the
Seminary, of many years' standing. Being a clergyman he
has been very often appointed by his associates to attend my
theological examinations. I have almost invariably, from
year to year, examined on the Church doctrine of the
Trinity. He knows, or is inexcusable if he does not know,
what I have taught. He knows, or ought to know, that I
have taught from year to year the doctrine of the Trinity,
the Church doctrine ; and that I " hold, maintain and inculcate " it, as I have done all along. I am thankful that it does

not devolve upon me to occupy your time in trying to explain why he has deemed it necessary to sign his name, in the professed interest of honesty of subscription, to a charge that I teach a modal Trinity, a charge which he knows full well, or is inexcusable if he does not know, is baseless and false, but unless he and his associates withdraw this charge and others equally preposterous, I must take time to refute them. Fortunately for the demands upon your time the strength of the list is in inverse ratio to its length.

Believing that you will appreciate the necessity laid upon me of reviewing in detail and with thoroughness these numerous accusations, and reminding you again of the two-fold, or three-fold necessities of evidence adequate to establish any one of these charges, I now proceed to their consideration.

The *first particular charge* is, that I "hold, maintain and inculcate that the Bible is not ' the only perfect rule of faith and practice,' but is fallible and untrustworthy even in some of its religious teachings."

What has there been in the evidence submitted on this point by the complainants which proves either that I hold what is charged, or that there is any thing in the article or citations adduced which affords any presumption that I thus teach, or that any thing which I teach or for which I am responsible is contrary to the Creed? I have not been able to detect a scintilla of evidence for either of these positions, each and all of which must be established or the charge falls.

Take first the article in the *Review* entitled "The Bible a Theme for the Pulpit." How or where does this show that, so far as appertains to my office, I fail in upholding the supreme authority of sacred Scripture? In what lies the proof that in the chapel pulpit, or in my lecture room, or in any public utterance whatsoever, I oppose the declaration of the Creed " that the word of God contained in the Scriptures of the Old and New Testaments is the only perfect rule of faith and practice"? Not only is no connection of this sort traced by the complainants, they have done nothing to lay the foundation for a presumption or suggestion in favor of such a connection. For there is no expression anywhere in the article of the thing charged. It contains not a syllable adverse to the requirement of the Creed. On the contrary, the article was written in the interest of the doctrine affirmed in the Creed. Its occasion was the discovery that some ministers, recognizing that many of their hearers hold to the old theory that the Bible in every part is equally authoritative and in every statement is infallible truth, and knowing also that such a proposition cannot be maintained, out of prudential motives have withdrawn from the teachings of the pulpit any instruction as to what the Bible is as the only perfect rule, and how it has become such a rule. The writer endeavored to enter into the thoughts and feelings of such ministers, to appreciate the reasons which influence them, to state those reasons, in order to point out to them that there is a better way, and one which it is the duty of the ministry of intelligent churches to follow. What now is the use made of this article by the complainants? First, five sentences are detached from that portion in which the embarrassments of the preacher are depicted. Then, a skip is made to the close of the article and a sentence picked up and so connected that its object is precisely reversed. It was written as a suggestion, at the close of a brief article, how, by pursuing a particular method of pulpit discussion, men disturbed by the results of modern critical study may be helped to a firm and immovable conviction of the trustworthiness and perfection of sacred Scripture as a rule of faith and practice. It is quoted as though it were designed to favor a treatment of the Bible "prejudicial to its sacredness and authority."

One is reminded that there is still need of the irony with which a bishop of the English Church two centuries ago discoursed upon "The Difficulties and Discouragements which attend the Study of the Scriptures in the way of Private Judgment; Represented in a letter to a young clergyman." He will subject himself to much toil in study, will be likely by the results of his labor to disturb the peace of the church and bring upon himself the reproach of being a *heretic*, "a term which there is a strange magic in. . . . It is supposed to include in it every thing that is bad; it makes every thing appear odious and deformed; it dissolves all friendships, extinguishes all former kind sentiments however just and well deserved. And from the time a man is deemed a heretic, it is charity to act against all the rules of charity; and the more they violate the laws of God in dealing with him, it is, in their opinion, doing God the greater service. . . . A search after truth will be called a love of novelty. The doubting of a single text will be scepticism; the denial of an argument the renouncing of the faith. . . . In a word orthodoxy atones for all vices and heresy extinguishes all virtues. . . . Turn yourself to the study of the heathen historians, poets, orators and philosophers. Spend ten or twelve years upon Horace or Terence. To illustrate a *billet-doux*, or a drunken catch; to explain an obscene jest; to make a happy emendation on a passage that a modest man would blush at, will do you more credit and be of greater service to you, than the most useful employment of your time upon the Scriptures; unless you can resolve to conceal your sentiments, and speak always with the vulgar. . . . You have two ways before you. *One* will enable you to be useful in the world, without great trouble to yourself. . . . The *other* . . . will draw on you an insupportable load of infamy, as a disturber of the church and an enemy to the orthodox faith, and in all probability end in the extreme poverty and ruin of yourself and family. Which God forbid should ever be the case of one who has no other views but to dedicate his life to God's service."

Who has forgotten the abuse which was rained upon Professor Stuart for his biblical studies? Writing (Oct. 7, 1813) to Dr. Spring, the son of a principal author of the Seminary Creed, he says — referring to the "exegesis of Canticles:" "For my humble self, if I doubt whether the forty-nine senses can all be applied to this book . . . and must be a heretic on this account, I say with Vitringa, *Ego sum in hac hæresi.* . . .

"I certainly," he continues, "do not think it worth the trouble of writing this to save myself from the imputation of heresy, among those who make all divinity heretical that is not *triangular.* . . . 'What, said Father Paoli to his brother Jesuit, who was less dexterous in combating for the mother church than himself. What did Scarpi say at the meeting of the order? — He said he doubted whether the infallibility of the Church could be predicated of the Pope alone, or whether it resided in an ecumenical council. — Most abominable! and what did you tell him? — I told him that the Pope was the successor of St. Peter. — Well, and what said he? — He said that he did not read in the New Testament of Peter's having appointed any successor, and challenged me to produce the passage. — Challenged you to produce the passage! — Yes; and I was not able to recollect it. — Able to recollect it! why did you not tell him that the Fathers believed as we do? — I did. — And what said he? — Why, that the Fathers were not the Pope, and so were not infallible. — Why didn't you tell him that he would endanger the faith of the whole Church by such *innovations?* — I did try to argue with him about them. — *Argue* with him! you stupid blockhead (*fatuus Diaboli*) — *argue with him!* Why did you not call him HERETIC . . .? These heretics are to be confounded by blows, not by arguments (*fustibus non argumentis confutandos*).'

"Thus," adds Professor Stuart, "believes brother Romeyn, as truly as Father Paoli, and for as good a reason. If you think strange of this, you have only to recollect that two pennyweights of brains are a sufficient apparatus for the purpose of guiding a march through the whole round of hard names and abusive insinuations, while it needs several pounds to manage an argument." . . .

May it please your Reverend and Honorable Body I have searched diligently through the printed specifications under this charge about the Scriptures, and have listened carefully

to catch any, even the faintest, suggestion of some utterance
for which I am responsible, which militates in the least
against the divine authority of the Scripture, but I have not
discovered it. Where is it found? Is an attempt to show
how a divine revelation has come to us, an attack upon revelation? The most cursory reading of either of the articles
named or cited, shows by constant incidental expressions,
and by its whole structure and design that the mind of
the writer assumes that we have in the Bible a trustworthy
and authoritative expression of the mind and will of God.
The complainants have not read to understand even that
which is perfectly patent and plain, much less to mark and
inwardly digest. They have been in search for means of
attack, on a rampage for accusations. Sentences are twisted
from their connections, quoted by jumping backwards and
then forwards,[1] divorced from qualifying declarations in the
immediate context, begun with capitals by omission of important connections and obliteration of every indication that
in the book they are not thus independent. It is easy to make
a slip in citation, as experience shows, and no generous critic
will deal severely with a mere inadvertence. But where
errors are numerous, where they always favor one side, where
they are artificial, they are properly regarded as evidence of
lack of candor. That the quotations are adduced for the purpose of specification does not help the matter. They are none
the less unfair citations.

I will adduce instances in point.

The third quotation from *Progressive Orthodoxy*—com-
mencing "Even if"—begins, in the book, "*And* even if," con-
necting with a different and natural explanation of our Lord's
method of reference to the Pentateuch and Isaiah. The sixth
citation,—beginning "When we recollect"[2]—is the second member of a sentence, whose first member reads "But
the slight blemishes in the very finest optical instruments
do not prevent our obtaining from them data which to the
human mind of finest training are exceedingly exact; and

---

[1] pp. 231, 227, 228. 207, 208, 209, 213, 214, 221, 222.
[2] Prog. Orth., p. 209.

when " etc. Half a sentence is taken. the connective omitted
without indication, and the whole covered up by altering the
capital letter.

The fifth quotation is followed in the paragraph from
which it is taken by an antithetic sentence, beginning: "But
this feature . . . is not its weakness but its strength," and
by further qualification in the next paragraph in the words:
" If the question mean, ' Must not such sin as still dwelt in
the apostles have tinged their religious conceptions and
teaching with error?' — we reply, This could not have been
unless they were more under the influence of moral evil than
we have any reason to suppose them to have been." That is,
the answer ' Yes ' is quoted and the answer ' No ' omitted;
and this when the negative refutes the charge of holding that
the Bible is "fallible and untrustworthy even in some of its
religious teachings."

The seventh quotation, — beginning, " The views of Christ,"
— recognizes that other ages than the apostolic have been
blessed with men in whom dwelt the Spirit of wisdom and
revelation.   It is overlooked that before the paragraph closes
allusion is made to ancient prophets, and that it is added:
" No teacher in the church has ever arisen or can ever arise
so filled with the Spirit as not to depend upon the apostles
for conceptions of God.   We can see that their situation and
their exceptionally exalted life make following teachers dependent upon them as they were not dependent upon any
predecessor except Christ; that their conceptions of our Lord
are the framework into which all the subsequent thoughts of
his church, about Him and his work, must be set; and the
norm by which the teaching of the church must shape itself."
And then the writer goes on to show that this follows " necessarily " from their historical relation to the Incarnation;
that beyond this intimate personal acquaintance with the
" Word of life," there was added "the inner revelation "
and *" pre-eminent endowment of the Spirit;"* that the hope
even must be excluded of other teachers arising superior to
them; that their conditions of spiritual endowment were
"absolutely unique;" that the greatest thinkers of the

church have never been able to correct one of their conceptions of Christ and that in them was fulfilled Christ's promise to lead them "into the whole truth."[1]

I will not go on with this exposure. These citations are
wholly insufficient for their purpose. They are vitiated, first,
by their irrelevancy. They fail, every one, as they stand, to
prove the charge, or even to specify it. They are wholly
defaulted, secondly, by being garbled. When taken in their
proper connections they turn into a positive refutation of the
charge — a refutation which would be repeated again and
again by further citation, by passages for instance which
may be found on pp. 10, 207, 214, 227, as well as on those
already adduced.

The specifications show only this, that sometimes in *Progressive Orthodoxy* the word imperfection is used, or its equivalent, whereas in the Creed the adjective "perfect" is employed. But it is not thereby shown that the book affirms
to be imperfect what the Creed says is perfect. The Creed
affirms perfection of the Word of God contained in the Scriptures of the Old and New Testaments as a rule of faith and
practice. I take no advantage, though I might on the theory
of a merely literal interpretation, of the words "contained
in." To me the Bible *is* the Word of God. But the perfection ascribed to it in the Creed is one of use and function.
It is the only perfect guide in a religious life, "in faith and
practice."

This formula did not originate with the framers of the
Seminary Creed. The Westminster Standards declare Holy
Scripture "to be the rule of faith and life,"[2] "the only rule
of faith and obedience,"[3] "the only rule to direct us how we
may glorify and enjoy Him."[4] And among the questions to
candidates for ordination is this one: "Do you believe the
Scriptures of the Old and New Testament to be the Word of
God. the only infallible rule of faith and practice?" This last
formula appears occasionally in local New England creeds.
The founders apply the word infallible to the "revelation

---

[1] Prog. Orth., pp. 210-213.
[2] *Confession*, Art. II.
[3] *Larger Catechism*, 3.
[4] *Shorter Catechism*, 2.

which God constantly makes of Himself in his works of creation, providence and redemption." Their phrase respecting the Scriptures is, "the only perfect rule of faith and practice." It is the Westminster formula with the change of "infallible" to "perfect." But the formula is older than the Westminster Standards. It summed up the universal Protestant contention against the Roman Catholic doctrine of Scripture. The Council of Trent exalted Tradition to a place of co-ordinate authority with Scripture. The Bible was not the only rule because there was another. It was not the only perfect rule because it was not a complete rule but partial. Practically it was not even an infallible rule because it needed to be supplemented by Tradition, and to be authoritatively interpreted by the Church, and with the Bible alone as his guide a man might go astray from its insufficiency. This great controversy brought into use such expressions as I have cited from the Westminster Standards, and similar ones with which we are familiar in our local confessions. If you will look into Chillingworth's great work on "The Religion of Protestants," in which he contended for the famous maxim that the Bible alone is this religion, you will find *passim* the expressions "a perfect rule of faith,"[1] "the only rule" and also abundant evidence that their meaning is what I have just explained, viz., that Sacred Scripture is "the only perfect rule of faith and practice," because it is a complete rule, needing no supplementing by tradition, a plain rule requiring no infallible interpreter, whether church or pope, council or creed, a sure rule for whoever follows its teachings will believe and do what is acceptable to God and find eternal life. In a word the formula as expounded by this acknowledged master has a negative and positive side. It denies that other rules are necessary for men either as a co-ordinate source of religious knowledge or as an indispensable interpreter, and it affirms that Scripture can make the man of God "perfect, thoroughly furnished unto all good works."[2] Scripture is thus "the only perfect rule of faith and practice."

See particularly Pt. I., c. 2.   [2] 2 Tim. iii. 17.

In perfect consistency with this exposition, Chillingworth opens the door for all the liberty that a sound historical criticism requires in the investigation of the method in which the Bible became such a rule of faith. There is not an utterance cited by the complainants which is not covered in principle by his masterly statement, and when the complainants attempt to put such expressions as they quote from *Progressive Orthodoxy* and the *Review* into antagonism to the Creed they are not only ineffective, but they show their ignorance of principles which were formulated in the beginnings of Protestantism and long since settled by one of its universally recognized and foremost champions. Why, even so familiar a book as Professor Stuart's *Old Testament Canon* contains many a sentence just as much and just as little objectionable as those picked out and up by the complainants.

Let me present a few of these which have been handed to me by one of my colleagues :

In regard to drawing the line between what is abrogated in the Old Testament and what is now of divine authority and obligation he says : "The ultimate appeal, then, is to understanding and reason ; not in order to establish the *principles* in question, for Christ and his apostles have established them, but to make a discriminating and judicious use of these principles in determining what still remains in full force." (p. 386.)

All that refers to Old Testament rites and forms of worship is abrogated. "It remains now only as the *history* of what is past, not the rule of action for the present or the future." It unfolds "in what manner divine Providence has been educating the human race ; by what slow and cautious steps religion has advanced, and how utterly impossible it is for a religion that abounds in rites and forms to make much *effectual* progress anywhere, either among Jews or Gentiles ; still more impossible that it should be a religion to convert the world." (p. 391.)

So too all statutes and ordinances that pertain merely to the form of the Jewish ecclesiastical and civil state. (pp. 404–405.)

"Rarely will one find any considerable portion of the Old Testament where there is nothing in it of the *local* and *temporal* that must be abstracted, in order for us to reduce it to practice." (p. 404.)

The devotional psalms, "the Psalms of complaint, of thanksgiving, of imprecation, and others, all have something which savors of time and place and circumstances. These we must omit, excepting that in the *exegesis* of the Psalm we must treat them as essential, but not in the practical use of it." (p. 405.)

" It is so with the Mosaic laws."

" Even the *ten commandments* are not altogether an exception to this." The reference here is to visiting iniquity to third and fourth generation, and to the promise that thy days may be long in the land.

With reference to the question what is of present practical value in the Old Testament he says : " How few [of the commentaries] have satisfied the claims of the *reason* and *understanding* of men ! "

" A commentary that would give us simply what is fairly to be learned from every part of the Old Testament in respect to present duty, or as to doctrine . . . is one of the things yet to be ; for I cannot think that it now is." (p. 406.)

" What can we say of those teachers who find just as full and complete a revelation in the Old Testament of every Christian doctrine, as in the New? (p. 407.) Instances Trinity, Immortality and Future State.

" We must attribute no more to the Old Testament than belongs to it. The glory of the gospel is not to be taken away and given to a mere introductory dispensation." (p. 408.)

" We should regard them (Old Testament books) in the light of a *preface* or of an *introduction* to the Gospel."

Of current abuse of Old Testament texts : " Books of such a peculiar nature as Job and Ecclesiastes, for example, are resorted to with as much confidence for *proof texts* as if they were all *preceptive* and not an account of disputes and doubts about religious matters." (p. 409.)

" The Psalms that breathe forth imprecations are appealed to by some, as justifying the spirit of vengeance under the gospel, instead of being regarded as the expression of a peculiar state of mind in the writer, and of his imperfect knowledge with regard to the full spirit of forgiveness."

He deprecates the " violence done to the understanding and to sober common sense " in exegesis, and says it " will be certain to avenge itself at last." (p. 410.)

" There are not a few persons, who seem to feel that if the Old Testament is a work of *inspiration* it must stand on the same level with the New, and be equally obligatory. There is something of truth in this, and not a little of error." (p. 413.)

"We have a *new* and a *better* Testament than the ancient. In itself it is a sufficient guide." (p. 414.)

"Of one thing I am fully persuaded, which is, that a proper use of the Old Testament will be made in all cases, by no one who cleaves to the notion, that because the Hebrew Scriptures were inspired they are therefore *absolutely* perfect. Such perfection belongs not to a prefatory or merely introductory dispensation. It is only a *relative* perfection that the Old Testament can claim; and this is comprised in the fact, that it answered the end for which it was given. It was given to the world, or to the Jewish nation, in its *minority*." (p. 415.)

"With the exception of such sins as were highly dishonorable to God and injurious to the welfare of men, the rules of duty were not in all cases strictly drawn."

"The Old Testament morality, in respect to some points of *relative* duty, is behind that of the Gospel" (p. 416).

"The Gospel is ever and always the *ultima ratio* in all matters of religion and morals. It is . . . the highest tribunal. Whatever there is in the Old Testament which falls short of this . . . is of course not obligatory on us" (p. 417.)

"The spirit of New Testament doctrine, morality, modes of worship (so far as modes are touched upon), is always to be applied to judging of our obligations to the ancient Scriptures."

"There are imperfections in the ancient system; but they are such as the nature of the case rendered necessary. They are in accordance with the principle of the slow and gradual amendment of the race of man." (p. 418.)

In arguing against Norton he emphasizes the divine origin and authority of the Hebrew Scriptures as admitted by Christ and his apostles and Christians generally and then says: "Mr. Norton has scanned Old Testament matters in the light of New Testament revelation, and then passed sentence of condemnation upon the imperfect, because it is not perfect. Is this equitable dealing? . . . Is it any satisfactory objection against this or that specific thing in the Old Testament that the New has better arranged or modified it? Is it conclusive against the history or character of David and other potentates, that they did things in war, which were common in those days, but which the Gospel and a better state of things now forbid?" (p. 419).

Particular 2. The complainants quote from the *Andover Review*, May, 1886, p. 522, but overlook the statement on p. 524:

" So long as the doctrines of universal sinfulness, of redemption and eternal life only through Jesus Christ the Saviour, who was TRUE GOD AND TRUE MAN, and the doctrine of eternal condemnation to those who do not believe on Christ, — so long as these doctrines are faithfully and generally preached we must conclude that the pulpit which is orthodox in name is in the best sense orthodox in fact." See also *Progressive Orthodoxy*, pp. 22 *sqq.*

Particular 3. In the words "are not found " (quoted from *Progressive Orthodoxy*, p. 47), there is an obvious reference to what is learned from history and observation. The discussion does not concern itself with exceptional cases, but with the broad and patent fact of the moral helplessness of mankind apart from Christ.

Pages 54–56 are then cited; but the extract opens, if we interpret aright the reference, with the declaration :

" But Christ's power to represent or be substituted for man is always to be associated with man's power to repent. The possibility of redeeming man lies in the fact that although he is by act and inheritance a sinner, yet under the appropriate influences he is *capable* of repenting. The power of repentance remains, and to this power the gospel addresses itself." " It is to this power that Christ, the holy and the merciful, attaches himself." " Now the power of repentance, which, so far as it exists, is the power of recuperation, is superior to the necessities of past wrong-doing and of present habit." (p. 55.)

It is indeed stated that " Man left to himself cannot have a repentance which sets him free from sin and death," and that the race, without Christ, " would be hopelessly destitute of " the requisite "powers for repentance and holiness." But here the writer is evidently contemplating a radical and complete restoration of men to sonship and freedom. Compare Paul's account of his own experience in the seventh of Romans, and these words in Ephesians ii. 11, 12, " Where-

fore remember, that aforetime ye, the Gentiles in the flesh,
. . . were at that time separate from Christ, having no hope
and without God in the world."

With the language quoted from p. 58, compare what is
said on pp. 59 and 60 : "Christ brings God the Person to
man the person, and in such manner that God is known as
the God of holy love, the loving and holy Father. The
goodness of God leads men to repentance." "Or reversing
the order and advancing to the ultimate fact that redemption
originates with God, we may say that man is the penitent
and obedient man because God in Christ is the reconciling
and forgiving God." The discussion deals with the great
facts of human recovery from sin. The distinction between
natural ability and moral inability is important ; but the
original Hopkinsians never thought of putting the stress
upon it which some later theologians have laid. Of one of
these it was said, when the remark was made that he claimed
to represent the Hopkinsians, 'Yes, with this difference :
they exalted divine efficiency; he, human efficiency.' The
writer of the article in *Progressive Orthodoxy* seeks to apprehend the real saving powers in the cross of Christ. His
critics appear to be fumbling over the distinction of natural
and moral ability.

Following their usual method, these complainants next
turn back a few pages and pick up a sentence on p. 55, and,
as is not unusual with them, overlook other sentences on the
same page which ought to have entirely relieved their dis-
tress. We need not quote over again what has just been
presented. Finally the sentence is taken from p. 126 ;
"Where in the realm of natural law, can the Spirit find
material or motive fitted to this most difficult of all tasks
— the convincement of sin?" As this is a question we
might wait perhaps for the complainants to answer it. Any
contribution they may thus make to Christian theology will
be cordially welcomed. Agassiz seems to have doubted
whether nature alone gives "any very clear mark of the
character of the Creator."[1] But this is not the point to be

[1] See Allen's Our Liberal Movement in Theology, p. 157.

here discussed. What is there in all that is adduced which shows any contrariety of opinion to the statements of the Creed? Man's natural powers of moral agency are not denied, but asserted. It is everywhere assumed that men are responsible for their sins. The discussion of the book relates to a different question, namely, How is man saved? The following extract from the early pages of the article on *The Atonement*, from which nearly all the specifications are taken, sufficiently shows this :

" Now the message of the gospel unquestionably is that man is not bound under ethical in the sense in which he is bound under physical necessity ; that forces are available for the moral and spiritual life by which man can be delivered from the worst consequences of sin, and can become a new creature. Transformation may be rapid and complete. Man may be translated from the dominion of merciless necessity into the life of freedom and love. The new and higher force is the revelation of God in Christ, through which the power of sin is broken and the penalty of sin remitted. If all this is true, the gospel gains a profounder meaning than it has ever yielded before. The church comes now to man, well aware that he cannot be separated from custom, habit, heredity, fixedness of character, the social organism of which he is part. It is seen that redemption must be grounded in reason, and must meet the actual conditions of life and character and society. Atonement must express and reveal God as the supreme Reason and perfect Righteousness, who cannot deny himself, and who cannot disregard nor annul the moral law which is established in truth and right. Christian thought, having established itself on the intrinsic, absolute right and on the inexorableness of law so firmly that these may be accepted as postulates in all the inquiry, agreeing so far forth with Anselm on the one hand and with the latest natural ethics on the other, is going forward now to learn if any ethical ends are secured by the revelation of God in Christ, and secured in such a way that God energizes in man and society for a moral transformation so radical and complete that it may be called salvation, redemption, eternal life, divine sonship. . . .

" This is the question to-day concerning atonement, — What moral and spiritual ends are secured by the sacrificial life and death of Christ? How does God's attitude towards man change, and man's attitude towards God change, so that there is sufficient power for the transformation of ethical and spiritual life as against the tendencies of moral corruption? Evidently the result is of a kind that cannot be brought about by sheer omnipotence, but only, if at all, by truth and love. Thought must move in the spiritual, not in the physical realm."

We add without comment a few sentences which show the point of view and the care exercised to suggest necessary qualifications.

" Regeneration thus acquires a large and an exact meaning under Christianity. We would not deny the existence of regenerate life outside Christianity. . . . If we say the least, we can say no less than that when we pass beyond the method of the conscious renewal of the spiritual life in Christ, we pass at once into what is exceptional, vague, and indeterminate. (pp. 127, 128.)

" The moral and spiritual recovery of mankind even as an aim of benevolent purpose, presupposes the provision of a power in motive, and a use of this power proportionate to the evil to be confronted, and the good to be accomplished. ' It was the good pleasure of the Father that in Him should all the fullness dwell.' The fullness was set over against the need. Christianity is not a matter of words, but of deed and of power. Whatever we may think of antecedent revelation the apostle teaches us the large fact and truth in the case when he says, even of the days of Jesus' earthly ministry, ' The Spirit was not yet given, for Jesus was not yet glorified.' " (p. 121.)

The Creed affirms " that every man is personally depraved ; " " that being morally incapable of recovering the image of his Creator, which was lost in Adam, every man is justly exposed to eternal damnation ; so that, except a man be born again, he cannot see the Kingdom of God ; " " that . . . the Son of God, and He alone, by his suffering and death, has made atonement for the sins of all men ; " " that the righteousness of Christ is the only ground of a sinner's justification ; that this righteousness is received through faith ; " " that regeneration and sanctification are effects of the creating and renewing agency of the Holy Spirit ; " . . . " that the ordinary means by which these benefits [of redemption] are communicated to us, are the word, sacraments, and prayer;" "that God's decrees perfectly consist with human liberty;" "that man has understanding and corporeal strength to do all that God requires of him; so that nothing, but the sinner's aversion to holiness, prevents his salvation."

Progressive Orthodoxy recognizes man's responsibility for his sins, affirms his moral ruin, and emphasizes the righteousness which is by faith in Christ and the renewing work of the Spirit. I am unable to see wherein this book fails to conserve the principles enunciated in the Creed on these topics. They seem to me to gain a new depth of meaning and a higher degree of reasonableness from the fact that the authors give to the universality of the Atonement and to the Incarnation the primary and central place in theology. Man's moral agency becomes the activity of a child of God, and sovereignty blends with fatherhood. The reality and guilt of sin grow darker, as the way of escape grows brighter. I do not the less accept the principles of moral agency contained in articles of the Creed which I have cited because they become more profound and far-reaching by reason of a doctrine which the Creed also contains, though without indicating its power of illumination; I refer to the article on the universality of the Atonement. If the Eternal Son became Man and died for all whose nature He made his own, then moral agency, in a world or age in which this is the central and supreme revelation of what is divine, necessarily transcends the bounds of either a legal or imperial sovereignty. I think that the fundamental principle of *Progressive Orthodoxy* is in the Creed, and that we have a right to interpret other associated doctrines by it. I maintain also that these doctrines, so far as they are not inconsistent with this principle, are better held the more they are connected with it and systematized by it.

Particular 4. I have already, in my Reply, called attention to the way in which the quotation marked as from page 64 is made up. I have also affirmed my belief that "every man who sins *is* lost, and is in danger of being remedilessly lost." I will now simply add a few quotations, several of them lying between the two page references, 55 and 64, which are given by the complainants in connection with this particular. Their point, it will be borne in mind as I read, is, that I hold, maintain and inculcate that men are not sinners unless they have heard of Christ, or at any rate are not "in danger of being lost." On page 44 and again on page 47 sinfulness is predicated of man universally. On page 48 it is said : " The consequences of holiness and of sin cannot be set aside by the will of God. On page 54 the garbled paragraph opens, in its second sentence, with recognizing " the fact " that man " is by act and inheritance a sinner," and its concluding sentence says that "on account of Christ *man* can be delivered from *condemnation.*" On the opposite page (57) we read: . . " God cannot be regardless of law nor indifferent to sin in saving man from *punishment.*" On the next page it is said: " The ideal relation of God is love, but the actual relation is wrath ;" on page 60, " He who is not moved to penitence and faith by Christ is under a *greater* condemnation ; " on page 61: " It is on account of Christ that God can forgive, on account of Christ that men are not left helpless and condemned under the necessities of unchangeable law." On page 177 the cause of missions is recognized as resting on "the postulates of universal sinfulness, universal atonement, and the indispensableness of faith." And in the concluding article of the book these postulates are re-affirmed, and it is added : We have accepted these postulates in their length and breadth. We have not reduced but rather have magnified their meaning." And yet in the face of these explicit statements we are charged with teaching that men are not sinners "save as they have received a knowledge of the historic Christ! "

Particular 5. I do not think that I need give any additional references here, and I will merely re-affirm the reply already submitted.

Particular 6. On page 33 there is a distinct recognition that the Apostle Paul teaches the propitiatory nature of Christ's sacrifice ; and on page 48 an equally clear acceptance of the Anselmic principle of a " necessity . . . in the ethical being

of God . . . which even his will cannot contradict nor super-
sede." ". . . God cannot be regardless of law nor indifferent
to sin in saving man from punishment." When it is said, "It
must be confessed, however, that it is not clear how the sufferings and death of Christ can be substituted for the punishment of sin," this is not a suggestion of doubt as to the fact
of Atonement but a statement of the problem, and the key to
the reasoning which follows. The complainants have confused two lines of approach to the subject (p. 57), and
failed to observe that the familiar one, on which their own
thoughts more naturally travel, is recognized but not pursued because it is so well understood. Perhaps if they
would kindly endeavor to think out what is suggested by
the word " realizing," in one of the closing sentences of the
article from which they quote, — " In the Atonement God
provided redemption for the world by realizing his holy love
in the eyes of all the nations " — their apprehensions would be
relieved. Will they suggest a thought or expression that
more deeply penetrates into the nature of the mysterious
sacrifice on Calvary than that by which it is opened to our
reverent gaze as a *Realization* in the fullness of time, at the
turning point of human history, through an incarnate Redeemer and for the purpose of man's redemption, of God's
righteous and holy love?

And then will the complainants, in addition, please to
point out what is the theory of the Atonement made binding
in the Creed as a condition of a trust? Where is it found,
and how is it expressed?

Particular 7. The most charitable interpretation of this
accusation is, that it is a sheer blunder, a blunder however
which nothing but the oppressive exigencies of this " friendly
suit" could have led sensible men to commit. It appears
that it was not the original intention of the complainants to
file charges and specifications themselves, but when your
Reverend and Honorable Body decided that, if they thought
the matter presented by them so serious as to require investigation, they should reduce their accusations to definite form,
their embarrassments became such that a civilized commu-

nity will treat their mistakes with appropriate levity. It is one
thing to indulge for four years in the almost unlimited license
of vague accusation permissible in the columns of religious
journalism, to call men Semi-Unitarians and Semi-Univer-
salists, and the like. But it is quite a different affair to make
a specific charge and to attempt to prove it. The editorial
habit, however, could not be easily resisted. A Semi-Unitarian
— what is he ? He must be a Sabellian. This is particularly
convenient, for the Professors at Andover promise to oppose
Sabellians, and we want in a friendly way to establish a violation of solemn promises and a breach of trust. We will
charge them then with holding that the Trinity is modal.
But either some special urgency of timeliness in pressing the
complaint, or some occult influence of superior power, or
some wholly mysterious cause, required such extreme rapid-
ity of execution, that these busy, active men, charged with
so many grave responsibilities, found no time to look up in
their Seminary note-books or some familiar text-book what is
the exact meaning of the words "modal and monarchian,"
as applied to the Trinity. They were caught by the word
" mode," just as before they had been, when dealing with the
Scriptures, with the word "perfect." The Creed says the
Bible is a perfect rule, the Professors talk of imperfections.
The Creed condemns Sabellians. Sabellians — perhaps they
remembered this much of their Seminary lore — hold to a
modal Trinity. Let us look and see if these same Professors
who have so trifled with Sacred Scripture are not equally
guilty in respect to the Holy Trinity. Thus searching they
discovered and triumphantly produced, when required so to
do, in the *amended* complaint, two passages from *Progressive
Orthodoxy*, each of which contains the word " mode " in application to a Person of the Trinity. Here surely is set forth
a modal Trinity, and a modal Trinity is Sabellian ! *Quid
obstat?* But I respectfully submit, Mr. President and Gentlemen, this question to your decision, whether any tyro in
theology could not have told these men that the distinction
between a modal or real Trinity is conveyed by the use of
the phrases mode of manifestation and mode of being. He

who affirms the latter predicate of a distinction in the Godhead uses the formula than which no other is more firmly
established in Christian Theology as the best word to dis-
criminate the church doctrine from every form of Monarchi-
anism. And this precise formula, or its equivalent, is the one
twice employed by the writer in *Progressive Orthodoxy* whose
sentences are quoted to prove that I hold to a modal Trinity.
It is as absurd as an attempt to prove that President Lincoln
was a believer in absolute monarchy because he used the
word government when he spoke at Gettysburg of government by the people.

The phrases I have used are, in the first passage cited,
" the divine nature as possessed by the Logos, or in that mode
which characterizes his existence." You have there all the
most characteristic forms of speech by which the Church
doctrine of the Trinity has been expressed for fifteen centuries. The Logos possesses, has as his own, the divine nature.
He possesses it, however, in a peculiar way or mode. This
mode of possession characterizes his being. It is his personal
property as the Larger Catechism says, — *his* characteristic.
In the next quotation the phrase employed is, " a particular
mode of the divine being," not, you observe, mode of manifestation, or relationship *ad extra*.

I think I need not stop to discuss the question of the meaning of the word " Person " as applied to the Holy Trinity.
When the article quoted from, referring to the three distinctions, or modes of being, in the godhead, affirms that " Neither
in itself is a Person," it uses the word Person as employed
when we speak of the one absolute Person, God. I hold, and
the writer of the article, judging by his language, agrees with ·
me in holding, that each distinction is personal, but that each
is a Person, (in the ordinary sense of personality, and as this
idea finds its supreme realization in the Infinite and Absolute
One), only in, with and through the other distinctions and as
possessing the one divine nature. And the orthodoxy of
this position can easily be established by the most approved
writers. A doctrine antagonistic to this, and at the same
time admitting personal distinctions, is sheer Tritheism, not
Trinitarianism.

I will subjoin a few quotations from authors of acknowledged standing and ability, which I have taken almost at random.

Dr. Shedd teaches that the word Person, as applied to the Trinity, designates a species of existence "anomalous," "unique," "totally *sui generis*."[1]

Dr. Schaff explains the doctrine established by the great Councils thus:

" In this one divine essence there are three *persons*, or, to use a better term, *hypostases*, that is three different modes of subsistence of the one same undivided and indivisible whole. . . . Here the orthodox doctrine forsook Sabellianism or modalism which, it is true, made Father, Son, and Spirit strictly co-ordinate, but only as different denominations and forms of manifestation of the one God."[2]

In 1819 Professor Moses Stuart, in his " Letters to the Rev. William E. Channing," gave this representation of the views of Trinitarians:

" The common language of the Trinitarian Symbols is, ' *That there are three* PERSONS *in the Godhead.*' In your comments upon this, you have all along explained the word *person*, just as though it were a given point, that we use this word here, in its *ordinary* acceptation as applied to *men*. But can you satisfy yourself that this is doing us justice? What fact is plainer from Church History, than that the word *person* was introduced into the creeds of ancient times, merely as a term which would express the disagreement of Christians in general, with the reputed errors of the Sabellians, and others of similar sentiments, who denied the existence of any *real distinction* in the Godhead, and asserted that Father, Son, and Holy Ghost were merely *attributes* of God. or the names of different ways in which he revealed himself to mankind, or of different relations which he bore to them, and in which he acted? The Nicene Fathers meant to deny the correctness of this statement, when they used the word *person*. They designed to imply by it, that there was some *real*, not merely *nominal* distinction in

[1] *History of Christian Doctrine*, I. 365.
[2] *History of the Christian Church*, III. 675.

the Godhead ; and that something more than a diversity of relation or action, in respect to us, was intended. They used the word *person*, because they supposed it approximated nearer to expressing the existence of a *real distinction*, than any other which they could choose. Most certainly neither they, nor any intelligent Trinitarian, could use this term, in such a latitude as you represent us as doing, and as you attach to it. We profess to use it merely from the poverty of language ; merely to designate our belief of a real distinction in the Godhead ; and NOT to describe independent, conscious beings, possessing *separate* and *equal essences*, and *perfections*. Why should we be obliged so often to explain ourselves on this point? . . . I could heartily wish, indeed, that the word *person* never had come into the Symbols of the Churches, because it has been the occasion of so much unnecessary dispute and difficulty." [1]

John Calvin, in his *Institutes*, remarks as follows : —

" The Latins having used the word *Persona* to express the same thing as the Greek ὑπόστασις, it betrays excessive fastidiousness and even perverseness to quarrel with the term. The most literal translation would be *subsistence*. Many have used *substance* in the same sense. Nor, indeed, was the use of the term Person confined to the Latin Church. For the Greek Church, in like manner, perhaps, for the purpose of testifying their consent, have taught that there are three πρόσωπα (*aspects*) in God. All these, however, whether Greeks or Latins, though differing as to the words perfectly agreed in substance." [2]

" Where names have not been invented rashly, we must beware lest we become chargeable with arrogance and rashness in rejecting them. I wish, indeed, that such names were buried, provided all would concur in the belief that the Father, Son, and Spirit, are one God, and yet that the Son is not the Father, nor the Spirit the Son, but that each has his peculiar subsistence [*proprietate*]. I am not so minutely precise as to fight furiously for mere words."

" But, if we hold, what has been already demonstrated from Scripture, that the essence of the one God, pertaining to the Father, Son and Spirit, is simple and indivisible, and again, that the Father differs in some special property from the Son, and the

[1] Op. cit , pp. 21-23, 2d ed., 1819.
[2] Op. cit. I. p. 148. Calv. Trans. Soc. Ed. 1845. [3] *Ib.* pp. 150, 151.

Son from the Spirit, the door will be shut against Arius and Sabel-
lius, as well as the other ancient authors of error." [1]

Particular 8. Perhaps I need do no more than repeat my
previous reply :

" The accusation is that I hold the work of the Holy Spirit to be
' chiefly confined to the sphere of historic Christianity ; ' or, as
more definitely specified by the citation, with its context, that the
' efficacious,' regenerating, saving work of the Spirit is thus ' chiefly confined.' The opposite proposition would be that this work is
' chiefly confined to ' paganism, or Judaism, or both. There can
be no doubt which of these propositions is more accordant with the
Creed, with orthodoxy, or with ' consistent ' Calvinism as explained
in the Creed. Substituting the words ' conducted within ' for
' confined to,' and not doubting a universal work of the Spirit, I
should admit the accusation."

I will only add that the subject is discussed in *Progressive
Orthodoxy* in the light of history, observation and missionary
experience — that is, as a question of fact. So far as we have
evidence, or judged by its fruits, Christianity alone offers the
requisite material in motive for the transformation of mankind into a spiritual temple and kingdom of God.

I think that this is implied in Pentecost, that it is the
teaching of John vii. 39, and of much Scriptural authority
besides. " Only when Jesus was glorified," is Dr. Milligan's
comment on the passage in John's Gospel (Dr. Schaff's *Popular Commentary*), . . " would men receive that spiritual
power which is the condition of all spiritual life."

Particular 9. I reaffirm but do not find occasion to ex-
pand my previous answer, save to add a few references to
passages on pp. 56, 57, 60, and 61, where the sinner's condemnation under law is abundantly recognized.

Particular 10. I repeat my former reply, and refer also to
my acceptance of the statement in the Creed that the Scriptures are the " only perfect rule of faith and practice." A
reasonable being must be guided by reason, but it is the dic-
tate of reason to submit to the word and authority of God.

[1] *Ib.* p. 173.

I believe, however, that reason is at the bottom of all things, the reason of the universal Creator and Redeemer. Therefore human reason may explore and question and hope to find more and more fully the truth. If the charge intends — which I do not allege — to cast a slur upon reason in matters of faith, I beg leave to refer to the nobler maxims of the leader of the party which had most to do with shaping the Seminary Creed. I quote from Dr. Park's Memoir of Samuel Hopkins.

" Our author's strength of character induced him to give an unusual prominence to the more difficult parts of theology, and thus it shaped his entire system. Whether his speculations be true or false, he has done a great work in promoting manly discussion, in convincing his readers that piety is something more than a blind sentimentalism, and that theology is something better than a superstitious faith. He has encouraged men to examine intricate theories, and the examination has saved them from scepticism. Hundreds have been repulsed into infidelity, by the fear of good men to encounter philosophical objections. Hopkins was too strong for such fears. He had that sterling common sense which loves to grapple with important truths, cost what they may of toil. The great problem of the existence of sin early awakened his curiosity, and moved the depths of his heart. A weaker man would have shrunk from the investigation of such a theme. But he was ready to defend all parts of what he loved to call ' a consistent Calvinism.' His readiness to encounter the hardest subjects and the sturdiest opponents, was foretokened by one of his early corporeal feats. It is reported that an insane man, stalwart and furious, was once escaping from his keepers with fearful speed; but the young divine intercepted him, and held him fast until the maniac gave up, and cried, ' Hopkins, you are my master.'

" Throughout the unpublished and published writings of Hopkins, there breathes a masculine spirit, which refuses to be satisfied by assertion instead of argument, and insists on the legitimate use of the faculties which God has given us. At the age of sixty-five, he writes to Dr. Hart: ' I ask what faith I shall have in the power of God, or what belief of any revealed truth, if I do not so far trust to my own understanding, as to think and be confident that I do understand that God has revealed certain truths, and what they

are.' In his thirty-fifth year, Hopkins seized at what he deemed a
tacit concession of Dr. Mayhew, that Arminianism could not be
sustained by reason. He writes to Bellamy: 'I think he [May-
hew] says that which may be fairly construed as a crying down
of reason, under the name of *metaphysical*, or some epithet tanta-
mount." Hopkins was too vigorous to leave such a concession
unnoticed. He turns the tables on his Arminian opposers, and
they censure him for his argumentative style, — the very thing for
which they have been censured, again and again, by their antago-
nists. Our stout champion says, that ' Pelagians and Arminians
have been, in too many instances, treated so by their opponents,
the professed Calvinists. The former have gloried in their reasoning against the latter, as unanswerable demonstration. The latter,
instead of detecting the weakness, fallacy, and absurdity of the
reasoning of the former, and maintaining their cause on this
ground, as well they might, have endeavored to defend themselves
from this weapon by bringing it into disgrace, and rejecting it
under the name of *carnal, unsanctified reason*, etc. This has been
so far from humbling or giving them the least conviction of their
errors, that it has had a contrary effect to a very great and sensible
degree. And no wonder ; for this was the direct tendency of it,
as it is an implicit confession that they felt themselves worsted at
reasoning.' " [1]

Particular 11. It is evident from a few extracts from *Progressive Orthodoxy* to which I will immediately call attention
that our views upon the subject here introduced have not
been presented in the unguarded way which is here assumed
to be true. What I am to read is a caveat to which marked
prominence is given in the book against such a misrepresentation. In the " Introduction " pains was taken to say :

" Problems are above the horizon which are not yet clearly
within the field of vision. Even their provisional and relative
solution is at present impracticable. Too early an attempt to
define and systematize is likely to cramp and repress inquiry, and
to promote a dogmatic self-satisfaction which is a deadly foe to
progress. The aim, accordingly, of the writers of these papers has
been to keep clearly within the range of what is immediately
necessary and practical. For the most part, a single line of

[1] *The works of Samuel Hopkins*, I. pp. 176-178.

inquiry has been followed, under the guidance of a central and vital principle of Christianity, namely, the reality of Christ's personal relation to the human race as a whole and to every member of it, — the principle of the universality of Christianity.

"This principle has been rapidly gaining of late in its power over men's thoughts and lives. It is involved in the church doctrine of the constitution of Christ's person. It is a necessary implication of our fathers' faith in the extent and intent of the Atonement. It is an indisputable teaching of sacred Scripture. It lies at the heart of all that is most heroic and self-sacrificing in the Christian life of our century. We have sought to apply this principle to the solution of questions which are now more than ever before engaging the attention of serious and devout minds. We have endeavored to follow its guidance faithfully and loyally, and whithersoever it might lead. We have trusted it wholly and practically. By the publication of this volume we submit our work to the judgment of a wider public. If we have anywhere overestimated or underestimated the validity and value of our guiding principle, we hope that this will be pointed out. Or if we have lost sight of any qualifying or limiting truth, we desire that this may be shown. On the other hand, if we have been true to a great and cardinal doctrine of our holy religion, and have developed its necessary implications and consequences, we ask that any further discussion of these conclusions should *recognize their connection with the principle from which they are derived, and their legitimacy, unless this principle is itself to be abandoned.*" [1]

On page 39 "a better understanding of the revealed central position of Christ in the universe, and of the absoluteness of Christianity," is claimed as a characteristic of the " New Theology." The presentation of the theory of future probation is prefaced by these remarks:

"At this point the discussion might terminate. The principle of judgment in accordance with which the destinies of men are determined we believe to be that which has now been defined. . . . We could stop here, but for a related question which has long perplexed and disturbed believers. It is a question as to the judgment and the destiny of those to whom the gospel is not made

[1] *Prog. Orth.*, pp. 3, 4, cf. pp. 13, 14, 16.

known while they are in the body. We must consider the discussion, then, in order to consider, as it may seem to deserve, this difficult question. It is, in our opinion, to be looked on as an appended inquiry, rather than as an essential question for theology. Still it is not wanting either in practical or speculative importance, and, at any rate, is at present much in dispute.

" B. A Related Question.

" What is the fate of those millions to whom Christ is not made known in this life, and of those generations who lived before the advent of Christ?

" This may, perhaps, be only a temporary question. The time may come, we think *will* come, when all will hear the messages of the gospel during the earthly lifetime, and will know the gospel so thoroughly that knowledge and corresponding opportunity will be decisive. Then there will be less occasion for perplexity, as there will be no apparent exclusion from those opportunities which at present are given to only part of the great human family.

" The question we have raised is not new. Nor are any of the proposed answers new, although some of the reasoning is the outcome of a more profound thought of the gospel than has been gained in preceding periods. An instructive lesson for impressing the difficulty of our inquiry is a history of the various opinions which have been held during the Christian centuries by honored leaders and revered saints ; such an historical sketch, for example, as Dean Plumptre gives in his recent book entitled, ' The Spirits in Prison.' No answer which has yet been given is entirely free from objections. Every one, unless he declines to accept any solution, has an alternative before him, and must rest in that conclusion which seems to him most nearly in accordance with the large meaning of the gospel, and which is exposed to the fewest serious objections. Certainly, any one should be slow to condemn those whose opinions on this vexed subject do not agree with his own hypothesis. There is no explicit revelation as to the destiny of those who on earth have had no knowledge of Christ. Therefore any inference that is drawn from the doctrines of the gospel, and from the interpretation of incidental allusions of Scripture, must be held with confession of some remaining ignorance on the part of the reasoner. The theory which we shall advance presently is offered under these conditions."

It is evident from these quotations that in our reply we might have met this entire charge by a simple and sheer denial. It is patent, by the book, that we do not, in the unqualified manner of the charge, make any opinion we entertain respecting future probation a central doctrine. In the strictest sense we do not treat it as a doctrine at all, but only as an inference from a doctrine or fundamental principle.

I do not wish, however, to avail myself of any refinements at this point. I claim full liberty under the Creed to hold in this matter whatever a true interpretation of Scripture, and of the "revelation which God constantly makes of Himself in his works of creation, providence and redemption," may make probable, and with a degree of faith as exactly proportionate to available evidence as I can measure; nay, I do not think I shall commit any sin against reason and Scripture and the God who speaks in Scripture and reason, nor violate any obligation under the Creed, if I allow myself to follow with a perfect trust wherever with the heart as well as with the head I can discover any traces of his holy and reconciling love.

I have not therefore in my reply availed myself of the opportunity given by the extravagance of the accusation to make a square denial of it. I have said: "In this unqualified form I do not admit that I hold, maintain and inculcate 'that there is and will be probation after death for all men who do not decisively reject Christ during the earthly life;' and that this should be emphasized, made influential, and even central in systematic theology." I have added: "God as revealed in Christ is to me central in theology. Whatever encourages hope that all men will have opportunity to be influenced by the motive of an offered Saviour is chiefly valuable in theology as a reflection of the character of God."

A theologian's duty, as well as a believer's, and indeed every man's, is primarily to God. What He is in his character and in his will concerning us, is the great, and all-absorbing question. This is emphatically a fundamental principle of "consistent Calvinism." The question about the

heathen has a deep interest to us because they are men ;
a deeper interest because they are men for whom Christ died,
each and every one ; the deepest interest because they are
children of the same God on whom all our personal hopes
depend and in whom all our lives are lived. A question of
this character is a fundamental question. Therefore when any
inquiry arises which in the smallest degree whatsoever involves His character, I will not protect myself by any man's
want of skill in attacking me. So far as the question of the
heathen comes into the sphere of the ethical character of
God and just so far as it is within even the faintest circles of
light which we may discern if we will, it is a part of the one
and the only central and fundamental question for every
man : What is God ? And I beg leave to emphasize that
this is the real central question we have discussed in *Progressive Orthodoxy*, and not the mere issue about Probation.

That there may be no ambiguity as to my position because,
on a question so vital, my assailants have blundered, I deny
even the last part of this accusation with this measure of
qualification.

The first part I deny, in my answer, by calling attention to
the fact that what I hold is an inference from what appears
to be evident, and is a reasonable inference, and that it seems
to be implied in the universality of Christ's Person, Atonement
and Judgment. This is a suggestion by example of the
grounds of hope, and the method of it. I then deny that
such an inference is inconsistent with any thing in the Creed.

Upon this basis there arise two questions. *First*, have the
complainants shown that we " hold, maintain and inculcate "
any thing more or other than what is here conceded ? No
evidence to this effect has been adduced, nor is there any.

Second. Is the drawing and accepting this inference such
a departure from the Creed as brings me into disharmony
with it, or into antagonism to it in my official service?

It devolves upon the complainants to prove such disharmony or antagonism. They must show, if they are to make
out their case, that the inference in question is necessarily
hostile to the Creed, that I cannot entertain it without being

hostile to the same, that I cannot receive it without violating my solemn promise " to maintain and inculcate the Christian faith as expressed in the Creed, . . . so far as appertains to my office, according to the best light God shall give me, and in opposition to" various errors.

In reviewing the effort to establish such antagonism I have a right to demand from the complainants entire definiteness of statement, and conclusiveness of argument. They must show that I actually take positions in what they prove, or in what I admit, that I hold, which contravene my official obligations under the Creed and Statutes.

Under the Creed. The question is not one of contrariety to opinions commonly held when the Seminary was founded, nor even to opinions held by the Founders, but simply of antagonism to what they have prescribed in their Statutes. Professor Park has said that the Professors at Andover "are now under the safeguard of that Creed. They cannot be required to believe more than is involved or implied in it." This is a cardinal principle. Not the opinions of the Founders, but what they have prescribed or implied in their Statutes, is the standard by which the charge of "heterodoxy" is to be tested." As I have previously stated I do not hereby waive or discredit any claim that may arise from a larger interpretation of the word heterodoxy, I simply disregard it for the present discussion, meeting my opponents on their chosen ground.

Coming now to the accusation I notice (1) *that the Creed contains no explicit declaration upon the question at issue.*

It says nothing whatever about the condition of men who die without opportunity to hear the gospel, or to accept or reject an offered Saviour, in the intermediate state between death and judgment. All that it affirms about men who do not die in faith is contained in these words: "but that the wicked will awake to shame and everlasting contempt and with devils be plunged into the lake that burneth with fire and brimstone forever and ever."

This is Biblical phraseology. It is the only instance in the entire Creed (with one possible exception which would confirm my argument) in which such a resort is made. Everywhere else the framers use their own terms, or the traditional language of the Catechism. An awe seems to come over them when they come to the awful destiny of incorrigible sinners. They will prescribe nothing themselves. Whatever their own interpretations of Scripture they will not introduce them into a Creed which they intend shall not be altered, and which they hope will endure till the end shall come. It probably never occurred to them that men would arise who would reject their doctrines as antiquated, and then claim that it is a breach of trust to follow the Scripture which they inserted in the Creed rather than to follow their opinions which they did not insert. I repeat: they simply on a subject so grave and terrible, use the phraseology of the Bible. Uninterpreted by them, left in its original form, it has the meaning of Scripture, as they quote it, and this meaning only.

I claim that this disposes conclusively, finally, of the whole question. I have no right, you have no right, to add to this Creed; to put an interpretation on this Scriptural language other than the language which is cited bears, to give it a meaning which they did not prescribe, and when they chose to leave it uninterpreted.

I know of but one qualification. It may be that a correct interpretation of the Hebrew original, whose translation in King James's version the Founders use, would make the passage less relevant than they supposed. It would not of course be fair to the Founders for any one to take an advantage of this — if such a supposition may be pardoned. For it obviously was the intention of the Founders to introduce into their Creed an article upon the final state of the wicked. They used for this purpose a passage about whose meaning they supposed there was no reasonable doubt. It is a text which in its phraseology as they accepted it plainly refers to the final resurrection. It was commonly so understood in their time, and by the best commentators with whom they were familiar. They would not have quoted it, if they had supposed it possible that it could refer to a revival of the Jewish nation under Antiochus Epiphanes, or any thing in the history of the Hebrews.

Beyond this they cannot go. They quoted what they understood to be plainly an eschatological passage, and left it wholly uninterpreted. No man has a right to go beyond this clear intent. All the language they used, as they use it, refers to the final resurrection and judgment.

This appears from an examination of it. " The wicked "— who are they? The "incorrigibly wicked at death," it has been argued. This is an addition. Besides, who are the incorrigibly wicked "at death"? The article speaks of the resurrection and final judgment. "The wicked" is the Founders' phrase, and they add no comment. It is a Biblical phrase. In the New Testament (King James's version), it is used but once with an eschatological reference. "So shall it be at the end of the world: the angels shall come forth and sever the wicked from among the just." "*At the end of the world.*" This is the point of view of the article in the Creed, and to select any other is to read into the article what this phrase does not require, and what the context excludes. The article continues: "the wicked will awake to shame and everlasting contempt," quoting the language of the prophet Daniel, which was understood to refer to the general resurrection at the end of the world, "and with devils be plunged into the lake that burneth with fire and brimstone for ever and ever," employing still Biblical language which describes what follows upon the final judgment.[1] There is in all this no allusion and no hint of an allusion to what ensues at death in the case of men who have not heard the Gospel, nor had opportunity to learn of a Saviour. Not a syllable. All reference to such a subject here is something added to the Creed, and is wholly without warrant or authority.

The case cannot be made stronger, but it is noteworthy that, as we should expect, such a necessary construction of the language harmonizes with the context.

The state of believers is considered at three stages, — in this life, at death, and at the resurrection. The state of unbelievers is considered at but one, — the final outcome of

---

Rev. xxi. 8 ; and perhaps Matt. xxv. 4.

their wickedness. The Shorter Catechism which is here followed so closely says nothing about the destiny of the wicked. The framers of the Creed were led by it through the three stages in the history of believers. They added something as to the final state of unbelievers. They had been brought to the final state of the righteous. They put in sharp contrast with this, and in Biblical and in part figurative language, the final state of the wicked. No one can rightfully add to their work as a condition of their trust.

2. *The Creed contains no implicit declaration adverse to the tenet that those who have had no opportunity to learn of a Saviour in this life may be granted such opportunity in the other life.*

It is contended that such an adverse conclusion may be deduced from the statement that " they who are effectually called do in this life partake of justification, adoption, and sanctification, and the several benefits which do either accompany or flow from them." This language, it is argued, implies that all who are saved are saved in this life. Consequently none can be supposed to have an opportunity of salvation beyond this life.

This is an attempt to find in the Creed a doctrine which is not taught in the place where it properly belongs. In an instrument so carefully drawn as the Creed, so well arranged, so studiously elaborated, such an endeavor is open to suspicion. The presumptions are against an incidental deliverance upon a question which, if the intention had been to pronounce upon it at all, would have certainly received the same pains-taking treatment which is everywhere else evinced. The character of the men who made the Creed and the character of the document are strongly adverse to the supposition that there was any purpose in this article to settle an important doctrine of eschatology. Such indirection is not the method of the Creed, nor is it the method of the men who composed it, nor of the theology of their time. In general, an incidental clause found in an article concerning one doctrine, ought to be inevitable and irresistible in its inference in order to make it equivalent to a direct statement which is wholly absent when and where it properly belongs.

It is further to be noticed that the object of the article cited is not to affirm, nor does it assert, that the effectually called are called in this life. This may be implied, but the purpose of the article is to state that certain blessings come in this life to the effectually called. The obvious purpose of the article therefore is not friendly to the supposition that it was intended to decide a wholly different question, namely whether some persons may be effectually called and saved in another life.

This brings to view another difficulty. The article before us does not deal with the number of the elect, or make any statement or involve any implication on this subject. Its purpose is not to define or determine who are effectually called, but simply to assure believers that the gospel has for them great and heavenly blessings which they may partake of in this life of conflict and toil. It is forcing language written for such a use to make it serve as the statement of a dogma respecting the question what opportunities may exist for the implantation and beginning of saving faith. The article is written for Christian believers. It is taken directly from the Shorter Catechism. It deals solely with believers, and presupposes their existence. The heathen are no more within its view than the angels. It is a violation of the accepted canons of interpretation to make it cover and decide questions of a different order, relating to a different class.

I think these considerations are sufficient of themselves to warrant the rejection of this method of proof. We are not, however, merely *warranted* in thus discarding it. A careful and thorough examination of the article leads to conclusions which absolutely require such a result. For it becomes evident that the interpretation I am opposing not merely forces the meaning of the article but makes it contradictory to the Standards of which its original formed a part, and puts it out of harmony with the Creed to which it has been transferred.

The article, as I have stated, is simply appropriated from the Shorter Catechism. Unless there is some decisive reason to the contrary it must bear the meaning as transferred which it has in its original appearance. Any interpretation which it is impossible to give to it as first written certainly cannot be necessary when it is simply repeated; and when, in addition, we find that the same impossibility also appears in its new connection, we are compelled wholly to reject such an explanation.

It will perhaps make my argument more clear if I first reduce the reasoning I am opposing to the syllogistic form, and then show where it fails. It may be stated thus:

The effectually called are the elect.

The effectually called receive salvation in this life.

Therefore the elect receive salvation in this life.

The elect are saved in this life.

None but the elect are saved.

Therefore none are saved except in this life.

This reasoning confuses certain specified blessings of salvation with the beginning or principle of salvation. But letting this pass it is valid only in case the minor premise of the first syllogism must mean: All the effectually called receive salvation in this life. But this indispensable extension of the minor premise is impossible on any just principles of interpretation of either the Catechism or the Creed, and therefore the reasoning breaks down. For if there may be some who are effectually called, and therefore are of the elect and therefore will be saved, who do not receive this salvation here they must be saved elsewhere; which is precisely the hope of *Progressive Orthodoxy*.

The Westminster Standards affirm that "elect infants, dying in infancy, are regenerated and saved by Christ through the Spirit, who worketh when, where, and how He pleaseth. So also are all other elect persons who are incapable of being outwardly called by the ministry of the word."

Now if the "effectually called," in the article quoted from the Catechism and adopted into the Creed, include all the elect, then we must hold that elect infants receive in this life the blessings which are enumerated, and so also must all other elect persons who are incapable of hearing the gospel. What now are these blessings? The article before us enumerates them in part. They are "justification, adoption, and sanctification and the several benefits which do either accompany or flow from them." In the Shorter Catechism these "benefits" are explained to be "assurance of God's love, joy in the Holy Ghost, increase of grace and perseverance therein to the end."

If, then, the effectually called referred to in the article under consideration embrace all the elect, and, as is expressly stated, there are "elect infants" and elect "other persons" who never are "outwardly called by the ministry of the word," it follows that all these infants who die in infancy, and these other persons who never hear the gospel, receive in this life the blessings included in justification, adoption and sanctification, and the other benefits described ; — that is, they experience in this life 'conviction of sin, enlightenment in the knowledge of Christ, renewal of will, the Spirit's persuasion and power to embrace Jesus Christ freely offered in the gospel, pardon and acceptance as righteous in God's sight, the imputation of Christ's righteousness which is received by faith alone, reception into the number and admission to all the privileges of the sons of God, ability more and more to die unto sin and live unto righteousness, assurance of God's love, peace of conscience, joy in the Holy Ghost, increase of grace and perseverance therein to the end.' Blessed infants! But who in his senses can think of putting an interpretation on this article which commits it to such absurdities?

We are still however far from being through with these consequences. For there is another alternative. If the "effectually called" in the article before us are all the elect, and all the elect consequently receive all these blessings in this life, it follows that only those are effectually called to whom such a description applies. Now it is impossible to apply it to the experience of infants and persons who know nothing of Christ. Hence we must conclude that there are no "elect infants," and no "other elect persons" beyond

the reach of the Christian ministry — not a soul imprisoned
here from the light which is so pleasant and the truth which
is life, among the elect ; not a pagan child or woman or man,
— not one elected; and therefore all are forever lost!

The simple truth is, as I have said, that the Catechism
was written for believers and their children, for Christian fam-
ilies and peoples.   It was not composed before the Fall,
or the Incarnation, nor in Africa.   Torture its definitions,
extort an unnatural meaning, and you make a consistent
interpretation of the Westminster statements concerning
effectual calling impossible.

It is important to notice that the Seminary Creed recognizes the Westminster and Savoy distinction between the
ordinary means of grace and those which the Spirit may
employ at his good pleasure.   It thus requires for its consistent interpretation that the article respecting the benefits
received in this life by the " effectually called " be not pressed
beyond its original purpose and scope.   Where the Creed
speaks of the way in which men become " partakers of the
benefits of redemption " it says: " the ordinary means by
which these benefits are communicated to us are the word
sacraments and prayer."   The phrase " the ordinary means "
is from the Westminster Standards and recalls the antithe-
sis already noticed.

The article in the Creed connects thus with the same
larger circle of thought recognized by the Westminster
divines.   It would be against the whole stream of history to
put upon a Creed prepared in New England at the beginning
of the nineteenth century as a basis of union of all phases of
Calvinism, a narrower construction than that intended for
the same words by theologians a century and a half earlier.
The Westminster divines admitted a wider working of God's
grace than they could define, and now the Andover Creed
which copies their words, and at the same time teaches a
universal atonement, is to be interpreted so as to shut the
door which even the men who held to a limited atonement,
to say the least, did not close !

And after all, supposing that the article before us were

thus perverted from its purpose, and made inconsistent with its history and the Creed, it would not then teach that the heathen can have no future opportunity of grace, but simply that they will not avail themselves of it any more than do the non-elect who have this opportunity here. And who can believe that the Founders both bungled and were irreverent in this fashion, as would be true of them if they intended to have this article construed as proposed.

A statement certainly ought to be absolutely decisive to justify an interpretation loaded with so many difficulties and even impossibilities. As it stands, so far is it from being thus conclusive that such a use of it turns it from its apparent purpose, attributes to it a design unsupported by evidence, puts it into contrariety with other declarations in the same Standards, and requires an interpretation of the Creed that makes it a condition of office at Andover to teach what never has been taught there from the beginning, namely, that all who do not hear the gospel in this life, including all infants and young children, and multitudes of the unfortunate who have lived in Christian lands without the requisite organs of mental and moral life, are not among the "effectually called," and therefore are not of the "elect," and therefore are lost forever. And such logic is to be applied to the Creed in order to squeeze out of it, if possible, what the framers of it would not write in it when they composed the article respecting the doom of the wicked.

Besides this inferential argument, I know of but one other which is employed in order to render it impossible for a Professor at Andover to hope that a universal gospel may have some provision of mercy for the millions upon millions who do not hear of it in this life.

It has been supposed that the Founders defined pretty clearly in their Creed the doctrinal test which they desired to impose. Until very lately no other has been so much as suggested. But the same ingenuity which has extracted a modal Trinity out of phraseology which used the long established and technical nomenclature of an ontological Trinity, and which has treated the articles of *Progressive Orthodoxy* as though they were a bushel of words out of which children might construct sentences to suit themselves, has discovered in the Statutes a new Creed. We have had before disputes over the Original Founders' Declaration, and the Creed of the Associate Founders; but now there appears a third one, never before known, nor suspected. Certainly these Statutes are progressive, if Orthodoxy is not. This new Creed is discovered in the Preamble to the Statutes.

In the deeply interesting, and I may say affecting, Preamble to the Statutes of the Associate Foundation, the Associate Founders mention some of the motives which led them to consecrate their gifts to the purpose of " increasing the number of learned and able Defenders of the Gospel of Christ, as well as of orthodox, pious, and zealous Ministers of the New Testament." Among these considerations they mention the fatal effects of the apostasy of man without a Saviour, the merciful object of the Son of God in assuming our nature and dying for our salvation, the institution of the Christian ministry, and the fact that " notwithstanding this appointment the greatest part of the human race is still perishing for lack of vision." These latter words have been seized upon and turned into an article of faith and a condition of the trust which has been instituted.

Such a use of them when explained will strike every candid mind as illegitimate. They are not a part of any declaration, creed or promise which these men saw fit to require of those to whom they committed their trust. They are simply declarations of a motive by which they were actuated in making their gift, to be respected as such, to be regarded so far as they express a permanent law and motive of Christian conduct, but not to be exalted to a position which the Founders themselves did not assign them; viz., that of a required article of faith.

I say this chiefly as a protest against the method of this argument of the complainants, rather than against its matter. For I " hold, maintain and inculcate," as my own belief and as a motive in life, that men are perishing for lack of vision, i.e., for the want of a knowledge of the gospel. Every sinner is perishing, and is in danger of perishing everlastingly, and will thus perish save as redeemed by Christ. Paul, as a friend has suggested, goes so far as to say, "For as many as have sinned without law, shall also perish without law." This is stronger language than that of the Founders. I submit to the Apostle. But how would Paul, were he on the earth, rebuke men who still persist, after the clearest demonstration that such was not his teaching, in claiming that his words compel us to hold that all the heathen actually perish, that not one will be saved. He believed that men were perishing for lack of vision, but not that this exhausted the divine purpose concerning them. Many of them did not perish, for through this same Apostle they heard of Christ, and believed in Him. Multitudes now are perishing, but whether everlastingly or not, depends on something not taken into account when such language is used.

It states the truth, but not the whole truth. It presents a motive which every Professor at Andover should be governed by, but it is not a statement of a doctrine which rules out all hope for the heathen, any more than does Paul's stronger declaration, "As many as have sinned without law shall also perish without law," for to some of such he afterwards wrote the letter known as the Epistle to the Ephesians, with its glowing representation of the revealed mystery, and its assurance that '*the dead in trespasses and sins, without Christ, having no hope, without God in the world, now had access by one Spirit unto the Father, and had become a habitation of God through the Spirit.*'

There is one other consideration, or class of considerations, to which I would invite your special attention before I leave this particular numbered eleven.

In the reply which I filed Nov. 30, referring to "opportunity to be influenced by the motive of an offered Saviour," the remark is made: "It seems to be implied in the universality of Christ's Person, Atonement, and Judgment." In *Progressive Orthodoxy*, this universality is often spoken of as a principle, "the reality of Christ's personal relation to the human race as a whole, and to every member of it, —

the principle of the universality of Christianity." This
principle is put forward as the key to the whole volume
(pp. 3, 4).

What I wish now to submit to you is, that this principle
is covered, and, I may say, is made prominent in the Creed.

The Creed affirms the Deity of Christ and his Eternal
Sonship. This Eternal Son became man and continues to
be God and Man in two distinct natures and one person forever. This is as distinct a doctrine as words can contain of
the universality of Christ's Person in its constitution. He
is God, — you cannot limit his relation, therefore, without
circumscribing his divinity. I speak not now of limitation
in method of revelation, but in nature or essence. He is
man, but so that his manhood unites in one person with the
Eternal Son ; he is not an individual member of the race,
therefore, like you and me, but its universal head. Now
take a step forward with the Creed : " [I believe] that, agreeably to the covenant of redemption, the Son of God, and
he alone, by his suffering and death, has made atonement for
the sins of all men." I shall endeavor to show further on
that here we have one of the two distinctive notes of this
Creed, that if anything in the Creed must be taken with
absolute literalness and in the full force of its language, this
a fortiori must be. It is enough now to leave it with this
repetition of its words, *Agreeably to the covenant of redemption, the Son of God, and He alone, by his suffering and
death, has made atonement for the sins of all men.*

Now the inference which my associates and myself have
drawn in the volume called *Progressive Orthodoxy*, is to our
view a legitimate and even necessary deduction from the principle thus emphasized in the Creed. So far were we from
supposing that we were teaching contrary to the Creed, that
we regarded ourselves as developing one of its most characteristic principles, namely that of the universality of the religion
of the cross of Christ. We were fortified in this conviction
by the fact that there is another principle in the Creed which
also aids to our conclusion. It, too, as I will subsequently
try to show, is a characteristic, a special note and feature of

the Creed. I refer to the principle that God's government of mankind deals with men as free moral agents, that sin and righteousness are not transferable quantities or qualities, nor passive states, but imply always personal agency. God deals not only with man, but with men, every man, and deals with each as a free moral agent. Put this and that together and grant the universality of Christianity, and that every man is dealt with in accordance with this universality as a free moral agent, and we have the entire premise of our argument. And this premise is not only in the Creed, but is there as its most distinctive feature.

I suppose no one will question that we have a right to the logic of the Creed. If a conclusion thus obtained contradicts some statement elsewhere made in the same document, a question of interpretation arises. But I need not stop to discuss this question here, for the Creed makes no statement inconsistent with our inference. We have a right, therefore, to our conclusion so far as the Creed is concerned. That, at any rate, does not estop us. It is not a condition of the trust we have received that no such inference be drawn, even if the inference be incorrect. The Founders have imposed upon your Reverend and Honorable Body serious responsibilities, but I think you will not regret that you are not made responsible for every instance of bad logic on the part of each Andover Professor.

I know not that I need weary you with any detailed reply to the remaining particulars in the Amended Complaint. I seem to myself to have said all that is necessary concerning them in the Reply which has been filed.

I think, also, that I have now covered the ground which has been definitely chosen for the present issue by the complainants. Everything else which they have introduced is not sufficiently specific and plain as an accusation to enable and require me to answer it.

I claim therefore that upon every one of the charges which are properly in issue the complainants have failed to show that I "hold, maintain and inculcate" in my office as Professor anything not in harmony with or antagonistic to the Creed and Statutes of the Seminary, and that I am therefore entitled to a complete acquittal. And here I might safely, I doubt not, rest my case.

But I ask your indulgence in the peculiar position in which I am placed, in submitting some further considerations, strictly relevant, as I conceive, to the preceding issue, but derived from a broader range of views than has been possible in following one by one particular accusations.

The official pledges and promises at Andover do not require the Professors to think and teach in all respects alike. They do, however, make it imperative that we should open and explain the Scriptures to our pupils with integrity and faithfulness. They impose upon us the sacred obligation to unfold the truths of the Creed in opposition to past heresies and current errors which are hazardous to men, *according to the best light God shall give us.* This is a law for the conscience of every Professor.

This I have promised. How am I to keep this promise? This inquiry involves these practical questions. How am I to accept the Creed of the Seminary? How ought I to accept it? How ought you to require me to accept it?

I raise deliberately this larger question, with all that it includes. I should have been glad, if instead of compelling me to wander through the long and tedious list of preposterous charges which I have reviewed, the complainants had raised directly the vital issue, although it is perhaps creditable to their sagacity that they have not.

I maintain — you will pardon me if, under the conviction of the utter unreasonableness of the attack which has been made upon our fidelity and our liberties, I do maintain — that we are entitled at your hands to something more than a technical acquittal. We have endeavored, in sincerity and good conscience, to put our Lord's money out to usury. It has well been said that if there are perils in such a course there are greater perils in the opposite course. The man who buried his talent was very faithful and very conservative, as some men understand fidelity and conservatism, but our Lord applied to him other designations. We have received the Creed of the Seminary as a sacred trust. We have sought to put its truths out to usury. No man, in my humble judgment, really takes the Creed of the Seminary, no man is fit to be a teacher of young men on its foundations, who does not thus endeavor. It has been said that eventually there will be two sets of Professors at Andover; one who will take the Creed and do little else, another that will give the lectures. I may be wrong, but I have not supposed this to be the "true intention" of the Founders.

Permit me then to state the principles by which I have been governed in my acceptance and use of the Creed, that is, in fulfilling my promise to maintain and inculcate the Christian faith as expressed in the Creed . . . "so far as may appertain to my office, according to the best light God shall give me . . ."

1. *I accept the Creed as it is written.* I have supposed my first duty to be to understand what it says, to gather its meaning from its own words, interpreting them by the ordinary and established rules of interpretation. With this understanding of the formula I take the Creed literally. I reject as dishonest the theories of creed-subscription designated by the phrases "private interpretation," "non-natural sense."

2. I accept the Creed *in the outcome and completeness of its meaning when compared part with part.* I do not find its meaning in one article alone, for there are, besides the Declaration, thirty-six distinct articles. I subscribe not merely to the words of the Creed, but rather to the meaning which the words yield when part is compared with part, article with article, clause with clause. Occasionally a single technical word may modify an entire article, as the word "constituted" which may be understood to contain a theory going back to the Council of Trent and into the scholastic disputes between the followers of Aquinas and those of Duns Scotus, or the word "Person" in the article on the Trinity, which has a history from the days of Tertullian; or the

word "personally" in the article on Depravity, which has in it the outcome of disputes between different schools of Calvinism, as well as between Calvinists and Arminians, which had been going on for centuries.

Whatever is the outcome of the Creed as a whole I accept.

An opposite, or apparently opposite theory of subscription has been asserted with great positiveness and argued with much force. It is that a Professor in signing the Creed accepts each article by itself. I admit the obligation to believe in every doctrine of the Creed, and to an acceptance of every article as it forms a consistent part of the whole; but I deny the binding force of each individual statement, taken apart from other statements. It is said: You affirm your belief in each. My reply is, that I cannot be required to believe in contradictions, and that the Creed must be allowed to interpret itself. I cannot suppose that in the same breath the Founders intended to require me to be a "consistent" Calvinist and to take an inconsistent Creed. They must therefore have intended to give me liberty of interpretation as respects particular articles.

Let me make this clear by an example. When the Creed comes to the topic of Redemption it takes three articles in succession from the Catechism and adds a fourth original to itself. The articles read : —

" [I believe] that God of his mere good pleasure from all eternity elected some to everlasting life, and that he entered into a covenant of grace to deliver them out of this state of sin and misery by a Redeemer; that the only Redeemer of the elect is the eternal Son of God, who for this purpose became man, and continues to be God and man in two distinct natures and one person forever; That Christ, as our Redeemer, executeth the office of a Prophet, Priest and King; that agreeably to the covenant of redemption, the Son of God, and He alone, by His suffering and death, has made atonement for the sins of all men."

Down to these last words we have the language, *the ipsissima verba*, of the Catechism. And even in this article we have the traditional formula " covenant of redemption."

Now if you take these articles, each as it stands, giving to each its natural, historical, full meaning, you are involved in an insoluble contradiction of belief. The first three articles state in unequivocal terms the doctrine of limited atonement: the fourth expresses plainly the doctrine of universal atonement. In other parts of the Creed it is claimed that phraseology is employed broad enough to admit the theories of all parties to the coalition, the Old or High Calvinists, the Moderate Calvinists, and the Hopkinsian Calvinists. However this may be, here, at least, the first party completely surrendered. It is just possible that if he had chosen so to do a High Calvinist might have said "made atonement for" means "sufficient for" and nothing more, but this puts a strain upon the words. They signified much more than this to the Hopkinsians. They meant more to the first Professor of Christian Theology at Andover, who received his nomination to their chair from the so-called Original Founders, as appears from his celebrated missionary sermon at Salem in 1812, in which he emphasizes the motive of an atonement not only " sufficient for Asiatics and Africans," but "made for them as well as for us." We may not doubt that they were understood in their evangelical sense by Moderate Calvinists who aided in the counsels from which the Seminary originated. Perhaps I spoke too strongly when I used of any Calvinist who had a part in the construction or institution of the Creed the word " surrendered "; there may have been no resistance, no disagreement at this point, though the earlier Calvinists of New England, represented by Samuel Willard, spurned even the concession that Christ's death was " sufficient " for all.

We have thus in the Creed new language, expressing what was still a novelty in Calvinistic doctrine, the truth that Christ on the cross died for all men, thrust into immediate sequence upon the established and traditional formulas which had affirmed for nearly all the preceding generations in New England that He died for the elect only. I say *only*, for though this word does not occur in these formulas, its meaning is indelibly impressed on them. It is there by the tech-

nical and well-understood use of terms, there emphatically
by the necessary connection and logic of the chosen articles,
there unmistakably and completely. First you have the
decree of election, then the covenant of grace which included the eternal covenant of Redemption between the
Father and the Son and the elect in Him; then, in pursuance of this electing decree, the incarnation of the Eternal
Son, who, as our Redeemer, i.e., as Redeemer of the elect,
executed the office not only of Prophet and King, but of
Priest, in which latter office, as the Catechism explains, and
the traditional theology fully agreed, He offered " up of himself a sacrifice to satisfy divine justice and reconcile us to
God," all, you notice, as Redeemer of the elect, and for the
elect, and in pursuance of the decree of election. I see not
how any man who takes these articles literally as they stand,
who sneers at taking the Creed " in the gross," and insists
on the acceptance of every doctrinal statement, can possibly
extricate himself from the necessity of first saying: " I believe that Christ executeth his office of priest under the
decree of election, and for the purpose of that election," and
then of immediately confessing " I believe that he executeth
this office of priest under a different decree and for another
purpose, namely, to die for the sins of the non-elect as well
as of the elect." There is, indeed, one supposable way out
of the contradiction, that of assuming that the whole race is
elected, or predetermined, to salvation, as Schleiermacher
believed; but this is only a temporary escape, for, apart from
the difficulty of interpreting the word " some " as meaning
all, the closing sentences of the Creed are unfriendly to a
doctrine of universal restorationism, and the subscriber would
find that he had only exchanged one contradiction for
another.

This antagonism in the Creed of two doctrines of the
atonement might be confirmed by tracing in detail the development of the two phrases " covenant of grace " and " covenant of redemption," and of the doctrine of the order of the
divine decrees, but I have said enough by way of illustration —
I am satisfied that it is simply impossible to take the Creed

in the way which I am opposing. I do not believe such a method ever would have been thought of but for the exigencies of controversy. There is a simple way out of these difficulties, — simple, but like many another simple principle it is found, when thoroughly applied, to be fruitful in important results. It is the path which the framers of the Creed must have intended should be followed, — *its acceptance as a whole and as it interprets itself.*

3. *I accept the Creed for substance of doctrine.* I employ this phrase under certain very careful restrictions. Were it not for the phrases " federal head and representative," "covenant of grace," " covenant of redemption," I should not need to use it at all, and I am not sure but that what I have said about taking the Creed as a whole comprehends whatever qualification I give to these terms. Still, for the sake of the utmost explicitness, I will state precisely what latitude I suppose this mode of taking the Creed permits. I do not understand that I am availing myself thereby of any other liberty than the framers intended should be used, or than was exercised while they were living and acting as Visitors, and than has been acknowledged and practised ever since.

The phrase " for substance of doctrine " appears in the *Preface* to the *Cambridge Platform*, adopted by the Synod of 1648. Referring to the Confession "agreed upon by the reverend assembly of divines at Westminster," the *Preface* says: " Finding the sum and substance thereof, in matters of doctrine, to express not their own judgment only, but ours also . . . we thought good to present . . . to our churches . . . our professed and hearty assent and attestation to the whole confession of faith (for substance of doctrine)." The Synod also passed unanimously a vote expressing " consent thereunto, for the substance thereof." From that early time on this method of accepting a Creed or Platform has obtained in New England. In his letters to Dr. Ware, the first Abbot Professor, enjoying the confidence of both sets of Founders of the Seminary and pre-eminent in his exertions to ensure the union, and writing only four years after a " perpetual union " was " established," remarked : " As it is one object of these Letters to make you acquainted with the real opinions of the Orthodox in New England, I would here say, with the utmost frankness, that we are not perfectly satisfied with the language used on this subject [Imputation] in the Assembly's Catechism. . . . Hence it is common for us, when we declare our assent to the Catechism, to do it with an express or implied restriction."[1] Dr. Woods subsequently modified his interpretation of the Catechism, but his testimony as to the custom and feeling of the Orthodox at that time and to his own liberty is not thereby affected. . Dr. Humphrey, President of Amherst College, and a Visitor of the Seminary, once remarked, "No mortal man, with a mind of his own, ever accepted the Westminster Catechism without qualifications of his own." " He was right," adds Professor Phelps, " the same is true of every Confession, — unless it be some brief compendium of historic *fact*, rather than of *doctrine*, like the Apostles' Creed."[2] And the editor of the *Congregationalist*, between four and five years since,[3] defending himself from the imputation of hostility to creeds, especially the Andover Creed, remarked, . . . "for substance we heartily accept it, as Professors Park and Phelps have always done."

Even that stern censor of former Professors at Andover, Rev. Daniel Dana, D.D., while contending against their heresies, made this noteworthy concession : " Nor will I contend that the man who has taken a lengthened creed should be trammelled by all the *minutiæ* which it may embrace.[4] And Dr. Hodge, in the *Princeton Review*, speaking for the Old School wing of the Presbyterian Church nearly a generation ago, remarked (I use this extract on the *a fortiori* principle) :

" It is a perfectly notorious fact, that there are hundreds of ministers in our Church, and that there always have been such ministers, who do not receive all the propositions contained in the Confession of Faith and Catechisms. . . . The principle that the

---

[1] *Letters to Unitarians*, Andover, 1820, p. 45.
[2] Quoted by Rev. Dr. Fiske in *The Creed of Andover Theol. Sem.*, 1882, p. 32
[3] June 21, 1882.
[4] *Sermon on the Faith of Former Times*, 1848, note to p. 16.

adoption of the Confession of Faith implies the adoption of all the propositions therein contained . . . is impracticable . . . "is more than the vast majority of our ministers either do or can do. To make them profess to do it is a great sin. It hurts their conscience. It fosters a spirit of evasion and subterfuge. It teaches them to take creeds in a ' non-natural sense.' It at once vitiates and degrades." [1]

A common method in New England may be illustrated by an extract from the covenant of the Church in Salem, of which Dr. Daniel Hopkins, the brother of Dr. Samuel Hopkins, was pastor from 1778 to 1814, — the church, it is of further special interest to note, with which the Associate Founder John Norris attended worship.

" Professing a belief in the Christian Religion as contained in the Scriptures of the Old and New Testament, and embracing that scheme of doctrine which is exhibited in what is called The Assembly's Shorter Catechism, as expressing, for substance, those important truths which God has revealed to us in his holy word." And again : " Knowing the necessity of order and discipline in every body of fallible men, we promise to submit ourselves to the government of Christ in his church agreeably to the directions on this subject contained in the eighteenth chapter of Matthew, and as more fully set forth in the Platform of Church Discipline drawn up by the Congregational Synod, at Cambridge, New England, A.D. 1648, which, in substance, we adopt, as agreeable to the rules and spirit of the gospel." [2]

In entire concurrence with the method familiar to Dr. Hopkins and Mr. Norris at Salem, and in the line of the testimonies already adduced, are the reminiscences and testimony of the venerable Gardiner Spring, a son of Dr. Samuel Spring, one of the authors of the Seminary Creed and one of the first Visitors. He says, referring to the Westminster Confession :

" Few, in this age of inquiry, *believe every word of it.* Nor did our fathers. I myself made two exceptions to it when I was re-

1 Reprinted in *Church Polity*, pp. 330-332.
2 *The Covenant of Third Church of Christ in Salem*, Salem, 1841, pp. 6, 7, 8.

ceived into the Presbytery of New York fifty-five years ago. Nor were those exceptions any barrier to my admission.[1] I am no bigot and no friend to innovations. Let our Confession and Catechism stand. . . . Witherspoon, Rodgers, McWhorter, Smith, Miller and Richards were not men of strife, nor did they lend their influence to awaken jealousies, heart burnings, and chilling alienations among those who ought to love as brethren. We have no Act of Uniformity to compel a perfect unanimity in every minute article of so extended a Confession. There are shades of thought and forms of expression, in regard to which men will not cease to think for themselves. I could specify many points in which not a few of our ministers and ruling elders do not exactly agree with our standards. Yet they are all HONEST CALVINISTS, and receive our standards as the most unexceptionable formularies ever drawn up by uninspired men, and receive them as a whole with all their hearts. The iron bed of Procrustes is not suited to the spirit of the age. Some modern Theseus will yet be raised up, and show to the church that there is small space for the couch of bigotry in the nineteenth century.[2] ''

I will add but one more testimony, and this not from a clergyman, but from a decision of the Supreme Court of Massachusetts rendered by Justice Thacher in the year 1815.

It was contended that a legacy to the Seminary was void, because " the original design of the founders of the Academy was to propagate Calvinism, as containing the important principles . . . of our holy Christian religion, as summarily expressed in the *Westminster Assembly's Shorter Catechism;* whereas, the design of the donors of the Associate Foundation is to add to *Calvinism* the distinguishing features of *Hopkinsianism,* a union or mixture inconsistent with the original design of the original founders of the Academy and of the theological institution." It was further contended, that if there were ' but one single article in the Creed contrary to Calvinism, or a single article omitted from the Creed which characterized Calvinism as understood at the time of the

[1] i.e. 1810. Two years after the Associate Foundation was established.
[2] *Life and Times of Gardiner Spring,* 11. pp. 21, 22.

foundation of the Academy,' the legacy was null and void. The Court overruled and rejected the principle that a Creed must be taken in its several articles irrespective of other articles or equally required statements of doctrine.

It confirmed as of legal validity the principle which I have stated already under number two (2). It further urged the duty of " charity of construction," by which " technical propositions, should not be pressed, by a construction "astute, narrow and uncharitable," into an antagonism which could be avoided ; and, applying this principle, the Judge said: " For myself, I confess that I do not clearly perceive any other sense than that in which the articles mean substantially the same thing, notwithstanding some diversity of expression, in which they can be said to be true and consistent with the Christian religion."

I quote this last opinion, not merely on account of its great weight as testimony, but because it indicates the true sense and application in the case before us of the phrases "substantially " and " for substance of doctrine."

These phrases are sometimes objected to, not without reason, as vague. Dr. Hodge makes this criticism. But their convenience and utility keep them in use, and as it were compel it. Dr. Hodge, after rejecting them, gives illustration upon illustration which implies his acceptance of just what they are commonly understood to mean.

These phrases do not mean that a signature for substance of doctrine can cover a method by which the substance of a creed is eliminated ; nor one by which any doctrine is rejected which belongs to a creed when it is regarded as a whole. They cover two points: first, a distinction between the necessary, integral parts or doctrines of a creed and those which are subsidiary and non-essential ; second, a distinction between contents [substance] and form.

In the first of these two senses it may be thought that the phrases " for substance of doctrine " or "substantially " can have no place in the interpretation of a creed so precise as that appointed by the Associate Founders. Such a use, it may be feared, would run into the objectionable method by which a doctrine accepted "for substance" is "substantially" rejected. I admit the necessity of care and explicitness. I deny, however, that the phrases have no application, or are of no service. They embody the principle expressed by Justice Thacher in the words "charity of construction."

A Creed like the Andover is not the work of one mind, but of many minds; not of one age, but of very many. Its traditional phraseology is the larger part of it. It deals with many subjects which are only approximately apprehended by the Church as a whole, and are somewhat differently apprehended by various schools of thought, and various theologians, all of whom, however, are in general agreement. Take what are called the mysteries of Christianity — the Trinity, the union of two natures in one Person. The Creed of Chalcedon, which is the standard orthodox symbol on this latter mystery, is called in the records a "boundary." It is a definition in the sense of pointing out certain errors to which faith is exposed and which the true doctrine will exclude, certain limits on either side, which cannot be passed without renouncing certain necessary elements of belief. The Creed says: 'The doctrine is — there are two natures; hold this theory or that, and you deny one nature or the other, the divine or the human. The doctrine is: There is one person; hold this theory or that, and you come into contradiction to this personal unity.' But no man in his senses ever thought that this definition gives us an exhaustive statement of the doctrine of the Person of Christ, or shuts up a man who confesses it to every subsidiary formula which men have invented in endeavoring more firmly to apprehend it, or more fully to appropriate it. It lies in the nature of the truths confessed in a creed, that they are not measurable nor ponderable nor definable like the commodities or currencies of commerce, like an acre of ground, or a house-lot, or a dollar whether gold or silver. One does not sign a creed precisely as he signs a note. There is a mischievous fallaciousness in the way in which men use such comparisons, and then proceed to impeach their brethren's honesty, simply because they do not know what they themselves are talking about.

This principle of "charitable construction" by which diversities of form in holding a doctrine are overlooked, has been employed in the history of the Seminary and under the eyes of its founders, so as to cover not merely a diversity as to the form but as to the substance of subsidiary or unessential doctrine. One perfectly plain tenet of the Creed, if an individual and important phrase is to be pressed, has never been required. At one time I presume most of those who subscribed, Professors and Visitors alike, did not accept it in its proper meaning as it stands in the Creed. I refer to the doctrine of the Eternal Sonship.

The Creed says: "[I believe] that the only Redeemer of the elect is the eternal Son of God, who for this purpose became man, and continues to be God and man in two distinct natures and one person forever." Every Professor, every Visitor, since the Seminary was founded, has signed this statement. One of the earliest signatures is that of Moses Stuart. In his *Letters to Rev. William E. Channing* ("1819, republished in five successive editions") Prof. Stuart repudiated, as is well known, the Nicene and historical church doctrine of Eternal Generation, or that the Son was always Son. He admitted an eternal distinction in the divine nature, that this distinction became incarnate and was called Son as incarnate, but denied that the name Son properly designates this distinction considered as eternal. In a word, the words Eternal Son did not mean to him what they had meant in the church, what they meant in the Catechism, whose words are here appropriated, what they meant in the traditional theology of New-England, what they meant to Dr. Samuel Hopkins and to Dr. Samuel Spring, both of whom are explicit even to the rejection and condemnation of any denial of this established traditional meaning. I know of no evidence that at the time the Creed was written they had gained any new accepted interpretation. They require in the Creed therefore their ordinary sense.

Professor Stuart rejected this tenet, and apparently without any hesitation or misgiving. He defined his position in respect to the creed of Nicea by saying that "the thing aimed at was in substance to assert the idea of a distinction in the Godhead," which is perfectly true as the history shows. He said later that the fathers were " in substance right, their pneumatic philosophy plainly inadmissible." [1] He must have explained to himself his disagreement with the language of the Catechism in the Seminary Creed on the same principle. He held what the phrase " Eternal Son," in its traditional sense, stood for, viz., the doctrine of the Deity of Christ. But the traditional form of this belief, as embodied in this phrase, he denied. That is, he held to the substance of the doctrine, as this is an integral and essential part of the Creed, but he rejected a subsidiary, and as he regarded it, unessential and unbiblical form of that doctrine in its substance, though this is a part of the substance of the Creed.

This was done by him while he was in most intimate relations with the early Founders of the Seminary, particularly with the Associate Founder William Bartlet, who continued to pay bills for German books, which Professor Stuart imported almost by the cart-load, and who never was disturbed, I presume, because small men and narrow men cried out against his Professor's neology. Professor Stuart was called to account by Dr. Miller of Princeton, and in reply published a heterodox book and assiduously followed up all this " heterodoxy " by excursus after excursus in his commentaries, and by articles in the *Biblical Repository* and the *Bibliotheca Sacra*.

I have had myself a little experience in relation to this doctrine. I have been led to accept the ordinary church doctrine, and that of the Catechism and the Creed. I do not wish to

> " Compound for sins [I am] inclined to
> By damning those [I] have no mind to ; "

but I am persuaded that Professor Stuart was wrong in the result of his exegesis on this point and in his interpretation of the history of the doctrine of the Eternal Sonship. I agree with the early Hopkinsians as well as with Charles Kingsley and Frederick D. Maurice in thinking this doctrine

[1] *Bibliotheca Sacra*, vii. p. 314.

an important one, and its rejection an error of some consequence. Coming early in my teaching at Andover to this
conclusion, I have maintained the Creed on this point as I
promised according to the best light God has given me.
I soon learned, by the fire of questions poured in upon me
that my pupils had been taught otherwise in another lecture
room. I made no allusions to such teaching, but simply
kept on with my own. It never occurred to me that somebody should be tried for "heterodoxy." If I had been a
lawyer, certainly if I could have been a judge, I should have
said that the article in the Creed was doubtless subscribed
by my pupils' teacher in Christian theology, who had subscribed to the phrase "Eternal Son" in the Catechism as
well as in the Creed, on the principle of "charitable construction," but being not a lawyer nor judge, but a Professor
of Ecclesiastical History, I thought and still think that he
subscribed on the principle which he now so vehemently
repudiates, and which is expressed in the venerable New
England formula, "for substance of doctrine."

This will I think make clear the full extent of my meaning. I reject all vague and loose applications of the phrase
"for substance," but it has, I hold, its legitimate place in
any requirement of subscription to the Seminary Creed
which has even a decent regard to past usage, whether at
Andover or in the church at large, or to the decisions of legal
tribunals, or to the true intentions of such men as founded
the Seminary whether Hopkinsians or Old Calvinists.

I know of but one important objection to this claim. It is
said that the purpose of the Hopkinsians, who put the
Creed into their Statutes, and came into the union on its
acceptance by the Andover Founders, was to compel the
Moderate Calvinists to greater strictness of belief at Andover
than could be secured by a general consent to the Catechism;
that in their opinion a general subscription or assent had let
into the ministry a great many men who were doctrinally
unsound, and that they intended to bar out such looseness.
If now their own Creed is to be subscribed for substance, as
the Catechism had been taken, the desired protection is

thrown away, and the assumed purpose of the Founders is frustrated.

I think this is a fair criticism upon such interpretations and uses of the formula, "for substance of doctrine," as I have rejected and condemned.

But it goes no further. It overlooks important facts.

1. The fact that the Creed is a union Creed. What was its origin and first form is uncertain. One account represents that it was constructed for the Newbury Seminary, which was not intended to be a mere Hopkinsian affair, but, broader. Another alleges that it was first presented to Dr. Spring by Dr. Pearson who represented the Andover Founders. All accounts agree that it was not intended for a mere party, and that it was finally accepted as a basis of union. It has from early times been called a "compromise" Creed. It certainly was designed to be comprehensive, and this is a more honorable description of it.

2. The fact that the Creed contains traditional phraseology which was accepted in its traditional meaning by some at least of those who entered into the union.

3. The fact that these men approved of this language being taken by other men with a new meaning, and that those who thus took it consented that such language should remain in the Creed.

One of these historical phrases is contained in the article: "[I believe] that Adam, the federal head and representative of the human race was placed in a state of probation and that in consequence of his disobedience all his descendants were constituted sinners." The phrase "federal head and representative" is the symbol of a distinct type of theology. In New England this had been, until the days of Jonathan Edwards, and particularly of Samuel Hopkins, the established system. It is the teaching of the Catechisms and the Confession. It was undergoing changes, but its essential idea that man's depravity comes to him not simply as an act of sovereignty but of law and justice was not yet abandoned. Emmons found it necessary to preach against it elaborately. Nor was it excluded from the Creed by the phrases "in consequence of " and " were constituted sinners." The latter is as old as the Vulgate.[1] It is Calvin's[2] language, and Turretin's.[3] Professor Park comments on it as though it were distinctive of Emmons. He says: "In one and the same discourse the doctor [Emmons] calls Adam 'a federal head of the race' and criticises the Assembly's Catechism for teaching that Adam entered into a literal covenant with his Maker. So in one and the same sentence the Creed excludes all that the Catechism says in regard to the covenant of works, quotes the very language of Emmons, that all Adam's '*descendants were constituted sinners*,' and also designates Adam as 'the federal head and representative of the race'. One sermon of Emmons is compressed into one article of the Creed." Unfortunately for this representation the sermon referred to was not preached until after the Creed was adopted, and the Seminary established; nor, so far as I can ascertain, was it published until 1860 in the edition of Emmons's works to which Dr. Park contributed a memoir. It is also well understood that Dr. Emmons was not entirely satisfied with the Creed. And, apart from all this, every old Calvinist could use the phrase "were constituted" and even "in consequence of," as well as the Hopkinsians. So that the article might with less forcing of its terms be harmonized with the Old Theology than with the New. Yet, on the other hand, it does not speak of the covenant of works, nor impute Adam's sin as guilt to his posterity, and the general shaping of the language in the context is all friendly to the new conceptions of moral agency which the Hopkinsians were zealously propagating. They too could live under this article in the Creed provided they could be allowed to accept the federal headship of Adam with a certain degree of latitude, in other words "for substance of doctrine." Professor Park really admits this to be the true explanation. For he adds to the words

---

[1] "Peccatores constituti sunt multi." Vulgate transl. of Rom. v. 19.

[2] " Quemadmodum enim per inobedientiam unius hominis peccatores constituti sunt multi : sic et per obedientiam unius justi constituentur multi." Com. on Rom. v. 19.

[3] " Eadem quippe ratione constituimur peccatores in Adamo qua justi constituimur in Christo." *Inst. Theol. Elenct.*, Pars Prima, Locus Nonus *De Peccato.* Q. IX. § xvi. ed. Lugd. Batav. 1696, Vol. I. p. 681.

I have just quoted the statement, " The disclaimer of a word in a *literal* sense need not be a disclaimer of it in a *figurative* sense," and earlier on the same page, he says: " Those Hop- kinsians, however, did not believe in any *literal* covenant of *works*. They could use the term figuratively, but would not insert the language of the Catechism into their Creed." *Their Creed!* It was not theirs alone. It was the Creed of the Federalists also, who could use the terms of this the- ology as the Hopkinsians could not. So that we are shut up to this conclusion. The Federalists put into, or found in, the Creed their favorite phrase " federal head and repre- sentative "; the Hopkinsians at least consented to its remain- ing there; and each party understood not only that it might bear a different meaning to the other, but that even if it did so, and the Creed were thus taken, it was satisfactorily taken, for it was accepted *for substance of doctrine*. Some criticism has been expended upon the Founders for their consenting to an ambiguous article. If the principle of the procedure were that each party should find his own doctrine by catch- ing at one clause and ignoring another, by interpreting *federal headship* " figuratively " and *constituted* " literally," or *vice versa*, I think the procedure could not be defended. I sup- pose it to have been a larger, a firmly established and well understood principle on which they acted, namely, that what- ever special theories these technical formulas suggested, and whatever preferences one person or another might entertain as respects these subsidiary forms of doctrine, the great fact was confessed of human depravity, so that men are acknowl- edged to be " morally incapable " of self-recovery, and to be in need of a Redeemer, and of regeneration by the Holy Spirit. Admit that the Article I have been considering can be accepted " for substance of doctrine," as I believe it has been subscribed from the first, and you simply apply to the Creed a well-known principle. Deny that this is legitimate, and you make an honest subscription impossible for any one but a Federal Calvinist, and discredit the entire history of the Seminary. It is discovered that Dr. Emmons once or twice, when he could not be misunderstood, used the older phraseology figuratively. And this is brought forward as a reason for giving the phrase the same interpretation in a carefully drawn Creed. In other words, because a preacher, in order to avoid a seemingly entire divorce of his thought from inherited principles, uses a familiar term in a way which suggests a connection between his own clearly explained and new views and the older theology, we have a right to understand such a phrase in a Creed to be *figurative*, and so are enabled to sign it literally, and avoid the offense of taking it substantially, as it has been taken from the time it was first written. I claim the right to abide by the accepted usage and the long established principle, and this not merely with reference to this article but wherever a similar exigency arises, always remembering the restrictions I have acknowledged.

There is one other general principle in the acceptance of theological creeds which was emphasized by Dr. Henry B. Smith, and which is of importance now. I remark therefore fourthly,

4. *I accept the Seminary Creed in its historical sense.*

I do not mean by this that opinions which it does not express may be read into it because they were entertained at the time it was written, and perhaps by the men who composed it ; nor that opinions which they put into it may be taken out of it because, perchance, if they were living now, they would appoint a different creed.

The Associate Founders reserved to themselves the right for seven years to amend the Creed. They prohibited subsequent alterations. This does not define the nature of subscription, as some have affirmed; but it doubtless does exclude, indirectly or by necessary inference, any mutilation of the Creed in its administration, either by adding to it a tenet which it does not authorize, or subtracting from it one that it requires. To this extent it supplies a rule for subscription.

I agree to this rule, and do not assert anything contrary to it when I affirm the historical sense of the Creed. I intend by this formula to emphasize several things.

(1) The language of the Creed must be interpreted historically. Its traditional terms, not otherwise explained, must

have their traditional meaning. Whatever of strictness, whatever of liberality, belongs to them when thus understood, enures to the subscriber now as at the first.

Such words and phrases are some already noticed: "only perfect rule of faith and practice," "three Persons," "same in substance," "equal in power and glory," "Adam, the federal head and representative," and so on.

Many Trinitarians hold to a personal or hypostatic subordination of the Son to the Father. So long as this is not understood to contradict what is affirmed by the phrase "same in substance," there is nothing in the Creed to exclude such a mode of belief. For the phrase "equality in power and glory" historically interpreted does not exclude either official or personal subordination, but only essential. One who denies the true Divinity of the Son could not sign the Creed honestly, but any believer in this doctrine, though a subordinationist, might accept it. We have here, as very often in the Creed, phrases which are not contracted but comprehensive, leaving room for many minor modifications of belief.

So the term "federal head," which also is left undefined, has a historical latitude of meaning. It came into vogue in opposition to an extreme type of Calvinism. It represented a new departure. It characterized a movement away from scholastic Calvinism in the direction of a Biblical Calvinism. It was a protest against an over-wrought doctrine of sovereignty, in the interest of human freedom. A man is not simply a creature, but a person, with whom God condescends to make a covenant. A distinguished theologian, to whom I have before referred, contends that the Creed must be taken in all its details, and cannot be taken as other Creeds are taken, but when he speaks of its federal terms he says, in language already partly quoted,[1] that the Founders " believed wisely in the ' covenant of redemption ' and in the ' covenant of grace,' as these terms were understood by the divines whom they deemed most authoritative. Those Hopkinsians, however, did not believe in any *literal* covenant of *works*. They would use the term *figuratively* . . . " Thus by a

[1] *The Associate Creed of And. Theol. Sem.*, pp. 44, 45.

" wise" interpretation and a "figurative" interpretation, *all*
the "details" of the Creed can be accepted literally!

But there is no need of such latitudinarian canons.

Taken historically all these terms are way-marks of progress along the line of modern theology, as it has more and
more realized the true character of God as revealed in Christ,
his overstepping the bounds of instituted law in the promises
of his grace, his dealing with men as persons endowed by
Him with inalienable rights. Professor Park has been wont
to say that the covenant of works was made in Holland. It
was — and it has in it the principle of liberty for which the
Netherlanders fought by land and sea. I would not miss from
the Creed Bullinger's "covenant of grace" or Cocceius's
"covenant of works" in the form of Adam's federal headship.
They are all there, and the signer of the Creed has his rights
under them and to them. They are still a standing protest
against an extreme type of Calvinism which after having
been modified by Federalism suddenly shot up like Jonah's
gourd in Emmonsism. The Creed, as Professor Park wisely
but not figuratively claims, is "protective," if historically
taken, and as a whole.

(2) Whenever traditional language is departed from and
new phraseology introduced we are brought into special
contact with the intention of the Founders.

In the legal interpretation of a document which is composed of printed matter and written statements, the latter ·
have the preference in interpreting the author's purpose.
They more especially express his mind and will.

This is an important principle in its application to the
Seminary Creed.

There are three parts of the Creed in which these novelties
of doctrine appear — the part which relates to original sin,
the one which treats of redemption, and the part which
treats of God's universal moral government; and the new
matter introduced consists of either an enlargement or correction of the traditional theology in respect to two points,
God's purpose of redemption, and the ethical principles by
which He is governed in dealing with men · these two aspects

of truth being indeed but one principle by which Theology always makes what progress it achieves, namely, a more thoroughly ethical or Christian apprehension of God.

The truth of what I have been saying will appear to any one who examines intelligently a copy of the Creed, like the one I have prepared which shows by Italics those portions which are copied from the Shorter Catechism, by Roman type and black ink where the thoughts of the Westminster Standards are reproduced, and by red ink what is new.

"Every Professor on this foundation shall be a Master of Arts of the Protestant Reformed Religion, an ordained Minister of the Congregational or Presbyterian denomination, and shall sustain the character of a discreet, honest, learned, and devout Christian, an orthodox and consistent Calvinist; and, after a careful examination by the Visitors with reference to his religious principles, he shall, on the day of his inauguration, publicly make and subscribe a solemn declaration of his faith in Divine Revelation, and in the fundamental and distinguishing doctrines of the Gospel as expressed in the following Creed, which is supported by the infallible Revelation which God constantly makes of Himself in his works of creation, providence, and redemption, namely: —

"I believe that *there is* one, and *but one, . . . living and true God;* that *the word of God, . . . contained in the Scriptures of the Old and New Testament,*[1] *is the only* perfect rule of faith and practice ; that agreeably to those Scriptures *God is a Spirit, infinite, eternal, and unchangeable in his being, wisdom, power, holiness, justice, goodness, and truth;* that *in the Godhead . . . are three Persons, the Father, the Son, and the Holy Ghost; and* that *these Three are One God, the same in substance, equal in power and glory;* that *God created man . . . after his own image, in knowledge, righteousness, and holiness;* that the **glory of God** *is man's chief end,* the **enjoyment of God** his supreme happiness ; that this enjoyment is derived solely from conformity of heart to the moral character and will of God ; that **Adam, the federal head and**

---

[1] *S. C.,* Testaments.

representative of the human race, was placed in a state of probation, and that in consequence of his disobedience all his descendants were constituted sinners; that by nature every man is personally depraved, destitute of holiness, unlike and opposed to God; and that previously to the renewing agency of the Divine Spirit all his moral actions are adverse to the character and glory of God; that being morally incapable of recovering the image of his Creator, which was lost **in Adam,** every man is justly exposed to eternal damnation; so that, except a man be born again he cannot see the kingdom of God; that *God, . . . of his mere good pleasure, from all eternity, elected some to everlasting life,* and that he *entered into a covenant of grace to deliver them out of* this state *of sin and misery . . . by a Redeemer;* that *the only Redeemer of* the *elect is the eternal Son of God, who* for this purpose *became man, and . . .* continue* *to be God and man in two distinct natures and one person forever;* that *Christ as our Redeemer executeth the office* [1] *of a Prophet, . . . Priest, and . . . King;* that agreeably to the covenant of redemption the Son of God, and he alone, by his suffering and death, has made atonement for the sins of all men; that **repentance, faith,** and holiness are the personal requisites in the Gospel scheme of salvation; that the *righteousness of Christ* is the *only* ground of a sinner's *justification;* that this righteousness is *received* through *faith,* and that this faith **is the gift of God;** so that our salvation is wholly of grace; that no means whatever can change the heart of a sinner and make it holy; that regeneration and sanctification are effects of the creating and renewing agency of the Holy Spirit, and that supreme love to God constitutes the essential difference between saints and sinners: that, by *convincing us of our sin and misery, enlightening our minds, . . . working faith in us, and renewing our wills,* [2] the *Holy Spirit* makes us *partakers of the* benefits of *redemption,* and that *the . . . ordinary means* by which these *benefits* are *communicated to us are the Word, sacraments, and prayer;* that *repentance* unto life. *faith to feed upon* Christ, *love* to God, *and new*

----

[1] *S. C.*, offices.   [2] *S. C.*, will.

obedience are the appropriate qualifications for *the Lord's Supper,* and that a Christian Church ought to admit no person to its holy communion before he exhibit credible evidence of his godly sincerity ; that perseverance in holiness is the only method of making our calling and election sure, and that the final perseverance of saints, though it is the effect of the special operation of God on their hearts, yet necessarily implies their own watchful diligence ; that *they who are effectually called do in this life partake of justification, adoption,* and *sanctification and the several benefits which . . . do either accompany or flow from them ;* that *the souls of believers are at their death made perfect in holiness, and do immediately pass into glory ;* that *their bodies, being still united to Christ,* will *at the resurrection* be *. . . raised up to glory,* and that the saints will be *made perfectly blessed in the full enjoy*ment *of God to all eternity ;* but that the wicked will awake to shame and everlasting contempt, and with devils be plunged into the lake that burneth with fire and brimstone for ever and ever. I moreover believe that God, *according to the counsel of his* own *will* and *for his own glory, hath foreordained whatsoever comes to pass,* and that all beings actions, and events, both in the natural and moral world, are under his providential direction : that God's decrees perfectly consist with human liberty, God's universal agency with the agency of man, and man's dependence with his accountability ; that man has understanding and corporeal strength to do all that God requires of him, so that nothing but the sinner's aversion to holiness prevents his salvation ; that it is the prerogative of God to bring good out of evil, and that he will cause the wrath and rage of wicked men and devils to praise him ; and that all the evil which has existed, and will forever exist, in the moral system, will eventually be made to promote a most important purpose under the wise and perfect administration of that Almighty Being who will cause all things to work for his own glory, and thus fulfil all his pleasure. And, furthermore, I do solemnly promise that I will open and explain the Scriptures to my Pupils with integrity and faithfulness ; that I will maintain and inculcate the Christian faith as expressed in the Creed by me now repeated, together with all the other doctrines and duties of our holy Religion, so far as may appertain to my office, according to the best light God shall give me, and in opposition not only to atheists and infidels, but to Jews, Papists, Mahometans, Arians, Pelagians, Antinomians, Arminians, Socinians, Sabellians, Unitarians, and Universalists, and to all other heresies and errors, ancient or modern, which may be opposed to the Gospel of Christ or hazardous to the souls of men; that by my instruction, counsel, and example I will endeavor to promote true Piety and Godliness; that I will consult the good of this Institution and the peace of the Churches of our Lord Jesus Christ on all occasions; and that I will religiously conform to the Constitution and Laws of this Seminary, and to the Statutes of this Foundation."

It follows from such a study of the Creed as I have indicated and from the application of the principle I have stated, that where contradiction would otherwise exist the controlling principle must be found in the interjected or new statement. The old cannot fetter the new; on the contrary the new may liberate the old.

Take the article about "federal head." If the Creed must be taken in its every detail, it asserts, as we have seen not figuratively but plainly and literally, the doctrine of the covenant of works. You cannot take this theory and at the same time accept one which contradicts it. But if any one should arise and take up the contention once so vigorously pressed against an Abbot Professor by Dr. Dana and Parsons Cooke and others, and insist that the Catechism and the Creed required that Professor to accept federal headship not in a figurative but in a literal sense, and that for nearly half a century he was guilty of a stupendous breach of trust and of violating his repeated solemn promises, a historical interpretation of the Creed will amply protect his good name. For if there is, as is claimed, a contradiction of theories in the Creed, the new formula has a superior power to the old, and so the Professor was quite in accord

with the Creed in his lifelong rejection of federal headship and advocacy of the theory recognized if not with
entire distinctness in the other portion of the article, at
least in this when interpreted in the light of the prominence elsewhere given to the principle of personal moral
agency.

Or take again the statement about a universal atonement.
You cannot evidently harmonize universal atonement and
limited atonement. Neither can you find in the Creed precisely the later theory of general atonement and particular
redemption. The general atonement of the Creed is something wrought out under the "Covenant of Redemption."
At the same time you cannot deny that under the phraseology of redemption is introduced a universal atonement ; and
this is not only unmistakably stated, but is the new element,
and therefore *par excellence* to be insisted upon. All the previous language, therefore, which embodies the older theory of
limited atonement must be qualified by this ruling article —
in other words the whole doctrine of the covenant of grace,
with particular election and redemption must be subsumed
under the doctrine of universal redemption, and this again,
so far as the covenant of redemption goes, must be adjusted
to personal responsibility and the doctrine of retribution for
the 'wicked at the day of final judgment.

Any one who takes the Creed in this way comes as near
as it is possible to come to the mind of those who framed it.
And it is no small honor to these men that at the early date
when the Creed was written they were willing thus to modify the traditional Calvinism in the interest of a new movement of thought and to put two essential principles of the
New Divinity — Universal Atonement and Personal Agency
— into the Creed, and require all who taught in the Seminary
to be faithful to them.

(3). There is room for a progressive interpretation and
systemization of the truths of the Creed.

Dr. Park has enunciated the first and most important part
of this proposition. He says, speaking of the Hopkinsian
founders, " They were in favor of progress in the interpre-

tation of the Creed, provided that the progress were toward the Hopkinsian interpretation of it." [1]

The Hopkinsian elements in the Creed have been already briefly characterized. They constitute the bulk of the additions to the Westminster statements. They include the principles of a universal atonement and personal agency.

But who will presume to say that these great principles had accomplished all their service for theology when they were put into the Creed, or at the close of any later period in the history of the Seminary? Who will doubt that the influence they already have exerted on the interpretation of other doctrines mentioned in the Creed must go on?

Historical interpretation gives us first the Creed in its meaning as understood by its framers: it also gives us the Creed as it proves to be a living fountain for others who receive it. No Creed is ever estimated aright or interpreted aright, until the principles in it which were vital to the authors of it are understood in their vitality, and vitality means always growth.

The other portion of my remark is no less true and important. The Creed admits of a progressive systematization of doctrine. I think it incites to such progress. It makes no attempt at systematic statement. It aims rather to enumerate the fundamental and distinguishing doctrines of the Gospel. Any work of systemizing is left to others. But its enumeration is the fruit of systemizing; and a historical interpretation, bringing to light its distinctive characteristics, shows how the inherited system is already modified, and how further changes are prophesied.

Put into the creed of old Calvinism, universal atonement, universal free moral agency, a higher conception of personality, and the system cannot remain what it was. The Hopkinsian founders were determined it should not, and the history of the Seminary proved they were right.

What a historical interpretation most emphatically suggests is the line along which this progress will move — what the direction of the systemizing process will be. It is from

---

[1] *The Associate Creed*, p. 94.

the formal to the real; from power to character, from work to person. So it has been in the entire history of theology as cultivated at Andover. Federalism gave way to the reality of a divine constitution, to laws of heredity and ethical responsibility. The work of Christ becomes more and more connected with his Person, the government of God with his character. The Creed opens the way to a more and more Christian conception of God and to a systemizing of all religious truth under this inspiration and with this centre. A Christocentric Theology — not a theology that centres in what is commonly understood by the words historic Christ, but one which centres in God as revealed in Christ — is just as admissible under the Creed at Andover as in any Church or School. For the Seminary Creed does not attempt to construct a completed system, nor to point out and prescribe in what the ultimate principle of the several truths it requires is to be found. The new elements are naturally thrown into special prominence, but they exclude nothing which is consistent with them. An experienced eye detects at once in this symbol the Creeds of Nicaea and Constantinople, the Creed of Chalcedon, the Augsburg Confession and the Westminster Standards, as well as the "improvements" of Edwards and Hopkins. And taking the whole into account it will be found to be a truer order and conception of its teaching to make the main historic root and stem of all Christian Theology its root and trunk rather than some one of its fruitful branches. Calvin had a true instinct when he arranged the topics of Christian faith, in the first edition of his *Institutes*, according to the scheme of the *Apostles' Creed*.

(4). The truths of the Seminary Creed may be adjusted to a larger knowledge and life than were open to its framers. A historical study and interpretation of the Creed shows that these truths came to these men as living and fruitful principles, and it is of the very nature of such truths to find new application and service in new forms.

It is one of the constant surprises to a student of the intellectual and moral history of man to find how differently a system, which has been superseded, appears when it is ap-

proached from the other side and followed through its period
of conflict to the time when it wins its victory, and for this
reason passes more and more out of sight. Its moving principles are not thus lost, rather they are now appropriated
and assimilated and become a part of the life and working
power of the Church. What if a man sees a larger truth
in election than individual salvation, is he denying his Calvinistic creed? What if he discern, that the principle of
probation, on the basis of atonement, when once admitted,
will not cramp itself to the meagre knowledge men had a
hundred years ago of the perishing millions of Africa and
Asia? Does he abandon this principle because he trusts it?
What if Christianity seems to him more and more to be the
key to history, more and more evidently to mean the powers
of recovery which God is pouring into the growing life of
the ages, and so with a simpler faith than ever before he
turns to the Cross and the Incarnation as the master light
of all his seeing, does he thereby renounce his connection with
men who could not stop when they had written the article
upon the doom of the wicked, but added a new close to their
Creed in this stately and comprehensive confession: "(I
believe) that it is the prerogative of God to bring good out
of evil, and that he will cause the wrath and rage of wicked
men to praise Him; and that all the evil which has existed,
and which will forever exist in the moral system will eventually be made to promote a most important purpose under the
wise and perfect administration of that Almighty Being who
will cause all things to work for His own glory, and thus fulfil
all His pleasure"?

When the controversy began, whose outcome is the present
trial, an editorial in the *Congregationalist* described the Seminary Creed, with the Visitorial system, "as a complicated and
iron-bound endeavor to anchor the orthodoxy of the future
as by chain cable to one of its particular phases in the past."
The issue thus made in the beginning is the real question at
the end. It is a testing question for you, Mr. President and
Gentlemen, as well as for me. You are on trial no less than
I. The Seminary is on trial. Is it committed to the main-

tenance of transient opinion, or is there a truer interpretation of its Creed? Is your office like that of a tither of
mint, anise and cummin, or are you interpreters of a religious Creed whose words are to be understood in their connections with the life of the Church and with Him whose
teaching is Spirit and life?

I plead for no license of interpretation, for no violation of
any just law of interpretation, for no departure from the
natural, grammatical, historic meaning of terms and phrases
— but I ask for breadth, insight and justice. I do not ask
you to make the Creed utter what we might suppose its
framers would say were they living now, but did not because
they flourished nearly a century ago — *ita Lex scripta est.*
This is the rule. But finding out what it says, I ask you to
interpret it as a whole, to admit the impossibility of making
every article in its obligation complete in itself, or any
phrase literally binding which is traditional and contradictory
to what is new in the Creed and therefore controlling, and I
especially ask your attention to the facts that at the beginning of my acceptance of the Creed I am reminded of God's
constant revelation of Himself, and near its close I make this
solemn promise, that I will teach the Christian faith as expressed in the Creed . . together with the other doctrines
and duties of our holy religion, so far as may appertain to
my office, ACCORDING TO THE BEST LIGHT GOD SHALL GIVE
ME. I have tried to follow this light. Until these recent
unhappy disputes I have never heard it questioned at Andover
but that the Creed could be taken on the principles I have
stated. I came with the understanding that it was thus liberally interpreted and administered. I supposed such a
policy to be as much a recognized part of the institution as
having a library or daily prayers. I believe that it alone
really fulfils the true intention of the Founders. Among my
reasons for such a faith are these:

1. The Seminary was organized and its Creed drawn to be a
means of union of the various parties, or as they were called,
denominations, of Orthodox Congregationalists then existing.
Few realize how many and deep were the divisions in those

days — leaving out of account the great schism which was hastening — how they fomented jealousies and suspicions and separated brethren into cliques and factions and arrayed them as supporters of this periodical or that, and even of different missionary organizations. The necessity of union was paramount in the minds of the leading men who founded the Seminary. It appears abundantly in their published correspondence, and will not I presume be disputed. Dr. Bacon at the Semi-Centennial of the Seminary expressed the common and undisputed opinion when he characterized the establishment of the Seminary as "an epoch in the history of New England theology," and added "It was founded, not for the special interest of any one locality or district, nor for the special system of any theological discoverer, but for the common interest of the churches, and for the common orthodoxy of Massachusetts and New England. It was pledged at the outset to a large and tolerant orthodoxy, as distinguished from the intolerance and contentiousness by which the little cliques and parties that arise in a particular locality and around a particular great man are too often characterized."[1] Unless there can be room in its Faculty for men who are loyal to what Dr. Bacon calls "the common orthodoxy of Massachusetts and New England" (by which he does not mean the ordinary opinion, or that of a majority), but who differ from others of their brethren as Dr. Stiles differed from Dr. Hopkins, or Emmons from Burton, or French from Spring, all of whom Dr. Bacon regards as within the purpose of the Creed,[2] the Seminary fails to fulfil the object for which it was founded.

2. The general structure of the Creed and the clauses respecting God's constant revelation and the promise which implies new light, favor the same conclusion.

3. The Constitution of the Seminary implies throughout the faith of the Founders in the advancement of religious knowledge. It bears throughout the impress of the broad and

---

[1] *Memorial of the Fiftieth Anniversary*, Andover: Published by Warren F. Draper, 1859, p. 101. See also *The Panoplist* IV. pp. 372, 373.

[2] *Memorial*, p. 99.

liberal mind of Dr. Pearson, as well as of the generosity and
public spirit of the donors. It was founded to increase " the
number of *learned* and *able* Defenders of the Gospel of Christ
as well as of orthodox, pious, and zealous Ministers of the
New Testament." A three years' residence was deemed "a
period scarcely sufficient for acquiring that fund of knowledge which is necessary for a Minister of the Gospel." Greek
and Hebrew were made obligatory through the course. Provision was made by which new foundations, whether chairs
of instruction or scholarships, should be increased. The cur-
riculum sketched at the outset is larger than has yet been
realized. A theological university, exceeding any thing before
known, was in mind. There was threatening what was regarded as a great religious defection. It was to be met not
simply with religious zeal and asserted authority of revelation, but with all available weapons of reason and learning.
A perusal of Mr. Abbot's will by which the Seminary received a most munificent bequest will satisfy any reader of
the generous purposes of knowledge with which the institution was started. But is it possible to suppose that all this
was done in the expectation that there would be no advancement in the understanding of truth, or that men would not
be allowed, while holding fast to the principles of the Creed,
to put them in new relations and gain new results?

What actually was done is well known in the case of Professor Stuart. His friends were at times anxious lest he was
verging to Sabellianism or rationalism, and he was always
under fire, but Mr. Bartlet went on with his remittances,
and when once a Committee of the Trustees remonstrated
at certain offences committed in the first edition of his commentary on Romans, Professor Stuart replied that he considered the interference "inquisitorial," and this ended the
matter. He taught in variance from the Creed all his life on
" The Eternal Sonship," and if, as I suppose to be true, his
opinion is now generally rejected, this also shows the wisdom
of trusting to the power of truth in such matters.

4. The character of the advisers of the Associate Founders,
their humility, and their faith in doctrinal progress, the school

of theology to which they belonged, concur to the same result. I have spoken thus far of the so-called Original Founders particularly, but not exclusively, for the Associate Foundation became a part of one and the same institution.

I turn now to the Hopkinsians. They had the spirit of their great leader whose words I will quote from the memoir by Dr. Park.

" When tired," says his biographer, " of hearing the stale charge that he had started new doctrines into life, he responds : ' I now declare, I had much rather publish *New Divinity* than any other. And the more of this the better, — if it be but true. Nor do I think any doctrine can be " too strange to be true." I should think it hardly worth while to write, if I had nothing *new* to say.' In his ' Animadversions on Mr. Hart's Late Dialogue,' Hopkins alludes to his having been falsely accused of propounding new theories, and replies : ' This he [Mr. Hart] has done over and over again, about a dozen times. He calls them " new doctrines," " a new system or rather chaos of divinity," " upstart errors," etc. And the teachers of them he calls " new apostles," " new divines," " new teachers," etc. — If this were true, I see not what reason there would be to make such a great outcry about it. There is really no evidence against these doctrines. It is at least *possible*, that there is some truth contained in the Bible, which has not been commonly taught ; yea, has never been mentioned by any writer since the apostles ; and whenever that shall be discovered and brought out, it will be *new*. And who knows but that some such *new* discoveries may be made in our day ? If so, unhappy and very guilty will be the man who shall attempt to fright people, and raise their prejudices against it, by raising the cry of New Divinity. Indeed, I question whether an author can, with a right temper and view, take this method to run any doctrine down, by appealing to the prejudices of people, and keeping up a constant loud cry of *new, upstart* divinity.' " [1]

" ' There is no reason to doubt,' he says in his seventy-second year, ' that light will so increase in the church, and men will be raised up, who will make such advances in opening the Scripture and in the knowledge of divine truth, that what is now done and

[1] Works of Samuel Hopkins, D.D. Boston, Doctrinal Tract and Book Society, 1852. Vol. I., pp. 177, 178.

written will be so far superseded as to appear imperfect and inconsiderable, compared with that superior light, with which the church will then be blessed.'"[1]

It should go without saying that if a Professor, following the best light which dawns upon him, finds himself wandering away from the Creed he is not to set up his private judgment and conceal his divergence, nor if the variation puts him in contradiction to the essential principles and the intent of the Creed do I raise any question as to his duty or yours.

What I maintain, and where I abide in good conscience is this: I have not thus violated my obligations under the Creed, even upon a close and technical construction of them. And if, as I also maintain, the Creed is a summary of principles which are to be applied and developed from generation to generation, I have done something far better and more faithful than a literal repetition of them — I have used them, and with them have confronted present great and important questions of religious thought and life.

What is proposed to be done? To remove, directly or indirectly almost, perhaps quite, an entire Faculty, and to proclaim to the world that an institution started as was Andover Seminary has outlived its usefulness. Not that men cannot be found to fill its chairs who may think that they are taking the Creed literally when they confess at once a limited atonement and an unlimited one, a federal headship which is figurative and an eternal Sonship which is temporal. Not that others still, if necessary, cannot be discovered who hold that when Paul says, "as many as have sinned without law shall also perish without law," he cuts off all hope for every heathen, and no offence need be taken at reading the word all into the Creed when it says that the effectually called receive the blessings of salvation in this life, or who still adhere to the theology of the covenants — but it will indeed be a new Andover when such principles of interpretation of the Creed are sanctioned. And how long can such a method of administration be perpetuated? If indeed the language of the instrument were perfectly plain, the argument from consequences would be irrelevant here. But instead of a perspicuous utterance there is at most silence, while for a liberal interpretation are the deep suggestions of its great doctrines of atonement and moral agency, of the Incarnation and an infinitely wise and benevolent and sovereign God, with his purpose binding together the ages, and the declaration of God's larger and constant revelation in his works, and the solemn promise exacted to look for light, and the happy auguries and peaceful promise and generous surroundings of its birth, and the expectation of the Founders that they had established an institution which should continue to bless the world so long as the sun and moon shall endure.

I am conscious of no desire paramount to the good of the Seminary. The finger of scorn is pointed at what is claimed to be the small support gained for the opinions expressed in Progressive Orthodoxy. We do not set up those opinions as a standard for Andover Professors. Some of our colleagues, esteemed and beloved, may not hold them. I really do not know where they all stand. And, besides, it *is* a new thing for men who demand fidelity to the Hopkinsian Founders to make the degree of present acceptance of a tenet the test of its truth! Writing in his seventy-fifth year Dr. Samuel Hopkins said,

" About forty years ago there were but few, perhaps not more than four or five, who espoused the sentiments which since have been called *Edwardean* and *New Divinity*, and, since after some improvement was made upon them, *Hopkintonian* or Hopkinsian sentiments. But those sentiments have so spread since that time among ministers, especially those who have since come on the stage, that there are now more than one hundred in the ministry, who espouse the same sentiments, in the United States of America. And the number appears to be fast increasing, and these sentiments appear to be coming more and more into credit, and are to be understood, and the odium which has been cast on them, and those who preached them, is greatly subdued." [1]

[1] Hopkins's Works, I., 237, 238.

His biographer adds that " the spirit of the new Divinity
was in the hearts of thousands, who did not favor it in all its
forms. The term ' Hopkinsian ' soon became the common des-
ignation of those evangelical or orthodox divines who favored
the doctrines of general atonement, natural ability, the active
nature of all holiness and sin, and the Justice of God in im-
puting to men none but their own personal transgressions. " [1]
That is, in 1756 there were five clergymen who dared believe
that men are not punished for a sin they did not commit, and
that Christ died for all men, and now I suppose there are not
so many in New England who would be willing to be known
as holding the opposite. Universal atonement is the orthodox
belief.

It is idle to question that in all lands, in all evangelical
churches to-day the question of the personal relation of Christ
to the entire race for which He died is receiving an attention
never before given to it. The Church at large has never yet
passed upon it. It was not before the minds of the authors
of the Catechism or of the Seminary Creed. It could not
be. Providence shapes problems for the Church. It puts
this one before us. It would be at least doubtful whether if
the Creed contained some expressions which might be used
to exclude the new doctrine it would not be an unwarrant-
able use of an incidental phrase to make it interdictive and
decisive of a question out of the purview of the framers.
Fortunately there is no such difficulty to be settled. The
Creed admits by its silence and by its principles, at least as
a legitimate inquiry, all that has been contended for by me
in the *Review* and in *Progressive Orthodoxy.*

I offer this as a complete and full justification against the
charges of the complainants.

[1] *Ibid.*, p. 238.

NOTE.

THE following are the particular charges which are specially considered, or referred to, in the foregoing argument : —

Page 103.

" 1. That the Bible is not ' the only perfect rule of faith and practice,' but is fallible and untrustworthy even in some of its religious teachings."

Page 114.

" 2. That Christ in the days of his humiliation was a finite being, limited in all his attributes, capacities and attainments; in other words, was not ' God and Man.' "

Page 114.

" 3. That no man has power or capacity to repent without knowledge of God in Christ."

Page 118.

" 4. That mankind, save as they have received a knowledge of ' the historic Christ,' are not sinners, or, if they are, not of such sinfulness as to be in danger of being lost. (' *Progressive Orthodoxy*,' p. 55.) "

Page 119.

" 5. That no man can be lost without having had knowledge of Christ. (' *Progressive Orthodoxy*,' pp. 63, 64.) "

Page 119.

" 6. That the atonement of Christ consists essentially and chiefly in his becoming identified with the human race through his incarnation, in order that, by his union with men, he might endow them with the power to repent, and thus impart to them an augmented value in the view of God, and so render God propitious towards them."

Page 120.

" 7. That the Trinity is modal, or monarchian, and not a Trinity of Persons."

Page 125.

" 8. That the work of the Holy Spirit is chiefly confined to the sphere of historic Christianity."

Page 125.

" 9. That without the knowledge of God in Christ, men do not deserve the punishment of the law, and that therefore their salvation is not ' wholly of grace.' "

Page 125.

" 10. That faith ought to be scientific and rational rather than scriptural."

Page 127.

" 11. That there is, and will be, probation after death for all men who do not decisively reject Christ during the earthly life ; and that this should be emphasized, made influential, and even central in systematic theology."

The " Reply " to which reference is made on page 118 and elsewhere, is the answer filed by the respondent with the Board of Visitors on Nov. 30, 1886, and extensively published by the daily press.

Q. ·(By Mr. BALDWIN.)   You are pastor of the First Church in New Haven?

A. Yes, sir.

Q. Were you formerly a student in Andover Seminary?

A. I was, sir.

Q. Did you ever attend the lectures of Professor Park?

A. I did, sir.

Q. Will you be kind enough to tell us whether you recollect in his lectures any statements which in any way attracted your attention as varying from the subordinate parts of the Creed, or from any parts of the Creed?

Mr. HOAR.   I do not see what it has to do with this inquiry, whether Dr. Park has broken the Creed.

Mr. BALDWIN.   We are simply pursuing the line of proof shown by our previous exhibits, that from the first there has been a large liberty of opinion at Andover, as has been so fully explained in the statement of Dr. Smyth.

Mr. HOAR.   If it goes beyond the Creed, then it has been unlawful; and if it does not go beyond the Creed, you need not prove it, because we are perfectly willing to admit it.

Mr. BALDWIN.   Do you object to it?

Mr. HOAR.   I have stated already my objection.   I do not see that it has any thing to do with the subject before us.

The CHAIRMAN.   It is understood that it is intended to bring out the customary principle as to the acceptance of the Creed.

Mr. BALDWIN.   Yes.

The CHAIRMAN.   As such it is admissible.

Q. Please state, then, whether any such remarks as I have

inquired concerning, were made by Dr. Park. Take, for instance, the eternal sonship.

A. I recollect distinctly, sir, and my notes of the lecture, which are taken partly in shorthand, show, that when Professor Park approached the doctrine of eternal sonship, he told us that here we come to a point of divergence between the old and the new divines, and that the new divines do not assert dogmatically a thing which should be asserted figuratively.

Q. And in regard to that special doctrine did he use any particular expression signifying his own view?

A. It was commonly understood, and I suppose it will not be denied, that he affirmed that the word son should be predicated of Christ in his humanity, rather than in his divinity, as denoting the constitution of Christ's person in the incarnation in the human life. He also asserted, of course, the divine distinction, — the *Logos* doctrine.

Q. In regard to the doctrine of sin, was there any divergence there?

A. I have not looked at my notes on that point.

Q. Please go on, then, to the time when you were elected a professor in Andover, and to your interviews at that time with the authorities of the Seminary in regard to your assenting to the Seminary statutes and Creed.

A. I had the pleasure on a former occasion of meeting the Board of Visitors, and I stated distinctly and definitely how I personally could subscribe to the Andover Creed. My memory is very distinct and definite upon this point, and I presume the Visitors will recollect it.

Q. What year was it, sir?

A. The event made more impression on me than the date; I think it was in 1882. I stated that I could accept and subscribe to the Andover Creed as a whole, interpreting its clauses by comparison among themselves, and in accordance with the terms of subscription which I understood had always been the usage of the Seminary, as sanctioned by the Board of Visitors. But I could not possibly subscribe to the Creed if I were required to take each clause and each article by itself. I instanced one clause in particular, which I could not take out of its connection with the whole contents of the Creed, namely, the clause relating to the Federal Headship, because I had been taught by my instructor in theology, Professor Park, not to believe in that. That was the manner in which I expressed my willingness to assent to the Creed, heartily and in good conscience and frankly as a whole, and according to what I understood to be the recognized principle of Creed subscription at Andover.

Q. How was that statement received by the Board?

A. I think we passed on to the theological examination.

Mr. BALDWIN. We shall desire to read at the proper time, in argument, the record of the action of the Board of Visitors on Dr. Smyth's case, and from his written publications.

TESTIMONY OF PROFESSOR HARRIS.

Q. (By Mr. BALDWIN.) State, if you please, Dr. Harris, what were the circumstances attending your assent to the statutes and Creed of the Seminary at the time of your receiving the appointment to the professorship you now hold.

A. Having been elected by the Board of Trustees to that office, a meeting of the Board of Visitors was held in this building in November, 1882, at which, besides the members of the Board, there were present Mr. Hincks, Mr. Taylor, and myself, all professors-elect. After some questioning on the part of members of the Board and quite full replies by us, it was stated by myself, I think, certainly by one of the three professors-elect, that there were some points in the statements of the Creed with which we found difficulty. It was proposed that the Creed should be read by the Secretary, and that either of us should interrupt the reading at any point to indicate our divergence from the Creed. Mr. Russell, then the secretary of the Board, read the Creed, and the interruptions occurred at various points.

I cannot remember all of the objections that were then made, but I do know that this doctrine of the Federal Headship was one, and that the statement made with regard to the covenants of grace and redemption as implying a limited atonement, was another.

At each point some member of the Board, and as I remember more especially Dr. Eustis, explained the sense in which these doctrines were held by him or by them, and could be held by us, showing the connection of the doctrines one with another, showing the bearing and meaning of the Creed as a whole, and so on. I remember that when the end of the

reading and the explanation had been reached, I remarked
that I wished I could take Dr. Eustis's explanations instead
of the Creed.

We then submitted to the Visitors — I think I was the
·person who submitted it — a proposal of the form in which
we were willing to take the Andover Creed, which, as nearly
as I remember, was this : "I accept" (my uncertainty is as
to that word "accept") "this Creed as expressing substantially the system of truth taught in the Holy Scriptures."
The proposal was, to accompany our signatures, either in
writing or orally, with this statement, when the Creed should
be publicly taken. To this the president of the Board replied
that there was no objection to it, and that for his own part,
he thought it would have a good effect in the existing state
of public opinion. I do not, of course, quote the language,
but the statement in general. I am not aware that the Board
of Visitors passed any formal vote in this matter, but it was
a distinct understanding, considered on our part as having
somewhat of the nature of an agreement with them, that we
should take the Creed under those conditions. When the
time of our induction into office came, the Creed was so taken
by each of us, with the statement which I have designated,
and, as we understood, with the sanction, not only of the
Board of Trustees, but also with the sanction of the Board
of Visitors.

Cross-Examination.

Q. (By Mr. FRENCH.) Was your attention at that time
called to this subject of future probation?

A. Yes, sir.

Q. Did you make any reply with reference to it?

A. Yes, sir.

Q. Were you questioned about it?

A. I was.

Q. At that time?

A. Yes, sir.

Q. What was said?

A. During the questioning on the part of the members of
the Board, and of the answering on the part of the profess-

ors, the question was raised as to my opinion concerning, — I think it was as definite as this, — concerning the probation of those who do not have the gospel. I am not certain as to that, but, however, I replied with regard to that point, and my reply in substance was this : That I recognized the liberty of clergymen, and the liberty of those who should take this Creed to hold the opinion that there might be for those who do not have the gospel a probation after this life ; that for myself I had not reached a definite conclusion concerning it, that I had not accepted it. I do not remember, I think, any thing more about that.

Q. That you had not at that time accepted it?

A. That I had not accepted it. I had emphasized, however, the liberty, not only of clergymen, but of those who might take the Creed, to hold that opinion.

Q. (By Mr. BALDWIN.) Will you state to the Board what occurred at the time of your examination and inauguration with regard to subscription to the Creed?

A. I met the Board of Visitors in company with Professor Harris and Professor Taylor, as stated by Professor Harris. The examination was conducted by President Seelye, who began the examination by asking me certain questions with respect to my views concerning the Holy Scriptures. These being answered, the examination passed on to Professor Harris, who was asked certain questions concerning Christian doctrine, which he answered. After the examination was over, the Creed was read by one of the Visitors, as Professor Harris has already stated. One of the three gentlemen who were under examination, expressed inability to take all the statements of the Creed separately, in minutely literal interpretation, to which Mr. Eustis replied that they themselves, the Visitors, did not take the Creed *verbatim et literatim*, and then went on explaining the Creed, as has been stated by Professor Harris. After the explanation of the Creed and our assent to it as expounded, Professor Harris made the proposal that we should employ at our inauguration the formula which he has already given, to which the president of the Board heartily consented, saying that in view of the existing state of feeling, he thought it would be a good thing to take the Creed in that way.

Q. Did you take it in that way?

A. When we were inaugurated we repeated this formula as our acceptance of the Creed, — "I assent to this Creed believing that it substantially contains the system of truth taught in the Holy Scriptures." That is as near as I can recollect the formula.

Q. No exception was taken by the Trustees to that method ?

A. No, sir.

TESTIMONY OF PROFESSOR TUCKER.

Q. (By Mr. BALDWIN.) Will you state, Professor Tucker, whether any thing was said by you as to your subscription to the Creed at the time of your induction into office ?

A. My election preceded, I think, by two years the election of the gentlemen who have testified. I find this statement which I made upon my subscription to the Creed July 1, 1880. I did not meet with the Board of Visitors upon my election, not having been notified by them of any call to that effect. When I took the Creed I took it reading this statement before subscription: "The Creed which I am about to read, and to which I shall subscribe, I fully accept as setting forth the truth against the errors which it was designed to meet. No confession so elaborate, and with such intent may assume to be the final expression of truth, or an expression equally fitted in language or tone to all times."

Cross-Examination.

Q. (By Mr. HOAR.) You say that accompanied your signature to the Creed?

A. It was not copied into the book; the reading of it accompanied the signature.

Q. You read that at the time when it was proposed to you, you should sign the Creed, and then you signed the Creed without putting down more than your name?

A. Simply my name.

Q. And to whom was this exposition given?

A. This was given in the presence of the Trustees and Visitors, so far as present. I do not remember who were there; it was a public inauguration.

Q. It was not a matter of consultation with the Visitors beforehand, as to whether that would be all that the constitution of the Seminary would require?

A. It was not. I made the statement before reading the Creed, then read the Creed, and, no objection being made, signed the Creed after that statement.

Mr. BALDWIN. That is all we have to offer.

Mr. FRENCH. We have nothing to offer in reply.

Mr. Chairman and Gentlemen of the Board:

My associates have requested me to open the defence, and to say, as I do so, that inasmuch as no opening has yet been made by my friends on the other side, stating the facts they intend to present to you, we trust that after the conclusion of what I have to say, they will be kind enough to open their case, so that my brethren who follow me may have the benefit of knowing what line of argument they ought to meet.

Mr. HOAR. We have heard that statement so often, sir, that I think we had better repudiate it once and for all. We did open our case. Judge French stated it at the original hearing. We have not duplicated that opening by going all over it with the same three gentlemen again, because we have divided these five complaints, which were lumped together, into five separate ones. We have taken for granted that the time which was spent was profitably spent, at any rate to save any repetition. Our case has been opened elaborately and stated. These gentlemen are charged with heterodoxy, by which I understand and mean, not the entertaining of any untrue or erroneous opinions, — that is all I meant when I said there was no charge of heresy. They may entertain the soundest opinions that ever were held, the most progressive, coming nearer and nearer to the light, and approved by God and man. Our position is that it is heterodoxy, because the framers of this Andover Creed have required a certain conformity to that Creed; and the sole question which we present for your decision as the Board of Visitors, is whether

they have departed substantially, — I should not criticise
very much all we have heard about the true mode of looking
at the Creed, within the limits of interpretation, consistently
with holding a more solid front of theological belief, —
whether they have departed from it or not. We have specified the particulars in which they have departed from it, and
how we can give them any greater information or understanding, I do not know. We have had it met by their client in a
perfectly manly, frank, honorable statement of what he con-
ceives to be the statement, which is just what we think; and
when we have heard all they say why our allegation is not
so, we propose to conclude our case, and we do not propose
to mix it up and discuss it a little piece at a time.

Mr. BALDWIN. Mr. President and gentlemen, it was the
hope of the pious founders of Andover Seminary that they
were constituting what would be a centre of Christian thought
and influence that would endure forever and ever; and I
think I may say that thus far they have not been disap-
pointed. They trusted that learned and able men would be
raised up generation after generation to make it this centre
by their teaching and example. It has been from its outset
a centre of thought and influence to American orthodoxy.
I think we may say that its teachings have often had their
influence across the sea, and certainly through the breadth of
our own country from its very first foundation.

Truth has been taught at Andover with a sincerity of conviction which was founded on a wide and generous scholarship. It has been the tradition of the Seminary that the
professors should not content themselves with the mere
routine of the lecture room, but that they should publish to
the world the fruits of their thought and study. They have
done that from the first. From the days of the old *Panoplist*
under Professor Woods, and the *Bibliotheca Sacra* under Professor Stuart and Professor Phelps and Professor Park and
their associates, down to the *Andover Review* of to-day, Andover has always had some channel of its own, through which
to communicate to the public its best thought.

The professors have not always been in accord on points

of detail in theology. Dr. Woods was not in accord with Professor Stuart. There were dissensions that we all know of when Professor Murdock was in the Seminary. Professor Emerson in his opinion as to the form of subscription to the Creed and Catechism differed from some of his associates, and Professor Park differed from some of his in his day. The German theology of Professor Stuart and some of his associates was very stoutly attacked by others then connected with the Seminary, mainly, I think, by those who did not know the German language. But now for several years there has been at Andover the most perfect harmony of fellowship and feeling among its faculty. Not, as has been stated by Professor Smyth, that they all think identically the same things in matters of detail and non-essentials, but that they have that harmony of spirit, and that feeling of a desire to stand for the peace of the churches and of the Seminary, which is inculcated so strongly by the language and the spirit of the statutes, and the Creed upon which it is founded.

But at the opening of the year that is now drawing to a close, one of the trustees saw fit to bring before the Board of Trustees, serious accusations against a number of the faculty of the institution. The Trustees proceeded to take action upon his proposal, but before they have gone so far as to commence a regular hearing, those proceedings are dropped, and Dr. Wellman comes before this Board, in his capacity as a Trustee at first, (I think now he claims only to act as an individual,) and presents here accusations which charge upon five of the professors, including the President of the faculty, heresies as to almost every cardinal feature of the Christian faith.

· At the time when these charges were first preferred before this Board last summer, it will be recollected that their form was general. The charges were made, but there were no specifications to support them. The charges were made against all, as for a joint offence ; and the charges themselves were indefinite and uncertain, — imposing from their very uncertainty. The Board required the complaint to be divided, and the charges to be supported by proper specifications. We have had the specifications, and we have heard the evidence adduced in their support, and the case has narrowed down to the simple compass of a book called " Progressive Orthodoxy," and a couple of articles in the " Andover Review."

The charges had declared that Professor Smyth " held, maintained, and taught," certain heretical doctrines. But the proof is wanting that he has taught a single doctrine which it is claimed by the prosecutors is erroneous.

Mr. FRENCH. I do not think you will find the word " taught " in the charges.

Mr. BALDWIN (reading from the complaint). " First, we charge that the said Egbert C. Smyth holds beliefs, has taught doctrines and theories, and has done other things as hereinafter enumerated, which are not in harmony with, but antagonistic to the Constitution and Statutes of the Seminary, and the true intention of its founders, as expressed in those Statutes.

" Secondly, we charge that the said Egbert C. Smyth . . . is not a man of sound and orthodox principles in Divinity ; . . . but that, on the other hand, he believes and teaches in several articles, hereinafter enumerated, what is antagonistic to the Seminary Creed.

" Thirdly, we charge that the said Egbert C. Smyth . . . believes and teaches, in several particulars, hereinafter enumerated, what is opposed to the Seminary Creed."

Mr. FRENCH. You have objected that every one of these charges is too general, and your case has been conducted upon Charge 4, and the specifications under Charge 4.

Mr. BALDWIN. Do you abandon the first three ?

Mr. FRENCH. No.

Mr. BALDWIN. Then three of your charges assert that they have taught things contrary to the Creed of the Seminary, and you have not a scintilla of proof to maintain your accusation. I call it a railing accusation, with no evidence to support it.

This solitary Trustee who comes before the Board with these charges, extraordinary in their amplitude of charge

and their poverty of proof, is supported by a corporal's guard
of individuals, one of whom is the editor of a well-known
journal of our denomination, which holds a position in Massachusetts, in which, perhaps, it claims to speak as the organ of
Massachusetts Congregationalism. The "Andover Review,"
published from the seat of the great Congregational Seminary
of Massachusetts, might put forth its claims to be considered
the organ of Massachusetts Congregationalism. I have no
doubt that the learned gentleman who has signed these
charges thinks that his organ is the better organ. Each belongs to a separate school of thinking. One of these schools,
that to which the *Congregationalist* belongs, is sedulous to
state old truths in old forms. The other school, to which
the "Andover Review" may be said to belong, is dominated by
the principle announced by Dr. Hopkins, " I never want to
write unless I have something new to say." They believe in
stating old truths, but in stating them, if they can, in fresh
lights, — lights calculated to impress them, with the conviction of freshness, on the human heart.

To the editor of one of these publications, it may seem a
stupendous breach of trust to clothe a seventeenth century
idea in a nineteenth century dress. It may seem to him
charitable and Christian to charge this as a crime hardly
equalled by embezzlements and forgeries, in an age not without many examples of such offences. But my client has
fought no battle in the newspapers. If his former pupils
have come before the public through the press with an indignant denial that they ever heard from his lips any of the
doctrines imputed to him by the prosecutors, it has been
done entirely without the knowledge or approval or assent of
the respondents, or any of them. We have preferred to
meet our accusers face to face in this presence, and utter our
defence here.

Progressive Orthodoxy, then, and the two articles from
the "Andover Review," are claimed to be contrary to the
obligations imposed upon Prof. Smyth by the statutes of
his foundation. We say that they are not; they say
that they are. And here is the precise question which

Judge Hoar has stated is before the Visitors, and which we accept.

The revelation of God's ways to men, say these Statutes, is twofold. It is given by the Scriptures, and it is given in the works of God. This idea that a progressive and constant revelation is being made of the divine character by the works of God, from year to year and age to age, was so dear to the founders of the professorship which Dr. Smyth holds, that they repeat it twice in their additional statutes, on pages 26 and 27. "The professor," they say, "shall, agreeably to the permanent Creed hereinafter mentioned, faithfully teach that revealed Holy Religion only which God constantly teaches men by His glorious works of creation, providence and redemption." And on the next page they say that "he shall subscribe a solemn declaration of his faith in divine revelation, and in the fundamental and distinguishing doctrines of the gospel as expressed in the following Creed, which is supported by the infallible revelation which God constantly makes of Himself in His works of creation, providence and redemption."

Why emphasize, Mr. Chairman and gentlemen, why emphasize so particularly by this iteration the fact that God is constantly revealing Himself from age to age more clearly, more clearly in one age than in the age before, by His works, and by His works of creation, providence and redemption? Is it not for one thing because the Westminster Catechism says that He is made known by His works, and then says these works are the works of creation and providence, and stops there? This Creed says God shows Himself infallibly, and more and more clearly as time goes on, by His works of creation, providence and redemption; and that word *redemption* stamps its character deep on the Creed of Andover Seminary, in its widest and most generous sense. The Bible, no doubt, is the key of the universe, but the Bible is not the universe. It tells us how to read the phenomena that science and inquiry bring to our eyes. We must accept the facts that astronomy gives us, the facts that geology gives us, the facts that biology gives us, the facts that evo-

lution gives us, and apply to them the key of the written
revelation of the Holy Scriptures; and that is the solemn
duty that this creed casts upon the Brown Professor of
Ecclesiastical History.

Let me read to the Visitors the definition of Calvinism by
Webster, in the edition of his dictionary of 1828, published
shortly after these documents took their shape: "Calvinism.
The distinguishing doctrines of this system are, original sin,
particular election and reprobation, particular redemption,
effectual grace in regeneration or a change of heart by the
spirit of God, justification by free grace, perseverance of the
saints, and the trinity." That is a list, no doubt fairly expressive of the Calvinism of the early part of the nineteenth
century, a definition which excludes from its distinguishing
features, most of those doctrines on which the weight of the
charges of the prosecutors rests. We find nothing here, for
instance, as to eschatology. We do find that particular
election and particular redemption are distinguishing doctrines of Calvinism. They are not, thank God, distinguishing doctrines of the Creed and Statutes of Andover Seminary.
The Creed of Andover Seminary, as the Board well know,
contains different statements of the truth of redemption and
of atonement. It tells us in one breath, in the familiar
phraseology of Calvinism, that redemption is for the few, is
for the elect; and then it follows with a wider message, that
redemption and that the atonement are for all men. And the
Creed of Andover Seminary closes with what is almost a
doxology of praise to God that in His good counsel and good
pleasure evil will finally give place to good. This declaration that all actions and events, both in the natural and
moral world are under His providential direction, that it is
the prerogative of God to bring good out of evil, and that
He will cause the wrath and rage of wicked men and devils
to praise Him, and that all the evil which has existed, and
will forever exist in the moral system, will eventually be
made to promote a most important purpose under the wise
and perfect administration of that Almighty Being, who
will cause all things to work for His own glory, this

ascription, I say, of homage to God, gives a character to the Andover Creed which is foreign to the old spirit of old Calvinism.

Take those two professions of this Creed, universal atonement and the universal change of evil to good in the far distant future, and add to it what they took from the Westminster Catechism, that Christ was the eternal Son of God, and you have three principles laid down, three principles combined for the first time, as has been said by my learned associate, in Christian theologic statement, from which deductions can be drawn and must be drawn of the most far-reaching character. It has been the business of the Andover professors to draw these deductions from these postulates for three-quarters of a century, and in so doing they have always had the adherents of the ancient system of narrow redemption, narrow election, and narrow atonement, against them. It has been constantly the Andover theology against Princeton theology, Dr. Miller against Dr. Stuart, the old school theology in Andover itself against the new school theology in Andover itself, Dr. Woods against his associates in the faculty, Dr. Dana against his associates among the Trustees. The Andover Creed is a nineteenth century Creed joined to a seventeenth century Creed, and where it differs from it, it must control it, as this Board held, your predecessors, in 1844, on the complaint of Prof. Woods and Dr. Dana, in regard to the non-subscription of the associate professors to the Westminster Catechism. I quote the language of the Board from page 430 of Woods' History of Andover Theological Seminary.

"XIV. The two creeds and declarations" (that is the declarations of the original Constitution and of the associate founders) "are *verbatim*, excepting that the associate declaration omits what is said of the catechism; but this omission, the original founders say, is supplied in the creed connected with it, and more than supplied because the Creed is the most explicit. We cannot therefore discover any *inconsistency* between the two taken as a whole."

Mr. FRENCH. What do you understand to be meant by

that; that there is nothing in the Creed that is not substantially in the Westminster Catechism ?.

Mr. BALDWIN. Perhaps it would be better for me to conclude my argument, and then you close.

Mr. FRENCH. Very well, I will not interrupt you again, sir.

Mr. BALDWIN. I have no hesitation, however, in replying to my friend Judge French, and in saying that if the Westminster Catechism does in any way conflict with the Associate Creed, and it is impossible to reconcile them, then the associate Creed must control, in my judgment. That they do accord in substance, which is all we have to inquire about to-day, has been decided by that Court which is superior to this Court, under the laws of the Commonwealth; and the law laid down by that Court in 1815 is, of course, the law for us in 1886. That case, the case of the Trustees of Phillips Academy *vs.* King, in the 12th Volume of Mass. Reports, it will be recollected, was one brought by the Trustees of Phillips Academy for a certain large legacy from the estate of Madam Norris. It was the contention of the Trustees that the legacy was good, because the Theological Seminary was built on a foundation broad enough to cover both Calvinism and Hopkinsianism; that the Associate Creed and the Westminster Catechism harmonized for substance, and that that was sufficient to support their title to the legacy. The Supreme Court took that view, and the legacy was obtained, and it is being used to-day by the Seminary for the support of its professors and its establishment.

Is there any doubt, Mr. Chairman and gentlemen, that the rule of law which gave that money to the Seminary dictates to the Seminary how that money is to be applied? If they got that legacy because the Westminster Catechism and the Associate Creed were in substantial harmony, must they not apply those funds, may they not apply those funds, in teaching on a platform which says that the Westminster Cate chism and the Associate Creed are in substantial harmony? Not that they are in literal harmony; not that in non-essentials they are not diametrically opposed. Take the letter for instance that I read from Dr. Spring, in putting in the evidence in this case, found in Woods' History, page 623. Says Dr. Spring, the author of the Associate Creed more than any one else, and a Visitor on the original Board, in speaking of the attack on the framers of the creed by a Unitarian periodical : " It has proved that we all have the Bible on our side when we depart from several answers in the Catechism. The transfer of sin, the sin of Adam, and the transfer of Christ's righteousness are scholastic nonsense and jargon." That was the language in which, in the form of an unofficial letter, Dr. Spring could characterize some of the language of the Catechism, which, together with the Creed formed the platform on which he stood as a member of the Board of Visitors.

So he says on page 594, in another letter to Dr. Morse : " We need not feel encumbered with the doctrine of eternal generation, because God is styled the Father and Christ the Son of God, any more than with the eternal fellowship of the trinity. The endearing words Father and Son are used to express the sublime eternal relation between the first two persons of the Godhead, because as I conceive no better words could be adopted. The relation is the most sublime and endearing."

We all know the poverty of human language to express the great thoughts of theology. Dr. Spring recognizes it there, and yet he says that eternal generation, which the term used seems to imply, is rejected. The term Son has no reference to a succession of age, to a descent from father to child. It refers, in the best word that human language can supply, to the sublime, endearing, eternal relation of the different subsistences of the Godhead.

It is Orthodox, then, to stand upon Andover Hill and teach the Westminster Catechism, and teach imputed sin, imputed righteousness. It is lawful also to stand there and teach what has been taught for generations, the wider doctrine of the Associate Creed.

The Creed of Andover Seminary is one, to understand which, you must read between the lines. Dr. Woods, in his History of the Seminary, has given us, on page 32, the tenets of Hopkinsianism, and they assert: " First, that all true virtue or real holiness consists in disinterested benevolence; second, that all sin consists in selfishness." Neither of these definitions is found in the Creed, and yet no Hopkinsian, like Dr. Spring or Dr. Woods, could have assented to that Creed without reading between the lines that sin was selfishness, and that disinterested benevolence was happiness and holiness. The omissions of the Creed mean as much as its propositions.

In the history of Dr. Woods, the Creed is frequently spoken of as a compromise Creed. It is better spoken of, I think, better described, in the language of Dr. Smyth as a comprehensive Creed. It is a Creed meant to be wide enough to bring within it all shades of belief comprised within the lines of evangelical doctrine. It is a Creed of the times, of this time, of this century. It is not so very far back to 1807 and 1808. Those were not times of dulness and inaction in the world. They were the times when the French Revolution and Napoleon were transforming Europe; when the whole circle of society was broken up with new movements and with new thoughts. It was in those times that this Creed arose as a new creation, expressive of the best thought of the day. And no higher conception has yet been formed of sin than that it is selfishness, or of holiness, than that it is disinterested benevolence.

It is of no consequence that any particular theory now held, future probation, for instance, if you please, was not in the minds, so far as we know, of the framers of the Creed. The only question is whether the language of the Creed necessarily excludes it. This question came before the Supreme Court of the United States sixty years ago, in a case of great magnitude, commonly known as the Dartmouth College case. The members of the Board will recollect that Dartmouth College exists under a charter from the British Crown. After the Revolution the Legislature of New Hampshire saw fit to pass an Act turning the college into a university in name, calling it Dartmouth University. They changed its mode of government by virtually deposing the

old Trustees named by the founders, or who had succeeded
to those thus named, and by adding to their number certain
State officers. The college applied to one of its great alumni,
Daniel Webster, to see if its franchise could not be protected ; and after study and reflection Mr. Webster told them
it could be, on this ground : That the National Constitution
declared that no State could pass any law impairing the
obligation of a contract. And what was a contract? Mr.
Webster argued to the Supreme Court of the United States
that the term *contract* included any gift made by one and
accepted by another; that that was an executed contract. A
charter was a tender by the State of certain franchises, and
its acceptance made a contract between the State and the
holder of the charter. And that contract, Mr. Webster contended, the State could not impair. The case was argued
with great ability by leading counsel, and the gentlemen on
the other side insisted that the framers of the Constitution
never could have had the thought of a charter in their minds,
— a charter from the British King, least of all. They were
talking of contracts such as notes and bonds, and not of
charters and grants of franchises. But when the great
Chief Justice Marshall came to dispose of the case in favor
of Dartmouth College, as he did, he said the question was
not whether the framers of the Constitution thought, when
they used the word *contract*, of charters, but whether the
word they used, whatever it was, was such that it might
be interpreted to cover charters. And Dartmouth College
held its own charter on the novel ground, to American
jurisprudence, that a charter was a contract, protected by the
Constitution of the United States.

And so, in construing this Creed, the question is not what
the founders meant by their words, when they put universal
atonement alongside of Christ as the eternal Son of God,
coupled with this doxology and ascription of praise to God as
he who would bring good out of all evil, but what may be
fairly derived from them by Christian teachers. What will it
allow them to hold, putting together these great principles and
drawing therefrom any and all legitimate deductions? That

principle governs this case, as it governed that of Dartmouth College.

And I need not say, Mr. Chairman, that no creed can mean the same thing to different men. We all look at truth, as the old warriors looked upon the shield, silver on one side and gold on the other, with a different aspect as we may approach it from a different side. I do not see you at this moment as my friend Judge French sees you. The point of view at which we stand creates the image which is presented to our minds. To a man of narrow range of scholarship and thought, a Creed means one thing; and the same words, to a man of philosophic insight, of deep reflection and of great scholarship, means something else. Which is right, the interpretation put upon it by the bigot, by the man who has not spent years of study to get at the real meaning of the words, or the judgment of the man who has given his life to unfolding the meaning of similar doctrines and searching to the very bottom to find out what truth is? "The letter killeth; the spirit giveth life."

And so this Andover Creed has been interpreted, as these books show, as our testimony has shown; and it is not denied. So has this Creed been interpreted for eighty years. Has there been any other mode of interpretation? Why have not my friends shown it? They have not shown it, because they could not show it. From the first Board of Visitors to the last there has been the same spirit of tolerance and catholicity in the construction of the Creed. The same construction has been put upon it that the Supreme Judicial Court of Massachusetts impressed upon it early in its history, in laying down the law for this case, and for every case that can ever arise, under the terms made use of in 1808.

I do not mean that the action of the Board of Visitors, of the Board of Trustees and of the professors, in adopting, in sanctioning, and in enforcing this liberal construction has passed unquestioned or unchallenged. If it had, the fact that such was the construction would not have half the force that it has now. No, from the very foundation of the Seminary there were men like the prosecutors of to-day, men who were hanging on the wheels of time trying to hold them back, who have opposed this doctrine on the part of the governing Board, and on the part of the teaching force of the Seminary. Let me read a word or two from what Dr. Dana wrote of Dr. Stuart and of Dr. Park. I read now from the 24th page of Dana's Letters to Stuart in opposition to articles in the " Biblical Repository" on the nature of sin : " In a word, my dear sir," says Dr. Dana, addressing himself to Prof. Stuart, " I cannot but apprehend that you are far too sanguine in anticipating the speedy disappearance of the doctrine in debate, — the doctrine of original sin. Unquestionably it is one of the grand pillars on which the Andover Institution rests. Can that which was true in 1808 be false in 1839? Rather let me ask, can a doctrine which the Church of Christ, from its first existence, has defended with such energy, and cherished with such ardor, be ever blotted out and lost? I have confidence that it will not."

Dr. Dana regarded the cause of Andover Seminary as lost when Stuart preached those doctrines, and Park afterwards came upon the stage to defend them. This is what Dr. Dana said of Prof. Park in 1853.

" His views of human ability are extravagant and extreme. They obviously tend to foster in men a spirit of pride, of self-sufficiency, of independence of God, and, emphatically, of procrastination. Is there no reason to fear that, in this very way, too many have found their eternal ruin? Is there no reason to fear that the unconcerned, the irreligion, and the false religion, which so sadly prevail at the present day, may be traced to the same source?"

And in another place he says:

" It is with real pain and grief that I make these statements. I have not a particle of enmity against the Professor. Far, far, rather, would I employ my pen in commending his fine talents. But if these talents are employed in opposition to fundamental truth, and in defence of dangerous error, their influence is only to be dreaded and discountenanced."

Like expressions might be found in the writings of Prof. Woods ; and Dr. Miller's letters to Prof. Stuart contain a similar criticism from a sister seminary. In the semi-centennial History of Andover there is quoted a remark by Dr. Spring on Dwight's Theology. The first volume of that work was published shortly before the foundation of the seminary, and Dr. Spring wrote of it thus : " Certainly the Lord must reign, or he would never have suffered such a book to be published." A year from that time Dr. Spring and Dr. Dwight were sitting together as members of this Board ; and that is a fair instance of the tolerance of difference of opinion on unessentials which has ever characterized the management of this institution. I read one other quotation from Dr. Dana's letters to Dr. Stuart, written in 1839, in reference to this same doctrine of Dr. Stuart on the nature of sin. Says Dr. Dana: " In view of the existing state of things, it is impossible adequately to describe the importance of our theological seminaries. From the very nature of the case, they must possess and wield an immense power either for good or for evil. While they are faithful to God and to His truth, the church will not fail to cherish them as her choicest hope, her richest, dearest treasure. But what if they should prove recreant to their high destiny? What if the streams which issue periodically from these fountains should become impure and polluted ? Alas, words cannot paint the bitter disappointment, the deep-felt grief, the disastrous, widespread and almost interminable evils which must ensue."

He therefore wanted Stuart to retract his views on the nature of sin ; but I need not say he did not.

Now, let me suggest this : That this doctrine of a possible future probation. which is attacked by the libel of the prosecutors, is one that has been found helpful to very many minds in grappling with the problems of evil and sin and human destiny. It has been found to be a powerful answer to agnosticism. Of all the forms of error that exist to-day among educated men. I think I am safe in saying that agnosticism is the most deadly, — the thought that there may be nothing above this world, that it is not worth while to inquire whether there is or is not. that we have not time for it, that we have not the ability for it, that we have not the

power to ascertain, and therefore that we have no incentive
to try. Agnosticism has sometimes taken the shape of theological treatises by eminent theologians, eminent in their
way, like Mansel. God is unknowable, they tell us, except
as he is explicitly revealed in his written word. No, says
the Andover Creed, the Andover Professors: He is also constantly revealing Himself in His works of creation, providence, and redemption. I think the doctrine of agnosticism
is met and silenced by this thought of a possible future probation, as it can be in no other way. Old Calvinism said
that God worked in His good pleasure when and how He
might for the salvation of the elect who were not outwardly
called in this life, who never heard the ministry of the Word,
and of the elect·infants. But how? Calvinism had no
answer, and therefore men, when they were led up to that
door and told they could go no further, became agnostics or
infidels. Here is a theory of thought and hope which shows
how God's ways in His dealings with man can be reconciled
with man's views of justice and what is due to himself. And
are these gentlemen to be blamed for putting before the
American public a view of that sort which has carried healing with it to many a wounded soul? As I compare a book
like *Progressive Orthodoxy* with the ancient and rigid statements of a former age, of the last century and of the century
before, it is almost like hearing St. Paul preach at Athens
about their worshipping the unknown God, when he had a
God openly to declare unto them. Here is a suggestion made
towards a better knowledge of God, a hope spoken of, not made
essential in Christian theology, but thrown out as a support to
those who need it, and seized with welcome by many hearts.

Unless, Mr. Chairman and gentlemen, the Andover Creed
can be accepted and interpreted hereafter as it has been in
the past, the hopes of the founders that that Creed would be
perpetually expounded by able and learned men will certainly
be frustrated. No learned and able man, in the true sense
of that word, will be found to come before you, as years go
on, and take that Creed in any other way than as you, gentlemen, have taken it, or these professors, who are on trial to-day,

have taken it. And suppose the day comes (as it may) when you cannot find anybody to accept each declaration of the Creed in a literal sense, and yet the Board of Visitors insists on a literal meaning of every word independent of every other, not looking at the whole, but taking it in its details, and calling for a subscription to every point without reference to it in its entirety. If that time ever comes, the time will have come too, when Congregationalists may well fear that the Supreme Judicial Court of Massachusetts, in the exercise of its high *Cy Pres* powers, will step down and order this institution to be closed, or changed into a foundation for some other mode of preaching the truth. This is the doctrine of administering trusts as near as may be to the will of the dead, when circumstances have so far changed that they cannot be exactly administered in accordance with the original intention, which has come here from the Courts of Great Britain. What have they done there? Formerly it was the law of Great Britain, as you know, that the Roman Catholic religion could not be publicly taught, could not be privately taught. Suppose in those days a good Catholic died leaving property for the benefit of his church. The Court of Chancery of Great Britain seized upon that fund. They said, true, the dead left it for a public and charitable purpose, and it shall be applied to a public and charitable purpose, but not to his. He wanted it to go to an illegal purpose; we will take it and apply it to the Church of England, the established church. Over and over again was that done under the *Cy Pres* doctrine in Great Britain. Is this Board willing to take one step which might tend to put Andover Seminary at the disposition of the Chancery Courts of this Commonwealth under that same doctrine? I trust not. I trust not as a Congregationalist who hopes that this Seminary will go on for centuries and be administered in the same way in which it has been administered from the very beginning of its history. Here is prosecuted the son-in-law of a former member of this Board, and I am glad that he is defended by the grandson of another Visitor who once held a seat, and the first seat, upon this Board, and by the grandnephew of another.

How easy it would be, Mr. Chairman and gentlemen, for these professors to draw their salaries and spend their lives in the pastoral quiet of Andover, without ever venturing into print and giving the world the benefit of their researches. They have been willing to spend their time and strength and thought in giving Andover a name in the theological world, in giving their best thoughts, their best hours, their best work, not simply to teaching, but to publishing their views. Are they to be censured for it? Certainly not, unless they have published something which is contrary to the true spirit and intent of the Statutes they have subscribed. If this prosecution rests on any thing, it is a breach of contract between them and the Trustees of Phillips Academy; and I need not say that to prove a breach of contract the plaintiff has the burden of the case, and must make it out by clear evidence. This idea of my friends on the other side, or their suggestion, that a theory thrown out tentatively in *Progressive Orthodoxy* is the assertion and teaching of a dogma, I repudiate. Let me read what Professor Park said once of a similar claim in regard to an expression of Tholuck as to a final restoration. " An opinion, when entertained in the shape of a subordinate and incidental theory, is as different in its influence from that same opinion when entertained in the shape of an essential and conspicuous doctrine, as the alcohol in bread is different in its effect from the alcohol in brandy." When we teach future probation as a dogma in Andover Seminary, and charge it upon our young men as a thing for them to teach and preach as a vital and fundamental and essential doctrine of religion, then it will be time for my friends to say that we are teaching doubts instead of truths.

The question as it seems to me is this : Is Andover Seminary to go on hereafter as it has gone on for eighty years? Is it to live forever and ever? It may, Mr. President and gentlemen, if you this day determine that the Creed and Statutes of the Seminary are to be read in the same spirit of union and harmony in which they were formed ; in the way in which every creed must be read which has in it the first elements of perpetuity.

HON. CHARLES THEODORE RUSSELL'S ARGUMENT.

Gentlemen of the Board of Visitors:

IF I know my purpose I am not here in the spirit of an advocate; much less of a partisan of any particular "phase of orthodoxy in the past" or in the present. I have heretofore subscribed the statutes under consideration, and for many years, in my humble way, I participated in their administration. For several of these years I had the pleasure to be associated with the two senior members of the present Board in such administration, — during all which I think we differed but upon a single occasion.

I am here to give you such aid as I may in meeting a duty in character most important and responsible; in result reaching far beyond present persons and present times. In a "judicial capacity" you are "to determine, interpret and explain the Statutes." And you come to this duty under a solemn pledge "to exert your abilities, to carry into execution the Statutes of the said Founders, and to promote the great object of the Institution."

It becomes then of primal importance to ascertain what principles of interpretation and construction are to be applied to these Statutes; and especially what principles these Founders themselves applied or intended should be applied. It is to this point that my argument will be addressed.

It is not necessary, after the elaborate, eloquent, and exhaustive exposition of Professor Smyth, yesterday and to-day, that I should, if I were able, deal with the theological questions in controversy. I am quite content to leave this part of the case where he has left it. I need hardly add that while I address you in behalf of the only respondent

Professor Smyth, now on trial, I intend my argument to apply without repetition to his associate Professors.

All courts of justice, before hearing a cause, require the parties to come, by their pleadings, or statements, to an issue in law or fact, single, certain and material ; which tendered by one party and accepted by the other, when decided by the Court, shall determine the controversy. Eminently necessary as such rule is to the rights of parties, it is equally so for any intelligible determination, from the record, of precisely what the tribunal did, and what it did not, decide. Still more essential, is such precision of statement, where the decision becomes a precedent, and an authoritative, perhaps conclusive, construction of such credal statutes as those now under discussion.

This rule, old as the common law, and in proceedings like these, everywhere, with us, guarded by Constitutional provision, is just as necessary to theological as legal controversies, especially where such controversies assume the now somewhat antiquated and repellent form of public complaint and prosecution for heresy.

That eminent theologian and scholar, Cardinal Newman, says, in one of his University Sermons, " Half the controversies in the world, could they be brought to a plain issue, would be brought to a prompt termination." " When men understand what each other means, they see, for the most part, that controversy is either superfluous or hopeless."

Recognizing this truth, and in no spirit of captious legal obstruction, this respondent asked for a clear and definite statement of the charges intended to be made. This would naturally and necessarily involve a statement of the particular parts of the creed, be it Calvinistic, Westminster Shorter Catechism, or associate, upon which the complainants relied, and the particular acts the respondent had done, or the particular opinions and doctrines he held, which violated such parts. Such specification the respondent has never obtained. We do not complain of dislocated and dismembered citations from the respondent's book, in allegation or evidence, so much as we do, that the complainants give us nowhere their hypothesis or construction of any parts of the creed, or even tell us the parts, which they say we violate. Till this is done we do not know whether our controversy is one of interpretation and construction, or of fact.

I began these preliminary suggestions with a citation from an eminent theologian of another country. May I close them with one from an equally eminent theologian of our country, — I mean Prof. Park? In the opening chapter of his pamphlet on "The Associate Creed of Andover Theological Seminary," published in 1883, he says: "There are several doctrines for the maintenance of which, in a special degree, the Andover Seminary was founded. In this chapter four of these doctrines are specified, because their practical importance is easily seen, and because their truth has been recently denied. Appended to the statement of each doctrine is a statement of the contrasted error" (p. 3).

"The first of these four doctrines is: The Bible, in all its religious and moral teachings, is entirely trustworthy. The contrasted error is: We are not authorized to confide in all the biblical teachings, even in all which relate to religion and morality. Some of them are false and hurtful; or some may be false and hurtful; or so far as any of them are in our view opposed to the Christian consciousness, we cannot positively believe them, even if we do not positively disbelieve them" (p. 3).

The citation of one of these specifications is sufficient to show the character of all. They at once reveal to us their author's conception of the creed and the alleged or contrasted error, and eliminate at once and clearly, either an issue of construction, or of fact.

Such specification is all the respondent has ever asked; and such the ablest of theologians, concurring with us, deems essential, at the very entrance, upon the same substantial discussion, which the complainants have forced upon us, without such specification.

We are told this is no trial for heresy: — but a friendly suit, to repress the greatest breach of trust of the century. It is said, the question is, not whether the respondent is right or wrong in his views; whether progressive orthodoxy is truer or better than Calvinistic orthodoxy; but simply, whether the views of these professors are inconsistent with any part of an ironclad creed, by which certain most eminent and progressive gentlemen, nearly a century ago, attempted by " a complicated and iron-bound endeavor to anchor the orthodoxy of the future, as by a chain cable, to one of its particular phases in the past." How far this is true, I will consider when I state the issue. I only say now, whether it be true or not, this is no such cold, comparative, impassive, impersonal question to you, Reverend and Honored Sirs.

Before you can take the seats, you so well fill, you have a solemn duty. Let me state it in the words of the Statutes : " He shall, moreover, in like manner, subscribe the same Theological Creed, which every Professor elect is required to subscribe, and a Declaration of his faith in the same Creed shall be repeated by him at every successive period of five years." Art. 19, Statutes.

Whatsoever it may be to others, this creed, ironclad or elastic, complicated or simple, with whatsoever construction or interpretation you put upon it, is to you, and each of you, to-day, a living, personal, present faith.

What then is the issue before you?

In April, 1863, the respondent, Egbert C. Smyth, was appointed Brown Professor of Ecclesiastical History and Pastoral Theology in the Theological Institution in Phillips Academy, Andover, as the successor of Dr. Shedd, upon the foundation established by Moses Brown under dates of Feb'y 8, 1819, Nov. 4, 1820, and June 14, 1824.

Deeds and Donations, 146–151.

The date of this Foundation, Feb'y 8, 1819, is important, as bearing materially upon a subsequent part of this argument.

By the terms of this Foundation " all the Articles of the Associate Statutes, which apply to Professors on that Foundation, viz. : the second, third, fourth, fifth, and sixth articles, shall apply equally and with the same force to the Professor on this my Foundation, and the said second, third, fourth, fifth, and sixth articles of the said Associate Statutes shall be for the regulation of this my said Professor forever, in the same manner as for the other Professors on the said Foundation."

The Foundation is then made " subject to visitation in the same manner as the said Associate Foundation is now subject to visitation."

Deeds and Donations, pp. 147–8.

Art. 2 of the Associate Statutes provides : —

Article II. Every Professor on the Associate Foundation shall be a Master of Arts, of the Protestant Reformed Religion, an ordained Minister of the Congregational or Presbyterian denomination, and shall sustain the character of a discreet, honest, learned and devout Christian ; an orthodox and consistent Calvinist; and after a careful examination by the Visitors with reference to his religious principles, he shall, on the day of his inauguration, publicly make and subscribe a solemn declaration of his faith in Divine Revelation, and in the fundamental and distinguishing doctrines of the Gospel, as expressed in the following Creed, which is supported by the infallible Revelation which God constantly makes of Himself in his works of creation, providence and redemption, namely : —

Then follows the Associate Creed and Declaration.

Art. 3 provides for the repetition of the Creed and Declaration every five years by the Professors.

Art. 4 provides for the honorable maintenance of the Professors.

Art. 5 is wholly devoted to regulations of their duties and services.

Art. 6 provides for filling vacancies.

Professor Smyth was appointed, subject to these Statutes, and these alone, by the Trustees.

I shall not stop to discuss at length, this proposition, because it is now so well settled by the established construction of this Board, as to be no longer open to question.

For nineteen years after the establishment of the seminary, no professor was required to, or did, sign any thing but the Associate Creed and Declaration. For a few years subsequent, from 1826 to 1842, under the action of the Trustees, all the professors were required to subscribe the declaration of the original Founders. But attention of the Visitors and Trustees was called to the matter, by the refusal of Dr. Emerson and Dr. Stuart to make such subscription, upon the ground it was not required. The question then passed under the careful adjudication of the Trustees, and subsequently of this Board, to which Dr. Woods made his elaborate and able plea, and Dr. Dana his earnest and solemn protest. The Board, then composed of Dr. Heman Humphrey, Dr. Codman and Judge Terry, rendered judgment upon it, in a very carefully drawn, exhaustive opinion in 1844. (Wood's Hist., pp. 424–432.)

Since then for forty-two years, under this judicial decision, no professor, upon the Associate Foundation, has subscribed, or been required to subscribe, any thing but the Associate Creed.

When the Brown professorship was established in 1819, the Professors were subscribing only the Associate Creed, and this under the inspection of the Board of Visitors, *of whom Mr. Brown was one.*

See Wood's Hist., pp. 368, 424.

Professor Smyth was, upon his appointment, carefully examined by the then Board of Visitors " with reference to his religious principles." Being found by them to be " a Master of Arts, of the Protestant Reformed Religion, an ordained Minister of the Congregational Denomination," and sustaining " the character of a discreet, honest and devout Christian ; an orthodox and consistent Calvinist," he was confirmed by them.

On the day of his inauguration, he publicly made and subscribed " a solemn declaration of his faith in Divine Revelation, and in the fundamental and distinguishing doctrines of the Gospel as expressed in the following creed, which is

supported by the infallible Revelation which God constantly
makes of Himself in his works of creation, providence, and
redemption, namely : " and he then repeated and subscribed
the Associate Creed.

This Creed and Declaration he has repeated every successive five years for thirteen years up to this time, and to-day
he repeats and subscribes it.

In doing this, his entire sincerity and good faith are asserted, and would be presumed by law, without assertion, and
are put beyond all question, by the eminent Christian character and intelligence of the respondent.

I repeat, what then is the issue ?

Simply this,

(1) Whether Professor Smyth has done any act, or holds,
maintains and inculcates any opinions, or theological doctrines, which are so inconsistent with any portion of this
creed, fairly, reasonably, rightly interpreted and construed,
as clearly to show that his subscription to, and adoption of,
it must be either dishonest, unintelligent, or evasive and
criminal.

(2) Whether he has done any acts, or holds, maintains, and
inculcates any opinion or theological doctrine, which take
from him " the character of a discreet, honest, learned and
devout Christian ; an orthodox and consistent Calvinist."

I do not understand that the complainants charge the
Respondent with " misbehavior, incapacity or neglect of the
duties of his office." But they do charge, with more or less
indefiniteness, that he has done acts, or holds, maintains
and inculcates opinions or doctrines, such as I have stated,
and that therefore Professor Smyth is guilty of " heterodoxy," under the 20th article of the Associate Statutes, and
ought to be removed or admonished by you according as
you shall find the " heterodoxy " to be of the first or second
degree.

This is the issue. They charge — we deny.

To determine this issue we must find what is the law,
under which it arises. In other words, what do the controlling Statutes and Creed mean and require? To settle

this it is of primal and transcendent importance to ascertain, by what principles and rules, these Statutes, and this Creed are to be construed and interpreted. I apprehend the whole controversy may turn upon this.

Before entering upon the discussion of these principles and rules, let me submit, that sincere and honest differences in the interpretation, construction or acceptance of these Statutes and this Creed, within just, intelligent, reasonable limits, do not constitute "heterodoxy." If they do, then, the compromising framers of the Creed, in its very origin, were heterodox and not orthodox one to the other. Eight distinguished, and all but one, reverend gentlemen, peers each of the other in character, intelligence, honesty, learning, Christian sincerity, and conscientiousness, have subscribed this creed and made it a personal faith. Three sit in your seats, and five in those of the Professors. The five are on trial before the three, for "heterodoxy" in a matter purely of interpretation, and construction. Your Statutes provide that a majority of your Board may decide all questions; and if only two are present, and divided in opinion, the vote of the President shall decide the question. Suppose two only present, and that they differ widely but honestly on the construction and interpretation of this creed, as Trustees, in days gone by, have, and perhaps, in the present day do, may your President not only decide, but impeach his associate of "heterodoxy" and admonish or remove him?

Before a Judge can take his seat upon the bench of the Supreme Court of the United States, he must make, not a declaration, but oath, that he will support the Constitution of the United States. Yet seven of these judges decide that the colored man is not a citizen, and two hold the opposite opinion. Five declare that Congress has no power to issue legal tender notes, and four again hold the opposite. And yet did anybody ever charge the minority with violation of their oath, or of the Constitution, or impeach them of "heterodoxy" to any of its provisions?

No. Honest and fair construction and interpretation, within just and reasonable limits of comprehension, are not "heterodoxy," nor culpable, though to others they may seem misconstructions and misinterpretations. And especially is this true, in matters of religious opinion and dogma. It is here little more than the assertion of the right of private judgment, the grand characteristic of the protestant church from the beginning. The right of fair, reasonable, honest, individual construction and interpretation of that he subscribes, is in every man, be his subscription to the Andover, or the Apostles' Creed, the great historic creeds, protestant or catholic, or that of the village churches of New England.

If there is any thing peculiar in this creed it is the manifest intention to make it, by adoption and repetition, an ever-living, personal, perpetual faith, to those who come under it. I do not contend that you can add to, or take from, it a word. Much less that you can pervert or evade it. Like some picture of the old masters, you may not put to it one touch of the pencil, but you may brush away its dust, set it in a new frame, and hang it in any brighter sunlight of heaven, and thereby bring out of it new and latent force, expression and beauty.

What this Creed is to you, it is, and was intended to be, to every soul who subscribes it; never a monumental relic of the past, but "as the sun and moon forever" a living faith, holding its protective power over the Institution, of which it was an incident, for "the defence and promotion of the Christian Religion" by increasing the number of learned and able Defenders, not of Calvin, nor of Hopkins, nor Emmons but "of the Gospel of Christ, as well as of orthodox, pious and zealous Ministers of the New Testament."

The Creed was made for the Seminary, not the Seminary for the Creed. The Seminary was founded, not for the times alone of its founders, but "as the sun and moon" for all time. Hence the long study, the careful preparation, the nice adjustment, the comprehensive and tolerant spirit of the Creed. Its framers, never, in a spirit of mutual jealousy and distrust framed their Creed to put one another, or you, or your professors into handcuffs and strait-jackets. In the polemic and anxious spirit of their time, they sought to guard and conserve the truths of religion, without sacrificing its freedom of thought or investigation. They built their ship of oak and iron, because they meant it to float on the tides of time and progress; not to strand on the rocks and shores. They met, representatives of the differing, almost hostile schools of orthodoxy, in a lofty spirit of Christian compromise, and not without thought, labor, perplexity, and sometimes discouragement, they framed a compromise creed, ironclad enough for security, comprehensive enough for the toleration of all orthodoxy, put together with such artistic Christian workmanship, that holders and emphasizers of some of its parts, could yet accept the others, without either breach of trust or heterodoxy.

When thus they founded their Seminary, and carefully protected it with their creed, they meant to plant by the river of God a tree, which, drawing thence its ever-living vitality, through root and trunk and branch, should ever shed its fruits for the healing of the nations. They did not, in a spirit of religious self-sufficiency, intend thereby, to set up a cold stony monument of all past attainment, and a boundary to all future progress, with their names upon its base, and inscribed in old black letter, upon its rocky sides, " Thus far and no farther forever."

I am confirmed in this by the modest and yet grandly sublime words in which they close their Statutes.

" To the Spirit of truth, to the divine Author of our faith, to the only wise God, we desire in sincerity to present our humble offering; devoutly imploring the Father of Light, richly to endue with wisdom from above, all his servants, the Visitors of this Foundation, and the Trustees of the Seminary, and with spiritual understanding the Professors therein; that being illuminated by the Holy Spirit, their doctrine may drop as the rain, and that their pupils may become trees of renown, in the Courts of our God, whereby He may be glorified."

Associate Stat. Art. 28.

I submit this is not the natural language of men, who intended to set an impassable limit within their Institution to all religious investigation, or who sought, " by a complicated and iron-bound endeavor to anchor the orthodoxy of the future, as by a chain cable to one of its particular phases in the past."

They doubtless intended to moor their ship with anchors and cables of more than ordinary solidity and strength, but in doing so, they were too good, and too old navigators, not to realize that if they would have her float, in safety even, they must pay out so much of cable, as, with the same ground tackle at the bottom, the same hull upon the surface, and the same flag at her mast-head, would allow her to rise with the tides, and veer her bows, now east, now west, now north, now south, just as the storms of assault came upon, or the winds of doctrine blew over her.

They anchored their ship, whatever the anchors and cables, to nothing, but "the defence and promotion of the Christian Religion, by making some provisions for increasing the number of learned and able Defenders of the Gospel of Christ, as well as of orthodox, pious and zealous Ministers of the New Testament ; " and they came to this anchorage, it may be, aided by the charts of Calvin, and Hopkins, and Emmons, and Spring, and Woods, but most of all because, in their own introductory words, they had been " seriously reflecting upon the fatal effects of the apostasy of man without a saviour, on the merciful object of the Son of God, in assuming our nature, and dying for our salvation, and upon the wisdom of his appointment of an order of men to preach his gospel in the world ; " and because they desired to raise up such an order of men, under the instruction of Professors " who should, agreeably to their permanent Creed " and " according to the best light God should give " them " faithfully teach that revealed Holy Religion only, which God constantly teaches men by his glorious works of Creation, Providence, and Redemption."

Surely this Creed is not more inflexible and absolute, than the law God gave his chosen people, as they gathered at

Sinai, or wandered in the desert. Our Divine Saviour declared that he came neither to destroy the law, nor the prophets, and that heaven and earth should pass away before one jot or one tittle should pass from the law. And yet, as he sat upon the slope of Olivet, teaching future teachers, he took this law up, and by interpretation and construction filled it with new and amazing life, vigor, beauty and obligation.

Upon the strictest construction, the Creed cannot exceed in any exaction it makes, the law of the Sabbath, which God himself so respected, as to withhold the manna in those sacred hours, whose rest, it was a capital offence for man to violate. Yet what new light broke out of this law, as it passed under the construction of the great Expounder, when he looked upon the suffering, or walked with his disciples through the fields of corn. " In it thou shalt do no work," said the Statute. " It is lawful to do good on the Sabbath day" said the Expounder. Construe by the intent and not the letter. " The Sabbath was made for man, not man for the Sabbath." This, to Jew and doctor, was new departure. " It is not lawful for thee to carry thy bed on the Sabbath day." " Behold thy disciples do that which is not lawful on the Sabbath day." And they said it, because they did not appreciate the distinction between law under the strictest letter, and law under divine construction and interpretation. They comprehended not the distinction between abrogating and destroying law, and filling it with new life and energy by rightful exposition and development.

I have dwelt thus long upon the proposition that this Creed is open to construction and interpretation, because, it seems to me to be practically contested by the ablest of the advocates of the strict, literal construction. Prof. Park, "Associate Creed of Andover Theological Seminary," p. 45, says: — " It is said that a professor may take the Associate Creed with abatements and reservations, because other creeds are so taken, but we reply : — This Creed is not other creeds. Examine its unique style.". . .

" Every distinct and complete statement begins in such a way that the man who reads it, declares that he believes it;

thus, the very structure of the Creed, in its warp and woof,
binds the articles together and holds them so that not one
shall drop out. Every article is to be believed on its own
account, and because it is woven in with the others, — believed as standing by itself, and as supported by those around
it."

I do not know by whom "it is said that a professor may
take the Associate Creed with abatements and reservations,
because other creeds are so taken." We do not say that the
Creed may be taken "with reservations and abatements," and
we are not aware that other creeds are so taken. We do say
that this Creed, like all creeds, from the Apostles down, may
be taken, and ought to be taken, subject to all the ordinary rules
and principles of construction and interpretation, and in this
I think we have the support of Prof. Park, notwithstanding
the language I have cited. For on page 78 of his pamphlet,
where he is attempting to supply what he felicitously calls
"a hiatus" in the Creed, "a mere vacuum," in reference to
the intermediate condition of the wicked immediately after
death, in regard to which the Creed says nothing in express
terms, he says, "The style of the Associate Creed resembles
that of many other creeds written by Congregational divines,
who have been distinguished for their strict Calvinism in regard to the intermediate state. We are bound to interpret it
by the usage prevailing at the time when the Creed was composed." He then states what "this usage indicates." If then
"the very structure of the Creed, in its warp and woof, binds
the articles together and holds them so that not one shall
drop out," it is still elastic enough to let in, by interpretation
and usage, what in the same pamphlet, page 78, is called "an
omission in the Andover Creed."

I think we have the support of this ablest of the literal
constructionists, farther, in the manly, earnest, and self respecting language in which he asserts his own fidelity to the
Creed, on pages 85, 6 and 7, — "I thought that I accepted
the Creed in all its details, as well as in substance. I now
think that I have taught all its doctrines in the sense intended by its chief framers" (p. 86).

And yet, if you will read the pamphlets I hold in my hand, by Dr. Dana, Dr. Lord of Dartmouth College, and a somewhat able lay writer, to say nothing of many others, you will find that they as sincerely believed the then Abbot Professor guilty of " heterodoxy," as Dr. Wellman and his associates now do the indicted Brown Professor. — Clearly, then, and there, there were two constructions of the Creed. — And had your predecessors sustained the narrow and literal construction, they would have taken from Andover, thirty years of the grand life, labor, and influence of the most eloquent, learned, and distinguished theologian of his generation.

This attempt to limit this compromise Creed, not by right and appropriate rules of construction, but by their own special dogmas and doctrines, somewhat aggressively asserted by eminent and sincere men, has met the administration of the Andover Institution all along its course. Dr. Woods encountered it in 1808. — Dr. Murdock in 1824, when he came to repeat his subscription, and the Trustees, previously to his subscription, requested him to answer this question : — " As the sermon on the atonement which you have published is differently understood by different persons, the Trustees ask you the following question, viz.: " Are all the sentiments contained in your sermon, in your view, in accordance with the Creed of this Seminary and with all those sentiments which the Statutes require its Professors to teach ? "

Dr. Murdock answered in the affirmative, and then repeated the Creed.

Trustee's Record, September 22, 1824.

This action must, of necessity, have had on inspection of this record, the supervision and approval of the Visitors.

Dr. Stuart encountered and conquered the attempt in his day. Dr. Park met it with most significant triumph in his day. To-day, his successor, with four of his associate Professors, confronts it in a public prosecution for " heterdoxy." Surely, the thing that has been, is the thing that shall be, and there is nothing new under the sun.

It is said, practically, this Creed must be construed as *sui gen, ris*. " This Creed is not other creeds. It differs from all other creeds." I do not concede this. I believe, rather, that "the style of the Associate Creed resembles that of many other creeds," and that " we are bound to interpret it," not only "by the usage, prevailing at the time when the Creed was composed," but by all the ordinary and usual rules and principles of Statute and Credal construction. While I am sure, if it differs from other creeds in the terms of its subscription, it is wholly upon the liberal side. Let me read the terms in which professors in Theological seminaries of the Presbyterian Church, in this country, are required to subscribe.

" In the presence of God and of the directors of this Seminary, I do solemnly and *ex animo* adopt, receive, and subscribe the Confession of Faith and Catechisms of the Presbyterian Church in the United States of America, as the Confession of my faith, or as a summary and just exhibition of that system of doctrine and religious belief which is contained in holy scripture, and therein revealed by God to man for his salvation ; and I do solemnly *ex animo* profess to receive the Form of Government of said Church as agreeable to the inspired oracles. And I do solemnly promise and engage not to inculcate, teach, or insinuate any thing which shall appear to me to contradict or contravene, either directly or impliedly, any thing taught in the said Confession of Faith or Catechisms ; nor to oppose any of the fundamental principles of Presbyterian Church Government while I shall continue a professor in this seminary."

To this declaration, confession, and promise, old school, and new school, together, now constituting the Presbyterian Church of the United States, alike *ex animo* subscribe. Would the prosecutors and defenders of the heresy charged upon Lyman Beecher, or Albert Barnes, construe and interpret all parts of this " system of doctrine and religious belief" in the same sense? And is the Andover Creed more narrow, or more liberal ; more explicit, or more general, than this? Can a subscriber, solemnly and *ex animo*, to this Presbyterian system of doctrine, subscribe to the Andover Creed without " heterodoxy " ?

This is not only a question of construction, but of some
practical significance; because Art. 2, Stat., requires every
professor to be " an ordained Minister of the Congregational
or Presbyterian denomination." And further, because if
under strict and iron construction the time shall arrive,
when no professor and no visitor will consent to subscribe
the Creed as it stands at present, so that "it will soon be,
if it is not now, antiquated and obsolete," Prof. Park gives
us the quieting assurance that, " the Seminary is free to
invite its professors and visitors from the Presbyterian
Church north, south, east, or west; and when the whole
Presbyterian Church in America has departed from the
Confession, the Seminary can import its professors from
Scotland."

The Associate Creed, etc., p. 97.

And so notwithstanding the long and painful discussions
and labors of the Founder's counsellors, the Creed is elastic
enough to take within its comprehension, professors, who
"solemnly and *ex animo*, adopt, receive, and subscribe the
Confession of Faith, and Catechism of the Presbyterian
Church in the United States of America as the confession
of their faith," and " the Form of Government of said
Church as agreeable to the inspired oracles." In view of
the history of the Statutes and Creed, this construction is
broadly liberal, and it is not surprising that the learned Professor should guard it from all application on the liberal side
of Orthodoxy, with this sentence. " The Seminary is liberal
towards all men of the two denominations, who adopt the
substance of the Shorter Catechism *as that substance is expressed* in the Creed, and is exclusive toward all men, who
do not adopt the substance of the Catechism, *as that substance is expressed* in the Creed."

The Associate Creed, p. 97.

As this respondent adopts whatever " substance is expressed in the Creed," he is clearly entitled, in like manner

with American and Scotch Presbyterians, to the consequent liberality of the Seminary.

If, then, these Statutes and this Creed are subject to the ordinary rules and principles of construction and interpretation, what are these rules and principles? They are not only everywhere fixed and settled, but they have been so conclusively determined, and asserted in their application to these precise Statutes and this Creed, that they are no longer open to doubt.

The first of the Statutes, those of Phillips and others, were made and accepted in August and September, 1807; the associate Statutes in March, 1808; and the additional Statutes of the original Founders, by which they came into *experimental coalition* with the associate Founders, in May, 1808. By all the Statutes, the Justices of the Supreme Judicial Court are made the Supreme Appellate Board of Visitors.

Judge Jackson, then at the bar, is said traditionally, to have examined and revised these Statutes.

And Prof. Park says, " Associate Creed, etc., p. 48, 9, " The provision for an appeal to the Supreme Court was made after a lengthened consultation with such eminent lawyers as Gov. Caleb Strong of Northampton, and Hon. George Bliss of Springfield."

By these Statutes it is provided that if after an experiment of " seven years coalition, upon visitatorial principles, it shall appear to the Board of Visitors that the visitatorial system is either unsafe or inexpedient," it may be dissolved as specially provided therein.

Art. 28, Associate Statutes.

By Art. 27, the Founders reserved the right within seven years " to make such amendments or additional articles," etc., " as upon experience and due consideration shall be deemed necessary, the more effectually to secure and promote the real design of this our Foundation."

At this time the associate Founders, with Mr. Abbot, Dr. Timothy Dwight, Hon. George Bliss, and Dr. Samuel

Spring were the visitors; and they so continued, with the exception of Mr. Abbot, and Mr. Norris who died, to the end of the seven years' experiment.

Associate Stat. Art. 12, Ad. Stat. Art. 2.

In 1811, Mrs. Norris, widow of John Norris, one of the associate Founders, died, and left a legacy of $30,000 to the associate Foundation, to which her husband had made his donation.

This legacy the heirs, or Executor of Mrs. Norris, keen as any theological doctor on the scent for heresy, refused to pay, upon the ground that *the Statutes and Creed of the associate Founders were so " heterodox " to, and inconsistent with, those of the original founders of Phillips Academy,* that the Trustees could not take the legacy.

It is not a little significant, that the first charge of heresy, or " heterodoxy," against any body connected with the Seminary, barring the objection of Dr. Dana to the appointment of Dr. Woods, was against the *associate Founders themselves.* It was practically charged upon them, and argued by the most eminent counsel in the Commonwealth, that they had established within the iron-guarded, Calvinistic precincts of Phillips Academy, an institution with statutes and creed utterly " heterodox " to the creed of the Phillipses.

The then Trustees of the Academy invoked the decision of the Supreme Court, and brought suit for the legacy. This suit was heard by the Court in November, 1814; and brought distinctly before the Court the Statutes of the Founders of the Academy, and the Statutes and Creed of the Associate Founders for construction and interpretation. The case was instituted and conducted under the supervision of the Treasurer, Mr. Samuel Farrar, who had been the legal draughtsman of the associate Statutes, and under that of the Trustees, among whom were three of the Phillips family, and Drs. Pearson, Dana, Morse, and Holmes. The case was argued for the Executor by Mr. Dexter, and Mr. Merrill, and for the

Trustees by Mr. Prescott and Nathan Dane. As I understand, neither of the eminent counsel of the Trustees sympathized in the religious views of the Trustees, — they must have presented the case, in argument, as specially instructed by them, and to their entire satisfaction — I infer, as I see by the records, they paid them some $2500 for the service. The Court reserved their decision four months, until March, 1815, when they gave it, as reported in Trustees Phillips Academy *vs.* King, Executor.

12 Massachusetts Report, 546.

To this decision I now ask attention. The earlier part of it is concerned with a question of technical law, whether a corporation is capable of taking and holding property as trustee (p. 553).

The other question discussed is the construction and interpretation of the Statutes. To this I call your attention in detail.

" Another objection is urged upon us, — ' That the legacy is void; because the trustees of Phillips Academy, by the act of June, 1807, were made capable only to hold property for the support of a theological institution, agreeably to the will of the donors, if consistent with the original design of the founders of the academy. And the original design of the founders of the said academy was to propagate Calvinism, as containing the important principles and distinguishing tenets of our holy Christian religion, as summarily expressed in the Westminster Assembly's shorter catechism : whereas the design of the donors of the associate foundation is to add to Calvinism the distinguishing principles of Hopkinsianism, an union or mixture inconsistent with the original design of the original founders of the academy and of the theological institution."

" This objection appears to me to be founded on a mistaken view of the original design of the founders of this academy ; which, as far as it can be collected from the case agreed, appears to have been to teach youth the great end and real business of living ; to convince them that goodness and knowledge must be united to form the most perfect character in human life ; that vice, in the most comprehensive sense, ought to be hated and avoided ; and that virtue, in an equally extensive sense, ought to be loved and praised : to cultivate, establish and perpetuate in the Christian church the true and fundamental principles of the Christian religion, as far as that institution might have influence, by an early inculcation of those principles on the minds of the pupils. And after detailing a number of particulars, as means to accomplish the end and design of the institution, it is declared that the first and principal object of the institution is the promotion of true piety and virtue ; the second the instruction of the English, Greek and Latin languages, together with writing, arithmetic, music, and the art of speaking ; the third, practical geometry, logic and geography ; and the fourth, such other of the liberal arts, sciences and languages, as opportunity might thereafter admit, and as the trustees should direct. The name of Calvin or Calvinism, as the end and object of the institution, is not mentioned. The objection therefore avails nothing against the legacy in question.

" The objection seems to have confounded the benefactors to the academy, on whose bounty the theological institution or seminary is established, with the original founders of the academy. For although it is true that Mr. John Phillips was one of the founders of the academy, we must, in this instance, distinguish between him as a founder and as an after donor or benefactor. In his will he directs the donation therein given to the trustees of this academy, to be appropriated to the support of such charity scholars as might be designed for the Gospel ministry, and having received the first part of their education at the academy, and before a theological professor should be instituted in this or in the Exeter academy, as was expected in some future time, they might be assisted in their theological studies under the direction of some eminent Calvinistic minister of the gospel ; until such time as an able, pious, orthodox instructor should be supported in one or other of those academies, as a professor of divinity, by whom they might be taught the important principles and distinguishing tenets of our holy Christian religion.

" It deserves notice, and is evidential of the good sense and vital Christianity of this holy man, that although this instruction was to be from some eminent Calvinistic minister, until an orthodox instructor (that is, one who should teach, explain and inculcate the important principles and distinguishing tenets of the religion of Jesus, as it had been delivered to the saints) should be instituted; yet he is to teach nothing but our holy Christian religion. He is not to teach Calvinism.

" If it be objected, that Calvinism and Christianity are identically the same, then it seems to me that the principle of the objection would be to give the preference to Calvin over Jesus as a religious instructor, and to rob the latter of some honor and glory, which I have ever considered as belonging to him over all his followers and other teachers."

" The deed from Mrs. Phœbe Phillips and others to the trustees of Phillips Academy, containing the constitution of the theological seminary, alludes to the Westminster Assembly's shorter catechism: but I can find nothing of Calvinism as the object of their intended foundation; except once, where they quote a passage from the will of Mr. John Phillips. And although the preamble to the statute of June 1807, enlarging the capacity of the trustees of Phillips Academy, has the words " in furtherance of the designs of the pious founders and benefactors of said academy," it is very clear that the legislature did not intend to comprehend the after benefactors of the academy with the original founders; because when the law directs how the increased revenue should be disposed of, it provides that it shall always be applied " to said objects " [that is, for the purpose of promoting the theological institution] " agreeably to the will of the donors, if " [that will or those objects be] " consistent with the original design of the founders of the said academy."

" It was but reasonable for the legislature, when increasing the capacity of the trustees, and enabling them to extend

the objects of education, to take care that this should be
done in a manner not inconsistent with the design of the
original founders, who were dead. But there was not the
same, or indeed any reason at all, for the legislature to interfere in what then was, or what might afterwards become a
matter of dispute between two sets of donors or benefactors ;
the bounty of neither of whom had been accepted by the
trustees, and who were capable of adjusting and appropriat-
ing their own bounties.

"I should not have thought it necessary to take any further notice of this objection, were it not that the counsel for
the defendant brought forward in the argument, and urged
upon the consideration of the court with great force, several
specific propositions or articles of two opposing creeds, or
which the counsel contended were directly contrary to each
other ; insisting that the intent of the founders was to maintain Calvinism, or the theology of Calvin ; and if there were
but one single article or proposition, in the creed of the
associate founders, contrary to Calvinism, the trustees of
the academy would have no right to take and appropriate
the legacy in question ; and should the creed imposed by the
associate founders omit a single article contained in the creed
of Calvin, or as Calvinism was understood at the time of the
foundation of the academy, it would be such a departure
from the intent, design and plan of the original founders,
that it must intercept the intended legacy, and prevent any
right from vesting in the plaintiffs. It was then stated to be
an essential article in the creed of Calvin, and what all Calvinists must necessarily believe, to make them Christians
according to the Calvinistic theology, 'that the original sin
of Adam is imputed to all his posterity, in some way or manner, that they are all and every one actual sinners ; ' whereas
the associate foundation did not admit this article in the
creed taught in their branch of the theological school, but
substituted the following article in lieu thereof, and made it
a necessary part of the religious creed of the professors, and
to be by them taught to the students in the institution ; viz.,
'Adam, the federal head and representative of the human

race, was placed in a state of probation, and in consequence
of his disobedience all his descendants were constituted sinners,' — which latter article, it was urged, is not only an article of a system of religion called Hopkinsianism, but it is
so inconsistent with, and contrary to the system of Calvinism in general, and particularly to the foregoing article of
the creed of Calvin, or of a Calvinistic Christian, as taught
in the assembly's shorter catechism, as could not be taught
in consistency and harmony with the design, views and intentions of the original founders of the academy : and thus
the legacy being given to promote Hopkinsianism in opposition to Calvinism, as explained in the said catechism, is void,
and ought not or rather cannot be recovered by the plaintiffs, who, as trustees of the academy, cannot take any donation or bequest contrary to the intent of the founders.

" To this objection, thus drawn out and explained nearly
in the words of the eloquent argument, it is enough to reply,
There is a clear, intelligible meaning, consistent with the
whole course of the providential government of God over
the natural and moral world by general laws, so far as the
subject has been investigated, which may be applied to the
two articles attempted to be contrasted, with no greater latitude in the use of language, than is frequently applied by
orthodox divines to words and phrases in the Bible, not
always to be taken literally : in which sense these propositions or articles will mean the same thing. And in such
sense they are consistent with the revelations contained in
the Bible ; which revelations make up the fundamental principles of the religion of Jesus. Hence there is no necessity
of conjecturing a variety of meanings, which the words may
possibly be susceptible of, in minds more habituated to dwell
on the theories of certain divines, than on the religion of
Jesus, as delivered by himself and those who are authorized
by God the Father to preach it. And I hesitate not to say,
that in all cases like this, we ought to be satisfied, whenever
we can reconcile the language of honest Christians by yielding to them that charity of construction, which it is allowed
by all that we should apply to the Holy Scriptures.

"For myself I confess that I do not clearly perceive any other sense, than that in which the two articles mean substantially the same thing, notwithstanding some diversity of expression, in which they can be said to be true, and consistent with the Christian religion. And, knowing as we all do, the founders, as well as the after-benefactors who have set up the associate foundation, to be persons of great piety and most sincere believers in the religion of Jesus; and that the first and principal object with all of them has been to establish, teach and enforce the belief and practice of that religion on the students of the institution, and through them on the whole world of mankind; — why should we now be called upon to apply *an astute, narrow* and *uncharitable* construction upon a few technical propositions, merely to divert the legacy of a pious woman from an object nearer to her than life itself? — And let me add, in this case, the object is great and noble, beyond almost any thing in our country.

"The same course of reasoning and observations would apply to the objection, as it was attempted to be applied to a supposed contradiction between some other tenets of the two supposed opposing systems of theology. But it cannot be necessary to protract this opinion more in detail, on this general objection."

It may be urged, and granted, that all that is here said is not necessary to the decision; and hence is *obiter dicta*. It may be said, the Justices of the court were Unitarian, and hence coming under one of the anathemas of the Creed, were incapable of making, or indisposed to make, the clear distinctions, or unable to appreciate the precise formulated doctrines of the great Masters of orthodox theology. — All this may, or may not be true, without touching, in the slightest, the force of my inferences and argument.

This court was the body, which the associate Founders had made, after mature deliberation, their appellate and supreme visitors. It was the tribunal before which they, and not their opponents, brought their case.

There can be no doubt but that the court, in this case, be it in decision or dicta, did discuss and determine the construction of these Statutes, and state distinctly the principles of interpretation to be applied to them.

When this decision was made in March, 1815, Bartlet and Brown of the associate Founders were living, and with Mr. Bliss, Dr. Dwight, and Dr. Spring, constituted the Board of Visitors. His Honor, William Phillips, Hon. John Phillips, Andover, Hon. John Phillips, Boston, Samuel Farrar, Drs. Morse, Pearson, Dana, and Holmes, were Trustees.

The experimental seven years' "coalition" of the Statutes expired in May, 1815, after this decision. This brought the whole matter of Statutes and Creed entirely within the control of Visitors and Trustees.

Associate Statutes, Art. 28, Stat. and Deeds, p. 99.

" If after an experiment of seven years' coalition, upon visitatorial principles, it shall appear to the Board of Visitors, that the visitatorial system is either unsafe or inexpedient, the coalition may, nevertheless, be continued upon such other principles,or system as may be then agreed upon by the Trustees and Visitors aforesaid, in consistency with the original design of this our Foundation," or the fund might be withdrawn, etc. " But if at the expiration of the seven years' experiment, or within the said term of seven years, the Board of Visitors and the Trustees aforesaid be well satisfied with the safety and expediency of the visitatorial system, and that a perpetual coalition is important, and desirable, union shall be established upon visitatorial principles, to continue, as the sun and moon, forever."

How opportune came this decision, at the moment this large responsibility devolved upon Visitors and Trustees, to help them meet it! How still more opportune, that it came in the lifetime of the Founders, — and while Dr. Dana was upon the Board of Trustees " to sound the alarm," and other eminent doctors, as well as several distinguished members of the Phillips family were there to take up its warning sound !

What did those Visitors and Trustees? Professor Park

234

says (The Associate Creed, etc., p. 81), "In the years 1815-16, the whole constitution of the Seminary was reconsidered by the two boards of visitors and trustees, and no change was made in it; there was no mitigation of its strictness."

No, "there was no mitigation of its strictness," because the Supreme Court had just considered it, and significantly asked why they "should be called upon to apply an *astute, narrow*, and *uncharitable* construction upon a few technical propositions;" and had declared "there is no necessity of conjecturing a variety of meanings which the words may *possibly* be susceptible of, in minds more habituated to dwell on the theories of certain divines than on the religion of Jesus, as delivered by himself and those who were authorized by God the Father to preach it. And I hesitate not to say, that in all cases like this, we ought to be satisfied whenever we can reconcile the language of honest Christians, by yielding to them that charity of construction, which it is allowed by all, that we should apply to the Holy Scriptures."

Visitors and Trustees had no reason to mitigate the strictness of Statutes, so construed and interpreted, and under which construction they had just claimed and taken a large legacy.— But what is more significant, they neither criticised, questioned, nor repudiated this construction: — more, they accepted and affirmed this construction. The whole constitution of the Seminary was reconsidered just after this decision, and certainly, in its light. — To this Seminary it was not only a decision in an important litigation, but the deliberate opinion of its ultimate visitors.

What was the result of this reconsideration by Visitors and Trustees, made just eighteen months after the decision of the Supreme Court?

Let me read it as it stands recorded, on pages 148 and 149 of the Trustees' Record for September, 1816.

Record, Deeds, and Donations, p. 136.

" The following communication was received from the Visitors, viz. : —

" At a meeting of the Board of Visitors of the Theological Seminary, in Andover, Sept. 25, 1816 — whereas by the twenty-eighth Article of the Statutes of the Associate Founders of said Institution it is provided, that if, after an experiment of seven years the Board of Visitors and the Trustees of Phillips Academy are well satisfied with the safety and expediency of the Visitatorial system, and that a perpetual coalition is important and desirable ; — union shall be established upon Visitatorial principles, to continue forever : — Voted, that the Board of Visitors are well satisfied with said system, and that a perpetual coalition upon said principles is, in their opinion, important and desirable, and that the concurrence of the Board of Trustees of Phillips Academy herein be requested.

SAMUEL SPRING, Secretary.

" Whereupon, Voted, that this Board are well satisfied with the safety and expediency of said system, and that a perpetual union is important and desirable, and they do concur with the request of the Board of Visitors, and declare that the perpetual union contemplated by the Statutes is established."

But this affirmation of the living associate Founders by no means stopped with their acts as visitors. In January and February, 1817, with this decision of the Court, and this action of the Visitors and Trustees open before, and participated in by, him, Mr. Bartlet provides the Seminary with a chapel, and on the 8th of May, and the 15th of September, 1818, conveyed it, with other lands, completed and furnished, to the Trustees, subject to these associate Statutes, just then construed by the court, and made permanent, without change, by himself and his associate Visitors.

Deeds and Donations, pp. 137, 139, 143.

February 8, 1819, only four years after the Court's decision, and three after that of himself and associate Visitors, practically confirming it, Moses Brown, the other surviving Founder, founded, with a donation of twenty-five thousand dollars, the professorship, which Professor Smyth now holds, and placed it under these same associate Statutes, just then so recently construed by the Court, and thereafter by himself and associate visitors made perpetual.

In March, 1820, Mr. Bartlet asked leave of the Trustees to put up another College for the use of the Seminary, and in September, 1821, tendered it complete to them, " to be forever used for the sole purpose of promoting the interests of said Seminary, according to the Constitution and Statutes of the same."

Deeds and Donations, p. 161.

In 1824 the Trustees and Visitors, by a unanimous vote, applied for and obtained an act of the Legislature, by which Moses Brown, William Bartlet, George Bliss, Calvin Chapin, and Jeremiah Day, the then Visitors, were made a corporation, by the name of the Visitors of the Theological Institution in Phillips Academy, in Andover. By the third section of this act, an appeal from the Visitors was given to any person aggrieved by any act of theirs " contrary to the Statutes of the Founders of said Institution," or in excess of their jurisdiction; to the Supreme Judicial Court, and they were further " authorized to declare null and void any decree or sentence of the Visitors, which they may consider contrary to the Statutes of the Founders, and beyond the just limits of the powers prescribed to them thereby," while nothing in the act contained was to be construed to limit or restrain the Court from exercising all such jurisdiction over the Visitors as " they might exercise had not this special provision been made."

Act Jan. 17, 1824, Deeds and Donations, p. 165.

They thus made these Statutes a Statute of the Commonwealth.

Can there be any doubt, after these, their acts and doings, and omissions to do, of the broad, tolerant, progressive and effective spirit, in which the Founders expected and intended these, their Statutes should be construed and accepted? To-day, seventy years after its utterance in the ears of the Founders, we simply ask you to adopt the language of the Supreme Court. "Knowing, as we all do, the Founders, as well as the after-benefactors, who have set up the associate foundation, to be persons of great piety, and most sincere believers in the religion of Jesus; *and that the first and principal object*, with all of them, has been to teach and enforce the belief and practice of that religion on the students of the institution, and through them on the whole world of mankind, why should we be now called upon to apply an *astute, narrow*, and *uncharitable* construction upon a few technical propositions?"

We simply ask you, with them, to say we "hesitate not to say that, in all cases like this, we ought to be satisfied, whenever we can reconcile the language of honest Christians by yielding to them that charity of construction, which it is allowed by all that we should apply to the Holy Scriptures."

12 Mass. Rep. 563-4.

Upon the construction made by the highest Court of the Commonwealth, and the designated appellate and ultimate Visitors of the Institution, in the lifetime of the Founders, and accepted, confirmed, and ratified, as thus shown by them, we take our stand.

But we go farther, and assert that this same construction was not only accepted, by the original Founders, Trustees, and Visitors, but that it has been adhered to by all Trustees and Visitors, from the impeachment of Dr. Woods, the first, to that of Dr. Harris, the last Abbot Professor.

There was one conscientious and able Trustee, heresy haunted and aggressive, who stood by the Seminary at its birth, and opposed the appointment of Dr. Woods, as first Abbot Professor, by the Founder himself, for that he suspected or feared in him " heterodoxy " to Calvinism or the Creed, one or both. — That he had some ground for this suspicion seems to be conceded by Dr. Woods, in his later and more conservative years, — when he had come into harmony, if not coalition, with his former accuser. Dr. Woods, after citing some passages from his " Letters to Unitarians," says (p. 180 Hist. Andover Seminary), —

"Now I must acknowledge that the passages, above quoted from my ' Letters,' are manifestly inconsistent with my professed belief and my promise as a Professor. And on reflection I cannot but think it strange, that the Trustees did not exercise the same watchful fidelity in this case, as they did afterwards in the cases above referred to ; and that neither they nor the Visitors ever admonished me for doing what was plainly at variance with the Constitution of the Seminary."

Upon these suspicions or charges, as is apparent, both Trustees and Visitors declined even so much as to make inquiry.

The next in the category was Dr. Stuart, of whom Dr. Woods says (Hist. p. 152-3), —

" After the lapse of about twenty years, it appeared that on some points of speculative divinity, particularly in anthropology, there was not an entire agreement between his opinions and those entertained by Dr. Porter and myself. But it was otherwise in regard to the great principles of experimental and practical godliness."

" The labors of Professor Stuart in his department contributed in a pre-eminent degree to the reputation and usefulness of the Seminary, and had a powerful influence in promoting in our country the study of the Scriptures in their original languages, and in settling the principles of exegesis. In the important improvements which have been made in this branch of sacred learning, during the last forty years, Professor Stuart had a leading agency.

" In regard to the plenary inspiration of the Scriptures, Professor Stuart, for a time, dissented somewhat from the common doctrine ; and he freely expressed his opinions on this subject in the lecture room, and hinted at them in some of his publications."

Next came Dr. Murdock's case in 1824. Page 178.

"A case occurred nearly twenty years since, in which the Trustees, in the discharge of the duty devolved upon them by the Founders, appointed a Committee to inquire into the opinions contained in a publication of one of the Professors. The Committee examined the publication, and, in a written communication to the Professor, pointed out various passages which seemed to them inconsistent with the Confession of Faith to which he had given his assent. This they did, not to bring against him the charge of heresy, but to ask of him a satisfactory explanation of what he had published, and to impress upon him the importance of guarding against any deviation, real or apparent, from the doctrinal standard appointed by the Founders."

Most significant was the result in this case, as I have stated. Dr. Murdock was required to answer this question with its preamble. "As the sermon on the Atonement which you have published is *differently* understood by different persons, the Trustees would ask you the following questions; viz.: Are all the sentiments contained in your sermon, *in your view*, in accordance with the Creed of this Seminary, and with all those sentiments which the Statutes require its professors to teach?" Dr. Murdock answered in the affirmative and then repeated the Creed. And so ended this impeachment of "heterodoxy,"—and it so ended under a Board of Trustees, of which Dr. Pearson, Dr. Morse, Dr. Dana, Dr. Holmes, Dr. Justin Edwards, His Honor William Phillips, Samuel Farrar, and Judge Samuel Hubbard were members.

In all the long and bitter controversy with Dr. Murdock, two years later, with his well-known views, no charge of "heterodoxy" or disregard of the doctrines of Creed or Statutes was made, and Dr. Murdock was removed on wholly different grounds.

Next came the conspicuous case of Prof. Park.—In his case, as in this, a dissenting Trustee, supported by a college President, brought, filed, urged, and at last published, in detailed specifications, charges against the Professor of Christian Theology.

Pages 8 and 9, Dr. Dana's Remonstrance, assert, —

" The present Professor of Christian Theology has, agreeably to the Constitution, solemnly declared and subscribed his assent to the doctrines of the Westminster Assembly's Shorter Catechism, and solemnly engaged to teach them, to the exclusion of all opposing doctrines and errors. That Catechism recognizes the doctrine of *original sin*. Is it consistent in the Professor to hold and teach that our nature is not sinful, and that original sin is not sin ? What though it be admitted, in the case of infants, that they need atonement and regeneration, in order to enter heaven ? Are not atonement and regeneration, where there is no sin, obviously supernumerary and absurd ?

" The Catechism recognizes a Regeneration, involving a real renovation by the Holy Spirit, and a restoration of the divine image. Is it consistent to hold and teach that Regeneration consists in a *change in the balance of the susceptibilities;* or in a change from sinful action to holy action ; or even in a change from a *nature* [not sinful] inclining to sinful acts, to a nature [not holy] inclining to holy acts ?

" The Catechism brings distinctly to view a Covenant made by God with Adam, the father of the race ; a covenant including all his posterity. This doctrine has ever been viewed by the greatest divines, as a kind of corner-stone in theology ; absolutely essential to explain many things in the gospel system, which otherwise would remain forever dark and inexplicable. It is therefore perfectly natural that the avowed enemies of religion should assail it, as they have actually done, with inveterate hostility, and with blasphemous ridicule. But can it be consistent, in a Professor who has taken the Catechism as his Creed, to explode the doctrine, by teaching that there is no evidence of any covenant of works between God and Adam, as the father of the race ; or with Adam, including his posterity ?

" The Catechism declares an Atonement, such as involves

a full satisfaction made by the Redeemer to the offended law and justice of God. It speaks of Christ as "undergoing the wrath of God" (meaning, the *manifestations* of his wrath), "and the cursed death of the cross." With what consistency can a Professor, who has declared his adhesion to the Catechism, maintain that it cannot be said that Christ's passive obedience frees us from punishment; and that in the case of the penitent, the demands of the law are *evaded*, or *waived?*

"In fine; the Catechism declares most explicitly, that we are justified by the righteousness of Christ, imputed to us, and received by faith. Where, then, is the consistency of maintaining that Christ needed obedience for himself, and could not perform a work of supererogation for others; that if Christ obeyed the law for us, we need not obey it for ourselves, for that the law does not require two obediences; neither in this case, is there any grace in our pardon; that Christ's obedience being imputed to us, involves a double absurdity."

"These are only *specimens* of the doctrines now taught in the Seminary. But they are specimens which comprehend the whole range both of doctrinal theology, and experimental religion. The doctrines are at irreconcilable war with the genuine doctrines of the gospel."

On page 10, he says :—

"I remark here, that there are many mistaken views of the Professor, which have come to my knowledge, which I have not specified. Such are the following: that there was a period when Christ *began* to be the Son of God — that if he was a man, and if he was a *holy* man, he must have had ability to sin — that temporal death makes no part of the penalty of the law, nor is it, properly speaking, the punishment of sin — that it is in the power of human beings to hinder the execution of some parts of the divine decrees. Assertions such as these, I must declare — begging the Professor's pardon — are very reckless, and very dangerous."

These charges were supported by Dr. Lord, and by an anonymous layman, and answered by the late Dr. George

Allen in a pamphlet entitled "The Andover Fuss, or Dr. Woods *vs.* Dr. Dana on the Imputation of Heresy against Prof. Park respecting the doctrine of Original Sin."

The Visitors, after examination of Prof. Park, utterly overruled Dr. Dana's protest against his appointment, and confirmed him : and the Trustees and Visitors entirely overruled or disregarded all Dr. Dana's subsequent charges.

Dr. Dana tells us that for forty-five years he had been a Trustee, — "With the venerable Founders of the Seminary I was intimately acquainted ; I knew their favorite objects and designs; I have carefully pondered their Constitution and Statutes, and I have watched with deep solicitude, the course of things in the Institution from its past inception to the present time."

Remonstrance, p. 5.

And he closes his Remonstrance thus : "But I have done. Should what I have written be successful, under the blessing of God, to promote true and pure religion ; to send a salutary alarm to the churches ; to check the progress of fatal error ; to induce Christians to grasp with new ardor the holy and saving doctrines of the Bible, and to *contend earnestly for the faith once delivered to the saints,* my object will have been attained, and I shall regard myself as the most favored of men."

And yet so variant was the action of the Trustees, under the liberal construction of the Court, from his ironclad notions, that he says he has been "painfully constrained to say their course, for some years, has been to him most mysterious, and inexplicable."

Remonstrance, p. 4.

And elsewhere he says, "My Brethren will permit me to say, that would we guard the Seminary from its dangers, and disencumber it of its evils, we must adopt a new system respecting creeds." — And the "*new system*" was required, because the Trustees refused to take cognizance of what he declares to be "deviations" "certainly essential," "for they are not only *erroneous explanations* of doctrines previously assented to, but contradictions and denials. Witness the cardinal doctrines of *original sin*, of *justification*, and of the *Covenant with Adam.*"

Remonstrance, p. 13.

It was a "new system respecting *creeds*" that Dr. Dana asked in his day, and it is a new system respecting Creeds, his successors ask to-day. They befriend new departures in law, if not in Theology.

Prof. Park, The Associate Creed, p. 86, after stating, among other things, that except Dr. Dana, not one of the Trustees or Visitors "ever intimated to me that he doubted my strict allegiance to the creed" says "I thought that I accepted the Creed in all its details, as well as in its substance. I now think that I have taught all its doctrines in the sense intended by its chief framers."

Nobody will doubt the sincerity and truth of these declarations. And I cite them in connection with Dr. Dana and Dr. Lord, only as confirmatory of how much, under just and proper construction, the Statutes and Creed take in and comprehend.

We come now to the last adjudication of Trustees and Visitors, under the Statutes and this Creed. And this touches again the Abbot Professorship.

On July 2, 1882, the Trustees elected Rev. Dr. Newman Smyth Abbot Professor of Christian Theology, to succeed Dr. Park. I suppose of all the "heterodoxies," and inconsistent holdings and beliefs, charged upon the Respondent, the one most relied upon is that contained in the 11th specification in these words. "That there is and will be, probation after death for all men, who do not decisively reject Christ during the earthly life," etc.

Perhaps no name in this country is more closely connected with the possible hypothesis covered by this charge, than that of Newman Smyth. When he was elected, his writings were before the Trustees, and in their deliberate judgment there was nothing in them, which should prevent the election of their author to his professorship.

The election came to the Visitors for confirmation, and had their most deliberate and careful consideration and judgment.

Let me read from this judgment — "The Board of Visitors of the Theological Institution at Andover, having been duly notified by the Trustees of the election of Rev. Newman Smyth as Abbot Professor of Theology, and having had, after repeated consideration by themselves of his election, a frank and full conference with the Professor elect at which a majority of the Board of Trustees were also present, have adopted the following minute which they hereby lay before the Trustees.

"The Visitors have been convinced of the general harmony of Dr. Smyth's theological views with those which have been identified with the history of the Andover Seminary from the beginning. He frankly and heartily accepts the creed to which the Abbot Professor must subscribe, and affirms that he is surprised to find after a careful study of this creed that it is in such accord with his own views.

"Some of the published works of Dr. Smyth have by many careful thinkers and earnest friends of the Seminary been interpreted as sanctioning views contrary to the doctrines commonly held by our churches and clearly declared in our articles of faith. These views especially relate to sin, the atonement and the future state. A teacher who should countenance, however unwittingly, a departure from the received faith on these points would evidently not be well fitted for the office of instructing young men in the truths of the Gospel. We have therefore carefully examined Dr. Smyth upon these, and also upon his general doctrinal opinions, and he with admirable frankness and with a sincerity which cannot be doubted has made it evident that however he may have been interpreted, his real views upon these themes are in substantial agreement with the characteristic doctrinal position of this Seminary."

Minute of Visitors.

To this minute, the Trustees by their Committee replied, March 23, 1882, from which reply I make the following extract.

"The Trustees of Phillips Academy have received your communication with regard to the election of the Rev. Newman Smyth, D.D., as Abbot Professor in the Theological Seminary which is in their care, and whose interests are, in part, committed to you. They have appointed us a Committee to present to you their reply. The Trustees wish to express their appreciation of the pains taken by the Visitors to reach an intelligent and trustworthy judgment upon the serious matter in which their concurrent action has been sought. They desire, also, to express their gratification that you concur in their judgment regarding the Theological belief of Dr. Smyth, and in their estimate of his character and ability.

"They are glad that the result of your deliberation and investigation is the conviction that the views of Dr. Smyth are in substantial agreement with the doctrines taught in the Seminary in the past, and in harmony with the creed to which the Abbot Professor is required to give his assent."

Trustees' Reply to Minute.

The Trustees conclude by renewing their request for the confirmation of Dr. Smyth.

The Visitors thereupon re-considered their action, and, by a majority of their number, refused to confirm his election. In the Minute then adopted the Board of Visitors say: —
"The Board of Visitors would again express their conviction that the theological views of Dr. Newman Smyth are in general harmony with those which have been identified with the history of the Andover Seminary from the beginning. After his full and explicit acceptance of the creed, and his frank additional statements in response to our inquiries, it is impossible for us to doubt his substantial agreement with the doctrinal position characteristic of this Institution. His natural frankness, his moral earnestness, and his Christian

sincerity are too evident to permit us after our conference with him to raise any question upon this point."

Visitors' Records.

Thus from 1807 to 1887, the construction and interpretation of these Statutes and Creed have been uniform, by Court, Visitors and Trustees. — Insinuations, suspicions, charges of heresy and " heterodoxy " to the Creed have run down the line of Seminary Administration, from the day a dissenting Trustee first raised them against a Founder's professor, to that in which his successor raises them against nearly the whole Faculty of the Institution, and all his associate Trustees. No " heterodoxy " has ever been eliminated, and until to-day no public prosecution has been entertained. Yet, in the administration of the Seminary, have been united, generation after generation, some of the most intelligent, conscientious, learned, orthodox men, clerical and lay, which this Commonwealth has produced.

For eighty years these Statutes and Creed have, without deviation, been construed in the manner I have stated : — strictly and firmly, in every necessity to security ; broadly, tolerantly, and liberally, in every essential to that intellectual, and spiritual freedom and progress, without whose conserving influences, creeds fall from living organisms, to fossils.

These liberal rules and principles of construction, so well established in relation to these identical Statutes, by Court, Trustees, and Visitors, are precisely those everywhere recognized by all Tribunals, civil or ecclesiastical.

They are clearly and distinctly announced by the English Courts in numerous cases, to only one of which I need refer, the great case of Voysey vs. Noble, decided in the Privy Council in 1871.

3 Privy Council Rep. 357.

The court say : —

" Before examining the charges and comparing the proofs adduced from Mr. Voysey's publications with the charges

founded thereon, and with the Articles and Formularies of
the Church alleged to have been contravened, it will be well
to enunciate, briefly, the rules of judicial exposition with
reference to the Articles and Formularies of the Church.

"In this respect we have the guidance of previous and
recent decisions of this Tribunal, expressed in clear and
definite language.

"In the cases arising on the work called '*Essays and
Reviews*,' *Williams* vs. *Bishop of Salisbury*, and *Wilson* vs.
Fendall, Lord *Westbury*, in delivering the opinion of the
Committee, said: 'Our province is, on the one hand, to
ascertain the true construction of those Articles of Religion
and Formularies referred to in each charge according to the
legal rules for the interpretation of Statutes and written
instruments; and, on the other hand, to ascertain the plain
grammatical meaning of the passages which are charged as
being contrary to or inconsistent with the doctrine of the
Church ascertained in the manner we have described.'

"But it is to be observed, that in inquiries of the nature
now before us, this Committee is not compelled, as in cases
affecting the right of property, to affix a definite meaning to
any given Article of Religion the construction of which is
fairly open to doubt, even should the Committee itself be of
opinion (on argument) that a particular construction was
supported by the greater weight of reasoning. Thus, Lord
Stowell, in the case of *Her Majesty's Procurator* vs. *Stone*,
thus expressed himself: 'I think myself bound at the same
time to declare that it is not the duty nor inclination of this
Court to be minute and rigid in applying proceedings of this
nature, and that if any Article is really a subject of dubious
interpretation it would be highly improper that this Court
should fix on one meaning, and prosecute all those who hold
a contrary opinion regarding its interpretation. It is a very
different thing where the authority of the Articles is totally
eluded, and the party deliberately declares the intention of
teaching doctrines contrary to them.'

"We have thought it right to refer to the canons of construction thus judicially expressed, because on the one hand

they allow to the party accused a fair and reasonable latitude
of opinion with reference to his conformity to the Articles
and Formularies of the Church, and on the other they afford
no sanction whatever to the contention of Mr. *Voysey*, that
unless there be found in the publication complained of a contradiction, *totidem verbis*, of some passage in the Articles, he
is at liberty to hold, or rather to publish, opinions repugnant
to or inconsistent with their clear construction.

" As regards those Articles of Religion as to the construction of which a reasonable doubt exists, the question may
arise how far opinions of a similar character to those charged
to be heretical, have been held by eminent Divines without
challenge or molestation, because the proof of their having
been so held may tend to show the *bona fides* of the doubt.
In this respect also we have ample guidance from authority ;
and it will be found that where the Article in question is
subject to reasonable doubt, and eminent Divines have held
opinions similar to those impugned in the case before the
Court, that circumstance alone has been held to be of great
weight in inducing the Court to allow a similar latitude of
construction to the party accused, without itself deciding
upon the construction of the Articles.

" Thus, in the case of *Williams* vs. *The Bishop of Salisbury*
the judgment of the Judicial Committee contains this passage : —

" ' It is obvious that there may be matters of doctrine in
which the Church has not given any definite rule or standard
of faith or opinion ; there may be matters of religious belief
on which the requisition of the Church may be less than the
Scripture may seem to warrant ; there may be very many
matters of religious speculation and inquiry on which the
Church may have refrained from pronouncing any opinion at
all. On matters on which the Church has prescribed no rule,
there is so far freedom of opinion that they may be discussed
without penal consequences. Nor in a proceeding like the
present are we at liberty to ascribe to the Church any rule or
teaching which we do not find expressly and distinctly stated,
or which is not plainly involved in or to be collected from that
which is written ' (pp. 385–7).

" In considering these first three charges, as in the consideration of those that follow, we have been most anxious to arrive at a fair construction of Mr. *Voysey's* writings, not only by examining the context which he has referred to as bearing on the passages cited, but also by attentively considering whether any previous writer, himself in Holy Orders, has been allowed, with impunity, to assert opinions similar to those of Mr. *Voysey*, so as to afford reasonable ground for holding that Mr. *Voysey* has merely availed himself of the privilege of adopting a possible interpretation of the language of the Articles, although it may appear to us that such interpretation is not sound or correct. But we can find nothing of the kind " (p. 391).

" We have fulfilled the duty of examining minutely the Articles of charge exhibited against the Appellant. We have not been unmindful of the latitude wisely allowed by the Articles of Religion to the Clergy, so as to embrace all who hold one common faith. The mysterious nature of many of the subjects associated with the cardinal points of this faith must, of necessity, occasion great diversity of opinion, and it has not been attempted by the Articles to close all discussion, or to guard against varied interpretations of Scripture with reference even to cardinal Articles of Faith, so that these Articles are themselves plainly admitted, in some sense or other, according to a reasonable construction, or according even to a doubtful, but not delusive, construction. Neither have we omitted to notice the previous decisions of the Ecclesiastical Courts, and especially the judgments of this Tribunal, by which interpretations of the Articles of Religion, which by any reasonable allowance for the variety of human opinion can be reconciled with their language, have been held to be consistent with a due obedience to the Laws Ecclesiastical, even though the interpretation in question might not be that which the Tribunal itself would have assigned to the Article " (pp. 404–5).

These rules are equally recognized by the authorities of the Presbyterian Church in this and other countries, as the just terms of credal subscription.

" The great dividing question is, how is the subscription or assent to our standards to be interpreted ? Or, with what degree of strictness is the phrase 'system of doctrines,' as it occurs in the ordination service, to be explained ? On this subject, which is one of vital importance, there are, if we do not mistake, two extremes equally to be lamented. On the one hand, there are some, who seem inclined to give the phrase in question, such a latitude that any one, who holds the great fundamental doctrines of the Gospel, as they are recognized by all evangelical denominations, might adopt it ; while on the other, some are disposed to interpret it so strictly as to make it not only involve the adoption of all the doctrines contained in the Confession, but to preclude all diversity in the manner of conceiving and explaining them. They are therefore disposed to regard those, who do not in this sense adopt the Confession of Faith and yet remain in the Church, as guilty of a great departure from moral honesty. This we think an extreme, and a mischievous one. Because it tends to the impeachment of the character of many upright men, and because its application would split the Church into innumerable fragments. These are among its most prominent evil tendencies. That it is an extreme, we think obvious, from the following considerations. It is making the terms of subscription imply more than they literally import. Two men may, with equal sincerity, profess to believe a doctrine, or system of doctrines, and differ in their mode of understanding and explaining them. 2. Such a degree of uniformity never was exacted, and never has existed. The Confession, as framed by the Westminster Divines, was an acknowledged compromise between different classes of theologians. When adopted by the Presbyterian Church in this country, it was with the distinct understanding that the mode of subscription did not imply strict uniformity of views. And from that time to this, there has been an open and avowed diversity of opinion on many points, among those who adopted the Confession of Faith, without leading to the suspicion of insincerity or dishonesty. 3. It is clearly impossible, that any considerable number of men can be brought to conform so exactly in their views, as to be able to adopt such an extended formula of doctrine precisely in the same sense."

3 Princeton Rev. 1831, p. 520–521.

" That this is the true interpretation is evident, 1. From the signification of the words as established by usage, which cannot be arbitrarily altered   The 'system of doctrine' contained in the Racovian Catechism is the Socinian system, and he who adopts that catechism before God and man professes himself to be a Socinian. The 'system of doctrine' contained in the ' Form of Concord ' is the Lutheran system ; that contained in the Apology for the Remonstrance is the Arminian system ; and by parity of reasoning the system of doctrine contained in the Westminster Confession is the Calvinistic system. No man therefore can honestly adopt that confession who is not a Calvinist ; and no man can honestly profess to be a Calvinist who does not adopt all the ' essential and necessary articles ' of Calvinism, as a known and historical form of faith. More than this the words do not signify. More than this no church court has the right to demand. And less than this no such court is authorized to accept. 2. This has been the interpretation put upon the formula in question from the beginning. No man has ever been subjected to discipline in our church for the denial of anything in our standards, which did not include the rejection either of some doctrine held in common by Calvinists and all other evangelical churches, (such as the doctrines of the Trinity, Incarnation, etc., etc.), or of some article of faith regarded as essential to the integrity of the Calvinistic system. 3. To demand more than this would be destructive to the unity of the church. There never was a period in our history in which all our ministers agreed in adopting every proposition contained in the Confession and Catechisms. It is notorious that such agreement does not now exist. On the other hand, to demand less than the adoption of the Calvinistic system in its integrity, would destroy the purity and harmony of the church."

37 Princeton Rev. p. 303–304.

Under the Vatican, in the infallible Roman Catholic Church, they are recognized rules and principles of construction and interpretation.

" Religious orders are not religious sects, having creeds of their own. The Dominican does not differ from the Augustinian, and both from the Jesuit, in the same way as Baptists, for instance, differ from Methodists, or Methodists from Episcopalians. Non-Catholic denominations disagree as to their belief, while Jesuits, Augustinians, and Dominicans have the *same faith*, and are united in the *same judgment*, as all other members of the Catholic Church. The variety of religious orders arises from the special way in which each practises the Evangelical counsels, in accordance with the special end for which it was established and sanctioned by the Church. The questions that gave rise to their different schools are those *outside* of the creed, or which the Church has not settled by any decision. So long as the Church does not speak, each may adhere to his own opinion, provided he be ready to submit his judgment to that of the Church, when in her authority she does speak. The controversy may sometimes seem to bear upon matters already defined; it is not, however, to disprove them, but to unfold them from a scientific point of view. In this doctors may disagree; the theory advanced by one may be in opposition with another's theory, and these again may widely differ from a third and fourth, proposed by other theologians; nor can it be otherwise; but as all of them leave the Catholic dogma untouched, their theorizing, without becoming a part of Catholic teaching, is left unchecked."

Prof. Russo, True Religion, 99.

" As this answer might seem to have been invented for the purpose of shielding ourselves against the attacks of the reformers, it is not out of place to remark that the doctrine thus laid down was not unknown fifteen centuries ago. ' What?' says Vincent of Lerins, ' is there no progress in the Church of Christ? There is progress in it, and very great progress, but it is indeed *progress* and not *change*, — *vere progressus sit ille fidei, non permutatio,* — for by progress a thing increases, remaining still itself; whereas by change it is transformed into something else.' And, after having shown how the human body passes through all the phases of its development, while still retaining its identity, 'even so,' he continues, 'must the Christian dogma, following the law of a similar progress, strengthen with years, increase with time, rise with age, yet still incorruptible and unalterable in its integrity.' "

Prof. Russo, True Religion, 103.

"Ever immutable, ever substantially the same, Catholic dogma, according as it advances in time, dilates its deep bosom, and discovers more and more that treasure which has its source in the Infinite. Now it dispels the lingering shadows of the past from a truth which is to illumine the future. Now it begets, at the appointed time, the conclusions which spring from its eternally fruitful principles, according as the assaults of error urge it on to the development of those divine seeds. Thus dogma goes on increasing without, brightening with all the truths which God raises over his Church, growing larger and clearer in the minds of men, but never changing, never transformed."

Prof. Russo, True Religion, 105.

I cite this work because it has been commended to me by high Church authority, as accurate and reliable.

These principles are impliedly and necessarily recognized in the Statutes themselves.

The Founders built their Institution, not merely for their own, but for all time. They protected it with a creed, compromised originally, but to be, not an anchor holding forever, those administering the Institution to "a phase of orthodoxy in the past," but ever and always to each of them a living, personal, present faith.

Over all they put a Board of Visitors, who having them-

selves first subscribed this creed, should construe and interpret it in all cases, brought judicially before them.

That such construction might be guarded from theological
bias, they put two clergymen and one layman on this Board.

That it might not suffer by the impetuous ardor of youth,
nor the freezing conservatism of age, they provided that no
one should be eligible as a Visitor till forty years of age,
and that no one should remain on the Board after seventy
years of age. The Board was to be one of acting, living
men, identified with the present, not with the past.

That they might be guarded against all inadvertence, they
are required to read the whole associate Statutes at each
annual meeting of the Board, and to renew their creed subscription every five years. So constituted they were to be
as in the Founders " place and stead," " the *Guardians, Over-
seers*, and *Protectors* of the Foundation forever," subject
only to the Supreme Visitors, " to determine, interpret, and
explain the Statutes of this Foundation," " and in general
to see that our true intentions, as expressed in these, our
Statutes, be faithfully executed; always administerting justice impartially, and exercising the functions of their office
in the fear of God, according to the said Statutes, the Constitution of the Seminary, and the Law of the Land."

The creation of so complicated an original and appellate
jurisdiction " to determine, interpret, and explain the Statutes of the Foundation " clearly indicates that the Founders
supposed questions upon their construction would arise in
the progress of the administration of the Seminary. — While
their ultimate Visitors, the Supreme Court, on a question
raised on the construction of these very Statutes, had unmistakably told them the principles which the " Laws of the
Land " would apply.

It only remains to ask if anything has been shown to have
been done or held by this Professor which makes him, in
subscribing this creed, guilty of evasion, untruth, and dishonesty. Modify as you please, generalize as you may, soften
all you can, in plain common words the charge comes to this.
if you find him guilty, I pray you as an act of justice, put

your finger on the act, or opinion condemned, that at last we may know what our crime is.

Burke said he could not indict a whole people, but these complainants, with more felicity, have practically embraced in their charges, a whole Faculty, all but one of a Board of Trustees, and a majority of the great denomination of which Andover is the cherished Institution, and you the honored representatives. — Under these charges the personal consequences of this trial are of great significance. But its public import is vastly more significant. You may indeed try to anchor this institution, and the denomination which sustains it, to " a particular phase of orthodoxy in the past," but I have so little confidence in the anchorage that I shall be only too glad, if you do not strand and shipwreck both in the hazardous attempt. I know you appreciate the magnitude and importance of your decision. I fervently pray it may be " according to the best light God shall give you."

EX-GOV. GASTON'S ARGUMENT.

May it please your Reverend and Honorable Body:

My words will be few, my speech will be brief; for I think that after Dr. Egbert C. Smyth appeared before you in the full proportions of a noble and Christian manhood, and made his defence, the day of his trial was over. Then what need of further speech from me or from any one? I should feel that I should trespass upon your time if I should undertake to reiterate in feebler form and phrase the words wh'ch you have heard from his lips.

I approach this discussion with diffidence, for it leads me aside from the ordinary duties of my professional labor, into fields that can be more appropriately occupied by those whose lives have been consecrated to the service of God, and whose duty it is to lead men upward and onward to eternal happiness and peace. But there are some matters which have not yet been presented at length, that I desire briefly to submit to your consideration.

And in the first place, what is this trial? What are its issues? what are its purposes? This is not a trial for breach of trust. These are not the prosecutors, this not the tribunal, and this not the respondent for such a case. What is it? It is a trial that should rise to a high moral and religious plane, and which should be conducted in the spirit of fairness, candor and truth. I do not remember any important trial where I ever acted as counsel before where there was not an opening of the case, — we have not had any thing in the nature of an

opening here ; and it seems to have been the policy of the
other side to prevent us from having any thing in the nature
of a statement of their case or of the particular grounds upon
which they intended to rely. We have their statements as
they appeared in print, at the first hearing on certain preliminary matters, and that is all we have, except certain
remarks which Judge Hoar has made, to which I shall hereafter respectfully invite your attention. Why is it, that in
the consideration of this great subject the ordinary method
has been departed from, and we have nothing from the complainants as to the course of argument which they intend to
pursue?

I have said, Mr. President, this is not a trial for breach of
trust. If the heirs of these donors, these great donors, great
in purpose and charity, see fit to go before the proper tribunal
and claim that the funds which their ancestors dedicated, as
they thought, to the service of God, are misapplied, then they
would go before the Court having jurisdiction of trusts, and
present the case there. The trustees, and not this respondent
hold the purse strings. It is not claimed that this respondent has any control of the moneys of the Institution at
Andover, or that he has the power to control them : and if
he attempted such misapplication, this is not the tribunal
to furnish the remedy.

My friend Prof. Baldwin rather complained in his address
of yesterday that we had not had the benefit of an opening,
and I make the same complaint to-day. In response to
Prof. Baldwin's complaint, Judge Hoar replied as follows:

" We have heard that statement so often, sir, that I think
we had better repudiate it once and for all. We did open
our case. Judge French stated it at the original hearing.
We have not duplicated that opening by going over it with
the same three gentlemen again, because we have divided
these three complaints, which were lumped together, into
five separate ones. We have taken for granted that the
time which was spent was profitably spent, at any rate to
save any repetition. Our case has been opened elaborately
and stated.

" These gentlemen are charged with heterodoxy, by which I understand and mean not the entertaining of any untrue or erroneous opinion. That is all I meant when I said there was no charge of heresy. They may entertain the soundest opinions that were ever held, the most progressive, coming nearer and nearer to the light, and approved by God and man. Our position is that it is heterodoxy, because the framers of the Andover Creed have required a certain conformity to that Creed, and the sole question which we present for your decision, as the Board of Visitors, is whether they have departed substantially. I should not criticise very much all we have heard about the true mode of looking at the Creed, within the limits of interpretation consistently with holding a more solid front of theological belief."

Therefore, I repeat this is not a suit for money, not a suit for redress for breach of trust. It is a prosecution for nonconformity to a certain Creed, and you are asked, if you find that there is such nonconformity, to pronounce your judgment and sentence. Prof. Egbert C. Smyth may be travelling in the pathway which leads to the gates of heaven, but that is of no importance here. The streams which issue from the institution of which he is the head, may be as " pure as Siloah's brook that flowed fast by the oracle of God," but no matter for that, this Reverend and Honorable tribunal is nevertheless requested to admonish or remove him. The motive and the animus of the prosecutors are as we think quite apparent. The respondent must interpret the Creed as they interpret it. He must consent to be bound by their fetters. If his belief is in substantial accordance with the Creed, that, I think, is not enough to satisfy these prosecutors. He may be travelling in the pathways which lead to eternal blessedness and truth, but, if there be any departure from the Creed in its severest and sternest construction and interpretation, he must be punished. The eminent senior Counsel of the complainants has with honesty stated what his position is. I desire to read his statement to you. I beg your attention to it. It is the statement made by a very able man, who is intellectually as well as morally honest. That statement is as follows : —

"I ought to say, perhaps, at the outset, Mr. Chairman and gentlemen, that I presume it would be very distinctly understood by the members of this tribunal, that I am not here to discuss any theological questions. I very much suspect that my clients would consider me entirely incompetent to be trusted with any such duty as that, and fear whether I might not, in my own private personal capacity, away from this reverend presence and these weighty considerations, fall back on Shakespeare's phrase, 'A plague on both your houses,' with great cordiality and good will. Yet that will not, I trust, interfere with my presenting, what I am employed to do, their views of the relation of this tribunal to the case before you, under the technical objections which have been so elaborately and at such length argued by the·distinguished and learned gentleman who has appeared for the respondents. The question here before you is, for your decision mainly, Have the terms of the trust on which certain citizens of Massachusetts chose to place their money been complied with by those having it in charge, or would it be complied with if they allowed a certain thing to be done or taught in the Seminary at Andover, which it is charged before you has been taught and done.

"Now, that is a matter which is to be determined upon certain legal rules. There are a great many persons in Massachusetts, of whom I confess I am one, who do not believe it is sound public policy ever to make a condition of the vesting of property beyond the life of one generation, on opinions. Nobody can tell where it will lead. Nobody can tell that the donors themselves would entertain all the opinions without modification. But it may be done under the laws of Massachusetts, and you gentlemen have, by accepting your place on the Board of Visitors, charged with the trust which the statute of the founders imposed upon you, undertaken to see that it is honestly and faithfully done.

"Now, if it were the Copernican system, or the Ptolemaic, that was in controversy, if a man under the laws of Massachusetts, who owns his money, which he has accumulated by honest industry, or which has come lawfully into his possession, which the law allows him to dispose of, provides that that money shall be appropriated to the vindication of the notion that the earth is flat, and that the sun goes around it day by day, and you undertake a trust in which that is to be maintained, if you find that the persons who are receiving the money are teaching something that differs decidedly from that, you do not execute your trust,—perhaps you would not hold so absurd a one as that,—but you do not execute your trust, if you do not decide that question honestly and fairly when it is before you for adjudication."

Now, there is the proposition, and I beg your Honor's attention to the illustration which my brother has given. If a man gives his money to teach the false doctrine that the earth is flat, then it is the duty of the persons who have that money in trust, to cause that falsehood to be taught. And, by analogy, if there be in this written Creed of Andover something which you know, and I know, and the world to-day knows, is false, you are invoked by the argument and the logic of my brother, to execute the trust in such a manner that the false things shall be taught under your direction. If that is the law, I respectfully suggest that these prosecutors might find better employment than seeking to enforce it.

So far, Mr. Chairman and gentlemen, I have discussed the general and the moral aspects of the case. I come now to this complaint, and I ask your attention to it. The rules of law (which in this regard are also the rules of common sense) require that when a man comes before any tribunal with grave charges against another man, it is his duty to prove them. That burden, by all moral and legal rules, rests upon these prosecutors. And what have they done? We have heard the sounding notes of preparation. It has been heralded forth that this respondent was to be proved guilty, not only of heterodoxy, but of heresy, and that this noble man, whose high character and learning nobody is bold enough to question, had broken solemn promises, and been false to his faith, and to his duty. That is the charge. In the name of all that is just, he who prefers such charges should be held by you up to the full measure of his duty, either to abandon the charges or to prove them.

Who is Professor Egbert C. Smyth, and who are his associates in this defence? Professor Egbert C. Smyth is a man of learning, a man of piety, a man of truth. He has been for more than a score of years a teacher in this institution which so many people love. Under his teachings have sat scores and hundreds of men, who have gone forth to the whole world, and through them the voice of Andover has been heard at home and abroad.

I think that all of the Professors, who are here accused of heresy or heterodoxy, are admitted to be men of piety, of ability, and of learning. No one ventures here to assert that any of them lack these important qualities.

How are the charges proved against this respondent and his associates? My brother French offered in evidence some extracts from a book written by these Professors or some of them called "Progressive Orthodoxy," and some extracts from two "Andover Reviews," and sat down. He then said in substance that that was his case. Progressive Orthodoxy! I do not think my brother or his clients love the word "progressive." It alarmed them, and if it had not been for that fatal word in the title, I doubt whether anybody would have found any heresy in the book. The word "progressive" suggests at once to them the ideas of heresy. "Progressive Orthodoxy" and two "Andover Reviews" are the proofs which these gentlemen bring of the grave offences charged "of a breach of trust which has scarcely a parallel in an age filled with them." Would you not have thought, Mr. Chairman, that some out of the scores and even hundreds of men who have been taught by Dr. Smith, who have heard his words, and have listened to his teachings would have been brought here to testify to his heresy or heterodoxy? What has he taught in the lecture-room at Andover? What has he proclaimed from the pulpit? Hundreds of living men have listened to his teachings, and know how he has discharged the duties of his office. Thousands have heard him from the pulpit. These men know whether he has taught or proclaimed any thing which is heretical in its character, or which is opposed to the Creed of Andover. None of these men are brought here to testify. Of his teachings in his office, you have learned nothing from the prosecutors. They rest their case upon these garbled extracts, torn from their context and perverted from their true meaning. That is all the evidence they have produced. And when my brother French said this was their case and sat down, as we thought, with a solemn and somewhat distressed countenance, we were amazed. As I looked at him, there came rushing upon my recollection at that moment a story which I once heard. It was given as a specimen of Scotch wit. A Scotch clergyman having wrought himself into tears, one of his parishioners turning to another said, " What is the minister grieving about ? " The reply was " Were you where he is, and had as little to say for yourself as he has, you would grieve too."

It is a well-established principle, established by that learned tribunal of which my brother Hoar was once an ornament, that the absence of testimony which can be produced, is a circumstance which courts and juries are to consider. Has Prof. Smyth taught any heresy in the lecture room at Andover, has he taught heterodoxy there? Where are the pupils? Where are the Trustees, under whose immediate supervision he performs his duty? Has any one of them heard it? Not one. Who has? Nobody has heard it; and the only proof of his heterodoxy given, is from perverted and garbled quotations to which I have referred.

I ask the attention of this Honorable Court to a statement of Prof. Smyth in his answer:

" In conclusion, I would respectfully call your attention to the number and character of the offences for which I am arraigned. I am charged with disbelieving the trustworthiness of the Scriptures as a religious guide ; with holding a humanitarian view of Christ ; with denying the doctrine of the Trinity ; with disowning man's free agency, his universal sinfulness and guilt, and exposure to the penalty of the law; with rejecting the doctrine of Atonement by the sufferings and death of Christ; with teaching that salvation is not 'wholly of grace;' and with breaking 'in repeated instances,' 'solemn promises.' Such accusations have no reality to me. I accept the Creed of the Seminary, interpreting it by no private opinion, but according to the well understood and commonly recognized laws of Creed-acceptance, laws which have been in vogue in this country from the earliest times, and which have governed subscriptions in the history of this Seminary from the beginning, and which have been recently recognized by your Reverend and Honorable Body. I welcome, if for any reason you deem such scrutiny necessary or useful, the most searching examination possible into the accusations now preferred, and I shall be pleased to expedite and facilitate such examination to the full extent of my power.

"At the same time, I hereby deny that I hold any beliefs, or have taught doctrines or theories not in harmony with or which are antagonistic to the Constitution or Statutes of the Theological Institution in Phillips Academy, Andover, in which I am Brown Professor of Ecclesiastical History, or contrary to the 'true intention' of its founders, as expressed in these Statutes, or that I believe or teach any thing antagonistic or opposed to the Creed of the said Institution, or in violation of the statutory requirements or the 'true intention' of the Founders as expressed in their Statutes."

Is Prof. Smyth an intelligent man? Does he know whereof he speaks? Is Prof. Smyth a truthful man? Then, if he be intelligent and true, that denial is worth whole pages of accusation. Suppose that these writings which have been put in here from "Progressive Orthodoxy" and from the "Andover Review" were his, although but very few of them are,—but he does not stand upon any such defence as that, —suppose they are his, and he comes in as a true and honest man and says what he has said in solemn phrase before you, does not that utterance sweep away all these accusations and meet and destroy all the evidence they have offered? You

have heard what he says, and who, Mr. President, shall gain-
say what Professor Smyth asserts? If what he says is true,
this is both an answer and a perfect and full defence. Who
shall say that Dr. Smyth does not believe in all the doctrines
of the Creed, when he says he does, and when he says he
has signed it conscientiously and has kept it faithfully?

I shall not go into any theological discussion, and the
suggestions which I am making seem to me to steer clear of
that. But this, I think, even with my limited information
and learning upon the question, I may say: That the Creed
of Andover is not that narrow, bigoted, confined Creed which
many people think it is and must be, remembering the time
of its origin. Taken in its entirety, and it cannot be properly
taken except in its entirety, the Creed is a broad one, comparatively, and is not confined to the narrow, limited construction which my brethren on the other side, or their
clients, attempt to place upon it. It is, Mr. Chairman and
gentlemen, no Procrustean bed, upon which the limbs of him
who is placed upon it, if they are not long enough to fill it,
are to be stretched to its length, or, if they are too long, are
to be lopped off, to meet its proportions. That is not the
Andover Creed. That is the Creed which our opponents
seek to have you impose upon the Seminary. That is the
kind of furniture you are asked to provide for the bed-cham-
bers at Andover. It is not such a Creed, by any just or by
any proper construction of words.

Prof. Smyth has gone over the matter in detail, with an
exhaustive learning, and with a fervid eloquence, and has
shown you, if human logic can show you, that these extracts
that have been put in evidence, if properly taken, upon any
honest construction, violate no article in that Creed. I have
said that it is a broad and a liberal Creed. I think I can
further say that it contains within itself some elements of
contradiction, because it was not the work of one mind, nor
was it the work of concurrent minds, meaning by concurrent,
minds which travel in the same pathway. It was the result
of a compromise, and as you, with your power of analysis,
look it over, you find that when it is separated into parts,

and disjointed, some parts of it oppose other parts. But that has not been the practical construction of it heretofore. The practical construction of the Andover Creed, as appears clearly from the historical matters which have been presented to you, has been to take it as a whole, and you cannot fairly take it any other way.

Now, then, I say for reasons which, if I should undertake to repeat them, would sound feeble in comparison with the way in which they have been put by Dr. Smyth and by my associates, there is nothing in the evidence which the complainants have produced which shows that any doctrine held by Dr. Smyth or by his associate professors, contravenes any substantial doctrine of the Creed.

I have said that the Creed was the work of several minds holding somewhat varied opinions, and that the framers of the Creed came as near together as men of varied opinions could come, and gave expression to their beliefs in the form of the Creed which has stood the test of years. I have said that it is a broad Creed. Were it otherwise in its general character, it would be redeemed by the clause which I propose now to read to you:

"And furthermore, I do solemnly promise, that I will open and explain the Scriptures to my pupils with integrity and faithfulness; that I will maintain and inculcate the Christian faith, as expressed in the Creed by me now repeated, together with all the other doctrines and duty of our Holy Religion, so far as may appertain to my office, according to the best light God shall give me."

I see here something more than the dawn of the light of religious freedom. I see that upon Andover Hill, years and years ago, the light of truth burst upon men. I see that upon Andover Hill shackles were broken. I learn that upon Andover Hill it was long ago determined that devout and Christian men might teach the doctrines of the Creed according to the best light God should give them. And has Prof. Egbert C. Smyth, by anybody's contention, done otherwise than to teach the doctrines of the Holy Religion and of the Creed, according to the best light God has given him? Did not that sentence, or part of a sentence, "according to the best light God shall give me," have a most significant meaning? Did not that open to religious and devout men, who agreed to the general and substantial doctrines of the faith, a certain degree of liberty, and was it not intended it should do so? Will anybody, Mr. Chairman and gentlemen, who recognizes his obligations to God, and his duties to man say, upon the facts which are before you, that Dr. Egbert C. Smyth has done any thing but teach the doctrines of his faith according to the best light God has given him? And if he has done that, he has done what he is permitted to do by this very Creed, and by the form of the obligations which he has assumed.

Now, let me repeat a little. I say that the proof has failed and ingloriously failed. Where are the living witnesses who can come here and by their speech condemn Prof. Smyth, if he is to be condemned? No voice from the lecture room comes here by any procurement of these prosecutors. No voice from any pulpit which he has filled comes here by any procurement of theirs. There has been none of that essential and important testimony which ought to have been adduced by those who make this charge of broken promises. The testimony from Progressive Orthodoxy, and those two Reviews, taken in the spirit in which they were written, and honestly interpreted prove nothing; and I challenge the reverend and legal gentlemen who shall respond, to meet, if they can, the candid and clear statements and forcible logic of Dr. Smyth.

You, Mr. Chairman and gentlemen, constitute a perpetual Court. It never ceases to exist. Different men may fill your seats, but the Court is perpetual. If what I have heard read here by Dr. Smyth and by my brother Russell, who is very familiar with matters connected with your institution, be true, then there has been no time in the history of Andover when so few charges of heterodoxy or heresy could have been made as now. You have heard the doctrines and utterances of the old divines. You have heard of old controversies at Andover, of differences of opinion in former years, which furnished better reasons for charges of heresy than now can possibly exist. I do not think from what I have learned that there has ever been an entire concurrence of opinion in matters of faith in the officers and teachers of this Institution. I do not think there ever can be such concurrence. Men will complain and if they bring all their complaints before you, you will be not only a perpetual court, but you will be in perpetual service. My brethren could find enough in these old documents which have been read for the employment of a dozen courts, if the authors had not passed away, and gone to their great account. But when I remember all this, and see what the practice of this Institution has been, I respect it the more, because it has allowed, within certain limits, the practice of free religious thought. It has been allowed, and I am happy to say that this tribunal has allowed it, — that we have proved here.

How did most of these five professors enter upon their sacred service at this Institution? It was done in the way which they have stated here, in which there was not an absolute taking of the Creed without qualification, which qualification was made before the Trustees and the Visitors in open assembly at the time of their being installed. What voice, Mr. President, was raised then to say that they should do that which my brother Hoar now claims they ought to have done? Who said to them: "If the Creed says the earth is flat, you, also, must say it is flat. You shall not qualify it. It is an ironclad Creed. The sternest interpretation, even in these days of light, shall be placed upon it, and if we can catch you tripping in any little detail, in any thing not essential, we will prosecute, or persecute, you for heterodoxy or heresy. Our Creed is chained to the past. Its chains shall not be broken. If you are in the road of progression, your ways are not our ways. Progression is heresy"?

Now let us see the spirit, Mr. Chairman and gentlemen, which, knowing this Board as I do I should expect, and the public would expect, would be manifested by it. One of the grave charges which the prosecutors make here is that

Prof. Smyth maintains, holds and inculcates a possible probation after death. Now, Prof. Newman Smyth had written a book, before he was presented as a professor at Andover, and this book was known. And I beg to read from it.

"Then there is a third truth which seems to be left in the shadows of the Gospel of the Kingdom; and that is the nature and intent of the divine administration of Hades — the place of departed spirits — from the time the dying leave the present world until the judgment day. There is a period of life after death; and before that last great day, when this world-age shall be over, of which the Bible gives us some intimation, but concerning which it affords no distinct revelation. It does tell us something concerning that intermediate state: enough at least to assure us that it shall not prove to be a loss of consciousness, and purposeless sleep of ages, for souls awaiting the great day of awakening."

"Such are the Biblical elements of the doctrine of the intermediate life, and they ought not to be quietly ignored by Orthodox theology, or left unadjusted to our whole teaching concerning the last things. If it be said that there is danger, that the consideration of these obscure passages might lead individuals to whom the Gospel is now preached to cherish fallacious hopes of a second probation after death, it is also true that the failure to take into account these hints and possibilities of Scripture, may involve for us, the righteousness of the government of God in great difficulty and betray us into an un-Scriptural dogmatism with regard to God's dealing with those who die without the Gospel. The only really dangerous thing is error — to go beyond or to fall short of, the truth of revelation — Romanism in Luther's day, had gone far beyond it; but that is no reason why Protestantism should now fall short of it."

These words were written by the Rev. Newman Smyth before his examination. If any as strong language has been used by his brother, Egbert C. Smyth, upon that question, I have failed to see it. What did this enlightened Board do? I hope that I may be corrected if I am mistaken; I state now what I have heard. What did this enlightened Board do? They did not confirm the nomination of this gentleman to his professorship, but expressly declared that it was not in consequence of any of his theological views. You followed in the light of the example of your predecessors. You rec ognized the spirit of religious freedom, and did not reject the nomination on account of the views of the candidate upon this question. But what are you asked to do now? You are asked to punish Dr. Egbert C. Smyth for entertaining the same views which his brother entertained, and which you have declared did not furnish a reason for rejection of the nomination of the latter for a professorship at Andover. You are asked for this among other reasons to say that his voice shall be heard no more at Andover.

There is one thing as to the purposes and wishes of our brethren and of these prosecutors, of which we have not been clearly informed. What do they wish you to do with Dr. Egbert C. Smyth? My brother, Judge Hoar, in the words which I have read to you, recognized the candor of this respondent, and he, as does everybody else, recognizes in him true manhood and the spirit of a devout Christian. What do the prosecutors want you to do with such a man, — a rare man, whose equal and peer in all respects it will be difficult to find? What do they want you to do with this great teacher and upright Christian man? Will you send him from the halls of Andover, or will you keep him there and fetter him? One or the other thing they must want you to do, or else they have no occasion to be present here. I suppose that is what Dr. Wellman wants, — one of the Trustees, who did not desire to trust his own body to do the duty which the Statutes imposed upon them, of investigating heresy and heterodoxy; did not like to trust them, but stepped out-side and came here, signing himself "Trustee." That is what Dr. Wellman, I suppose, wants, but I think he will de-sire it long before he will get it. And he wants these other gentlemen, a magnificent Faculty, removed, or trammelled, or censured. If you send them away, that will of course be the end of them at Andover, but not elsewhere. If you fetter them, or trammel them, or admonish them, the days of their

usefulness at Andover will be over. What are you going to
do? For what purpose was this high, grave and important
tribunal called together but to do one or the other of these
things? But with the most profound respect for this tribunal, I say that to do either one of these things would be, —
I measure my words, — an outrage. While I respect all
tribunals (and especially this), that have in charge matters
of important public concern, I must be pardoned for saying
that there is a tribunal that is above and over them all. I
allude now not to that great tribunal, to which we all must
at length submit ourselves, but to that human tribunal, the
tribunal of intelligent, honest and Christian public opinion,
a tribunal, as Mr. Webster said, which men, associations, and
even nations must regard.

Now, to do what these gentlemen ask you to do, would
be not only to outrage honest, true, public sentiment, but
to outrage the principles of religion, justice and law.

Mr. Chairman, I began by saying that I had but a few
words to utter. I fear I have gone beyond my suggestion,
certainly I have gone beyond my intention. Andover is a
place of much religious importance. I would like to read at
this point, possibly a little out of its connection, an extract
from the words of the donors. It sometimes, perhaps not
very often, happens that God gives to large hearts large
means — it was so here. Let me read it, and commend it to
the attention of the four gentlemen who institute and prosecute these proceedings.

" To the Spirit of Truth, to the Divine Author of our
faith, to the Only Wise God, we desire in sincerity to present
this our humble offering ; devoutly imploring the Father of
Lights, richly to indue with wisdom from above all His servants, the Visitors of the Foundation, the Trustees of the
Seminary ; and with spiritual understanding the Professors
therein ; that, being illuminated by the Holy Spirit, their
doctrine may drop as the rain ; and that their pupils may
become trees of renown in the courts of our God, whereby
He may be glorified."

Suppose, Mr. President, a word of yours could bring these

Founders back to life, that they might look upon this scene. Suppose in obedience to your call, they should come here filled with the spirit in which that last utterance of theirs was made, what do you think they would say? Would they look at Egbert C. Smyth, and say to him "Abandon your office, leave the Institution, which our benefactions have founded!"? Can you not imagine that they might say to him, "You have ability, piety and learning. You have been true and faithful. Continue in your service. Point out to men the paths which lead to blessedness and peace, with the best light God has given you"? Might they not say to these prosecutors, "Cease this strife, and obtain, if you can, the spirit under which we made our gifts to this Institution"?

Andover is loved by large numbers of those who believe in the doctrines taught there. It is respected by those outside of it. Its history has been filled with achievements worthy of the love of religion and learning which inspired its origin. Keep it! Keep it faithfully! Let it not become the plaything of human passions, or the instrument of a bigot's zeal. Save it! Rescue it from these troubles, and men will bless you for the service!

STATEMENT OF PROFESSOR WILLIAM J. TUCKER.

Mr. President, and Gentlemen of the Board of Visitors:

IT is not my intention, nor the intention of the respondents who may follow me, to traverse the ground covered in the argument of our honored colleague. We adopt by common consent the views therein expressed in regard to the Creed of the Seminary, and the terms of subscription to it, and we accept the answer therein made to the charges and specifications of the complainants. If now we make further demands upon your time in this hearing — and our demands will not be large — to meet the charges as preferred against us in person, it is because of personal relations which we severally hold to the Creed of the Seminary. There are obligations which apply to us in common, and there are obligations and requirements which derive a special meaning and force from their application to the departments which we individually represent.

Before I pass to my personal defense, I ask your indulgence for the moment to an incidental matter of general interest. During the progress of this hearing, frequent reference has been made in somewhat depreciatory language to the interposition of counsel on behalf of the respondents. I call up the fact of the employment of counsel not for apology but for explanation. The first intimation which we received of these proceedings was in the receipt of a communication from your honorable body containing the charges and specifications of the complainants, accompanied by an order that we file an answer within fifteen days. We had no knowledge whatever of the affair beyond that which was conveyed in the communication before us. We knew nothing of the origin or motive or resources of the prosecution. It seemed to be an organized movement and representative of something, for one of the prosecutors signed himself "a trustee" and the others "a committee of certain of the Alumni."

To this communication we made reply at the specified time, not only without counsel, but without having taken legal advice; and each man made reply for himself, not as in the answer to the amended complaint, when we united in a common reply. It was not until the case began to assume a judicial character under the subsequent orders of your Board, that we introduced counsel, and from that time the case has gone on upon its legal or theological side as either issue has for the time been uppermost. I have recalled this fact, in reference to our first answer, to your knowledge, because it has been overlooked and obscured. You will bear us witness that the original reply anticipated all legal procedures, and that it was direct, frank and specific upon the theological questions at issue.

The charge, Mr. President, upon which I appear before you in this hearing, I now understand to be that of heterodoxy in respect to the Creed, involving the more special charge upon myself in connection with Professor Smyth, according to the terms of our foundations, that I am "not an orthodox and consistent Calvinist." Up to the closing argument for the complainants, there seemed to be no little confusion between the complainants and their counsel as to the exact nature of this prosecution, whether it were for breach of trust or for heresy. The argument to which I have referred seems to settle this question. The Counsel said; "There is no breach of trust suggested against Professor Smyth by me, and there has not been. It must have been only casually, by inference, if it has ever been introduced into these proceedings. We never expected any such thing would be done." And again "I should suppose that if any doctrine, held as a distinctive doctrine by this interesting company of persons, not intended in any way to be approved,

commended or forwarded by the Foundation of the Andover
Theological Seminary, who seemed to be grouped here at the
end of the creed, almost on the principle of the tares, binding them in bundles to burn them, — ' In opposition not only
to Atheists and Infidels, but to Jews, Papists, Mahometans,
Arians, Pelagians, Antinominians, Arminians, Socinians, Sabellians, Unitarians, and Universalists, and all other heresies
and errors,' — I should suppose that there could be no doubt
that if there were anything which could be included in that
list, could be proved and established in this theological discussion as having been taught by a professor at Andover,
you would have no difficulty about it."

Assuming from these admissions that the charge is that of
heterodoxy in regard to the Creed of the Seminary, I will
say that I accept without question, whatever of responsibility may attach to the publication of the articles, and of the
book, from which the citations in support of the charges
have been drawn. I make no distinction between what I
teach and what I publish, alone or in responsible connection
with others, save in this regard — and upon this distinction
I do insist — I endeavor to teach according to the natural
proportion of truth ; I publish according to the exigencies of
public discussion, claiming in this regard the unvexed right
of publication, subject only to fidelity to the Constitution
and Creed of the Seminary in the subject-matter of what I
publish.

My defense is twofold. It covers my personal and my official relation to the Creed.

I answer first ; that the theology of " Progressive Orthodoxy " is a natural and legitimate outcome of the Creed of
the Seminary, especially at the point of greatest contention,
that of probation for all men under the gospel. I may be
allowed to say that there is a presumption in favor of this
theology as consistent with the teachings of Andover, because it is held and put forth by men who are theologically
the product of Andover or of the influences which made
Andover.

In the original form under which the charges were pre-

ferred, three of the four complainants signed themselves as a
Committee of " certain of the Alumni." This term alumni
has in itself a significance which does not necessarily attach
to any merely official connection with the Seminary. It is
suggestive of the more sensitive, if less responsible, relations
of loyalty and affection. In this respect to be an alumnus
is more than to be a professor or a trustee or a visitor.
When therefore a case is made up of certain alumni against
certain professors, it seems to be a case in the interest of
loyalty.

But, in the present instance, of the five accused professors
four are alumni, and of the one who is not an alumnus, though
for a considerable time a graduate student, it may fairly be
said that in what belongs to him by inheritance. and in what
he has earned by long and devoted service, he represents more,
than any other one of us, of this quality of affectionate loyalty. Another professor, I refer to Professor Churchill, passed
immediately upon graduation into the service of the Seminary.
And of the remaining three, Professors Harris, Hincks and
myself, graduating within two or three years of one another,
we came back into the service of the Seminary chiefly because we were alumni. We were not ambitious of the positions which we now fill. Content and satisfied in the work of
the pastorate we returned to Andover at its call because we
loved Andover. We had its traditions ; our roots were in
its soil. And coming to our chairs from the pastorate, not
from fields of speculative thought, but from contact with
men, we brought with us those conceptions of Christian
truth which we have since tried to unfold. For myself it is
absolutely true, that I am conscious of holding no other gospel to-day, in any other spirit or with any other conclusion,
than that which I held in my active ministry, and it never
occurred to me, though in the course of my ministry I crossed
and recrossed the line of my denomination that Andover
would ever summon me to account for my holding of the
gospel as contrary to her traditions, her teachings and her
spirit. I speak now as an alumnus, not as a professor. And
in so speaking I think that I represent at least " certain of

the Alumni." For I remember that when attempts have been made at regularly constituted alumni meetings to inaugurate proceedings like the present, they have ignominiously failed.

I am singled out, Mr. President, in connection with Professor Smyth upon the charge, related, I suppose to the theory of a Christian probation, that I am not an "orthodox and consistent Calvinist." You will allow me to say, without argument, that if I am not "an orthodox and consistent Calvinist," according to the Creed, in my theological convictions and methods, I am nothing. Without permitting myself to put that which is of a name or of a school above that which is of Christ, I believe in Calvinism, not as the Creed found it but as the Creed tried to leave it. I believe in its ruling idea and method as against the idea and method to which it is historically opposed. I locate the hope of man in the power and purpose of God, not in exaggerated and unreal notions of man's ability. Christianity is to me above all things a religion of motives. Calvinism is a religion of motives. It emphasizes the "power of God" unto salvation, though in its older and higher forms it limits the application of the power, shutting it up within an arbitrary election. The Creed takes up this idea of power which inheres in Calvinism and gives it breadth and freedom. To me it is an inspiration, remembering the struggle of which the Creed bears ineradicable marks, which makes the Creed a thing of life and not an instrument of bondage — to me it is an inspiration to follow this idea of divine power and purpose, which the Creed inherits from the Catechism, as it feels its way along till it finds the gateway of universal Atonement, through which it pours its now free and invigorating current. The current which runs through the Creed is Calvinism. The Creed widens its banks. And the natural culmination of the Calvinism of the Creed lies to my mind in the very hope of which I am chiefly called in question, the hope which I reverently entertain without equivocation and without excuse, that God according to the eternal purpose which he purposed in Christ, will see to it that every soul comes into some real relation to Christ's atoning sacrifice before any soul passes into the eternal condemnation. And in the name of the Calvinism of the Creed I protest against the contention of those who, reaching in some other way a like conclusion, who are indignant if a theology with a narrower conclusion is imputed to them, do yet charge me with being heterodox toward the Creed, if I believe that God is saving such as are being saved in the way of consistent Calvinism and of orthodox Christianity.

I have used the latter term, orthodox Christianity, advisedly. For as I believe the philosophy of those who deny the possibility of a Christian probation to all men, leads away from orthodox Christianity. If there be any in these days who accept the dogma of the universal perdition of the race outside Christianity, these are removed from any interest or concern in existing controversies. But among those who refuse to accept the dogma, there can be but two parties, those who look upon man as the subject of redemption, and therefore accessible in some way and at some time to the motives of redemption, and those who look upon man as having a sufficiency of motive in himself under the light of nature, and under the work of the Spirit independent of the cross of Christ. Can there be any doubt as to which of these theories is the more closely related to Calvinism and which to Unitarianism? Can there be any doubt toward which the Creed of the Seminary inclines? If Andover Seminary was established to oppose and counteract any influence it was that of Unitarianism. For this object the more extreme parties in orthodoxy were willing to sink their differences and unite. This is an historic fact which none will dispute. Now I do not charge upon those who hold the theory of salvation under the light of nature that they are Unitarians, but I do wish to suggest to you that in their eagerness to use any and all arguments to combat the theory of a Christian probation, they are making themselves exceedingly familiar with the old time arguments of Unitarians in regard to Christian Missions. And I wish to suggest further that in the impending conflict in this country between Christianity and Naturalism it is of some consequence which way the influence of Andover counts. The present controversy may seem provincial. It is called so by some who have not discovered its larger bearings. But it is the door through which New England theology is to enter in and take its part in the contention to which I have referred, the contention between Christianity and Naturalism. And my study of the Creed convinces me that Andover has in hand a weapon of exceeding keenness and power if its edge is not turned in the very opening of the conflict.

My second answer has to do with my official relation to the Creed. I am a teacher of Homiletics. It is my duty to instruct in regard to the subject-matter and the method of preaching, and show how the truth can be made the instrument of conviction and persuasion in bringing men to Christ.

I answer then in the second place that the method of the theology which is called in question best satisfies the requirements of the Creed in respect to the conduct of my professorship. I am called upon in that Creed to teach the truth in opposition to all errors which are "hazardous to the souls of men." To me this is the most serious part of the Creed. Even in the enumeration of errors which gives to the Creed a somewhat belligerent tone one detects the earnestness and scope of its intention. It was this part of the Creed which chiefly arrested my attention when examining it with a view to subscription. And the terms of my subscription, according to the testimony which I have given you, were in these words — "The Creed which I am about to read, and to which I shall subscribe, I fully accept as setting forth the truth against the errors which it was designed to meet." How was I to carry out the terms of my subscription? How was I to fulfil the intention of the Creed? The question was one of method. I tried to answer it according to my experience. I came to my professorship after a pastoral service of twelve years. The two communities in which my pastorates were served gave me ready and full access to the thoughts of men, especially to the thoughts of men in their scepticism and oppositions to Christianity. And under the study which this intercourse gave me I discovered that error has two means of livelihood. A given error lives because of the truth in it. No error is all error. And it lives because of the error in the truth which opposes it. Error thrives upon all insincerities and exaggerations in the holding of truth. Mohammedanism, to take a remote example of the errors which I am to oppose, lives upon the truth which inheres in it, the truth of God in His unity and sovereignty: a truth so profound and vital that it is impossible for any but the purest type of Christianity to live beside it : a truth which makes it, in the presence of an impure Christianity, a perpetual "scourge of God." Take now an error specified in the Creed which is close at hand and most involved in the present controversy, that of Universalism. Upon what does Universalism rely for its increase? Not simply upon the truths which it holds, for most of these are held in common with the Evangelical denominations. Universalism thrives upon the errors of orthodoxy, upon all exaggerated, untenable, insincere assertions of the orthodox faith. My complainants charge "Progressive Orthodoxy" with teaching toward Universalism. What is their alternative under the Creed? The interpretation which they have sought to put upon the Creed to counteract this tendency is to be seen in their use of the clause respecting those who are effectually called as *in this life* partaking of justification, adoption and sanctification. What must this clause say to be of use to them? Why this, that those only who do *in this life* share in the results of effectual calling, justification, adoption, sanctification and the like, are effectually called, that is saved : all others, including the mass of the heathen, and, by logic, all infants are lost. Now if this is the true interpretation of the Creed it is to be taught. I am to teach my pupils to preach it. Suppose they do preach it ; what better means can they take to build up Universalism ? Is this the way to meet that error ? What is the intellectual difficulty which Universalism seeks to meet and solve ? I have not found many men who disbelieved in future punishment. I have not found it difficult to gain a response from any congregation when preaching upon this doctrine. The intellectual difficulty does not lie in the doctrine itself, fearful as it is, but in the injustice and inequalities of application which attach to it under some representations of it. The state of the public mind in respect to this doctrine of future punishment, so far as I have observed, is precisely like that which existed fifty years ago in respect to the doctrine of election. Men were not then in revolt against the sovereignty of God. They were in revolt against the narrow and arbitrary application of it. They are in revolt to-day against a like narrow and arbitrary application of the Divine justice; they are in revolt against the assertion of a dogma, which assigns the greater part of the human race to perdition without the opportunity of accepting or rejecting its Redeemer.

This much for the Creed on its apologetic side as related to the pulpit. I am more concerned with the Creed on its evangelistic side, for the great end which it has in view is the conversion of men under the proclamation of the gospel. But here it is charged that "Progressive Orthodoxy" takes away the urgency of the gospel, that it changes the accent of the gospel, in the emphasis which it naturally lays on the present. To which I reply that the view there set forth ought to produce, and does produce when accepted, precisely the opposite effect. Why is the preacher able to say to men, "Now is the accepted time." "Now is the day of salvation"? Is it not because of the offer of salvation which has gone before? Suppose a missionary to go up and down Africa and without first offering Christ to men to say to them "Now is the accepted time!" what meaning would his words convey? Words take their meaning from their connection. It is the incoming of Christianity, the offer of salvation, which puts such a meaning into the "now" of men's lives. So the Baptist as he saw the Jewish skies beginning to flush under the dawn of Christianity cried out with a new meaning, "Repent, the kingdom of heaven is at hand." So Peter at Pentecost standing in the shadow of the cross, and beside the open

grave of Christ, could say to men with such result as followed, "Repent and be baptized every one of you for the
remission of sins." And so Paul at Athens, proclaiming a
risen Christ could declare that the times of ignorance God
had overlooked, but now he commandeth all men everywhere to repent. We are so familiar with the call to repentance that we forget that it assumes the gospel. Herein lay
the irrelevancy of all the passages quoted by Dr. Dexter from
the sermons of the early New England divines to prove their
opinion upon the question of a future probation. They all
assumed that their hearers had now the full opportunity of
accepting Christ and therefore there would be no other and
better one, an inference with which we are in full agreement. Herein too lay the significance of the sermon introduced by Dr. Wellman into his argument, in which he
tried to show how those who believed in the possibilities of
men in Christ because of their vital relation to him even in
their sin, would preach to sinners. Listening to that sermon,
even under its unsympathetic statement of the idea, I forgot
for the time the argument, I became indifferent to the irony,
I felt the truth. So I try to teach men to preach Christ to
their fellow-men so that they can say to them, *now*, and now
only, is the accepted time; for now, you have your possibilities in Christ; now your decision is full and final.

Now am I right or am I wrong in this conception of the
Creed as related to preaching? I ask your opinion. I want
to know in some authoritative way whether or no this is
heterodoxy. I ask for no charitable construction of the
Creed in any other than the legal sense of the term. I want
to know what its working construction is. I want to know
how I am to handle the creed in my endeavor to train men
to preach the truth, whether they are dealing with error, or
whether they are dealing with the glorious imperatives of the
gospel.

I conclude this personal statement with a brief reference
to the changes which have taken place since my official connection with the Seminary. I came to Andover in 1880.
That was two years before the present disturbance. My

term of service covers the transition from what is called the
old to what is called the new. The term new departure is
not our term. Two years before the election of Dr. Newman
Smyth to the chair of Theology, that is in the year 1880,
the class entering the Seminary numbered ten. The year
following, 1881, the entering class numbered five. If charges
are brought against the present administration of Andover,
tending to show its decline, let care be taken in the matter
of dates. To-day there are forty-eight undergraduate students at Andover, — this does not include fourth year men or
fellows — giving the Seminary the second place in numbers
among the four Congregational Seminaries of New England
and if I am not mistaken the second place among the Congregational Seminaries in the country in the number of
regular students. And during these years of suspicion and
opposition the graduates of the Seminary have passed without exception into the service of the churches. They all fill
honored pastorates in New England and throughout the
country. Meanwhile I know of no function of the Seminary
which has been reduced. I know of no relation to the
churches which has been broken, not even that relation
which allows the return to the Seminary of gifts of money.
During the past year not less than eighty thousand dollars
have been added intelligently to the funds of the Seminary.
Andover is furnishing to-day as always men for the established pastorates, for arduous and difficult service on the
frontier; she has her quota of men knocking and in waiting
at the doors of the American Board. So far as I can discover as an alumnus the Andover that is, is in spirit and in
method and in result the Andover that was. The true continuity, the real succession is there, and there along the line
of present development, I most assuredly believe that the
true continuity, the real succession will give, under any and
all possible contingencies, the Andover of the future. If I
did not believe this in the loyalty of my heart as an alumnus
of the Seminary, I should not for a moment remain in its
official service. Indeed Mr. President I may say without
affectation that as this hearing has proceeded my chief interest

and concern has changed. I came here anxious to vindicate
my rights in my present holding of truth under the Creed
of the Seminary. It is for you to judge whether the vindication has been made. But my greater anxiety in your
decision is for the Seminary itself. A right is a right in
respect to any man and his work. But what are the interests of five men as compared with the interests of an institution. I agree with the position of the complainants which
subordinates our personal and professorial interests to those
which are higher. I have asked for no charitable construction of the Creed in behalf of our teachings. I ask for no
kind of charity in dealing with our personal interests.

But for the Seminary my thought is more urgent. Under-
neath any rights which inhere in my professorship, I am
conscious of the assertion of the deeper and inalienable rights
which belong to me as an alumnus of Andover, and as such
I venture to ask in my anxiety — what is to be its future?
I ask it in the name of its past. Who has the right to affirm
of the past of any time that it is conservative and not progressive? Who has the right to say this of Andover in the
light of its history? The men who founded Andover builded
well, consciously well, but they builded even better than they
knew, and I believe that they to-day rejoice that they builded
better than they knew — that the principles which they forced
into the Creed were wider and more far reaching than they
dared to conceive.

I ask in the name of a great number of living and working alumni, many of whom are in intellectual sympathy
with its current theology, and many more in sympathy with
its working principles and its general position.

I ask in the name of the natural constituency of the
Seminary, among the young men in our colleges and churches,
whose decision touching Andover awaits your decision.

And yet, even in behalf of these interests, no more than
in behalf of my own, do I dare to ask for charity; for I
have learned to believe that when great interests are at issue
between man and man, and the hearts of men are quick,
the fairest thing on the face of the earth in the eyes of
all, is justice unadorned.

STATEMENT OF PROFESSOR GEORGE HARRIS.

May it please your Reverend and Honorable Body :

My object in addressing you is to explain in part my reasons for assenting to the Seminary Creed when I was inaugurated in 1883, with my reasons for continuing to assent to it, and to add a correction of certain misapprehensions which appear to exist relative to the doctrine of Atonement as it is discussed in Progressive Orthodoxy. As I first took the Creed after the present theological controversy began my relation to it was assumed at the outset in the full light of nearly all the objections which have been urged during this hearing.

When it was proposed to me to become Abbot Professor of Christian Theology in the Seminary, I was engaged in the active duties of the pastorate in Providence and had no intention of changing either the form or the place of my Christian service. I was acquainted with the issues which had been raised by the election of Rev. Newman Smyth to the same professorship, but had not made a thorough examination of the Andover Creed. Before the Trustees took action I studied the Creed and Statutes with more carefulness. When I began this study I was by no means confident that I could give a sincere assent to them nor was I certain that I could subscribe to the Westminster Shorter Catechism with the qualifications of the Creed, as the Abbot Professor is required to do. My attention was first given to the doctrines which are now considered most important and concerning which wide differences of opinion prevail, — the doctrines of the Bible, the Person and Work of Christ, and Eschatology. I was at once favorably impressed with the breadth of statement on these doctrines. Great facts are given but no specific theories are proposed. For example I found that the Creed goes no farther than to indicate the religious function of the Bible and that it distinguishes the Word of God from the Scriptures or writings which contain it. Although I held that every part of the Scriptures in connection with the whole is vitally related to the Divine Revelation it conveys, yet it was at once evident that no theory of a verbally inspired or of an infallible Book free from imperfections in every respect could be required. The Word of God is not the very same thing with the *words* of men into which it has been expressed. I saw that the doctrine of the Creed is identical with the doctrine of Paul as stated to Timothy. "Every Scripture inspired of God is also profitable for teaching, for reproof, for correction, for instruction which is in righteousness; that the man of God may be complete, furnished completely unto every good work." The field of fact is left open to inquiry in order that investigation may discover the relation of divine and human elements in the Sacred Scriptures.

The doctrine of the Person of Christ I found expressed in the well-known and generally accepted statement of the Symbol of Chalcedon than which a better formula has not been framed concerning the fact of the union of two natures in one person. The union of divine and human in Christ is generally admitted to present the most difficult problem of theology, and when I heard one of the complainants arguing that problem as against our views in thirteen propositions I entertained for the moment the pious wish of one of the scholars of the Reformation who near the end of his life said that he should welcome a change of worlds for two reasons, one that he might comprehend the union of the two natures, the other that he might be delivered, to use his very language, from the *rabies theologorum*.

The doctrine of Atonement I could not fail to see is stated in a general form and with complete reserve as to what is called the philosophy of Atonement. It emphasizes the fact, the object, and the extent of Atonement made by the sufferings and death of Christ, but the only approach to a theory is the declaration that Christ exercised the priestly office.

The doctrine of Eschatology, as stated in the Creed presented no difficulty except that the language in which the fate of the wicked is described I found to be somewhat more expressive of physical suffering than other Scriptural language which I myself should have selected to express the same belief; namely, the final and irreversible doom of those who are incorrigibly wicked. I assumed that the framers of the Creed held opinions on that subject somewhat more materialistic than the opinions which are held at present. At that time, as I have already stated in my testimony, I had reached no settled conclusion concerning God's dealing with those to whom the gospel is not presented. It then seemed to me that the Scriptures touch that question only incidentally, and that they give no unmistakable utterance. I had, as Bushnell used to put it, hung the question up in my mind. I did not, however, discover that the Creed required one to hold the distinct opinion that no person who is deprived in this life of the ordinary means of grace can have any other opportunity of salvation. The Creed seemed to me to be treating Eschatology and all other doctrines on the basis of a received gospel and of man's duty and destiny in view of the fact that he has the gospel. Although I had not then accepted the opinion for which I am now blamed I did not understand that I must definitely reject it. One, that is, could at least be Agnostic concerning the intermediate state of those who do not have the gospel, since the Creed says nothing about it. If I had then known what I now understand to be the opinion of my colleague in the Stone professorship, which amounts to a confession of ignorance on the subject, I should not have supposed that the Creed requires him to go farther than that. If the Creed obliges one to hold an absolute and exhaustive negative concerning God's dealing with heathen nations I could not have assented to it, nor could I assent now. I understand my accusers to maintain that the Creed imposes the opinion that for all human beings without any exception whatever there is no opportunity of salvation but

that which is given in the earthly life. I should not have
dreamed of ascertaining the relation of the Creed to the
possibility of Christian probation for the heathen by surmising
what the Founders *would* have thought *if* the question had
been presented to them. I think there would have been a
variety of answers, and that some of them would have said
they did not know. I supposed that the only proper course
is to bring given opinions concerning which the Creed is
silent into the light of the principles or essential doctrines of
the Creed, and in such a relation to reach, if it were possible,
a conclusion. I turned to the Catechism, which as some have
held, dominates the Creed, and discovered that it is entirely
silent concerning the fate of the wicked, even of those who do
have the gospel. I also believed, as I subsequently declared to
the Visitors, that under the Creed there is liberty to hold the
opinion that those who do not have the gospel in this life may
have it in the life to come. I was also aware that their decision in the case of Rev. Newman Smyth covered this opinion.
I had never believed that any man has a second probation
under the gospel, and in this respect agreed heartily with the
opinions of the Founders — as I agree now.

I then turned to other portions of the Creed concerning
original sin, election, natural ability, the covenants, etc. It
was not till then that difficulties arose. As a theory of moral
heredity the doctrine of Federal Headship was repugnant to
me. The distinctions of natural and moral ability seemed to
me metaphysical refinements, to which I did not care to commit myself, although my judgment of them is now more favorable. These and kindred clauses pertaining to man, and not
the clauses which embody revealed truth concerning God,
were to me the defective portions of the Creed. It was not
the theology, but the psychology and anthropology of the
Creed before which I hesitated. I remembered indeed that the
only instructor in theology I ever had, my distinguished predecessor in the Abbot professorship, who, as I knew, had had
long practice in taking this very Creed, I remembered that he
poured derision and ridicule on the doctrine of Federal Headship, and that he declared the covenants of grace and redemp-

tion to be figurative and poetical expressions, in order to reach the conclusion that no objection could be made against a figure of speech. Still, I must decide for myself, and at length I reached the conclusion of common sense, that these statements stand for essential facts and doctrines; that Federal Headship signifies the doctrine of depravity and moral heredity as including the entire race, that theories of ability and inability signify man's responsibility and opportunity under the gospel, that the doctrine of election signifies that the individual's confidence of salvation does not rest merely on his own purpose of yesterday, and that it is certain God will redeem to himself a holy people ; and all of these opinions were real to me. That is to say, I accepted the substance of doctrine represented by these statements, a substance which in several cases was to me so vital and solid, that in comparison the statements of the Creed seemed to be but the shadow. I felt, sir, as it is said some of the Puritans who lived before the Westminster Confession was framed felt with regard to the phrases of the thirty-nine articles which they considered too lax, that I could take these inadequate statements of the Creed with "a godly interpretation." However, I could not be entirely satisfied without submitting my difficulties to the Board of Visitors, and having the benefit of their advice and judgment. The result was an agreement that the Creed should be taken as expressing substantially the system of truth taught in the Holy Scriptures.

It is noticeable, gentlemen, that the charges most urgently pressed by the complainants do not touch opinions which are covered by specific and clear statements of the Creed, but only opinions concerning doctrines which the Creed introduces in the most general terms. The weight of this accusation bears on our views of the Bible, Atonement, and Eschatology concerning which the Creed is indefinite and reserved. At other points it would have been much easier to argue disagreement. That is to say, the doctrines selected are those which happen just at present to be most in dispute, and it is evident we are opposed not so much because on these doctrines we are antagonistic to the Creed, but rather because our opinions differ from the opinions of our accusers. Such difference we do not for a moment deny.

After my confirmation by your Board, the Creed passed almost entirely out of my thoughts. I remained through the winter with my parish, and at the end of four months was dismissed by Council. Then followed the preparation of an Inaugural address, the fitting up of a house at Andover, and also a growing and appalling sense of what I had undertaken as a teacher of Christian theology. I confess to you, sir, that at times I was profoundly thankful that the Seminary was reduced in numbers and that my first year's course would be heard by only a handful of students.

In addition to the heavy burdens which, as I often felt, I had unwisely assumed, I was made aware at the time of my inauguration of conditions which would make my work still more arduous. It then appeared, in the discussions of the only public and regularly called meeting of the Alumni which within the last four years has considered the theological status of the Seminary, that a determined opposition was to be expected. It was not known that any of the new professors, or indeed that any member of the entire faculty, save one, entertained hope for the unevangelized heathen. But we were not even to have a fair opportunity to prove ourselves. The impressions I then received from intimations and public threats have been abundantly verified. There have been petty insinuations, and constructions offered which if they were not misrepresentations were astonishing misunderstandings. The Seminary was few in numbers as we took it from a former administration, and we had no expectation, with so many untried teachers, of large additions at the outset, yet a journal edited by one of the complainants condescended to make a calculation which by reckoning in lecturers, retired professors, and even the librarian, showed that to each instructor in Andover Seminary there was in attendance one student and five-sevenths of a student. Although our growth has not been rapid, for no efforts have been spared publicly or privately to turn students away from us, similar calculations were not made last year, nor has attention ever been as distinctly called in that quarter to the considerable growth which the Seminary has had. I have been tempted, and have sometimes yielded to the temptation, to review every sentence of mine which would be printed to ascertain if by any possibility the opponents of the Seminary could construe it to our disadvantage. I have not dared at times (I may have been too timid) to trust an article as a whole, and have modified or omitted sentences which had, as I thought, some point, lest advantage should be taken of a turn of expression. Possibly some of the vagueness of which my accusers complain may be due to such revisions.

I mention all this as part of my experience in the Seminary, and to remind you that opposition did not begin with the appearance of Progressive Orthodoxy in 1885, nor with articles in the " Andover Review " for April and May 1886.

During the last five months I have become better informed in respect to the circumstances under which the Seminary Creed was formulated, and as must be true of all in attendance, I also have learned during the progress of this hearing not a little that was not known before. I have learned from the paper read Friday by Dr. Dexter, or rather have had new illustrations of the fact, that the founders had in view the condition and destiny of men in Christendom, under the gospel. I also judge from that paper that the motive of fear was then worked in too large as it now is worked, according to my judgment, in too small proportion. It has also been made clear to me that the original union included parties which differed as widely as our accusers differ from ourselves. The difference was perhaps even wider, for universality of Atonement as against limitation, and free agency as against inability meant at the time and still mean contrasts as great as any which exist in this present controversy. I have learned that the founders and their friends drove in chaises, wrote precisely worded letters, were not above some logrolling, tried to influence one man through another man, to get at merchants of Newburyport through their minister, that they suspected the motives of opponents and used rather harsh language towards them, that they were men of like passions with ourselves, that, there was more of what we call human nature in them than in their Creed, but also that they were eager for union and were willing to make proper concessions, that they had for their time remarkable breadth of view, above all that they had the courage to put vital principles, of the consequences of which they were not afraid, into their union creed. They did not, I believe, understand how much is involved in the universality of the person and atonement of Christ, nor in the freedom and rationality of man in accordance with which he is saved or lost. But they ventured out. Those principles and doctrines of revelation gained a place in the Creed. They did not know, we do not know, how large results are involved in those truths of Divine revelation. And the fact has been that while some of their statements about man have lost in importance, till they seem to us an almost outgrown metaphysic and ethic, the revealed truths concerning God and his ways with man, which are higher than our thoughts, have enlarged in the apprehension of their descendants and are to enlarge more and more by reverent study of God's works in creation, providence and redemption, by clearer knowledge of the Bible, and by the deepening spiritual experience which believers gain in their " minds and hearts."

I have also examined the relation of Creed and Catechism, a relation in which I am the only living person who has a directly responsible interest, and have come to a conclusion which I believe to have been expressed by my predecessor, that in the case of the Abbot Professor a legal reference to the Catechism is appropriate, but that the Creed determines the sense in which those portions of the Catechism shall be taken which are found in both instruments. I am not able to understand the satisfaction my colleagues on the Associate foundation take in their freedom from the Catechism, even as interpreted by the Creed, for with the exception of the doctrine of limited atonement, which the Creed corrects, I consider the Westminster Catechism, as a doctrinal formulary, superior to the Andover Creed.

One point has perhaps been overlooked by the complainants.

The Catechism teaches that the world was made in the space of six days. There is no doubt in my mind that the Westminster Divines meant by that 144 hours. The statement is not modified by the Creed. But I do not believe that the world was created in six solar days. I believe that the universe was created in no time. As Augustine said, the world was not created *in tempore*, but *cum tempore*. Or, if by creation is meant the time from the appearance of matter to the appearance of man, I should prefer to assume millions rather than even thousands of years. Nor have we yet done with the consequences which come in with a recognition of the time required for the evolution of the existing order, since this change of opinion may prove to involve essential doctrines.

We may expect our accusers next to turn their attention to the Presbyterian body, for the clergymen and theological professors of that denomination take the Catechism without the modifications of a later Creed, yet many of them hold to the universality of atonement.

On the whole, more careful study of the origin of the Creed, to which this trial has invited me has not substantially changed my understanding of it. Neither have my opinions substantially changed. I have not, let me hope, stopped thinking, even if premiums have been offered to encourage cessation of thought. Neither, let me also hope, have I ceased to receive the light which God gives to those who honestly seek the truth. My changes of doctrinal view have been in respect to proportion, emphasis and clearness. I do find it easier to reconcile the significance and scope of atonement with the opinion that the knowledge of it will be given to all men before the final judgment than with the opinion that the light of nature is essentially the knowledge of Christ, or with the opinion that all knowledge of God in Christ, except that which is given in this life, is withheld from the perishing heathen. My difficulty, sir, is with the alternatives. I only say that upon the hypothesis which I entertain some serious objections disappear, and that it harmonizes certain essential doctrines of the gospel with the Providence of God, but that it is of secondary rather than primary value, in the sense that it is an inference from essential doctrines rather than itself an essential doctrine. I would also say that if the Creed requires me to hold definitely that no member of the unevangelized nations has other knowledge of God for his salvation than that which he gains in this life, I desire to be emancipated from such a creed at the earliest possible moment. But I do not interpret your former decision as shutting one up to such a conclusion. I understand that the Creed requires no more than the essentials of faith as given in other evangelical symbols. In our own denomination, council after council has decided that the opinion I hold on the probation of the heathen does not override any essential article of faith.

The most serious charge which has been brought against me is in my judgment to my opinions on the Atonement. The gospel in its very essence is the redemption of sinful man through Jesus Christ, and to be in error concerning it is more reprehensible than to believe that the Bible contains some blemishes incidental to the human media through which its truth was given, or to hold a certain opinion concerning God's grace to the heathen. I do not propose to discuss the doctrine but to correct some misapprehensions. As I listened to the paper which was devoted chiefly to that topic, I perceived that while it condemned my view it indicated the view, and apparently the only view which the writer considers correct, or tenable under the Creed. I observed that he understands the Creed to be committed to the so-called governmental theory of Atonement. As the reading proceeded, the ideas presented, the expressions used, the turns given to phrases, the repetition of favorite words were such that if the voice had not been different and I had closed my eyes I should have believed myself to be back again where I was nearly a score of years ago in the middle class lecture-room at Andover listening to the Abbot Professor of Theology as he gave his interesting expositions of the Grotian theory of Atonement. Now I believe that theory to be permissible under the Creed, although to my thinking, since it finds the principal effect of Atonement in the exhibition it makes to sinners and to the universe of God's regard for his law, it is in the last analysis, a moral influence theory.

But I call attention to the fact that whatever is true in the Grotian or governmental theory of Atonement is included in the presentation of the subject in Progressive Orthodoxy. It is stated on page 57 that the sufferings and death of Christ realize God's hatred of sin and the righteous authority of law, and that therefore punishment need not be exacted. This line of reflection was not followed out because, as stated in the article, it is so familiar. "Its meaning is" says the book "that God cannot be regardless of law nor indifferent to sin in saving man from punishment." That is the pith of the governmental theory. Then comes the passage urged so emphatically in the complaint. "It must be confessed that it is not clear how the sufferings and death of Christ can be substituted for the, punishment of sin" (but we have not reached the end of the sentence) "how because Christ made vivid the wickedness of sin and the righteousness of God, man is therefore any the less exposed to the consequences of sin. We must go on to the fact that Christ makes real *very much more* than God's righteous indignation against sin. The punishment of sin does not save men. It only vindicates . God and his law. Christ while declaring God's righteousness reveals God seeking men at the cost of sacrifice." It is not the error but the inadequacy of the governmental theory which is criticised.

The entire discussion is on the basis of propitiation. The fundamental position is that because God is reconciled to man therefore man is forgiven, rather than that God forgives by reason of any thing that man does. First God is reconciled, then man repents. Not first man repents and then God is reconciled. Much space is given to an inquiry concerning the offering which humanity makes to God in the sacrifice of Christ. I quote — "Humanity may thus be thought of as offering something to God of eminent value. When Christ suffers the race suffers. When Christ is sorrowful the race is sorrowful." Why did Dr. Wellman's quotation stop here? Let us go on. "Christ realizes what humanity could not realize for itself. The race may be conceived as approaching God, and signifying its penitence by pointing to Christ, and by giving expression in him to repentance which no words could utter." And then with but a sentence between comes this statement. "The representative power which belongs to man in his various relations comes to its perfect realization in Christ. In the family, in government, in business, in society, representative or substitutionary relations are the rule not the exception. Much more has Christ the power perfectly to represent us or to be substituted for us, because there is no point of our real life where he is not in contact with us."

But the most singular part of the objection is the criticism made on my belief in the union of Christ with the race. Because the Incarnation, which is the true humanity of Christ, helps us to understand the Atonement, it is concluded that Incarnation has been put in the place of Atonement. The article was endeavoring to express the opinion that Christ's union with the race gives large part of its significance to his sufferings and death. "For verily not of angels doth he take hold, but he taketh hold of the seed of Abraham. Wherefore it behooved him in all things to be made like unto his brethren that he might be a merciful and faithful high priest in things pertaining to God to make propitiation for the sins of the people." The fact that Christ in his incarnation became a real man in organic relation with the human race gives the most profound conception of his Atonement. It should also be observed that in the statement concerning incarnation it is perfectly clear that something other is meant than the completed union of Christ with the believer. And this view of Christ's proper humanity is argued to be in opposition to the statement of the Creed that Jesus Christ and he *alone* made atonement for the sins of all men; as if "alone" means that he has no organic union with the men for whom he laid down his life. This is as complete a reversal of an author's meaning as it was ever my misfortune to hear. I believe the framers of the Creed were not desir-

ous of propounding any *theory* of Atonement but of emphasiz-
ing its extent.

In a similar vein the opinions presented on man's power
to repent were discussed. There is, in the article cited,
an inquiry concerning fact, concerning man's real rather
than his formal freedom. The word "cannot" is Paul's
"cannot" when he said, "I cannot do the things which
I would." I understood that the view we are required to
hold under the creed, in the opinion of our accusers, is that
man does all of his repenting by his own unaided power
and that after he has achieved a complete repentance, God
forgives him on account of the sacrifice of Christ. I had
supposed that man does his sinning by his own unaided
power, but that when it comes to holiness, especially that
radical choice in which real repentance largely consists and
which is a true turning to God, he is to no small degree
dependent on the Holy Spirit of God taking the things of
Christ and showing them unto him. In that opinion I believe I am in most substantial accord with the Seminary
Creed.

Some of these speculations to which we have listened made
the impression on me that it is extremely difficult for what
may be called the logical school of evangelical belief to enter
into a sympathetic appreciation of the beliefs of the spiritual
school. I am prepared to abate somewhat the feeling that
our accusers and their associates *refuse* to understand us as
we mean, for it has been borne in on me during this hearing
that they probably are *unable* so to understand us — I do not
intend this observation as a slur, but as the statement of a
fact. I do not deny that our writings may sometimes have
been vague. But I am satisfied that the real difficulty lies
deeper, and that the two parties or wings are separated somewhat as parties in the church have been separated in almost
every period of its history — because they approach truth from
opposite sides, or rather because the one party approaches
from without on the circumference, the other party from
within at or near the centre. This difference is partly constitutional and so cannot be avoided. It is a remark made first

I think by Schelling, although attributed to Coleridge, that every man as to philosophy is born either a Platonist or Aristotelian. It is equally true that as to theology some men are endowed with spiritual, others more largely with logical apprehension. It seems to me that our opponents almost completely fail to apprehend that movement of religious thought of the last thirty years in this and other countries which has been the advancing supremacy of the rational, ethical and spiritual habit of thought in place of a syllogistic, logical and therefore rationalizing habit. If I had time, sir, I should like to maintain that the later developments of New England theology have been more rationalistic than any theological movement since the Scholastic period.

If I may be pardoned a generalization without prefatory discussion I should say that one school of thought looks at truth in its objective forms as an external thing, that the re-action is mysticism which evolves beliefs out of subjective feeling, and that the newer school of thought in our own time appropriates external truth by reason and spirit into living faiths, uniting the objective and subjective. Whenever these contrasted parties have been contemporaneous it has been easier for the spiritual or intuitional school to comprehend the merely logical than for the logical to comprehend the spiritual. Paul understands James better than James understands Paul. John understands Peter better than Peter understands John. But it is easier for the logical than for the other school to state its opinions clearly and to defend them adroitly. The Anselmic (at least as it is frequently stated) and the Grotian theories of Atonement, for example, can be put in a nutshell and made intelligible to any one, and that is the trouble with them. They make Atonement a device and do not see that it is God seeking men. Now, not to dwell on this distinction, what is true in other denominations is true in ours that one party is moved on by the deeper currents of rational and spiritual impulse while the other does not escape the syllogistic and formal methods to which it has become accustomed. These are the differences which confront us at this trial.

That which to the one school is the vital, organic, real relation of Christ to men is to the other school mysticism and vagueness.

The complainants will say that this very state of things is fatal to us for the admission is made that we are on another track than that on which all Christians travelled at the beginning of this century. But, on the contrary, I contend that the two parties which entered into this union were really unlike in these very respects. On the one side were mechanical, artificial opinions concerning imputation, representation, Divine Sovereignty; on the other side were character in freedom, an organic relation of man to man, and of man to Christ, and a purpose of God running through history and revealing him as the God of reason and love. Then as now, and as always, there were the contrasts of legal and spiritual, external and internal, conservative and progressive, old and new. Since the beginning there have been alternations in the teachings at Andover. Much of the time both schools have been represented. Both schools are represented there to-day. It is doubtless well for the church and the world that both types of thought exist and, to some degree, work harmoniously side by side. The fruitfulness of the great truths of revelation and of the advancing kingdom of Christ produces various types. The doctrinal Paul, the mystical John, the ecclesiastical James are reflected and reproduced in all the great bodies of Christendom. If the tenure of either party under the Creed is in doubt it is of that party which to-day opposes us, since the Creed crowded hard on formal views of the external relations of men to each other and to Christ. We should claim that we are more nearly in the line of that vigorous movement which enlarged the old faith into new meaning and scope. But the Seminary Creed was then and is still a platform for the two principal schools of evangelical faith.

In my judgment the particular opinion which is held of the opportunities of heathen men is of less importance than that there be a firm hold on those great postulates of the gospel's truth from which we think our theory properly pro-

ceeds. I could not as I have said assent to the Creed if it
compels me to maintain a negative concerning the unevangelized nations, much less if it shuts me up to theories of
Atonement and of the Bible which have been represented
here as alternative to my own. I had supposed that Andover with its origin, history and traditions is a good institution for the advancement of Christian doctrine. But if I
must try to squeeze my opinions into any given phraseology
and to institute at every point a microscopic comparison with
the Creed I should decline thus to sacrifice spontaneity, en-
thusiasm and progress. You very well know that none of us
care for the salaries we receive since every one of us remains
at Andover at a pecuniary sacrifice, but we do care for the
advantage of our positions to advance the gospel of Christ,
and we do care for saving the institution to its intended uses.
It was not established as an asylum for orthodoxy, but as a
school for " increasing the number of learned and able De·
fenders of the Gospel of Christ, as well as of orthodox, pious,
and zealous Ministers of the New Testament "; for the production of character and influence devoted to the service of
Christ.

I beg only, in addition, to call your attention to a phrase in
the Statutes which has been misapplied. Emphasis has been
laid on the direction that the Creed should never be altered
in any particular. But it never has been altered. It is identically the same as at the first. The intention was to prevent
the Trustees or Visitors from repealing any clauses, or adding
new clauses. There was to be no more legislation on that
subject. It was rather a safeguard against retrogression than
a bar to advance. The true inference from that provision is
that there is all the more reason for allowing a liberal and
Christian construction of a Creed which is itself forever unchangeable.

STATEMENT OF PROFESSOR EDWARD Y. HINCKS.

THE work assigned to me by the Trustees of Andover Seminary with the concurrence of your honorable Body, is that of interpreting the Scriptures. This task of interpretation includes not only the correct rendering of the words of the inspired writers, but the tracing out of their leading thoughts, and their subordinate ideas in their connection with these. It also includes such discussion of the historical questions pertaining to the respective date, authorship, and immediate purpose of the Sacred writings as is essential to a correct understanding of their contents. In doing this work I have tried to be true to the province required of me by the constituted authorities of the Seminary "to open and explain the Scriptures to my pupils with integrity and faithfulness."

I assume that an honest and faithful expositor will try to ascertain as nearly as possible the meaning of the language used by the inspired writers, by the use of such grammatical, etymological and illustrative helps as are at his command. I also take for granted that he will try to enter into sympathy as far as possible with the religious feelings and motives which animated these writers. Having done this he will, I likewise assume, declare their thoughts, according to his best understanding of them ; not allowing his representations to be modified by his own prejudices or those of others. Such unbiassed interpretation I have tried to give to those of the Scriptures which I have had occasion to expound. In deciding upon the questions involving facts relating to these Scriptures, I have acted upon the principle, that the laws which govern historical research in one field must govern it in every field ;

and that problems for which revelation does not furnish means
of solution must be solved by strictly historical methods.

At the same time these principles of interpretation and
research have been employed under the avowed conviction
that the Scriptures are a supernaturally given source of spiritual enlightenment and carry the absolute authority of the
Divine Redeemer. I have endeavored to show that the divine
communications made to our Lord and his apostles, and those
given to the ancient prophets have passed over into them and
make them the prime source of religious knowledge, and
the final test of Christian belief.

If I have not claimed for them perfect accuracy in all
statements lying outside of the sphere of religious truth, and
if I have assigned to them functions of varying value in revealing God's character and ways, it is because this is necessarily
involved in showing the connection with Christ in the light
of which alone their authority can be appreciated and their
meaning understood. Since God's revelation to man centres
in Him, all parts of that revelation must be seen as related to
that centre to be understood. This implies the historical
study of Scripture, its examination in the light of contemporaneous facts and events. Such examination implies of
course the faithful use of historical methods and the honest
recognition of their results. A firm conviction that the
Scriptures contain the religious conceptions of Christ and his
apostles forbids any shrinking from such candid research.
The wish to keep that conviction fresh is an unceasing stim-
ulus to pursue it. I may remind you that to this part of the
work of a Biblical teacher in Andover Seminary great importance was attached by its Founders as appears from Article VI.
of the original constitution, which I beg permission to read.

Article VI. Under the head of Sacred Literature shall be
included Lectures on the formation, preservation and transmission of the Sacred Volume; on the languages in which
the Bible was originally written; on the Septuagint version
of the Old Testament and on the peculiarities of the language
and style of the New Testament, resulting from this version
and other causes; on the history character use and authority

of the ancient version of the Old and New Testaments; on the canons of Biblical criticism; on the authenticity of the several books of the sacred Code; on the apocryphal books of both Testaments; on modern translations of the Bible, more particularly on the history and character of our English version; and also critical Lectures on the various readings and difficult passages in the sacred writings.

While I have aimed to present the Scriptures in their historical and living connection with Christ, and thus to establish for them a higher value than such as comes from a purely formal authority, I have never reached conclusions as regards their nature or their teachings at variance with the Creed or any of the Christian doctrines expressed in it. I desire at this point in behalf of my associates and myself to correct representations made by one of the Complainants in his plea, of the meaning of certain cited passages from the articles on the Scriptures submitted as evidence by the prosecution.

From the editorial entitled "The Bible a Theme for the Pulpit" the following sentence (And. Rev. v. 409) was quoted by him as proof that the article advocates a covert opposition to the orthodox doctrine of inspiration, on the part of ministers. "A minister who should begin to preach a series of sermons about the Bible by saying that he expected to show that the notion of inspiration in which his hearers had been trained was an erroneous one, would probably find a considerable part of his congregation resolutely opposed to his teaching from the outset." To this I would add the sentence which follows — "The misunderstanding as to his conception of the Bible created by his injudicious remark — (injudicious because misrepresenting the real nature of the proposed teaching), could hardly be removed by any subsequent explanations." It is here plainly implied that the teaching suggested is not really at variance with the evangelical view of the Scriptures.

The following sentences which I will not stay to cite make the implication yet more evident. I will add a word, explaining another sentence from this editorial discussed by the same gentleman, " Then, as inspired life is shown expressing itself in inspired teaching, — as for example the connection between Paul's written teaching and his own inner life and his apostolic work is traced, or the apostolic tradition is shown embodying itself in the Synoptic Gospels — the conviction will gradually be created that the Scripture is the vehicle by which the divine revelation is conveyed to men, and in no true sense the revelation itself." The word " revelation " is used here in its Scriptural sense, of a supernatural disclosure of truth to inspired teachers. Paul e.g. says in the Epistle to the Galatians that God revealed his Son in him that he might preach Him. Paul's epistles bring the revelation which he received to us. They are not the revelation itself, for it expressed itself in them. There are important ends, it is thought, in pointing out the distinction. The charge that it is derogatory to the Scriptures is as absurd as would be the claim that one depreciated Christ's parables in saying that they were the vehicle by which his ideas were conveyed to the mind of the people. I must also correct the same gentleman's interpretation of a sentence belonging to the article on the Scriptures in " Progressive Orthodoxy " (p. 221). " We are finding out that the seat of the prophetic teaching was the moral and religious nature of the inspired seer alone." It was elaborately urged that this refers the teaching of the prophets to a purely human source. Indeed the word source was used as a synonym for " seat " in interpreting the sentence. But the claim could hardly have been made if the sentence had been read in its context. For it is preceded by these words.

" That conception of the prophet which regarded him as merely a voice, uttering words which his own inner life had no share in producing is rapidly disappearing before the intelligent study of the Old Testament." And we pass over but one sentence to come to these words . . . " It is not denied that they were sometimes evidently conscious of receiving special messages from God. Nor would we claim that the conceptions of God's kingdom in its present state and coming development, given them by the Spirit, were so thor-

oughly wrought into their own thinking as the apostles'
conceptions of Christ and his Kingdom were united with
their own thought."

One more instance of misrepresentation in the use of the
same article must be pointed out. The following words are
found on page 231.

" Whatever else comes to us as from God must present its
credentials to Christ's truth in our minds and hearts."

These last words, it is said, show that the writer recognized no objective divine revelation. But let me read the
context.

"If Christ is the supreme and final Revelation, He is the
test of all preceding revelation. If we accept Him as God's
supreme and final revelation, we must bring preceding revelation to this test. We cannot escape the process of comparison if we would. He brings us his own conception of God, of
life, of duty. It claims to cover the whole horizon of truth,
and demands possession of every spiritual and rational faculty.
If we will have it as ours we must hold it separate from and
above every other. Whatever else comes to us as from God
must present its credentials to Christ's truth in our minds
and hearts."

The two last sentences are evidently to be read in close
connection. Their obvious meaning is that if we will take
Christ's truth into our hearts we must give it royal authority
over them, and make it judge of every thing that claims to
come empowered by God to enter them. Not our notions,
but Christ's truth within us is to rule our inner being.

The earlier sentences expressly emphasize the supremacy of
the objective Christian revelation.

I repeat that I have been both in belief and teaching true
to " the principles of the Creed;" to quote words of Professor Stuart cited by the prosecution.

I will frankly admit however my belief that the Creed itself gives me a degree of liberty in interpreting its tenets.
In the pledge which it exacts the promise " to open and explain the Scriptures to my pupils with integrity and faithfulness" precedes that " to maintain and inculcate the Christian

faith, as expressed in the Creed by me now repeated." That promise has, I conceive, especial force for those who are called to teach the Bible in the Seminary. They at any rate are required by it to make the exposition of the Scriptures "according to the best light God shall give" them, the shaping and paramount principle of their teaching. They are to explain the Bible with integrity; giving no interpretations but such as are the fruit of their own study and research, and carry their own conviction; they are to explain it with faithfulness, counting subservience to human opinion unfaithfulness not only to the Scripture, but to the Seminary which requires a fair exposition of the word of God. This to men who like the Founders, regarded the Bible as the depository of divine truth must have implied the expectation of a progressive unfolding of that truth on the part of the teachers of sacred literature. It would have been absurd to require a promise to "open and expound the Scriptures with integrity and faithfulness," if the conclusions reached were expected to be absolutely identical with those already arrived at and set forth. Indeed, the word " open " seems to imply an advance into undeveloped riches of divine truth.

If I am correct in believing that the Founders laid this promise of a progressive teaching of Scripture upon the Biblical teachers in the Seminary, I may assume that they expected those teachers to interpret the creed in the light of that promise. To claim that they regarded their statement of belief as an absolutely perfect representation of the doctrinal contents of the Bible is to impugn not only their good judgment but their sincerity, since they have put the Scriptures above the creed as " the only perfect rule of faith and practice." To put such an interpretation upon the creed therefore as would prevent the teachers in the Seminary from keeping abreast of contemporaneous Biblical Scholarship by the use of legitimate methods (if such an interpretation were possible) would thwart their wishes both by making the Creed, not the Bible the ultimate test of the teaching of the institution as well as the " only perfect rule " of its professors' belief, and by robbing its Biblical instruction of that manifest and avowed loyalty to the Scriptures as the one unquestionable and paramount authority which the Founders intended it should have.

It is not meant of course, that the several articles of the creed have not a meaning for every one who teaches under it. No one could claim e.g. that one could go on teaching in the Seminary who had become satisfied that the Scriptures furnished no reason for believing in the doctrine of the Trinity. The enactment requiring a renewed subscription at the expiration of each five years;—which recognizes a necessary movement of mind engaged in the study of divine truth, provides that such movement shall be bounded by the great doctrinal lines plainly indicated by the Creed. I for one would not retain my position five years nor one year, had I abandoned any of the doctrines enunciated there. But I do not think retaining it inconsistent with the belief that the Scriptures may yet afford the means of giving one or more of those doctrines a better expression. For I am sure that such Biblical teaching as they exact by solemn pledge implies this belief.

I close by declaring my full and hearty belief " that the word of God, contained in the Scriptures of the Old and New Testament is the only perfect rule of faith and practice," and by denying that I have in the lecture-room or out of it made statements inconsistent with this belief, or inconsistent with my promise to " open and explain the Scriptures to my pupils with integrity and faithfulness," to " maintain and inculcate the Christian faith as expressed in the Creed of the Seminary," together with all the other doctrines and duties of our Holy Religion, so far as may appertain to my office, according to the best light God shall give me."

STATEMENT OF PROFESSOR J. W. CHURCHILL.

May it please your Reverend and Honorable Board : —

IN filing my exception to the charges against me for holding, maintaining, and inculcating opinions that are contrary
to the Associate Creed of Andover Theological Seminary,
I desire that it be understood as explicitly as language
can express my position that I am not seeking to evade
in the slightest degree my share of the editorial responsibility
in the purpose and conduct of " The Andover Review;" or to
avoid whatsoever consequences may follow from an adverse
decision against my co-editors upon the citations from the
Review as evidence of teaching and maintaining opinions in
nonconformity to the Seminary Creed. The fate of one
editor is the fate of all the editors. Nor do I wish to suggest
the inference that I am not in perfect sympathy with the
spirit and aim that animate and control the movement and
tendency in contemporary religious thought known as Progressive Orthodoxy. I adhere to the principles of the movement, although I do not accept every inference from some
of its positions. Neither let it be inferred that I consider my
adherence to Progressive Orthodoxy as inimical to the Associate Creed, which I conscientiously subscribed to on my inauguration into the Jones Professorship of Elocution, which
I have since twice repeated as an act of solemn obligation in
the presence of the Trustees of the Seminary, and to which
I am still loyal as it has been interpreted and administered
for more than half a century. Nor do I desire, in filing this
exception, to add to the already numerous complications of
this perplexing public Inquiry into the Orthodoxy of the ed-

itors of " The Andover Review." Much less do I wish to embarrass your reverend and honorable Board with untimely or irrelevant demands upon your attention. Still less would I convey the impression that I do not wish, or that I ought not, to be placed under your supervision, or that I resist any claim that your reverend and honorable Body may lawfully make for its Visitorial jurisdiction over the Jones Professorship.

But the question occasionally has been discussed in high quarters, and especially during the last few months, whether or not the Jones Professorship is strictly under the control of the Visitors of the Associate Foundation. In the Statutes of the various Chairs of Instruction that have been founded since the establishment of the Associate Creed, there seem to be three classes of conditions: one class, represented by the Taylor Professorship of Biblical Theology and History, now held by Professor Taylor, distinctly places the chair under the Visitorial supervision of your reverend and honorable Board; a second class, represented by the Stone Professorship of the Relations of Christianity to the Secular Sciences, now held by Professor Gulliver, distinctly states the exemption of the chair from your Visitorial control; the third class, represented by the Jones Professorship of Elocution, makes no reference whatsoever to the relation of the chair to any Visitorial supervision.

It is for the sole purpose of permanently determining the question of your Visitorial relation to the Jones Professorship that I filed my eleventh exception. I have availed myself of the occasion of this trial to submit the test; because, if the Jones Professorship is not under your Visitorial jurisdiction, then the complainants have no case against me upon which your reverend and honorable Board can adjudicate; if, on the other hand, it shall be decided that the Jones Professorship is under your Visitorial supervision, I shall cheerfully conform to your requirements in the premises, and shall respond to the charges preferred against me in such a manner as your Board shall direct.

Since it has been determined that it is advisable for me to make a statement in connection with the statements of my colleagues, I have thrown together this morning the few expressions following that partially may answer the present purpose of meeting the charges preferred against me.

It will be remembered by your reverend and honorable Board that in reply to your requisition of July 27, 1886, to present a written answer to the original charges within fifteen days that I conformed to your requirements within a very few days after the allotted time. The reply was made before the indicted professors had engaged counsel to defend them; but this fact was overlooked, inadvertently, I am willing to believe, in the counsel's argument for the prosecution in the case of my colleague, Professor Smyth, and through the omission an erroneous and injurious impression must have been conveyed to you and to the public concerning our action in the early history of this case.

You will also recall the fact that, in answer to the Amended Charges, there was presented to you a written reply from each of my colleagues, and that no reply was sent in by me, but that I added to the general Bill of Exceptions a special exception claiming that my Professorship was not under your jurisdiction. I withheld my answer to the Amended Charges until I should learn your decision on the point in question. Had I received the decision before this Court opened the case of Professor Smyth I should have sent in my written reply couched in the same language that was employed in the replies of my colleagues. I should also have prepared a more complete and careful statement than this, and of a different character, to meet the demands of the present time and place. But, inasmuch as no decision has been rendered upon my special exception, and also for the sake of brevity, I ask permission of your reverend and honorable Board to refer to the answer of my colleagues as being identical with my own; since what was common to those answers is expressed in the same language, and was discussed and drawn up in my presence, and with my voluntary co-operation as being equally indicted with them.

I would also respectfully ask permission, under the circumstances, to refer for ampler defence to the exposition of the

Seminary Creed as given by the Rev. D. T. Fiske, D.D., the venerable and honored President of the Board of Trustees of Andover Theological Seminary. I doubt not that I can safely rely upon your familiarity with that document. My intellectual and moral attitude towards the Creed is exactly defined in Dr. Fiske's Exposition. The high character, theological attainments, wisely conservative temper, and candid spirit of Dr. Fiske, are a sufficient guaranty to me of a competent and accurate representation of the Creed in his account of its origin, its subsequent history, its character, the significance of subscription to it, the history of its administration, and the source of responsibility in deciding the orthodoxy of the Professor in relation to the Creed. I refer to Dr. Fiske's Exposition and rely upon it, because its original intention was neither polemical in tone, nor inimical in its spirit towards any individual connected with the Board of Instruction or of Administration. It was not written for any Star-chamber assembly in secret conclave with the purpose of ultimately making it an iron heel to crush the advocate of some obnoxious doctrine: it was written solely for the information of the North Essex Ministerial Association with which he is connected, and with no intention of subsequent publication. Dr. Fiske's paper was entirely successful in removing previous unfortunate misconceptions, and conveyed much valuable information to his ministerial associates. That accomplished theologian, the late Rev. Raymond H. Seeley, D.D., of Haverhill, gave it his cordial endorsement. The Exposition afforded such general satisfaction that it was published at the request of the Association. The Rev. Ray Palmer, D.D., a former Visitor of the Seminary, has declared Dr. Fiske's Essay to be "a fair and honest statement of the essential facts of the case, and well adapted to set the public — those who *wish* to be set right — in a position to judge of the whole matter." He affirms that the view of the Creed, so clearly and ably presented, and the meaning of subscription to it was that which he himself entertained when he subscribed to it. "It was that," he adds, "of Drs. Dwight and Smith when they became Visitors." (See Prefatory Note to Dr.

Fiske's Exposition : Cupples, Upham & Co., Boston, Dec. 17, 1886.)

Upon my election to office in the Seminary I consulted my honored professor of Sacred Rhetoric concerning the manner in which the Creed was to be taken, for I had often heard it spoken of as an iron-clad affair of a past age, which had mostly lost its force and was only loosely binding upon the teachers of the present. Professor Phelps answered : " You must take the Creed as the rest of us have taken it — in its historic sense, and for substance of doctrine." His explanation of those terms (which I do not now recall in his language) satisfied me that an honest man could take the Creed honestly ; but it also disclosed to me the fact that the Creed required interpretation.

Accepting Dr. Fiske's exposition as my *vade mecum* in the interpretation of the Creed, I affirm my deliberate and conscientious conviction that if the Creed had the inherent power to effect the union of conflicting schools of religious thought in the days of its origin, it has the very same inherent power in the present day to prevent division and separation.

I cannot suppose that my personal views on the Ethics of Creed-Subscription are of the slightest importance to your reverend and Honorable Board. Nevertheless, they are of vital importance to me ; and I find myself in such hearty accord with the principles of Creed subscription as enunciated by Professor Austin Phelps, that I venture to make reference to the chapter in one of his works, — " My Portfolio," and entitled the " Rights of Believers in Ancient Creeds." Many of the illustrations in that clear, comprehensive, and conservative discussion are drawn from the Seminary Creed and the history of its administration (see p. 41 *et seq.*). I may safely assume your acquaintance with Professor Phelps's views upon this important topic. I refer to Dr. Fiske and to Professor Phelps as reflecting more perfectly and more vividly my own views, and for the purpose of brevity at this late stage of the proceedings.

In this manner, also, I express my sincere reverence for the framers of the Creed in their strenuous efforts to secure a true expression of theological doctrine. As time goes on, my veneration for those wise and able men is deepened, and my confidence in the greatness of their purpose, and my admiration for their achievement, are confirmed. Their elaborate formulary is not an antiquated relic, but is an impressive and living memorial of their insight into religious Truth, and of their theological prowess. They were guided by the promised Spirit of Truth, who has never been absent from the church in its work of creed-construction, and who is still in the hearts of men that are called upon to interpret the religious symbols of a former time.

I am glad to express my sympathy with the doctrinal conclusions at which they arrived. Every theological and Scriptural *fact* they registered in that Creed is true, and always will be true. Their skill in putting those truths into logical and vital relations is remarkable, and it remains a noble expression of the tenets of consistent Calvinism. But who shall call it a final expression of truth? It contains truth so far as it goes, but it does not exhaust it. Every Creed is a monument of man's imperfection. I believe this Creed, but I never can relinquish my right to think upon theological topics independently of the Creed, and outside of its terms, provided that, in the use of my conclusions, I am not inharmonious with a sound interpretation of the Creed or antagonistic to it. The responsibility of subscription ultimately rests upon the Professor himself. Any man likely to be elected to any chair in the Seminary is supposed to be intelligent and honest enough to decide for himself whether he can or cannot conscientiously subscribe, or maintain his subscription, to the Creed; and no man has a right to go behind the subscriber's conscience, or try to displace it by substituting some other man's interpretation.

In saying this, I mean to imply the inadequacy of this, and any existing Creed, to cover all the subjects of theological inquiry and discussion that constantly emerge in the gradual development of the aspects of Truth. Religion is a life, the life of God in the soul of man; but Theology is the Science

of Religion. Theology, with all the sciences, is bound to
regard changing data, and constantly must be passed under
review for revision and re-adjustment. There is new light
in Philosophy, new light in History, new light in Science,
new light in Criticism, that is constantly breaking forth. If
fresh light in any of these departments of thought and endeavor that are organically related to the facts and truths of
theological science can be allowed to flash out in Yale Seminary or in Union, — and it is flashing there — then I want
its brightness in Andover, to make the Creed still more an
illuminating power; and through Andover to shine in upon
the spiritual darkness of the nations. If a narrow construction of the Creed is to act as an extinguisher, or as a min-
imizing agent in denying me the benefits or the use of any
new light, I shall see to it that I do not suffer the condemnation of those who love darkness rather than light.

Wonder has often been expressed that a Professor of Elocution should be accused of heretical teaching of Theology.
My offence arises in the fact that I am a responsible co-
editor of the heretical "Andover Review." I have already
expressed my willingness to share every thing that editorial
responsibility carries with it. As editors we work and express ourselves in the plural and not in the singular. In
explanation of my arraignment it has been said in pleasantry
that I have been indicted for giving to the enunciation of
"Sheol" a circumflex inflection as expressing doubt. Not
so; on the contrary, and all jesting apart at a time of serious-
ness, I enunciate "Sheol," and teach my pupils to enunciate
it, and every word symbolizing a revealed fact of solemn
import, with the firm, downward inflection expressive of the
affirmation of the reality of a positive personal conviction.
Not one of my colleagues is so poor a theologian or so un-
skilful a speaker as to confound a downright inflection with
a circumflex.

I have not yet found the term "Probation" a necessity
for my theology or my view of life, here or hereafter. I do
not find it in the Creed, excepting as it refers to Adam's probation in his relation as the federal head of the race; nor

is it a biblical word, although the idea is admitted to be scriptural. I have been accustomed to regard this earthly scene and God's relation to it, not as a court-room, nor even a school-room, but as a scene of moral education in which the Father of Spirits is training the nations and individuals composing His great human family for the Eternal Life beyond life. As I think I stated in my former answer to you, I cannot believe that every soul's life in the Fatherhood of God will have its moral discipline ended with its earthly career; but, undoubtedly, there are souls existing both in this world and the next that forever will resist the Divine purpose and means in discipline. But it is not needful that I should enlarge upon this view in order to guard it, or to defend it, or to show its harmony with the Creed. The spiritual results in holy character in the great multitude of the Redeemed in the Eternal World are the same in my view of the future life that the advocates of a continued probation for the mass of the evangelically Unprivileged hope to see gloriously realized.

I know the history of the so-called Andover hypothesis of Continued Probation, from the first syllable of its utterance to the present hour. I have been in most intimate relations, day in and day out, year in and year out, with its supporters. I know a hundred times better than those who have misunderstood and consequently have misrepresented them, the spirit and manner, the limitations, lights and shades, and the conditions of development in which the hypothesis has been maintained. But little value may be attached to a personal opinion; nevertheless, the circumstances of this public statement make it proper for me to say that, inasmuch as I am convinced that this hypothesis does not militate against the doctrines of the Depravity of Man, the Necessity of Regeneration, the Trinity of the Godhead, the Universal Atonement of Christ, or the Eternity of Future Rewards and Punishments, which doctrines are authoritatively declared to be the distinguishing, essential, and pivotal doctrines in the system of Truth which the Seminary Creed, and all the great historic confessions affirm, — therefore, in view of such harmony with these tests of Orthodoxy, I earnestly claim for my colleagues their liberty of opinion, teaching, and discussion concerning this hypothesis. More than this : I believe that there is Reason and Scripture in it.

In making answer in this special form demanded by the present exigency of the case, I trust that I have again affirmed my sincere, reverent, and hearty loyalty to the elaborate symbol that I am called upon to sign as a Professor in Andover Theological Seminary. Whatsoever minor diversities of formal expression or of individual interpretation my colleagues or myself may demand as our rights as believers in the Creed, I sincerely believe that they are held in accordance with sound and recognized principles of Creed-Subscription. I sincerely believe that such modifications of belief or statement do not impair the integrity of doctrine as expressed in our authoritative standard. They are simply changed aspects of unchangeable truths. I sincerely believe that the intention of the Framers of this Creed was to make forever secure the teaching of a large, an enlarging, and a tolerant Orthodoxy; that they were intent upon making the teaching in the Seminary a synonym for a true, consistent, and catholic theology. Moreover, I sincerely and intelligently affirm that there exists in the religious community a wide-spread and positive judgment, that organized opposition to competent and conscientious teaching on the doctrinal basis laid by the Founders of the Seminary, is inconsistent with a true liberty of teaching within the limits of the Creed ; and that such organized opposition is subversive of the stability of true theology,—a permanence that must ever be conditioned upon freedom of theological teaching and discussion as an inalienable right under any creed of the protestant faith.